EDITED BY MARTIN H. GREENBERG

# HAUNTED HOUSES
## THE GREATEST STORIES

MJF BOOKS
NEW YORK

Published by MJF Books
Fine Communications
322 Eighth Avenue
New York, NY 10001

Library of Congress Catalog Card Number 97-70825
ISBN-10: 1-56731-168-7
ISBN-13: 978-1-56731-168-6

*Haunted Houses: The Greatest Stories*
Copyright © 1997 by Tekno-Books

Manufactured in the United States of America.

MJF Books and the MJF colophon are trademarks of Fine Creative Media, Inc.

QM      10  9   8   7   6   5   4   3   2

# Contents

# Haunted Houses: The American Nightmare

On any given night, a person can walk down any suburban street and see row upon row of houses stretching off in the distance. Large or small, A-frame or ranch, colonial or southwestern—the choice is limited only by the owner's imagination.

For many, owning a house is still the American dream. To set foot in a place that you know is yours! Not an apartment, through which dozens of people have come and gone before you, but solid walls and a door that you can walk through and know that no matter what, you're home. A place that is your own, with no one to answer to but yourself. There is a satisfying comfort in that knowledge, a feeling that you are now more than just one person; you now have an attachment to this land upon which you have built your home.

If you're lucky to have a family that traces its history back far enough, you may have an ancestral home, housing multiple generations throughout the decades, an everlasting monument to the achievements of your forefathers. In it you might feel a palpable sense of history, of noble or not so noble deeds from long ago.

Sometimes, though, these deeds do more than just linger in

the homes in which they were committed. They replay themselves, over and over. Or they drive new generations to repeat these acts, fulfilling a cycle of violence that visits families over and over again. Several films have illustrated this idea quite well, from *The Amityville Horror* to *Poltergeist*, playing on the fear of discovering an unknown evil in the place which is supposedly a sanctuary for your family, and making it perhaps the greatest terror of all.

If a house in a story or film is found out to be haunted, the reader's first reaction may be sympathy for the main characters. After all, they're just trying to find shelter, to provide a basic human need. It's not their fault that the dwelling they chose had a sometimes unspeakable history that's now causing them to suffer.

But if you look at the situation from the other side, who is the interloper? Aren't the people who move in trying to impose their own sense of history on the house, replacing what happened years ago with their memories, their emotions? Some houses may resist this change. Some may resist violently.

Perhaps it is not realistic to attribute characteristics of life to houses. But, as we're sure anyone can tell you, there is hardly a person out there who can't say that certain houses they enter give them a "feeling" of some kind. Whether it's good or bad, well, that all depends on what kind of house it is, and what went on there in its past.

The stories in this collection span a wide range of styles and settings, from the English countryside to the New England hills, from a restored country home in whose basement rests unspeakable evil to a stately mansion that resists any attempt to tear it down with deadly force. These stories will make anyone think twice about becoming a homeowner.

# The Rats in the Walls

## by H.P. Lovecraft

On July 16, 1923, I moved into Exham Priory after the last workman had finished his labors. The restoration had been a stupendous task, for little had remained of the deserted pile but a shell-like ruin; yet because it had been the seat of my ancestors, I let no expense deter me. The place had not been inhabited since the reign of James the First, when a tragedy of intensely hideous, though largely unexplained, nature had struck down the master, five of his children, and several servants; and driven forth under a cloud of suspicion and terror the third son, my lineal progenitor and the only survivor of the abhorred line.

With this sole heir denounced as a murderer, the estate had reverted to the crown, nor had the accused man made any attempt to exculpate himself or regain his property. Shaken by some horror greater than that of conscience or the law, and expressing only a frantic wish to exclude the ancient edifice from his sight and memory, Walter de la Poer, eleventh Baron Exham, fled to Virginia and there founded the family which by the next century had become known as Delapore.

Exham Priory had remained untenanted, though later allotted to the estates of the Norrys family and much studied because of its peculiarly composite architecture; an architecture involving Gothic towers resting on a Saxon or Romanesque substructure, whose foundation in turn was of a still earlier order or blend of orders—Roman, and even Druidic or native Cymric, if legends speak truly. This foundation was a very singular thing, being merged on one side with the solid limestone of the precipice from whose brink the priory overlooked a desolate valley three miles west of the village of Anchester.

Architects and antiquarians loved to examine this strange relic of forgotten centuries, but the country folk hated it. They had hated it hundreds of years before, when my ancestors lived there, and they hated it now, with the moss and mould of abandonment on it. I had not been a day in Anchester before I knew I came of an accursed house. And this week workmen have blown up Exham Priory, and are busy obliterating the traces of its foundations. The bare statistics of my ancestry I had always known, together with the fact that my first American forbear had come to the colonies under a strange cloud. Of details, however, I had been kept wholly ignorant through the policy of reticence always maintained by the Delapores. Unlike our planter neighbors, we seldom boasted of crusading ancestors or other mediaeval and Renaissance heroes; nor was any kind of tradition handed down except what may have been recorded in the sealed envelope left before the Civil War by every squire to his eldest son for posthumous opening. The glories we cherished were those achieved since the migration; the glories of a proud and honorable, if somewhat reserved and unsocial Virginia line.

During the war our fortunes were extinguished and our whole existence changed by the burning of Carfax, our home on the banks of the James. My grandfather, advanced in years, had perished in that incendiary outrage, and with him the envelope that had bound us all to the past. I can recall that fire today as I saw it then at the age of seven, with the Federal soldiers shouting, the women screaming, and the negroes howling and praying. My father was in the army, defending Richmond, and after many formalities my mother and I were passed through the lines to join him.

When the war ended we all moved north, whence my mother had come; and I grew to manhood, middle age, and ultimate wealth as a stolid Yankee. Neither my father nor I ever knew what our hereditary envelope had contained, and as I merged into the grayness of Massachusetts business life I lost all interest in the mysteries which evidently lurked far back in my family tree. Had I suspected their nature, how gladly I would have left Exham Priory to its moss, bats, and cobwebs!

My father died in 1904, but without any message to leave to me, or to my only child, Alfred, a motherless boy of ten. It was this boy who reversed the order of family information, for although I could give him only jesting conjectures about the past, he wrote me of some very interesting ancestral legends when the late war took him to England in 1917 as an aviation officer. Apparently the Delapores had a colorful and perhaps sinister history, for a friend of my son's, Capt. Edward Norrys of the Royal Flying Corps, dwelt near the family seat of Anchester and related some peasant superstitions which few novelists could equal for wildness and incredibility. Norrys himself, of course, did not take them so seriously; but they amused my son and made good material for his letters to me. It was this legendry which definitely turned my attention to my transatlantic heritage, and made me resolve to purchase and restore the family seat which Norrys showed to Alfred in its picturesque desertion, and offered to get for him at a surprisingly reasonable figure, since his own uncle was the present owner.

I bought Exham Priory in 1918, but was almost immediately distracted from my plans of restoration by the return of my son as a maimed invalid. During the two years that he lived I thought of nothing but his care, having even placed my business under the direction of partners.

In 1921, as I found myself bereaved and aimless, a retired manufacturer no longer young, I resolved to divert my remaining years with my new possession. Visiting Anchester in December, I was entertained by Capt. Norrys, a plump, amiable young man who had thought much of my son, and secured his assistance in gathering plans and anecdotes to guide in the coming restoration. Exham Priory itself I saw without emotion, a jumble of tottering mediaeval ruins covered with lichens and honeycombed with rooks' nests, perched perilously upon a precipice, and denuded of floors or other interior features save the stone walls of the separate towers.

As I gradually recovered the image of the edifice as it had been when my ancestors left it over three centuries before, I began to hire workmen for the reconstruction. In every case I was forced to go outside the immediate locality, for the Anchester villagers had an almost unbelievable fear and hatred of the place. This sentiment was so great that it was sometimes communicated to the outside laborers, causing numerous desertions; whilst its scope appeared to include both the priory and its ancient family.

My son had told me that he was somewhat avoided during his visits because he was a de la Poer, and I now found myself subtly ostracised for a like reason until I convinced the peasants how little I knew of my heritage. Even then they sullenly disliked me, so that I had to collect most of the village traditions through the mediation of Norrys. What the people could not forgive, perhaps, was that I had come to restore a symbol so abhorrent to them; for, rationally or not, they viewed Exham Priory as nothing less than a haunt of fiends and werewolves.

Piecing together the tales which Norrys collected for me, and supplementing them with the accounts of several savants who had studied the ruins, I deduced that Exham Priory stood on the site of a prehistoric temple; a Druidical or ante-Druidical thing which must have been contemporary with Stonehenge. That indescribable rites had been celebrated there, few doubted, and there were unpleasant tales of the transference of these rites into the Cybele-worship which the Romans had introduced.

Inscriptions still visible in the subcellar bore such unmistakable letters as "DIV . . . OPS . . . MAGNA. MAT . . ." sign of the Magna Mater whose dark worship was once vainly forbidden to Roman citizens. Anchester had been the camp of the third Augustan legion, as many remains attest, and it was said that the temple of Cybele was splendid and thronged with worshippers who performed nameless ceremonies at the bidding of a Phrygian priest. Tales added that the fall of the old religion did not end the orgies at the temple, but that the priests lived on in the new faith without real change. Likewise was it said that the rites did not vanish with the Roman power, and that certain among the Saxons added to what remained of the temple, and gave it the essential outline it subsequently preserved, making it the center of a cult feared through half the heptarchy. About 1000 A.D. the place is mentioned in a chronicle as being a substantial stone priory housing a strange and powerful monastic order and surrounded by extensive gardens which needed no walls to exclude a frightened populace. It was never destroyed by the Danes, though after the Norman Conquest it must have declined tremendously; since there was no impediment when Henry the Third granted the site to my ancestor, Gilbert de la Poer, First Baron Exham, in 1261.

Of my family before this date there is no evil report, but something strange must have happened then. In one chronicle there is a reference to a de la Poer as "cursed of God" in 1307, whilst village legendry had nothing but evil and frantic fear to tell of the castle that went up on the foundations of the old temple and priory. The fireside tales were of the most grisly description, all the ghastlier because of the frightened reticence and cloudy evasiveness. They represented my ancestors as a race of hereditary daemons beside whom Gilles de Retz and the Marquis de Sade would seem the veriest tyros, and hinted

whisperingly at their responsibility for the occasional disap-
pearances of villagers through several generations.

The worst characters, apparently, were the barons and their
direct heirs; at least, most was whispered about these. If of
healthier inclinations, it was said, an heir would early and mys-
teriously die to make way for another more typical scion. There
seemed to be an inner cult in the family, presided over by the
head of the house, and sometimes closed except to a few members. Temperament rather than ancestry was evidently the basis
of this cult, for it was entered by several who married into the
family. Lady Margaret Trevor from Cornwall, wife of Godfrey,
the second son of the fifth baron, became a favorite bane of
children all over the countryside, and the daemon heroine of a
particularly horrible old ballad not yet extinct near the Welsh
border. Preserved in balladry, too, though not illustrating the
same point, is the hideous tale of Lady Mary de la Poer, who
shortly after her marriage to the Earl of Shrewsfield was killed
by him and his mother, both of the slayers being absolved and
blessed by the priest to whom they confessed what they dared
not repeat to the world.

These myths and ballads, typical as they were of crude superstition, repelled me greatly. Their persistence, and their application to so long a line of my ancestors, were especially
annoying; whilst the imputations of monstrous habits proved
unpleasantly reminiscent of the one known scandal of my immediate forbears—the case of my cousin, young Randolph Delapore of Carfax, who went among the negroes and became a
voodoo priest after he returned from the Mexican War.

I was much less disturbed by the vaguer tales of wails and
howlings in the barren, windswept valley beneath the limestone cliff; of the graveyard stenches after the spring rains; of
the floundering, squealing white thing on which Sir John
Clave's horse had trod one night in a lonely field; and of the
servant who had gone mad at what he saw in the priory in the
full light of day. These things were hackneyed spectral lore,

and I was at that time a pronounced skeptic. The accounts of vanished peasants were less to be dismissed, though not especially significant in view of mediaeval custom. Prying curiosity meant death, and more than one severed head had been publicly shown on the bastions—now effaced—around Exham Priory.

A few of the tales were exceedingly picturesque, and made me wish I had learnt more of the comparative mythology in my youth. There was, for instance, the belief that a legion of batwinged devils kept witches' sabbath each night at the priory—a legion whose sustenance might explain the disproportionate abundance of coarse vegetables harvested in the vast gardens. And, most vivid of all, there was the dramatic epic of the rats—the scampering army of obscene vermin which had burst forth from the castle three months after the tragedy that doomed it to desertion—the lean, filthy, ravenous army which had swept all before it and devoured fowl, cats, dogs, hogs, sheep, and even two hapless human beings before its fury was spent. Around that unforgettable rodent army a whole separate cycle of myths revolves, for it scattered among the village homes and brought curses and horrors in its train.

Such was the lore that assailed me as I pushed to completion, with an elderly obstinacy, the work of restoring my ancestral home. It must not be imagined for a moment that these tales formed my principal psychological environment. On the other hand, I was constantly praised and encouraged by Capt. Norrys and the antiquarians who surrounded and aided me. When the task was done, over two years after its commencement, I viewed the great rooms, wainscotted walls, vaulted ceilings, mullioned windows, and broad staircases with a pride which fully compensated for the prodigious expense of the restoration.

Every attribute of the Middle Ages was cunningly reproduced, and the new parts blended perfectly with the original walls and foundations. The seat of my fathers was complete, and I looked forward to redeeming at last the local fame of the line which ended in me. I would reside here permanently, and prove that a de la Poer (for I had adopted again the original spelling of the name) need not be a fiend. My comfort was perhaps augmented by the fact that, although Exham Priory was mediaevally fitted, it's interior was in truth wholly new and free from old vermin and old ghosts alike.

As I have said, I moved in on July 16, 1923. My household consisted of seven servants and nine cats, of which latter species I am particularly fond. My eldest cat, "Nigger-Man," was seven years old and had come with me from my home in Bolton, Massachusetts; the others I had accumulated whilst living with Capt. Norrys' family during the restoration of the priory.

For five days our routine proceeded with the utmost placidity, my time being spent mostly in the codification of old family data. I had now obtained some very circumstantial accounts of the final tragedy and flight of Walter de la Poer, which I conceived to be the probable contents of the hereditary paper lost in the fire at Carfax. It appeared that my ancestor was accused with much reason of having killed all the other members of his household, except four servant confederates, in their sleep, about two weeks after a shocking discovery which changed his whole demeanor, but which, except by implication, he disclosed to no one save perhaps the servants who assisted him and afterward fled beyond reach.

This deliberate slaughter, which included a father, three brothers, and two sisters, was largely condoned by the villagers, and so slackly treated by the law that its perpetrator escaped honored, unharmed, and undisguised to Virginia; the general whispered sentiment being that he had purged the land of immemorial curse. What discovery had prompted an act so terrible, I could scarcely even conjecture. Walter de la Poer must have known for years the sinister tales about his family, so that this material could have given him no fresh impulse.

Had he, then, witnessed some appalling ancient rite, or stumbled upon some frightful and revealing symbol in the priory or its vicinity? He was reputed to have been a shy, gentle youth in England. In Virginia he seemed not so much hard or bitter as harassed and apprehensive. He was spoken of in the diary of another gentleman adventurer, Francis Harley of Bellview, as a man of unexampled justice, honor, and delicacy.

On July 22 occurred the first incident which, though lightly dismissed at the time, takes on a preternatural significance in relation to later events. It was so simple as to be almost negligible, and could not possibly have been noticed under the circumstances; for it must be recalled that since I was in a building practically fresh and new except for the walls, and surrounded by a well-balanced staff of servitors, apprehension would have been absurd despite the locality.

What I afterward remembered is merely this—that my old black cat, whose moods I know so well, was undoubtedly alert and anxious to an extent wholly out of keeping with his natural character. He roved from room to room, restless and disturbed, and sniffed constantly about the walls which formed part of the Gothic structure. I realize how trite this sounds—like the inevitable dog in the ghost story, which always growls before his master sees the sheeted figure—yet I cannot consistently suppress it.

The following day a servant complained of restlessness among all the cats in the house. He came to me in my study, a lofty west room on the second story, with groined arches, black oak panelling, and a triple Gothic window overlooking the limestone cliff and desolate valley; and even as he spoke I saw the jetty form of Nigger-Man creeping along the west wall and scratching at the new panels which overlaid the ancient stone.

I told the man that there must be some singular odor or emanation from the old stonework, imperceptible to human senses, but affecting the delicate organs of cats even through the new woodwork. This I truly believed, and when the fellow suggested the presence of mice or rats, I mentioned that there had been no rats there for three hundred years, and that even the field mice of the surrounding country could hardly be found in these high walls, where they had never been known to stray. That afternoon I called on Capt. Norrys, and he assured me that it would be quite incredible for field mice to infest the priory in such a sudden and unprecedented fashion.

That night, dispensing as usual with a valet, I retired in the west tower chamber which I had chosen as my own, reached from the study by a stone staircase and short gallery—the former partly ancient, the latter entirely restored. This room was circular, very high, and without wainscotting, being hung with arras which I had myself chosen in London.

Seeing that Nigger-Man was with me, I shut the heavy Gothic door and retired by the light of the electric bulbs which so cleverly counterfeited candles, finally switching off the light and sinking on the carved and canopied four-poster, with the venerable cat in his accustomed place across my feet. I did not draw the curtains, but gazed out at the narrow north window which I faced. There was a suspicion of aurora in the sky, and the delicate traceries of the window were pleasantly silhouetted.

At some time I must have fallen quietly asleep, for I recall a distinct sense of leaving strange dreams, when the cat started violently from his placid position. I saw him in the faint auroral glow, head strained forward, forefeet on my ankles, and hind feet stretched behind. He was looking intensely at a point on the wall somewhat west of the window, a point which to my eye had nothing to mark it, but toward which all my attention was now directed.

And as I watched, I knew that Nigger-Man was not vainly excited. Whether the arras actually moved I cannot say. I think it did, very slightly. But what I can swear to is that behind it I heard a low, distinct scurrying as of rats or mice. In a moment the cat had jumped bodily on the screening tapestry, bringing the affected section to the floor with his weight, and exposing a damp, ancient wall of stone; patched here and there by the restorers, and devoid of any trace of rodent prowlers.

Nigger-Man raced up and down the floor by this part of the wall, clawing the fallen arras and seemingly trying at times to insert a paw between the wall and the oaken floor. He found nothing, and after a time returned wearily to his place across my feet. I had not moved, but I did not sleep again that night.

In the morning I questioned all the servants, and found that none of them had noticed anything unusual, save that the cook remembered the actions of a cat which had rested on her windowsill. This cat had howled at some unknown hour of the night, awaking the cook in time for her to see him dart purposefully out of the open door down the stairs. I drowsed away the noontime, and in the afternoon called again on Capt. Norrys, who became exceedingly interested in what I told him. The odd incidents—so slight yet so curious—appealed to his sense of the picturesque, and elicited from him a number of reminiscences of local ghostly lore. We were genuinely perplexed at the presence of rats, and Norrys lent me some traps and Paris green, which I had the servants place in strategic localities when I returned.

I retired early, being very sleepy, but was harassed by dreams of the most horrible sort, I seemed to be looking down from an immense height upon a twilit grotto, knee-deep with filth, where a white-bearded daemon swineherd drove about with his staff a flock of fungous, flabby beasts whose appearance filled me with unutterable loathing. Then, as the swineherd paused and nodded over his task, a mighty swarm of rats rained down on the stinking abyss and fell to devouring beasts and man alike.

From this terrific vision I was abruptly awakened by the motion of Nigger-Man, who had been sleeping as usual across my feet. This time I did not have to question the source of his snarls and hisses, and of the fear which made him sink his claws into my ankle, unconscious of their effect; for on every side of the chamber the walls were alive with nauseous sound—the verminous slithering of ravenous, gigantic rats. There was now no aurora to show the state of the arras—the fallen section of which had been replaced—but I was not too frightened to switch on the light.

As the bulbs leapt into radiance I saw a hideous shaking all over the tapestry, causing the somewhat peculiar designs to execute a singular dance of death. This motion disappeared almost at once, and the sound with it. Springing out of bed, I poked at the arras with the long handle of a warming-pan that rested near, and lifted one section to see what lay beneath. There was nothing but the patched stone wall, and even the cat had lost his tense realization of abnormal presences. When I examined the circular trap that had been placed in the room, I found all of the openings sprung, though no trace remained of what had been caught and had escaped.

Further sleep was out of the question, so, lighting a candle, I opened the door and went out in the gallery toward the stairs to my study, Nigger-Man following at my heels. Before we had reached the stone steps, however, the cat darted ahead of me and vanished down the ancient flight. As I descended the stairs myself, I became suddenly aware of sounds in the great room below; sounds of a nature which could not be mistaken.

The oak-panelled walls were alive with rats, scampering and milling, whilst Nigger-Man was racing about with the fury of a baffled hunter. Reaching the bottom, I switched on the light, which did not this time cause the noise to subside. The rats continued their riot, stampeding with such force and distinctness that I could finally assign to their motions a definite direction. These creatures, in numbers apparently inexhaustible, were engaged in one stupendous migration from inconceivable heights to some depth conceivably or inconceivably below.

I now heard steps in the corridor, and in another moment two servants pushed open the massive door. They were searching the house for some unknown source of disturbance which had thrown all the cats into a snarling panic and caused them to plunge precipitately down several flights of stairs and squat, yowling, before the closed door to the sub-cellar. I asked them if they had heard the rats, but they replied in the negative. And when I turned to call their attention to the sounds in the panels, I realized that the noise had ceased.

With the two men, I went down to the door of the sub-cellar, but found the cats already dispersed. Later I resolved to explore the crypt below, but for the present I merely made a round of the traps. All were sprung, yet all were tenantless. Satisfying myself that no one had heard the rats save the felines and me, I sat in my study till morning, thinking profoundly and recalling every scrap of legend I had unearthed concerning the building I inhabited.

I slept some in the forenoon, leaning back in the one comfortable library chair which my mediaeval plan of furnishing could not banish. Later I telephoned to Capt. Norrys, who came over and helped me explore the sub-cellar.

Absolutely nothing untoward was found, although we could not repress a thrill at the knowledge that this vault was built by Roman hands. Every low arch and massive pillar was Roman —not the debased Romanesque of the bungling Saxons, but the severe and harmonious classicism of the age of the Caesars; indeed, the walls abounded with inscriptions familiar to the antiquarians who had repeatedly explored the place—things like "P. GETAE. PROP . . . TEMP . . . DONA . . ." and "L. PRAEC . . . VS . . . PONTIFI . . . ATYS . . ."

The reference to Atys made me shiver, for I had read Catullus and knew something of the hideous rites of the Eastern god, whose worship was so mixed with that of Cybele. Norrys and I, by the light of lanterns, tried to interpret the odd and nearly effaced designs on certain irregularly rectangular blocks of stone generally held to be altars, but could make nothing of them. We remembered that one pattern, a sort of rayed sun, was held by students to imply a non-Roman origin, suggesting that these altars had merely been adopted by the Roman priests from some older and perhaps aboriginal temple on the same site. On one of these blocks were some brown stains which made me wonder. The largest, in the center of the room, had certain features on the upper surface which indicated its connection with fire—probably burnt offerings.

Such were the sights in that crypt before whose door the cats howled, and where Norrys and I now determined to pass the night. Couches were brought down by the servants, who were told not to mind any nocturnal actions of the cats, and Nigger-Man was admitted as much for help as for companionship. We decided to keep the great oak door—a modern replica with slits for ventilation—tightly closed; and, with this attended to, we retired with lanterns still burning to await whatever might occur.

The vault was very deep in the foundations of the priory, and undoubtedly far down on the face of the beetling limestone cliff overlooking the waste valley. That it had been the goal of the scuffling and unexplainable rats I could not doubt, though why, I could not tell. As we lay there expectantly, I found my vigil occasionally mixed with half-formed dreams from which the uneasy motions of the cat across my feet would rouse me.

These dreams were not wholesome, but horribly like the one I had had the night before. I saw again the twilit grotto, and the swineherd with his unmentionable fungous beasts wallowing in filth, and as I looked at these things they seemed nearer and more distinct—so distinct that I could almost observe their features. Then I did observe the flabby features of one of them—and awaked with such a scream that Nigger-Man started up, whilst Capt. Norrys, who had not slept, laughed considerably. Norrys might have laughed more—or perhaps less—had he known what it was that made me scream. But I did not remember myself till later. Ultimate horror often paralyses memory in a merciful way.

Norrys waked me when the phenomena began. Out of the

same frightful dream I was called by his gentle shaking and his urging to listen to the cats. Indeed, there was much to listen to, for beyond the closed door at the head of the stone steps was a veritable nightmare of feline yelling and clawing, whilst Nigger-Man, unmindful of his kindred outside, was running excitedly around the bare stone walls, in which I heard the same babel of scurrying rats that had troubled me the night before.

An acute terror now rose within me, for here were anomalies which nothing normal could well explain. These rats, if not the creatures of a madness which I shared with the cats alone, must be burrowing and sliding in Roman walls I had thought to be of solid limestone blocks . . . unless perhaps the action of water through more than seventeen centuries had eaten winding tunnels which rodent bodies had worn clear and ample. . . . But even so, the spectral horror was no less; for if these were living vermin why did not Norrys hear their disgusting commotion? Why did he urge me to watch Nigger-Man and listen to the cats outside, and why did he guess wildly and vaguely at what could have aroused them?

By the time I had managed to tell him, as rationally as I could, what I thought I was hearing, my ears gave me the last fading impression of the scurrying; which had retreated *still downward*, far underneath this deepest of sub-cellars till it seemed as if the whole cliff below were riddled with questing rats. Norrys was not as skeptical as I had anticipated, but instead seemed profoundly moved. He motioned to me to notice that the cats at the door had ceased their clamor, as if giving up the rats for lost; whilst Nigger-Man had a burst of renewed restlessness, and was clawing frantically around the bottom of the large stone altar in the center of the room, which was nearer Norrys' couch than mine.

My fear of the unknown was at this point very great. Something astounding had occurred, and I saw that Capt. Norrys, a younger, stouter, and presumably more naturally materialistic

man, was affected fully as much as myself—perhaps because of
his lifelong and intimate familiarity with local legend. We could
for the moment do nothing but watch the old black cat as he
pawed with decreasing fervor at the base of the altar, occasionally
looking up and mewing to me in that persuasive manner which
he used when he wished me to perform some favor for him.

Norrys now took a lantern close to the altar and examined
the place where Nigger-Man was pawing; silently kneeling and
scraping away the lichens of the centuries which joined the
massive pre-Roman block to the tesselated floor. He did not
find anything, and was about to abandon his efforts when I noticed a trivial circumstance which made me shudder, even
though it implied nothing more than I had already imagined.

I told him of it, and we both looked at its almost imperceptible manifestation with the fixedness of fascinated discovery
and acknowledgment. It was only this—that the flame of the
lantern set down near the altar was slightly but certainly flickering from a draught of air which it had not before received,
and which came indubitably from the crevice between floor
and altar where Norrys was scraping away the lichens.

We spent the rest of the night in the brilliantly lighted study,
nervously discussing what we should do next. The discovery
that some vault deeper than the deepest known masonry of the
Romans underlay this accursed pile; some vault unsuspected
by the curious antiquarians of three centuries; would have been
sufficient to excite us without any background of the sinister.
As it was, the fascination became two-fold; and we paused in
doubt whether to abandon our search and quit the priory forever in superstitious caution, or to gratify our sense of adventure and brave whatever horrors might await us in the unknown
depths.

By morning we had compromised, and decided to go to London to gather a group of archaeologists and scientific men fit to
cope with the mystery. It should be mentioned that before leaving the sub-cellar we had vainly tried to move the central altar

which we now recognized as the gate to a new pit of nameless fear. What secret would open the gate, wiser men than we would have to find.

During many days in London Capt. Norrys and I presented our facts, conjectures, and legendary anecdotes to five eminent authorities, all men who could be trusted to respect any family disclosures which future explorations might develop. We found most of them little disposed to scoff, but, instead, intensely interested and sincerely sympathetic. It is hardly necessary to name them all, but I may say that they included Sir William Brinton, whose excavations in the Troad excited most of the world in their day. As we all took the train for Anchester I felt myself poised on the brink of frightful revelations, a sensation symbolized by the air of mourning among the many Americans at the unexpected death of the President on the other side of the world.

On the evening of August 7 we reached Exham Priory, where the servants assured me that nothing unusual had occurred. The cats, even old Nigger-Man, had been perfectly placid; and not a trap in the house had been sprung. We were to begin exploring on the following day, awaiting which I assigned well-appointed rooms to all my guests.

I myself retired in my own tower chamber, with Nigger-Man across my feet. Sleep came quickly, but hideous dreams assailed me. There was a vision of a Roman feast like that of Trimalchio, with a horror in a covered platter. Then came that damnable, recurrent thing about the swineherd and his filthy drove in the twilit grotto. Yet when I awoke it was full daylight, with normal sounds in the house below. The rats, living or spectral, had not troubled me; and Nigger-Man was still quietly asleep. On going down, I found that the same tranquillity had prevailed elsewhere; a condition which one of the assembled savants—a fellow named Thornton, devoted to the psychic— rather absurdly laid to the fact that I had now been shown the thing which certain forces had wished to show me.

All was now ready, and at 11 A.M. our entire group of seven men, bearing powerful electric searchlights and implements of excavation, went down to the sub-cellar and bolted the door behind us. Nigger-Man was with us, for the investigators found no occasion to despise his excitability, and were indeed anxious that he be present in case of obscure rodent manifestations. We noted the Roman inscriptions and unknown altar designs only briefly, for three of the savants had already seen them, and all knew their characteristics. Prime attention was paid to the momentous central altar, and within an hour Sir William Brinton had caused it to tilt backward, balanced by some unknown species of counterweight.

There now lay revealed such a horror as would have overwhelmed us had we not been prepared. Through a nearly square opening in the tiled floor, sprawling on a flight of stone steps so prodigiously worn that it was little more than an inclined plane at the center, was a ghastly array of human or semi-human bones. Those which retained their collocation as skeletons showed attitudes of panic, fear, and over all were the marks of rodent gnawing. The skulls denoted nothing short of utter idiocy, cretinism, or primitive semiapedom.

Above the hellishly littered steps arched a descending passage seemingly chiseled from the solid rock, and conducting a current of air. This current was not a sudden and noxious rush as from a closed vault, but a cool breeze with something of freshness in it. We did not pause long, but shiveringly began to clear a passage down the steps. It was then that Sir William, examining the hewn walls, made the odd observation that the passage, according to the direction of the strokes, must have been chiseled *from beneath*.

I must be very deliberate now, and choose my words.

After ploughing down a few steps amidst the gnawed bones we saw that there was light ahead; not any mystic phosphorescence, but a filtered daylight which could not come except from unknown fissures in the cliff that overlooked the waste valley. That such fissures had escaped notice from outside was hardly remarkable, for not only is the valley wholly uninhabited, but the cliff is so high and beetling that only an aeronaut could study its face in detail. A few steps more, and our breaths were literally snatched from us by what we saw; so literally that Thornton, the psychic investigator, actually fainted in the arms of the dazed man who stood behind him. Norrys, his plump face utterly white and flabby, simply cried out inarticulately; whilst I think that what I did was to gasp or hiss, and cover my eyes.

The man behind me—the only one of the party older than I—croaked the hackneyed "My God!" in the most cracked voice I ever heard. Of seven cultivated men, only Sir William Brinton retained his composure, a thing the more to his credit because he led the party and must have seen the sight first.

It was a twilit grotto of enormous height, stretching away farther than any eye could see; a subterraneous world of limitless mystery and horrible suggestion. There were buildings and other architectural remains—in one terrified glance I saw a weird pattern of tumuli, a savage circle of monoliths, a low-domed Roman ruin, a sprawling Saxon pile, and an early English edifice of wood—but all these were dwarfed by the ghoulish spectacle presented by the general surface of the ground. For yards about the steps extended an insane tangle of human bones, or bones at least as human as those on the steps. Like a foamy sea they stretched, some fallen apart, but others wholly or partly articulated as skeletons; these latter invariably in postures of daemoniac frenzy, either fighting off some menace or clutching other forms with cannibal intent.

When Dr. Trask, the anthropologist, stopped to classify the skulls, he found a degraded mixture which utterly baffled him. They were mostly lower than the Piltdown man in the scale of evolution, but in every case definitely human. Many were of higher grade, and a very few were the skulls of supremely and sensitively developed types. All the bones were gnawed, mostly by rats, but somewhat by others of the half-human drove. Mixed with them were many tiny bones of rats—fallen members of the lethal army which closed the ancient epic.

I wonder that any man among us lived and kept his sanity through that hideous day of discovery. Not Hoffman or Huysmans could conceive a scene more wildly incredible, more frenetically repellent, or more Gothically grotesque than the twilit grotto through which we seven staggered; each stumbling on revelation after revelation, and trying to keep for the nonce from thinking of the events which must have taken place there three hundred, or a thousand, or two thousand, or ten thousand years ago. It was the antechamber of hell, and poor Thornton fainted again when Trask told him that some of the skeleton things must have descended as quadrupeds through the last twenty or more generations.

Horror piled on horror as we began to interpret the architectural remains. The quadruped things—with their occasional recruits from the biped class—had been kept in stone pens, out of which they must have broken in their last delirium of hunger or rat-fear. There had been great herds of them, evidently fattened on the coarse vegetables whose remains could be found as a sort of poisonous ensilage at the bottom of huge stone bins older than Rome. I knew now why my ancestors had had such excessive gardens—would to heaven I could forget! The purpose of the herds I did not have to ask.

Sir William, standing with his searchlight in the Roman ruin, translated aloud the most shocking ritual I have ever known; and told of the diet of the antediluvian cult which the priests of Cybele found and mingled with their own. Norrys, used as he was to the trenches, could not walk straight when he came out of the English building. It was a butcher shop and kitchen—he had expected that—but it was too much to see familiar English implements in such a place, and to read familiar English *graffiti* there, some as recent as 1610. I could not go in that building—that building whose demon activities were stopped only by the dagger of my ancestor Walter de la Poer.

What I did venture to enter was the low Saxon building whose oaken door had fallen, and there I found a terrible row of ten stone cells with rusty bars. Three had tenants, all skeletons of high grade, and on the bony forefinger of one I found a seal ring with my own coat-of-arms. Sir William found a vault with far older cells below the Roman chapel, but these cells were empty. Below them was a low crypt with cases of formally arranged bones, some of them bearing terrible parallel inscriptions carved in Latin, Greek, and the tongue of Phrygia.

Meanwhile, Dr. Trask had opened one of the prehistoric tumuli, and brought to light skulls which were slightly more human than a gorilla's, and which bore indescribably ideographic carvings. Through all this horror my cat stalked unperturbed. Once I saw him monstrously perched atop a mountain of bones, and wondered at the secrets that might lie behind his yellow eyes.

Having grasped to some slight degree the frightful revelations of this twilit area—an area so hideously foreshadowed by my recurrent dream—we turned to that apparently boundless depth of midnight cavern where no ray of light from the cliff could penetrate. We shall never know what sightless Stygian worlds yawn beyond the little distance we went, for it was decided that such secrets are not good for mankind. But there was plenty to engross us close at hand, for we had not gone far before the searchlights showed that accursed infinity of pits in which the rats had feasted, and whose sudden lack of replenishment had driven the ravenous rodent army first to turn on the living herds of starving things, and then to burst forth from the priory in that historic orgy of devastation which the peasants will never forget.

God! those carrion black pits of sawed, pricked bones and opened skulls! Those nightmare chasms choked with the pithecanthropoid, Celtic, Roman, and English bones of count-

less unhallowed centuries! Some of them were full, and none
can say how deep they had once been. Others were still bot-
tomless to our searchlights, and peopled by unnamable fancies.
What, I thought, of the hapless rats that stumbled into such
traps amidst the blackness of their quests in this grisly Tar-
tarus?

Once my foot slipped near a horribly yawning brink, and I
had a moment of ecstatic fear. I must have been musing a long
time, for I could not see any of the party but the plump Capt.
Norrys. Then there came a sound from that inky, boundless,
farther distance that I thought I knew; and I saw my old black
cat dart past me like a winged Egyptian god, straight into the
illimitable gulf of the unknown. But I was not far behind, for
there was no doubt after another second. It was the eldritch
scurrying of those fiend-born rats, always questing for new
horrors, and determined to lead me on even unto those grinning
caverns of earth's center where Nyarlathotep, the mad faceless
god, howls blindly in the darkness to the piping of two amor-
phous idiot flute-players.

My searchlight expired, but still I ran. I heard voices, and
yowls, and echoes, but above all there gently rose that impious,
insidious scurrying; gently rising, rising, as a stiff bloated
corpse gently rises above an oily river that flows under endless
onyx bridges to a black, putrid sea.

Something bumped into me—something soft and plump. It
must have been the rats; the viscous, gelatinous, ravenous army
that feast on the dead and the living. . . . Why shouldn't rats eat
a de la Poer as a de la Poer eats forbidden things? . . . The war
ate my boy, damn them all . . . and the Yanks ate Carfax with
flames and burned the Grandsire Delapore and the secret. . . .
No, no, I tell you, I am *not* that demon swineherd in the twilit
grotto! It was *not* Edward Norrys' fat face on that flabby fungous thing! Who says I am a de la Poer? He lived, but my boy
died! . . . Shall a Norrys hold the lands of a de la Poer? . . . It's
voodoo, I tell you . . . that spotted snake. . . . Curse you,

Thornton, I'll teach you to faint at what my family do! . . .
'Sblood, thou stinkard, I'll learn ye how to gust . . . wolde ye
swynke me thilke wys? . . . *Magna Mater! Magna Mater! . . .
Atys . . . Dia ad aghaidh's ad aodaun . . . agus bas dunach ort!
Dhonas's dholas ort, agus leatsa! . . . Ungl . . . ungl . . .
rrlh . . . chchch . . .*

That is what they say I said when they found me in the
blackness after three hours; found me crouching in the blackness over the plump, half-eaten body of Capt. Norrys, with my
own cat leaping and tearing at my throat. Now they have blown
up Exham Priory, taken my Nigger-Man away from me, and
shut me into this barred room at Hanwell with fearful whispers
about my heredity and experience. Thornton is in the next
room, but they prevent me from talking to him. They are trying, too, to suppress most of the facts concerning the priory.
When I speak of poor Norrys they accuse me of a hideous
thing, but they must know that I did not do it. They must know
it was the rats; the slithering scurrying rats whose scampering
will never let me sleep; the demon rats that race behind the
padding in this room and beckon me down to greater horrors
than I have ever known; the rats they can never hear; the rats,
the rats in the walls.

# The Doll

## by Joyce Carol Oates

*M*any years ago a little girl was given, for her fourth birthday, an antique dolls' house of unusual beauty and complexity, and size: for it seemed large enough, almost, for a child to crawl into.

The dolls' house was said to have been built nearly one hundred years before, by a distant relative of the little girl's mother. It had come down through the family and was still in excellent condition: with a steep gabled roof, many tall, narrow windows fitted with real glass, dark green shutters that closed over, three fireplaces made of stone, mock lightning rods, mock shingleboard siding (white), a veranda that nearly circled the house, stained glass at the front door and at the first floor landing, and even a cupola whose tiny roof lifted miraculously away. In the master bedroom there was a canopied bed with white organdy flounces and ruffles; there were tiny window boxes beneath most of the windows; the furniture—all of it Victorian, of course—was uniformly exquisite, having been made with the most fastidious care and affection. The lampshades were adorned with tiny gold fringes, there was a marvelous old tub with claw feet, and nearly every room had a chandelier. When she first saw the dolls' house on the morning of her fourth birthday the little girl was so astonished she could

not speak: for the present was unexpected, and uncannily
"real." It was to be the great present, and the great memory, of
her childhood.

Florence had several dolls which were too large to fit into
the house, since they were average-size dolls, but she brought
them close to the house, facing its open side, and played with
them there. She fussed over them, and whispered to them, and
scolded them, and invented little conversations between them.
One day, out of nowhere, came the name *Bartholomew*—the
name of the family who owned the dolls' house. Where did you
get that name from, her parents asked, and Florence replied
that those were the people who lived in the house. Yes, but
where did the name come from? they asked.

The child, puzzled and a little irritated, pointed mutely at the
dolls.

One was a girl-doll with shiny blond ringlets and blue eyes
that were thickly lashed, and almost too round; another was a
red-haired freckled boy in denim coveralls and a plaid shirt. It
was obvious that they were sister and brother. Another was a
woman-doll, perhaps a mother, who had bright red lips and
who wore a hat cleverly made of soft gray-and-white feathers.
There was even a baby-doll, made of the softest rubber, hairless and expressionless, and oversized in relationship to the
other dolls; and a spaniel, about nine inches in length, with big
brown eyes and a quizzical upturned tail. Sometimes one doll
was Florence's favorite, sometimes another. There were days
when she preferred the blond girl, whose eyes rolled in her
head, and whose complexion was a lovely pale peach. There
were days when the mischievous red-haired boy was obviously
her favorite. Sometimes she banished all the human dolls and
played with the spaniel, who was small enough to fit into most
of the rooms of the dolls' house.

Occasionally Florence undressed the human dolls, and
washed them with a tiny sponge. How strange they were, without their clothes . . . ! Their bodies were poreless and smooth

and blank, there was nothing secret or nasty about them, no
crevices for dirt to hide in, no trouble at all. Their faces were
unperturbable, as always. Calm wise fearless staring eyes that
no harsh words or slaps could disturb. But Florence loved her
dolls very much, and rarely felt the need to punish them.

Her treasure was, of course, the dolls' house with its steep
Victorian roof and its gingerbread trim and its many windows
and that marvelous veranda, upon which little wooden rocking
chairs, each equipped with its own tiny cushion, were set. Visitors—friends of her parents or little girls her own age—were
always astonished when they first saw it. They said: Oh, isn't
it beautiful! They said: Why, it's almost the size of a real house,
isn't it?—though of course it wasn't, it was only a dolls' house,
a little less than thirty-six inches high.

Nearly four decades later while driving along East Fainlight
Avenue in Lancaster, Pennsylvania, a city she had never before
visited, and about which she knew nothing, Florence Parr was
astonished to see, set back from the avenue, at the top of a
stately elm-shaded knoll, her old dolls' house—that is, the
replica of it. The house. The house itself.

She was so astonished that for the passage of some seconds
she could not think what to do. Her most immediate reaction
was to brake her car—for she was a careful, even fastidious
driver; at the first sign of confusion or difficulty she always
brought her car to a stop.

A broad handsome elm- and plane tree–lined avenue, in a
charming city, altogether new to her. Late April: a fragrant,
even rather giddy spring, after a bitter and protracted winter.
The very air trembled, rich with warmth and color. The estates
in this part of the city were as impressive, as stately, as any she
had ever seen: the houses were really mansions, boasting of
wealth, their sloping, elegant lawns protected from the street
by brick walls, or wrought-iron fences, or thick evergreen
hedges. Everywhere there were azaleas, that most gorgeous of

spring flowers—scarlet and white and yellow and flamey-orange, almost blindingly beautiful. There were newly culti-vated beds of tulips, primarily red; and exquisite apple blos-soms, and cherry blossoms, and flowering trees Florence recognized but could not identify by name. *Her* house was sur-rounded by an old-fashioned wrought-iron fence, and in its enormous front yard were red and yellow tulips that had pushed their way through patches of weedy grass.

She found herself on the sidewalk, at the front gate. Like the unwieldy gate that was designed to close over the driveway, this gate was not only open but its bottom spikes had dug into the ground; it had not been closed for some time and could probably not be dislodged. Someone had put up a hand-lettered sign in black, not long ago: 1377 EAST FAINLIGHT. But no name, no family name. Florence stood staring up at the house, her heart beating rapidly. She could not quite believe what she was seeing. Yes, there it was, of course—yet it *could* not be, not in such detail.

The antique dolls' house. *Hers.* After so many years. There was the steep gabled roof, in what appeared to be slate; the old lightning rods; the absurd little cupola that was so charming; the veranda; the white shingleboard siding (which was rather weathered and gray in the bright spring sunshine); most of all, most striking, the eight tall, narrow windows, four to each floor, with their dark shutters. Florence could not determine if the shutters were painted a very dark green, or black. What color had they been on the dolls' house . . . She saw that the gingerbread trim was badly rotted.

The first wave of excitement, almost of vertigo, that had over-taken her in the car had passed; but she felt, still, an unpleasant sense of urgency. Her old doll's house. Here on East Fainlight Avenue in Lancaster, Pennsylvania. Glimpsed so suddenly, on this warm spring morning. And what did it mean . . . ? Obvi-ously there was an explanation. Her distant uncle, who had built the house for his daughter, had simply copied this house, or another just like it; no doubt there were many houses like this one. Florence knew little about Victorian architecture but she supposed that there were many duplications, even in large, costly houses. Unlike contemporary architects, the architects of that era must have been extremely limited, forced to use again and again certain basic structures, and certain basic ornamentation—the cupolas, the gables, the complicated trim. What struck her as so odd, so mysterious, was really nothing but a coincidence. It would make an interesting story, an amusing anecdote, when she returned home; though perhaps it was not even worth mentioning. Her parents might have been intrigued but they were both dead. And she was always careful about dwelling upon herself, her private life, since she halfway imagined that her friends and acquaintances and colleagues would interpret nearly anything she said of a personal nature according to their vision of her as a public person, and she wanted to avoid that.

There was a movement at one of the upstairs windows that caught her eye. It was then transmitted, fluidly, miraculously, to the other windows, flowing from right to left. . . . But no, it was only the reflection of clouds being blown across the sky, up behind her head.

She stood motionless. It was unlike her, it was quite uncharacteristic of her, yet there she stood. She did not want to walk up to the veranda steps, she did not want to ring the doorbell, such a gesture would be ridiculous, and anyway there was no time: she really should be driving on. They would be expecting her soon. Yet she could not turn away. Because it *was* the house. Incredibly, it was her old dolls' house. (Which she had given away, of course, thirty—thirty-five?—years ago. And had rarely thought about since.) It was ridiculous to stand here, so astonished, so slow-witted, so perversely vulnerable . . . yet what other attitude was appropriate, what other attitude would not violate the queer sense of the sacred, the otherworldly, that the house had evoked?

She would ring the doorbell. And why not? She was a tall,

rather wide-shouldered, confident woman, tastefully dressed in a cream-colored spring suit; she was rarely in the habit of apologizing for herself, or feeling embarrassment. Many years ago, perhaps, as a girl, a shy, silly, self-conscious girl: but no longer. Her wavy graying hair had been brushed back smartly from her wide, strong forehead. She wore no makeup, had stopped bothering with it years ago, and with her naturally high-colored, smooth complexion, she was a handsome woman, especially attractive when she smiled and her dark staring eyes relaxed. She *would* ring the doorbell, and see who came to the door, and say whatever flew into her head. She was looking for a family who lived in the neighborhood, she was canvassing for a school millage vote, she was inquiring whether they had any old clothes, old furniture, for . . .

Halfway up the walk she remembered that she had left the keys in the ignition of her car, and the motor running. And her purse on the seat.

She found herself walking unusually slowly. It was unlike her, and the disorienting sense of being unreal, of having stepped into another world, was totally new. A dog began barking somewhere near: the sound seemed to pierce her in the chest and bowels. An attack of panic. An involuntary fluttering of the eyelids. . . . But it was nonsense of course. She would ring the bell, someone would open the door, perhaps a servant, perhaps an elderly woman, they would have a brief conversation, Florence would glance behind her into the foyer to see if the circular staircase looked the same, if the old brass chandelier was still there, if the "marble" floor remained. Do you know the Parr family, Florence would ask, we've lived in Cummington, Massachusetts, for generations, I think it's quite possible that someone from my family visited you in this house, of course it was a very long time ago. I'm sorry to disturb you but I was driving by and I saw your striking house and I couldn't resist stopping for a moment out of curiosity. . . .

There were the panes of stained glass on either side of the

oak door! But so large, so boldly colored. In the dolls' house they were hardly visible, just chips of colored glass. But here they were each about a foot square, starkly beautiful: reds, greens, blues. Exactly like the stained glass of a church.

I'm sorry to disturb you, Florence whispered, but I was driving by and . . .

I'm sorry to disturb you but I am looking for a family named Bartholomew, I have reason to think that they live in this neighborhood. . . .

But as she was about to step onto the veranda the sensation of panic deepened. Her breath came shallow and rushed, her thoughts flew wildly in all directions, she was simply terrified and could not move. The dog's barking had become hysterical.

When Florence was angry or distressed or worried she had a habit of murmuring her name to herself, Florence Parr, Florence Parr, it was soothing, it was mollifying, Florence Parr, it was often vaguely reproachful, for after all she *was* Florence Parr and that carried with it responsibility as well as authority. She named herself, identified herself. It was usually enough to bring her undisciplined thoughts under control. But she had not experienced an attack of panic for many years. All the strength of her body seemed to have fled, drained away; it terrified her to think that she might faint here. What a fool she would make of herself. . . .

As a young university instructor she had nearly succumbed to panic one day, mid-way through a lecture on the metaphysical poets. Oddly, the attack had come not at the beginning of the semester but well into the second month, when she had come to believe herself a thoroughly competent teacher. The most extraordinary sensation of fear, unfathomable and groundless fear, which she had never been able to comprehend afterward. . . . One moment she had been speaking of Donne's famous image in "The Relic"—a bracelet of "bright hair about the bone"—and the next moment she was so panicked she could hardly catch her breath. She wanted to run out of the classroom, wanted to run out of the building. It was as if a demon had appeared to her. It breathed into her face, shoved her about, tried to pull her under. She would suffocate: she would be destroyed. The sensation was possibly the most unpleasant she had ever experienced in her life though it carried with it no pain and no specific images. Why she was so frightened she could not grasp. Why she wanted nothing more than to run out of the classroom, to escape her students' curious eyes, she was never to understand.

But she did not flee. She forced herself to remain at the podium. Though her voice faltered she did not stop; she continued with the lecture, speaking into a blinding haze. Surely her students must have noticed her trembling . . . ? But she was stubborn, she was really quite tenacious for a young woman of twenty-four, and by forcing herself to imitate herself, to imitate her normal tone and mannerisms, she was able to overcome the attack. As it lifted, gradually, and her eyesight strengthened, her heartbeat slowed, she seemed to know that the attack would never come again in a classroom. And this turned out to be correct.

But now she could not overcome her anxiety. She hadn't a podium to grasp, she hadn't lecture notes to follow, there was no one to imitate, she was in a position to make a terrible fool of herself. And surely someone was watching from the house. . . . It struck her that she had no reason, no excuse, for being here. What on earth could she say if she rang the doorbell? How would she explain herself to a skeptical stranger? I simply must see the inside of your house, she would whisper, I've been led up this walk by a force I can't explain, please excuse me, please humor me, I'm not well, I'm not myself this morning, I only want to see the inside of your house to see if it *is* the house I remember. . . . I had a house like yours. It was yours. But no one lived in my house except dolls; a family of dolls. I loved them but I always sensed that they were blocking the way, standing between me and something else. . . .

The barking dog was answered by another, a neighbor's dog. Florence retreated. Then turned and hurried back to her car, where the keys were indeed in the ignition, and her smart leather purse lay on the seat where she had so imprudently left it.

So she fled the dolls' house, her poor heart thudding. What a fool you are, Florence Parr, she thought brutally, a deep hot blush rising into her face.

The rest of the day—the late afternoon reception, the dinner itself, the after-dinner gathering—passed easily, even routinely, but did not seem to her very real; it was not very convincing. That she was Florence Parr, the president of Champlain College, that she was to be a featured speaker at this conference of administrators of small private liberal arts colleges: it struck her for some reason as an imposture, a counterfeit. The vision of the dolls' house kept rising in her mind's eye. How odd, how very odd the experience had been, yet there was no one to whom she might speak about it, even to minimize it, to transform it into an amusing anecdote. . . . The others did not notice her discomfort. In fact they claimed that she was looking well, they were delighted to see her and to shake her hand. Many were old acquaintances, men and women, but primarily men, with whom she had worked in the past at one college or another; a number were strangers, younger administrators who had heard of her heroic effort at Champlain College, and who wanted to be introduced to her. At the noisy cocktail hour, at dinner, Florence heard her somewhat distracted voice speaking of the usual matters: declining enrollments, building fund campaigns, alumni support, endowments, investments, state and federal aid. Her remarks were met with the same respectful attention as always, as though there were nothing wrong with her.

For dinner she changed into a linen dress of pale blue and dark blue stripes which emphasized her tall, graceful figure, and drew the eye away from her wide shoulders and her stolid thighs; she wore her new shoes with the fashionable three-inch heel, though she detested them. Her haircut was becoming, she had manicured and even polished her nails the evening before, and she supposed she looked attractive enough, especially in this context of middle-aged and older people. But her mind kept drifting away from the others, from the handsome though rather dark colonial dining room, even from the spirited, witty after-dinner speech of a popular administrator and writer, a re-tired president of Williams College, and formerly—a very long time ago, now—a colleague of Florence's at Swarthmore. She smiled with the others, and laughed with the others, but she could not attend to the courtly, white-haired gentleman's as-tringent witticisms; her mind kept drifting back to the dolls' house, out there on East Fainlight Avenue. It was well for her that she hadn't rung the doorbell, for what if someone who was attending the conference had answered the door; it was, after all, being hosted by Lancaster College. What an utter fool she would have made of herself. . . .

She went to her room in the fieldstone alumni house shortly after ten, though there were people who clearly wished to talk with her, and she knew a night of insomnia awaited. Once in the room with its antique furniture and its self-consciously quaint wallpaper she regretted having left the ebullient atmo-sphere downstairs. Though small private colleges were in trou-ble these days, and though most of the administrators at the conference were having serious difficulties with finances, and faculty morale, there was nevertheless a spirit of camaraderie, of heartiness. Of course it was the natural consequence of peo-ple in a social gathering. One simply cannot resist, in such a context, the droll remark, the grateful laugh, the sense of cheer-ful complicity in even an unfortunate fate. How puzzling the human personality is, Florence thought, preparing for bed, moving uncharacteristically slowly, when with others there is a public self, alone there is a private self, and yet both are real. . . . Both are experienced as real. . . .

She lay sleepless in the unfamiliar bed. There were noises in the distance; she turned on the air conditioner, the fan only, to drown them out. Still she could not sleep. The house on East Fainlight Avenue, the dolls' house of her childhood, she lay with her eyes open, thinking of absurd, disjointed things, wondering now why she had *not* pushed her way through that trivial bout of anxiety to the veranda steps, and to the door, after all she was Florence Parr, she had only to imagine people watching her—the faculty senate, students, her fellow administrators—to know how she should behave, with what alacrity and confidence. It was only when she forgot who she was, and imagined herself utterly alone, that she was crippled by uncertainty and susceptible to fear.

The luminous dials of her watch told her it was only 10:35. Not too late, really, to dress and return to the house and ring the doorbell. Of course she would only ring it if the downstairs was lighted, if someone was clearly up. . . . Perhaps an elderly gentleman lived there, alone, someone who had known her grandfather, someone who had visited the Parrs in Cummington. For there *must* be a connection. It was very well to speak of coincidences, but she knew, she knew with a deep, unshakable conviction, that there was a connection between the dolls' house and the house here in town, and a connection between her childhood and the present house. . . . When she explained herself to whoever opened the door, however, she would have to be casual, conversational. Years of administration had taught her diplomacy; one must not appear to be *too* serious. Gravity in leaders is disconcerting, what is demanded is the light, confident touch, the air of private and even secret knowledge. People do not want equality with their leaders: they want, they desperately need, them to be superior. The superiority must be tacitly communicated, however, or it becomes offensive. . . .

Suddenly she was frightened: it seemed to her quite possible that the panic attack might come upon her the next morning, when she gave her address ("The Future of the Humanities in American Education"). She was scheduled to speak at 9:30, she would be the first speaker of the day, and the first real speaker of the conference. And it was quite possible that that disconcerting weakness would return, that sense of utter, almost infantile helplessness. . . .

She sat up, turned on the light, and looked over her notes. They were handwritten, not typed, she had told her secretary not to bother typing them, the address was one she'd given before in different forms, her approach was to be conversational rather than formal though of course she would quote the necessary statistics. . . . But it had been a mistake, perhaps, not to have the notes typed. There were times when she couldn't decipher her own handwriting.

A drink might help. But she couldn't very well go over to the Lancaster Inn, where the conference was to be held, and where there was a bar; and of course she hadn't anything with her in the room. As a rule she rarely drank. She never drank alone. . . . However, if a drink would help her sleep: would calm her wild racing thoughts.

The dolls' house had been a present for her birthday. Many years ago. She could not recall how many. And there were her dolls, her little family of dolls, which she had not thought of for a lifetime. She felt a pang of loss, tenderness. . . .

Florence Parr who suffered quite frequently from insomnia. But of course no one knew.

Florence Parr who had had a lump in her right breast removed, a cyst really, harmless, absolutely harmless, shortly after her thirty-eighth birthday. But none of her friends at Champlain knew. Not even her secretary knew. And the ugly little thing turned out to be benign: absolutely harmless. So it was well that no one knew.

Florence Parr of whom it was said that she was distant, even guarded, at times. You can't get close to her, someone claimed.

And yet it was often said of her that she was wonderfully warm and open and frank and totally without guile. A popular president. Yet she had the support of her faculty. There might be individual jealousies here and there, particularly among the vice presidents and deans, but in general she had everyone's support and she knew it and was grateful for it and intended to keep it.

It was only that her mind worked, late into the night. Raced. Would not stay still.

Should she surrender to her impulse, and get dressed quickly and return to the house? It would take no more than ten minutes. And quite likely the downstairs lights would *not* be on, the inhabitants would be asleep, she could see from the street that the visit was totally out of the question, she would simply drive on past. And be saved from her audacity.

If I do this, the consequence will be. . . .

If I fail to do this. . . .

She was not, of course, an impulsive person. Nor did she admire impulsive "spontaneous" people: she thought them immature, and frequently exhibitionistic. It was often the case that they were very much aware of their own spontaneity. . . .

She would defend herself against the charge of being calculating. Of being overly cautious. Her nature was simply a very pragmatic one. She took up tasks with extreme interest, and absorbed herself deeply in them, one after another, month after month and year after year, and other considerations simply had to be shunted to the side. For instance, she had never married. The surprise would have been not that Florence Parr had married, but that she had had time to cultivate a relationship that would end in marriage. I am not opposed to marriage for myself, she once said, with unintentional naiveté, but it would take so much time to become acquainted with a man, to go out with him, and talk. . . . At Champlain where everyone liked her, and shared anecdotes about her, it was said that she'd been even as a younger woman so oblivious to men, even to attentive men, that she had failed to recognize a few years later a young linguist whose carrel at the Widener Library had been next to hers, though the young man claimed to have said hello to her every day, and to have asked her out for coffee occasionally. (She had always refused, she'd been far too busy.) When he turned up at Champlain, married, the author of a well-received book on linguistic theory, an associate professor in the Humanities division, Florence had not only been unable to recognize him but could not remember him at all, though he remembered her vividly, and even amused the gathering by recounting to Florence the various outfits she had worn that winter, even the colors of her knitted socks. She had been deeply embarrassed, of course, and yet flattered, and amused. It was proof, after all, that Florence Parr was always at all times Florence Parr.

Afterward she was somewhat saddened, for the anecdote meant, did it not, that she really *had* no interest in men. She was not a spinster because no one had chosen her, not even because she had been too fastidious in her own choosing, but simply because she had no interest in men, she did not even "see" them when they presented themselves before her. It was sad, it was irrefutable. She was an ascetic not through an act of will but through temperament.

It was at this point that she pushed aside the notes for her talk, her heart beating wildly as a girl's. She had no choice, she *must* satisfy her curiosity about the house, if she wanted to sleep, if she wanted to remain sane.

As the present of the dolls' house was the great event of her childhood, so the visit to the house on East Fainlight Avenue was to be the great event of her adulthood: though Florence Parr was never to allow herself to think of it, afterward.

It was a mild, quiet night, fragrant with blossoms, not at all intimidating. Florence drove to the avenue, to the house, and was consoled by the numerous lights burning in the neighborhood: of course it wasn't late, of course there was nothing extraordinary about what she was going to do.

Lights were on downstairs. Whoever lived there was up, in the living room. Waiting for her.

Remarkable, her calmness. After so many foolish hours of indecision.

She ascended the veranda steps, which gave slightly beneath her weight. Rang the doorbell. After a minute or so an outside light went on: she felt exposed: began to smile nervously. One smiled, one soon learned how. There was no retreating.

She saw the old wicker furniture on the porch. Two rocking chairs, a settee. Once painted white but now badly weathered. No cushions.

A dog began barking angrily.

Florence Parr, Florence Parr. She knew who she was, but there was no need to tell *him*. Whoever it was, peering out at her through the dark stained glass, an elderly man, someone's left-behind grandfather. Still, owning this house in this part of town meant money and position: you might sneer at such things but they do have significance. Even to pay the property taxes, the school taxes. . . .

The door opened and a man stood staring out at her, half smiling, quizzical. He was not the man she expected, he was not elderly, but of indeterminate age, perhaps younger than she. "Yes? Hello? What can I do for . . . ?" he said.

She heard her voice, full-throated and calm. The rehearsed question. Questions. An air of apology beneath which her confidence held firm. ". . . driving in the neighborhood earlier today, staying with friends. . . . Simply curious about an old connection between our families. . . . Or at any rate between my family and the people who built this. . . ."

Clearly he was startled by her presence, and did not quite grasp her questions. She spoke too rapidly, she would have to repeat herself.

He invited her in. Which was courteous. A courtesy that

struck her as unconscious, automatic. He was very well man-
nered. Puzzled but not suspicious. Not unfriendly. Too young
for this house, perhaps—for so old and shabbily elegant a
house. Her presence on his doorstep, her bold questions, the
bright strained smile that stretched her lips must have baffled
him but he did not think her *odd*: he respected her, was not
judging her. A kindly, simple person. Which was of course a relief. He might even be a little simple-minded. Slow-thinking.
He certainly had nothing to do with . . . with whatever she was
involved in, in this part of the world. He would tell no one
about her.

". . . a stranger to the city? . . . staying with friends?"

"I only want to ask: does the name Parr mean anything to
you?"

A dog was barking, now frantically. But kept its distance.

Florence was being shown into the living room, evidently
the only lighted room downstairs. She noted the old staircase,
graceful as always. But they had done something awkward
with the wainscoting, painted it a queer slate blue. And the
floor was no longer of marble but a poor imitation, some sort
of linoleum tile. . . .

"The chandelier," she said suddenly.

The man turned to her, smiling his amiable quizzical worn
smile.

"Yes . . . ?"

"It's very attractive," she said. "It must be an antique."

In the comfortable orangish light of the living room she saw
that he had sandy red hair, thinning at the crown. But boyishly
frizzy at the sides. He might have been in his late thirties but
his face was prematurely lined and he stood with one shoulder
slightly higher than the other, as if he were very tired. She
began to apologize again for disturbing him. For taking up his
time with her impulsive, probably futile curiosity.

"Not at all," he said. "I usually don't go to bed until well past
midnight."

Florence found herself sitting at one end of an overstuffed sofa. Her smile was strained but as wide as ever, her face had begun to grow very warm. Perhaps he would not notice her blushing.

". . . insomnia?"

"Yes. Sometimes."

"I too . . . sometimes."

He was wearing a green-and-blue plaid shirt, with thin red stripes. A flannel shirt. The sleeves rolled up to his elbows. And what looked like work-trousers. Denim. A gardener's outfit perhaps. Her mind cast about desperately for something to say and she heard herself asking about his garden, his lawn. So many lovely tulips. Most of them red. And there were plane trees, and several elms. . . .

He faced her, leaning forward with his elbows on his knees. A faintly sunburned face. A redhead's complexion, somewhat freckled.

The chair he sat in did not look familiar. It was an ugly brown, imitation brushed velvet. Florence wondered who had bought it: a silly young wife perhaps.

". . . Parr family?"

"From Lancaster?"

"Oh no. From Cummington, Massachusetts. We've lived there for many generations."

He appeared to be considering the name, frowning at the carpet.

". . . *does* sound familiar. . . ."

"Oh, does it? I had hoped. . . ."

The dog approached them, no longer barking. Its tail wagged and thumped against the side of the sofa, the leg of an old-fashioned table, nearly upsetting a lamp. The man snapped his fingers at the dog and it came no further; it quivered, and made a half growling, half sighing noise, and lay with its snout on its paws and its skinny tail outstretched, a few feet from Florence. She wanted to placate it, to make friends. But it was such an ugly creature—partly hairless, with scruffy white whiskers, a naked sagging belly.

"If the dog bothers you . . ."

"Oh no, no. Not at all."

"He only means to be friendly."

"I can see that," Florence said, laughing girlishly. ". . . He's very handsome."

"Hear that?" the man said, snapping his fingers again. "The lady says you're very handsome! Can't you at least stop drooling, don't you have any manners at all?"

"I haven't any pets of my own. But I like animals."

She was beginning to feel quite comfortable. The living room was not exactly what she had expected but it was not *too* bad. There was the rather low, overstuffed sofa in which she sat, the cushions made of a silvery-white, silvery-gray material, with a feathery sheen, plump, immense, like bellies or breasts, a monstrous old piece of furniture yet nothing one would want to sell: for certainly it had come down in the family, it must date from the turn of the century. There was the Victorian table with its coy ornate legs, and its tasseled cloth, and its extraordinary oversized lamp: the sort of thing Florence would smile at in an antique shop, but which looked fairly reasonable here. In fact she should comment on it, since she was staring at it so openly.

". . . antique? European?"

"I think so, yes," the man said.

"Is it meant to be fruit, or a tree, or . . ."

Bulbous and flesh-colored, peach-colored. With a tarnished brass stand. A dust-dimmed golden lampshade with embroidered blue trim that must have been very pretty at one time.

They talked of antiques. Of old houses. Families.

A queer odor defined itself. It was not unpleasant, exactly.

"Would you like something to drink?"

"Why yes I—"

"Excuse me just a moment."

Alone she wondered if she might prowl about the room. But it was long and narrow and poorly lighted at one end: in fact, one end dissolved into darkness. A faint suggestion of furniture there, an old spinet piano, a jumble of chairs, a bay window that must look out onto the garden. She wanted very much to examine a portrait above the mantel of the fireplace but perhaps the dog would bark, or grow excited, if she moved.

It had crept closer to her feet, shuddering with pleasure.

The redheaded man, slightly stooped, brought a glass of something dark to her. In one hand was his own drink, in the other hand hers.

"Taste it. Tell me what you think."

"It seems rather strong. . . ."

Chocolate. Black and bitter. And thick.

"It should really be served hot," the man said.

"Is there a liqueur of some kind in it?"

"Is it too strong for you?"

"Oh no. No. Not at all."

Florence had never tasted anything more bitter. She nearly gagged.

But a moment later it was all right: she forced herself to take a second swallow, and a third. And the pricking painful sensation in her mouth faded.

The redheaded man did not return to his chair, but stood before her, smiling. In the other room he had done something hurried with his hair: had tried to brush it back with his hands, perhaps. A slight film of perspiration shone on his high forehead.

"Do you live alone here?"

"The house does seem rather large, doesn't it?—for a person to live in it alone."

"Of course you have your dog. . . ."

"Do *you* live alone now?"

Florence set the glass of chocolate down. Suddenly she remembered what it reminded her of: a business associate of her father's, many years ago, had brought a box of chocolates back from a trip to Russia. The little girl had popped one into her mouth and had been dismayed by their unexpectedly bitter taste.

She had spat the mess out into her hand. While everyone stared.

As if he could read her thoughts the redheaded man twitched, moving his jaw and his right shoulder jerkily. But he continued smiling as before and Florence did not indicate that she was disturbed. In fact she spoke warmly of the living room's furnishings, and repeated her admiration for handsome old houses like this one. The man nodded, as if waiting for her to say more.

". . . a family named Bartholomew? Of course it was many years ago."

"Bartholomew? Did they live in this neighborhood?"

"Why yes I think so. That's the real reason I stopped in. I once knew a little girl who—"

"Bartholomew, Bartholomew," the man said slowly, frowning. His face puckered. One corner of his mouth twitched with the effort of his concentration: and again his right shoulder jerked. Florence was afraid he would spill his chocolate drink.

Evidently he had a nervous ailment of some kind. But she could not inquire.

He murmured the name *Bartholomew* to himself, his expression grave, even querulous. Florence wished she had not asked the question because it was a lie, after all. She rarely told lies. Yet it had slipped from her, it had glided smoothly out of her mouth.

She smiled guiltily, ducking her head. She took another swallow of the chocolate drink.

Without her having noticed, the dog had inched forward. His great head now rested on her feet. His wet brown eyes peered up at her, oddly affectionate. A baby's eyes. It was true that he was drooling, in fact he was drooling on her ankles, but of course he could not help it. . . . Then she noted that he had wet on the carpet. Only a few feet away. A dark stain, a small puddle.

Yet she could not shrink away in revulsion. After all, she was a guest and it was not time for her to leave.

". . . Bartholomew. You say they lived in this neighborhood?"

"Oh yes."

"But when?"

"Why I really don't . . . I was only a child at the. . . ."

"But when was this?"

He was staring oddly at her, almost rudely. The twitch at the corner of his mouth had gotten worse. He moved to set his glass down and the movement was jerky, puppet-like. Yet he stared at her all the while. Florence knew people often felt uneasy because of her dark over-large staring eyes: but she could not help it. She did not *feel* the impetuosity, the reproach, her expression suggested. So she tried to soften it by smiling. But sometimes the smile failed, it did not deceive anyone at all.

Now that her host had stopped smiling she could see that he was really quite mocking. His tangled sandy eyebrows lifted ironically.

"You said you were a stranger to this city, and now you're saying you've been here. . . ."

"But it was so long ago, I was only a . . ."

He drew himself up to his full height. He was not a tall man, nor was he solidly built. In fact his waist was slender, for a man's—and he wore odd trousers, or jeans, tight-fitting across his thighs and without zipper or snaps, crotchless. They fit him tightly in the crotch, which was smooth, seamless. His legs were rather short for his torso and arms.

He began smiling at Florence. A sly accusing smile. His head jerked mechanically, indicating something on the floor. He was trying to point with his chin and the gesture was clumsy.

"You did something nasty on the floor there. On the carpet."

Florence gasped. At once she drew herself away from the dog, at once she began to deny it. "I didn't—It wasn't—"

"Right on the carpet there. For everyone to see. To smell."

"I certainly did not," Florence said, blushing angrily. "You know very well it was the—"

"Somebody's going to have to clean it up and it isn't going to be *me*," the man said, grinning.

But his eyes were still angry.

He did not like her at all: she saw that. The visit was a mistake, but how could she leave, how could she escape, the dog had crawled up to her again and was nuzzling and drooling against her ankles, and the redheaded man who had seemed so friendly was now leaning over her, his hands on his slim hips, grinning rudely.

As if to frighten her, as one might frighten an animal or a child, he clapped his hands smartly together. Florence blinked at the sudden sound. And then he leaned forward and clapped his hands together again, right before her face. She cried out for him to leave her alone, her eyes smarted with tears, she was leaning back against the cushions, her head back as far as it would go, and then he clapped his hands once again, hard, bringing them against her burning cheeks, slapping both her cheeks at once, and a sharp thin white-hot sensation ran through her body, from her face and throat to her belly, to the pit of her belly, and from the pit of her belly up into her chest, into her mouth, and even down into her stiffened legs. She screamed for the redheaded man to stop, and twisted convulsively on the sofa to escape him.

"Liar! Bad girl! Dirty girl!" someone shouted.

She wore her new reading glasses, with their attractive plastic frames. And a spring suit, smartly styled, with a silk blouse in a floral pattern. And the tight but fashionable shoes.

Her audience, respectful and attentive, could not see her trembling hands behind the podium, or her slightly quivering knees. They would have been astonished to learn that she hadn't been able to eat breakfast that morning—that she felt depressed and exhausted though she had managed to fall asleep the night before, probably around two, and had evidently slept her usual dreamless sleep.

She cleared her throat several times in succession, a habit she detested in others.

But gradually her strength flowed back into her. The morning was so sunny, so innocent. These people were, after all, her colleagues and friends: they certainly wished her well, and even appeared to be genuinely interested in what she had to say about the future of the humanities. Perhaps Dr. Parr knew something they did not, perhaps she would share her professional secrets with them. . . .

As the minutes passed Florence could hear her voice grow richer and firmer, easing into its accustomed rhythms. She began to relax. She began to breathe more regularly. She was moving into familiar channels, making points she had made countless times before, at similar meetings, with her deans and faculty chairmen at Champlain, with other educators. A number of people applauded heartily when she spoke of the danger of small private colleges competing unwisely with one another; and again when she made a point, an emphatic point, about the need for the small private school in an era of multiversities. Surely these were remarks anyone might have made, there was really nothing original about them, yet her audience seemed extremely pleased to hear them from her. They *did* admire Florence Parr—that was clear.

She removed her reading glasses. Smiled, spoke without needing to glance at her notes. This part of her speech—an amusing summary of the consequences of certain experimental programs at Champlain, initiated since she'd become president—was more specific, more interesting, and of course she knew it by heart.

The previous night had been one of her difficult nights. At

least initially. Her mind racing in that way she couldn't control, those flame-like pangs of fear, insomnia. And no help for it. And no way out. She'd fallen asleep while reading through her notes and awakened suddenly, her heart beating erratically, body drenched in perspiration—and there she was, lying twisted back against the headboard, neck stiff and aching and her left leg numb beneath her. She'd been dreaming she'd given in and driven out to see the dolls' house; but of course she had not, she'd been in her hotel room all the time. *She'd never left her hotel room.*

She'd never left her hotel room but she'd fallen asleep and dreamt she had but she refused to summon back her dream, not that dream nor any others; in fact she rather doubted she did dream, she never remembered afterward. Florence Parr was one of those people who, as soon as they awake, are *awake*. And eager to begin the day.

At the conclusion of Florence's speech everyone applauded enthusiastically. She'd given speeches like this many times before and it had been ridiculous of her to worry.

Congratulations, handshakes. Coffee was being served.

Florence was flushed with relief and pleasure, crowded about by well-wishers. This was her world, these people her colleagues, they knew her, admired her. Why does one worry about anything! Florence thought, smiling into these friendly faces, shaking more hands. These were all good people, serious professional people, and she liked them very much.

At a distance a faint fading jeering cry *Liar! Dirty girl!* but Florence was listening to the really quite astute remarks of a youngish man who was a new dean of arts at Vassar. How good the hot, fresh coffee was. And a thinly layered apricot brioche she'd taken from a proffered silver tray.

The insult and discomfort of the night were fading; the vision of the doll's house was fading, dying. She refused to summon it back. She would not give it another thought. Friends—acquaintances—well-wishers were gathering around her, she knew her skin was glowing like a girl's, her eyes were bright and clear and hopeful; at such times, buoyed by the presence of others as by waves of applause, you forget your age, your loneliness—the very perimeters of your soul.

*Day* is the only reality. She'd always known.

Though the conference was a success, and colleagues at home heard that Florence's contribution had been particularly well received, Florence began to forget it within a few weeks. So many conferences!—so many warmly applauded speeches! Florence was a professional woman who, by nature more than design, pleased both women and men; she did not stir up controversy, she "stimulated discussion." Now she was busily preparing for her first major conference, to be held in London in September: "The Role of the Humanities in the 21st Century." Yes, she was apprehensive, she told friends—"But it's a true challenge."

When a check arrived in the mail for five hundred dollars, an honorarium for her speech in Lancaster, Pennsylvania, Florence was puzzled at first—not recalling her speech, nor the circumstances. How odd! She'd never been there, had she? Then, to a degree, as if summoning forth a dream, she remembered: the beautiful Pennsylvania landscape, ablaze with spring flowers; a crowd of well-wishers gathered around to shake her hand. Why, Florence wondered, had she ever worried about her speech?—her public self? Like an exquisitely precise clockwork mechanism, a living mannequin, she would always do well: you'll applaud too, when you hear her.

# Lizzie Borden Took An Axe . . .

## by Robert Bloch

*"Lizzie Borden took an axe
And gave her mother forty whacks.
When she saw what she had done
She gave her father forty-one."*

Men say that horror comes at midnight, born of whispers out of dreams. But horror came to me at high noon, heralded only by the prosaic jangling of a telephone.

I had been sitting in the office all morning, staring down the dusty road that led to the hills. It coiled and twisted before my aching eyes as a shimmering sun played tricks upon my vision. Nor were my eyes the only organs that betrayed me; something about the heat and the stillness seemed to invade my brain. I was restless, irritable, disturbed by a vague presentiment.

The sharp clangor of the phone bell crystallized my apprehension in a single, strident note.

My palms dripped perspiration-patterns across the receiver. The phone was warm, leaden weight against my ear. But the voice I heard was cold; icy cold, frozen with fear. The words congealed.

"Jim—come and help me!"

That was all. The receiver clicked before I could reply. The phone slid to the desk as I rose and ran to the door.

It was Anita's voice, of course.

It was Anita's voice that sent me speeding toward my car; sent me racing down the desolate, heat-riddled road toward the old house deep in the hills.

Something had happened out there. Something was bound to happen, sooner or later. I'd known it, and now I cursed myself for not insisting on the sensible thing. Anita and I should have eloped weeks ago.

I should have had the courage to snatch her bodily away from this atmosphere of Faulkneresque melodrama, and I might have, if only I had been able to *believe* in it.

At the time it all seemed so improbable. Worse than that, it seemed *unreal*.

There are no legend-haunted houses looming on lonely hill-sides. Yet Anita lived in one.

There are no gaunt, fanatical old men who brood over black books; no "hex doctors" whose neighbors shun them in superstitious dread. Yet Anita's uncle, Gideon Godfrey, was such a man.

Young girls cannot be kept virtual prisoners in this day and age; they cannot be forbidden to leave the house, to love, and marry the man of their choice. Yet Anita's uncle had her under lock and key, and our wedding was prohibited.

Yes, it was all sheer melodrama. The whole affair struck me as ridiculous when I thought about it; but when I was with Anita, I did not laugh.

When I heard Anita talk about her uncle, I almost believed; not that he had supernatural powers, but that he was cunningly, persistently attempting to drive her mad.

That's something you can understand, something evil, yet tangible.

There was a trust fund, and Gideon Godfrey was Anita's legal guardian. He had her out there in his rotting hulk of a house—completely at his mercy. It might easily occur to him to work on her imagination with wild stories and subtle confirmations.

Anita told me. Told me of the locked rooms upstairs where the old man sat mumbling over the moldering books he'd hidden away there. She told me of his feuds with farmers, his open boastings of the "hex" he had put on cattle, the blights he claimed to visit upon crops.

Anita told me of her dreams. Something black came into her room at night. Something black and inchoate—a trailing mist that was nevertheless a definite and tangible presence. It had features, if not a face; a voice, if not a throat. It whispered.

And as it whispered, it caressed her. She would fight off the inky strands brushing her face and body; she would struggle to summon the scream which dispelled spectre and sleep simultaneously.

Anita had a name for the black thing, too.

She called it an *incubus*.

In ancient tracts on witchcraft, the incubus is mentioned—the dark demon that comes to women in the night. The black emissary of Satan the Tempter; the lustful shadow that rides the nightmare.

I knew of the incubus as a legend. Anita knew of it as a reality.

Anita grew thin and pale. I knew there was no magic concerned in her metamorphosis—confinement in that bleak old house was alchemy enough to work the change. That, plus the sadistically in-spired hintings of Gideon Godfrey, and the carefully calculated at-mosphere of dread which resulted in the dreams.

But I had been weak, I didn't insist. After all, there was no real proof of Godfrey's machinations, and any attempt to bring issues to a head might easily result in a sanity hearing for Anita, rather than the old man.

I felt that, given time, I would be able to make Anita come away with me voluntarily.

And now, there was no time.

*Something* had happened.

The car churned dust from the road as I turned in toward the tottering gambrels of the house on the hillside. Through the flickering heat of a midsummer afternoon, I peered at the ruined gables above the long porch.

I swung up the drive, shot the car past the barn and side-build-ings, and parked hastily.

No figure appeared at the open windows, and no voice called

a greeting as I ran up the porch steps and paused before the open door. The hall within was dark. I entered heedless of knocking, and turned towards the parlor.

Anita was standing there, waiting, on the far side of the room. Her red hair was disheveled about her shoulders; her face was pale—but she was obviously unharmed. Her eyes brightened when she saw me.

"Jim—you're here!"

She held out her arms to me, and I moved across the room to embrace her.

As I moved, I stumbled over something.

I looked down.

Lying at my feet was the body of Gideon Godfrey—the head split open and crushed to a bloody pulp.

## 2.

Then Anita was sobbing in my arms, and I was patting her shoulders and trying not to stare at the red horror on the floor.

"Help me," she whispered, over and over again. "Help me!"

"Of course I'll help you," I murmured. "But—what happened?"

"I don't—know."

"You don't *know?*"

Something in my intonation sobered her. She straightened up, pulled away, and began dabbing at her eyes. Meanwhile she whispered on, hastily.

"It was hot this morning. I was out in the barn. I felt tired and dozed off in the hayloft. Then, all at once, I woke and came back into the house. I found—him—lying here."

"There was no noise? Nobody around?"

"Not a soul."

"You can see how he was killed," I said. "Only an axe could do such a job. But—where is it?"

She averted her gaze. "The axe? I don't know. It should be beside the body, if someone killed him."

I turned and started out of the room.

"Jim—where are you going?"

"To call the police, naturally," I told her.

"No, you can't. Don't you see? If you call them now, they'll think *I* did it."

I could only nod. "That's right. It's a pretty flimsy story, isn't it Anita? If we only had a weapon; fingerprints, or footsteps, some kind of clue—"

Anita sighed. I took her hand. "Try to remember," I said, softly. "You're sure you were out in the barn when this happened? Can't you remember more than that?"

"No, darling. It's all so confused, somehow. I was sleeping— I had one of my dreams—the black thing came—"

I shuddered. I knew how *that* statement affected me, and I could imagine the reaction of the police. She was quite mad, I was sure of it; and yet another thought struggled for realization. Somehow I had the feeling that I had lived through this moment before. Pseudo-memory. Or had I heard of it, read of it?

Read of it? Yes, that was it!

"Try hard, now," I muttered. "Can't you recall how it all began? Don't you know why you went out to the barn in the first place?"

"Yes. I think I can remember. I went out there for some fishing sinkers."

"Fishing sinkers? In the barn?"

Something clicked, after all. I stared at her with eyes as glassy as those of the corpse on the floor.

"Listen to me," I said. "You're not Anita Loomis. You're— Lizzie Borden!"

She didn't say a word. Obviously the name had no meaning for her. But it was all coming back to me now; the old, old story, the unsolved mystery.

I guided her to the sofa, sat beside her. She didn't look at me. I didn't look at her. Neither of us looked at the thing on the floor. The heat shimmered all around us in the house of death as I whispered the story to her—the story of Lizzie Borden—

## 3.

It was early August of the year 1892. Fall River, Massachusetts lay gasping in the surge of a heat-wave.

The sun beat down upon the home of Fall River's leading citizen, the venerable Andrew Jackson Borden. Here the old man dwelt with his second wife, Mrs. Abby Borden, stepmother of the two girls, Emma and Lizzie Borden. The maid, Bridget "Maggie" Sullivan, completed the small household. A house guest, John V. Morse, was away at this time, visiting. Emma, the older Borden girl, was also absent.

Only the maid and Lizzie Borden were present on August 2nd, when Mr. and Mrs. Borden became ill. It was Lizzie who spread the news—she told her friend, Marion Russell, that she believed their milk had been poisoned.

But it was too hot to bother, too hot to think. Besides, Lizzie's ideas weren't taken very seriously. At 32, the angular, unprepossessing younger daughter was looked upon with mixed opinion by the members of the community. It was known that she was "cultured" and "refined"—she had traveled in Europe; she was a churchgoer, taught a class in a church mission, and enjoyed a reputation for "good work" as a member of the WCTU and similar organizations. Yet some folks thought her temperamental, even eccentric. She had "notions."

So the illness of the elder Bordens was duly noted and ascribed to natural causes; it was impossible to think about anything more important than the omnipresent heat, and the forthcoming Annual Picnic of the Fall River Police Department, scheduled for August 4th.

On the 4th the heat was unabated, but the picnic was in full swing by 11 o'clock—the time at which Andrew Jackson Borden left his downtown office and came home to relax on the parlor sofa. He slept fitfully in the noonday swelter.

Lizzie Borden came in from the barn a short while later and found her father asleep no longer.

Mr. Borden lay on the sofa, his head bashed in so that his features were unrecognizable.

Lizzie Borden called the maid, "Maggie" Sullivan, who was resting in her room. She told her to run and fetch Dr. Bowen, a near neighbor. He was not at home.

Another neighbor, a Mrs. Churchill, happened by. Lizzie Borden greeted her at the door.

"Someone has killed father," were Lizzie's words.

"And where is your mother?" Mrs. Churchill asked.

Lizzie Borden hesitated. It was hard to think in all this heat. "Why—she's out. She received a note to go and help someone who is sick."

Mrs. Churchill didn't hesitate. She marched to a public livery stable and summoned help. Soon a crowd of neighbors and friends gathered; police and doctors were in attendance. And in the midst of growing confusion, it was Mrs. Churchill who went directly upstairs to the spare room.

Mrs. Borden rested there, her head smashed in.

By the time Dr. Dolan, the coroner, arrived, questioning was already proceeding. The Chief of Police and several of his men were on hand, establishing the fact that there had been no attempt at robbery. They began to interrogate Lizzie.

Lizzie Borden said she was in the barn, eating pears and looking for fishing sinkers—hot as it was. She dozed off, was awakened by a muffled groan, and came into the house to investigate. There she found her father's hacked body. And that was all—

Now her story of a suspected poisoning was recalled, with fresh significance. A druggist said that a woman had indeed come into his shop several days before and attempted to procure some prussic acid—saying she needed it to kill the moths in her fur coat. She had been refused, and informed by the proprietor that she needed a doctor's prescription.

The woman was identified, too—as Lizzie Borden.

Lizzie's story of the note summoning her mother away from

the house now came in for scrutiny. No such note was ever discovered.

Meanwhile, the investigators were busy. In the cellar, they discovered a hatchet with a broken handle. It appeared to have been recently washed, then covered with ashes. Water and ashes conceal stains. . . .

Shock, heat, embarrassment all played subtle parts in succeeding events. The police presently withdrew without taking formal action, and the whole matter was held over, pending an inquest. After all, Andrew Jackson Borden was a wealthy citizen, his daughter was a prominent and respectable woman, and no one wished to act hastily.

Days passed in a pall of heat and gossip behind sweaty palms. Lizzie's friend, Marion Russell, dropped in at the house three days after the crime and discovered Lizzie burning a dress.

"It was all covered with paint," Lizzie Borden explained.

Marion Russell remembered that dress—it was the one Lizzie Borden had worn on the day of the murders.

The inevitable inquest was held, with the inevitable verdict. Lizzie Borden was arrested and formally charged with the slayings.

The press took over. The church members defended Lizzie Borden. The sobsisters made much of her. During the six months preceding the actual trial, the crime became internationally famous.

But nothing new was discovered.

During the thirteen days of the trial, the bewildering story was recounted without any sensational development.

Why should a refined New England spinster suddenly kill her father and stepmother with a hatchet, then boldly "discover" the bodies and summon the police?

The prosecution was unable to give a satisfactory answer. On June 20th, 1893, Lizzie Borden was acquitted by a jury of her peers, after one hour of deliberation.

She retired to her home and lived a life of seclusion for many,

many years. The stigma had been erased, but the mystery remained unsolved with her passing.

Only the grave little girls remained, skipping their ropes and solemnly chanting:

> *"Lizzie Borden took an axe*
> *And gave her mother forty whacks.*
> *When she saw what she had done*
> *She gave her father forty-one."*

## 4.

That's the story I told Anita—the story you can read wherever famous crimes are chronicled.

She listened without comment, but I could hear the sharp intake of breath as I recounted some singularly significant parallel. *The hot day . . . the barn . . . the fishing sinkers . . . a sudden sleep, a sudden awakening . . . the return to the house . . . discovery of a body . . . took an axe. . . .*

She waited until I had finished before speaking.

"Jim, why do you tell me this? Is it your way of hinting that I—took an axe to my uncle?"

"I'm not hinting anything," I answered. "I was just struck by the amazing similarity of this case and the Lizzie Borden affair."

"What do you think happened, Jim? In the Lizzie Borden case, I mean."

"I don't know," I said slowly. "I was wondering if you had a theory."

Her opal eyes glinted in the shadowed room. "Couldn't it have been the same thing?" she whispered. "You know what I've told you about my dreams. About the incubus."

"Suppose Lizzie Borden had those dreams, too. Suppose an entity emerged from her sleeping brain; an entity that would take up an axe and kill—"

She sensed my protest and ignored it. "Uncle Gideon knew of

such things. How the spirit descends upon you in sleep. Couldn't such a presence emerge into the world while she slept and kill her parents? Couldn't such a being creep into the house here while I slept and kill Uncle Gideon?"

I shook my head. "You know the answer I must give you," I said. "And you can guess what the police would say to that. Our only chance now, before calling them, is to find the murder weapon."

We went out into the hall together, and hand in hand we walked through the silent ovens that were the rooms of this old house. Everywhere was dust and desolation. The kitchen alone bore signs of recent occupancy—they had breakfasted there early in the day, Anita said.

There was no axe or hatchet to be found anywhere.

It took courage to tackle the cellar. I was almost certain of what we must find. But Anita did not recoil, and we descended the dark stairwell.

The cellar did not yield up a single sharp instrument.

Then we were walking up the stairs to the second floor. The front bedroom was ransacked, then Anita's little room, and at last we stood before the door of Gideon Godfrey's chamber.

"It's locked," I said. "That's funny."

"No," Anita demurred. "He always kept it locked. The key must be downstairs with—him."

"I'll get it," I said. And I did so. When I returned with the rusty key, Anita stood quaking in the hallway.

"I won't go inside with you," she breathed. "I've never been inside his room. I'm afraid. He used to lock himself in and I'd hear sounds late at night—he was praying, but not to God—"

"Wait here, then," I said.

I unlocked the door, opened it, stepped across the threshold.

Gideon Godfrey may have been a madman himself. He may have been a cunning schemer, bent on deluding his niece. But in either case, he did believe in sorcery.

That much was evident from the contents of his room. I saw the books, saw the crudely drawn chalk circles on the floor; literally dozens of them, hastily obliterated and repeated endlessly. There were queer geometric configurations traced in blue chalk upon one of the walls, and candle-drippings covered walls and floors alike.

The heavy, fetid air held a faint, acrid reek of incense. I noted one sharp instrument in the room—a long silver knife lying on a side-table next to a pewter bowl. The knife seemed rusty, and the rust was red. . . .

But it was not the murder weapon, that was certain. I was looking for an axe, and it wasn't here.

I joined Anita in the hall.

"Isn't there anywhere else?" I asked, Another room?"

"Perhaps the barn," she suggested.

"And we didn't really search in the parlor," I added.

"Don't make me go in there again," Anita begged. "Not in the same room where he is. You look there and I'll go through the barn."

We parted at the foot of the stairs. She went out the side entrance and I walked back into the parlor.

I looked behind the chairs, under the sofa. I found nothing. It was hot in there; hot and quiet. My head began to swim.

Heat—silence—and that grinning thing on the floor. I turned away, leaned against the mantel, and stared at my bloodshot eyes in the mirror.

All at once I saw it, standing behind me. It was like a cloud—a black cloud. But it wasn't a cloud. It was a *face*. A face, covered by a black mask of wavering smoke; a mask that leered and pressed closer.

Through heat and silence it came, and I couldn't move. I stared at the swirling, cloudy smoke that shrouded a face.

Then I heard something swish, and I turned.

Anita was standing behind me.

As I grasped her wrists she screamed and fell. I could only

stare down at her, stare down as the black cloud over her face disappeared, oozed into air.

The search was over. I'd found the murder weapon, all right; it rested rigidly in her hands—the bloodstained axe!

### 5.

I carried Anita over to the sofa. She didn't move, and I made no attempt to revive her.

Then I went out into the hall, carrying the axe with me. No sense in taking any chances. I trusted Anita still, but not that thing—not that black mist, swirling up like smoke to take possession of a living brain and make it lust to kill.

Demoniac possession it was; the legend spoken of in ancient books like those in the room of the dead wizard.

I crossed the hall to the little study opposite the parlor. The wall telephone was here; I picked it up and rang the operator.

She got me the Highway Police headquarters. I don't know why I called them, rather than the sheriff. I was in a daze throughout the entire call. I stood there holding the axe in one hand, reporting the murder in a few words.

Questions rose from the other end of the wire; I did not answer them.

"Come on out to the Godfrey place," I said. "There's been a killing."

What else *could* I say?

What would we be telling the police, half an hour from now, when they arrived on the scene?

They wouldn't believe the truth—wouldn't believe that a demon could enter a human body and activate it as an instrument for murder.

But I believed it now. I had seen the fiend peering out of Anita's face when she tried to sneak up behind me with the axe. I had seen the black smoke, the conjuration of a demon lusting for bloody death.

Now I knew that it must have entered her as she slept; made her kill Gideon Godfrey.

Perhaps such a thing had happened to Lizzie Borden. Yes. The eccentric spinster with the overactive imagination, so carefully repressed; the eccentric spinster, sleeping in the barn on that hot summer day—

> *"Lizzie Borden took an axe*
> *And gave her mother forty whacks."*

I leaned back, the verse running through my head.

It was hotter than I had believed possible, and the stillness hinted of approaching storm.

I groped for coolness, felt the cold axeblade in my hand as I leaned the weapon across my lap. As long as I held onto this, we were safe. The fiend was foiled, now. Wherever that presence lurked, it must be raging, for it could not take possession.

Oh, that was madness! The heat was responsible, surely. Sunstroke caused Anita to kill her uncle. Sunstroke brought on her babblings about an incubus and dreams. Sunstroke impelled that sudden, murderous attack upon me before the mirror.

Sympathetic hallucination accounted for my image of a face veiled by a black mist. It had to be that way. The police would say so, doctors would say so.

> *"When she saw what she had done*
> *She gave her father forty-one."*

Police. Doctors. Lizzie Borden. The heat. The cool axe. Forty whacks. . . .

### 6.

The first crash of thunder awakened me. For a moment I thought the police had arrived, then realized that the heat-storm was breaking. I blinked and rose from the armchair. Then I realized that something was *missing*.

The axe no longer rested across my lap.

It wasn't on the floor. It wasn't visible anywhere. The axe had disappeared again!

"Anita," I gasped. I knew without conscious formulation of thought how it must have happened. She had awakened while I slept—come in here and stolen the axe from me.

What a fool I had been to sleep!

I might have guessed it . . . while she was unconscious, the lurking demon had another chance to gain possession. That was it; the demon had entered into Anita again.

I faced the door, stared at the floor, and saw my confirmation scrawled in a trail of red wetness dotting the carpet and outer hall.

It was blood. Fresh blood.

I rushed across the hall, re-entered the parlor.

Then I gasped, but with relief. For Anita was still lying on the couch, just as I had left her. I wiped the sudden perspiration from my eyes and forehead, then stared again at the red pattern on the floor.

The trail of blood ended beside the couch, all right. But did it lead *to* the couch—or *away* from it?

Thunder roared through the heat. A flicker of lightning seared the shadows of the room as I tried to puzzle it out.

What did it mean? It meant that perhaps Anita was not possessed of a demon now while she slept.

*But I had slept, too.*

Maybe—maybe the demon had come to *me* while *I* dozed off!

All at once, everything blurred. I was trying to remember. Where was the axe? Where could it possibly be, *now?*

Then the lightning came again and with it the final confirmation—the revelation.

I saw the axe now, crystal-clear—the axe—buried to the hilt in the top of Anita's head!

# The Yellow Wallpaper

## by Charlotte Perkins Gilman

It is very seldom that mere ordinary people like John and myself secure ancestral halls for the summer.

A colonial mansion, a hereditary estate, I would say a haunted house, and reach the height of romantic felicity—but that would be asking too much of fate!

Still I will proudly declare that there is something queer about it.

Else, why should it be let so cheaply? And why have stood so long untenanted.

John laughs at me, of course, but one expects that in marriage.

John is practical in the extreme. He has no patience with faith, an intense horror of superstition, and he scoffs openly at any talk of things not to be felt and seen and put down in figures.

John is a physician, and *perhaps*—(I would not say it to a living soul, of course, but this is dead paper and a great relief to my mind)—*perhaps* that is one reason I do not get well faster.

You see he does not believe I am sick!

And what can one do?

If a physician of high standing, and one's own husband,

assures friends and relatives that there is really nothing the matter with one but temporary nervous depression—a slight hysterical tendency—what is one to do?

My brother is also a physician, and also of high standing, and he says the same thing.

So I take phosphates or phosphites—whichever it is, and tonics, and journeys, and air, and exercise, and am absolutely forbidden to "work" until I am well again.

Personally, I disagree with their idea.

Personally, I believe that congenial work, with excitement and change, would do me good.

But what is one to do?

I did write for a while in spite of them: but it *does* exhaust me a good deal—having to be so sly about it, or else meet with heavy opposition.

I sometimes fancy that in my condition if I had less opposition and more society and stimulus—but John says the very worst thing I can do is to think about my condition, and I confess it always makes me feel bad.

So I will let it alone and talk about the house.

The most beautiful place! It is quite alone, standing well back from the road, quite three miles from the village. It makes me think of English places that you read about, for there are hedges and walls and gates that lock, and lots of separate little houses for the gardeners and people.

There is a *delicious* garden! I never saw such a garden—large and shady, full of box-bordered paths, and lined with long grape-covered arbors with seats under them.

There were greenhouses, too, but they are all broken now.

There was some legal trouble, I believe, something about the heirs and coheirs; anyhow, the place has been empty for years.

That spoils my ghostliness, I am afraid, but I don't care—there is something strange about the house—I can feel it.

I even said so to John one moonlight evening but he said what I felt was a *draught*, and shut the window.

I get unreasonably angry with John sometimes. I'm sure I never used to be so sensitive. I think it is due to this nervous condition.

But John says if I feel so, I shall neglect proper self-control; so I take pains to control myself—before him, at least, and that makes me very tired.

I don't like our room a bit. I wanted one downstairs that opened on the piazza and had roses all over the window, and such pretty old-fashioned chintz hangings! But John would not hear of it.

He said there was only one window and not room for two beds, and no near room for him if he took another.

He is very careful and loving, and hardly lets me stir without special direction.

I have a schedule prescription for each hour in the day; he takes all care from me, and so I feel basely ungrateful not to value it more.

He said we came here solely on my account, that I was to have perfect rest and all the air I could get. "Your exercise depends on your strength, my dear," said he, "and your food somewhat on your appetite; but air you can absorb all the time." So we took the nursery at the top of the house.

It is a big, airy room, the whole floor nearly, with windows that look all ways, and air and sunshine galore. It was nursery first and then playroom and gymnasium. I should judge; for the windows are barred for little children, and there are rings and things in the walls.

The paint and paper look as if a boy's school had used it. It is stripped off—the paper—in great patches all around the head of my bed, about as far as I can reach, and in a great place on the other side of the room low down. I never saw a worse paper in my life.

One of those sprawling flamboyant patterns committing every artistic sin.

It is dull enough to confuse the eye in following, pronounced enough to constantly irritate and provoke study, and when you follow the lame uncertain curves for a little distance they suddenly commit suicide—plunge off at outrageous angles, destroy themselves in unheard of contradictions.

The color is repellent, almost revolting; a smoldering unclean yellow, strangely faded by the slow-turning sunlight.

It was a dull yet livid orange in some places, a sickly sulphur tint in others.

No wonder the children hated it! I should hate it myself if I had to live in this room long.

There comes John, and I must put this away—he hates to have me write a word.


We have been here two weeks, and I haven't felt like writing before, since that first day.

I am sitting by the window now, up in this atrocious nursery, and there is nothing to hinder my writing as much as I please, save lack of strength.

John is away all day, and even some nights when his cases are serious.

I am glad my case is not serious!

But these nervous troubles are dreadfully depressing.

John does not know how much I really suffer. He knows there is no *reason* to suffer, and that satisfies him.

Of course it is only nervousness. It does weigh on me so not to do my duty in any way!

I meant to be such a help to John, such a real rest and comfort, and here I am a comparative burden already!

Nobody would believe what an effort it is to do what little I am able—to dress and entertain, and order things.

It is fortunate Mary is so good with the baby. Such a dear baby!

And yet I *cannot* be with him, it makes me so nervous.

I suppose John never was nervous in his life. He laughs at me so about this wallpaper!

At first he meant to repaper the room, but afterward he said that I was letting it get the better of me, and that nothing was worse for a nervous patient than to give way to such fancies.

He said that after the wallpaper was changed it would be the heavy bedstead, and then the barred windows, and then that gate at the head of the stairs, and so on.

"You know the place is doing you good," he said, "and really, dear, I don't care to renovate the house just for three months' rental."

"Then do let us go downstairs," I said, "there are such pretty rooms there."

Then he took me in his arms and called me a blessed little goose, and said he would go down to the cellar, if I wished, and have it whitewashed into the bargain.

But he is right enough about the beds and windows and things.

It is an airy and comfortable room as any one need wish, and, of course, I would not be so silly as to make him uncomfortable just for a whim.

I'm really getting quite fond of the big room, all but that horrid paper.

Out of one window I can see the garden, those mysterious deepshaded arbors, the riotous old-fashioned flowers, and bushes and gnarly trees.

Out of another I get a lovely view of the bay and a little private wharf belonging to the estate. There is a beautiful shaded lane that runs down there from the house. I always fancy I see people walking in these numerous paths and arbors, but John has cautioned me not to give way to fancy in the least. He says that with my imaginative power and habit of story-making, a nervous weakness like mine is sure to lead to all manner of excited fancies, and that I ought to use my will and good sense to check the tendency. So I try.

I think sometimes that if I were only well enough to write a little it would relieve the press of ideas and rest me.

But I find I get pretty tired when I try.

It is so discouraging not to have any advice and companionship about my work. When I get really well, John says we will ask Cousin Henry and Julia down for a long visit; but he says he would as soon put fireworks in my pillowcase as to let me have those stimulating people about now.

I wish I could get well faster.

But I must not think about that. This paper looks to me as if it *knew* what a vicious influence it had!

There is a recurrent spot where the pattern lolls like a broken neck and two bulbous eyes stare at you upside down.

I get positively angry with the impertinence of it and the everlastingness. Up and down and sideways they crawl, and those absurd, unblinking eyes are everywhere. There is one place where two breadths didn't match, and the eyes go all up and down the line, one a little higher than the other.

I never saw so much expression in an inanimate thing before, and we all know how much expression they have! I used to lie awake as a child and get more entertainment and terror out of blank walls and plain furniture than most children could find in a toy-store.

I remember what a kindly wink the knobs of our big, old bureau used to have, and there was one chair that always seemed like a strong friend.

I used to feel that if any of the other things looked too fierce I could always hop into the chair and be safe.

The furniture in this room is no worse than inharmonious, however, for we had to bring it all from downstairs. I suppose when this was used as a playroom they had to take the nursery things out, and no wonder! I never saw such ravages as the children have made here.

The wallpaper, as I said before, is torn off in spots, and it sticketh closer than a brother—they must have had perseverance as well as hatred.

Then the floor is scratched and gouged and splintered, the

plaster itself is dug out here and there, and this great heavy bed which is all we found in the room, looks as if it had been through the wars.

But I don't mind it a bit—only the paper.

There comes John's sister. Such a dear girl as she is, and so careful of me! I must not let her find me writing.

She is a perfect and enthusiastic housekeeper, and hopes for no better profession. I verily believe she thinks it is the writing which made me sick!

But I can write when she is out, and see her a long way off from these windows.

There is one that commands the road, a lovely shaded winding road, and one that just looks off over the country. A lovely country, too, full of great elms and velvet meadows.

This wallpaper has a kind of sub-pattern in a different shade, a particularly irritating one, for you can only see it in certain lights, and not clearly then.

But in the places where it isn't faded and where the sun is just so—I can see a strange, provoking, formless sort of figure, that seems to skulk about that silly and conspicuous front design.

There's sister on the stairs!

Well, the fourth of July is over! The people are all gone and I am tired out. John thought it might do me good to see a little company, so we just had mother and Nellie and the children down for a week.

Of course I didn't do a thing. Jennie sees to everything now.

But it tired me all the same.

John says if I don't pick up faster he shall send me to Weir Mitchell in the fall.

But I don't want to go there at all. I had a friend who was in his hands once, and she says he is just like John and my brother, only more so!

Besides, it is such an undertaking to go so far.

I don't feel as if it was worthwhile to turn my hand over for anything, and I'm getting dreadfully fretful and querulous.

I cry at nothing, and cry most of the time.

Of course I don't when John is here, or anybody else, but when I am alone.

And I am alone a good deal just now. John is kept in town very often by serious cases, and Jennie is good and lets me alone when I want her to.

So I walk a little in the garden or down that lovely lane, sit on the porch under the roses, and lie down up here a good deal.

I'm getting really fond of the room in spite of the wallpaper. Perhaps *because* of the wallpaper.

It dwells in my mind so!

I lie here on this great immovable bed—it is nailed down, I believe—and follow that pattern about by the hour. It is as good as gymnastics, I assure you. I start, we'll say, at the bottom, down in the corner over there where it has not been touched, and I determine for the thousandth time that I *will* follow that pointless pattern to some sort of conclusion.

I know a little of the principle of design, and I know this thing was not arranged on any laws of radiation, or alternation, or repetition, or symmetry, or anything else that I never heard of.

It is repeated, of course, by the breadths, but not otherwise.

Looked at in one way each breadth stands alone, the bloated curves and flourishes—a kind of "debased Romanesque" with *delirium tremens*—go waddling up and down in isolated columns of fatuity.

But, on the other hand, they connect diagonally, and the sprawling outlines run off in great slanting waves of optic horror, like a lot of wallowing seaweeds in full chase.

The whole thing goes horizontally, too, at least it seems so, and I exhaust myself in trying to distinguish the order of its going in that direction.

They have used a horizontal breadth for a frieze, and that adds wonderfully to the confusion.

There is one end of the room where it is almost intact, and there, when the crosslights fade and the low sun shines directly upon it, I can almost fancy radiation after all—the interminable grotesques seem to form around a common center and rush off in headlong plunges of equal distraction.

It makes me tired to follow it. I will take a nap I guess.

I don't know why I should write this.

I don't want to.

I don't feel able.

And I know John would think it absurd. But I *must* say what I feel and think in some way—it is such a relief!

But the effort is getting to be greater than the relief.

Half the time now I am awfully lazy and lie down ever so much.

John says I mustn't lose my strength, and has me take cod liver oil and lots of tonics and things, to say nothing of ale and wine and rare meat.

Dear John! He loves me very dearly, and hates to have me sick. I tried to have a real earnest reasonable talk with him the other day, and tell him how I wish he would let me go and make a visit to Cousin Henry and Julia.

But he said I wasn't able to go, nor able to stand it after I got there; and I did not make out a very good case for myself, for I was crying before I had finished.

It is getting to be a great effort for me to think straight. Just this nervous weakness I suppose.

And dear John gathered me up in his arms, and just carried me upstairs and laid me on the bed, and sat by me and read to me till it tired my head.

He said I was his darling and his comfort and all he had, and that I must take care of myself for his sake, and keep well.

He says no one but myself can help me out of it, that I must use my will and self-control and not let any silly fancies run away with me.

There's one comfort, the baby is well and happy, and does not have to occupy this nursery with the horrid wallpaper.

If we had not used it, that blessed child would have! What a fortunate escape! Why, I wouldn't have a child of mine, an impressionable little thing live in such a room for worlds.

I never thought of it before, but it is lucky that John kept me here after all. I can stand it so much easier than a baby, you see.

Of course I never mention it to them any more—I am too wise—but I keep watch of it all the same.

There are things in that paper that nobody knows but me, or ever will.

Behind that outside pattern the dim shapes get clearer every day.

It is always the same shape, only numerous.

And it is like a woman stooping down and creeping about behind that pattern. I don't like it a bit. I wonder—I begin to think—I wish John would take me away from here!

It is so hard to talk with John about my case, because he is so wise, and because he loves me so.

But I tried it last night.

It was moonlight. The moon shines in all around just as the sun does.

I hate to see it sometimes, it creeps so slowly, and always comes in by one window or another.

John was asleep and I hated to wake him, so I kept still and watched the moonlight on the undulating wallpaper till I felt creepy.

The faint figure behind seemed to shake the pattern, just as if she wanted to get out.

I got up softly and went to feel and see if the paper *did* move, and when I came back John was awake.

"What is it, little girl?" he said. "Don't go walking about like that—you'll get cold."

I thought it was a good time to talk, so I told him that I really was not gaining here, and that I wished he would take me away.

"Why darling!" said he, "our lease will be up in three weeks, and I can't see how to leave before.

"The repairs are not done at home, and I cannot possibly leave town just now. Of course if you were in any danger, I could and would, but you really are better dear, whether you see it or not. I am a doctor, dear, and I know. You are gaining flesh and color, your appetite is better, I feel really much easier about you."

"I don't weigh a bit more," said I, "nor as much; and my appetite may be better in the evening when you are here, but it is worse in the morning when you are away!"

"Bless her little heart!" said he with a big hug, "she shall be as sick as she pleases! But now let's improve the shining hours by going to sleep, and talk about it in the morning!"

"And you won't go away?" I asked gloomily.

"Why, how can I, dear? It is only three weeks more and then we will take a nice little trip of a few days while Jennie is getting the house ready. Really, dear, you are better!"

"Better in body perhaps—" I began, and stopped short, for he sat up straight and looked at me with such a stern, reproachful look that I could not say another word.

"My darling," said he, "I beg of you, for my sake and for our child's sake, as well as for your own, that you will never for one instant let that idea enter your mind! There is nothing so dangerous, so fascinating, to a temperament like yours. It is a false and foolish fancy. Can you not trust me as a physician when I tell you so?"

So of course I said no more on that score, and we went to sleep before long. He thought I was asleep first, but I wasn't and lay there for hours trying to decide whether that front pattern and the back pattern really did move together or separately.

On a pattern like this, by daylight, there is a lack of sequence, a defiance of law, that is a constant irritant to a normal mind.

The color is hideous enough, and unreliable enough, and infuriating enough, but the pattern is torturing.

You think you have mastered it, but just as you get well underway in following, it turns a back-somersault and there you are. It slaps you in the face, knocks you down, and tramples upon you. It is like a bad dream.

The outside pattern is a florid arabesque, reminding one of a fungus. If you can imagine a toadstool in joints, an interminable string of toadstools, budding and sprouting in endless convolutions—why, that is something like it.

That is, sometimes!

There is one marked peculiarity about this paper, a thing nobody seems to notice but myself, and that is that it changes as the light changes.

When the sun shoots in through the east window—I always watch for that first long, straight ray—it changes so quickly that I never can quite believe it.

That is why I watch it always.

By moonlight—the moon shines in all night when there is a moon—I wouldn't know it was the same paper.

At night in any kind of light, in twilight, candle light, lamplight, and worst of all by moonlight, it becomes bars! The outside pattern I mean, and the woman behind it is as plain as can be.

I didn't realize for a long time what the thing was that showed behind, that dim sub-pattern, but now I am quite sure it is a woman.

By daylight she is subdued, quiet. I fancy it is the pattern that keeps her so still. It is so puzzling. It keeps me quiet by the hour.

I lie down so much now. John says it is good for me, and to sleep all I can.

Indeed he started the habit by making me lie down for an hour after each meal.

It is a very bad habit I am convinced, for you see I don't sleep.

And that cultivated deceit, for I don't tell them I'm awake— O no!

The fact is I am getting a little afraid of John.

He seems very queer sometimes, and even Jennie has an inexplicable look.

It strikes me occasionally, just as a scientific hypothesis— that perhaps it is the paper!

I have watched John when he did not know I was looking, and come into the room suddenly on the most innocent excuses, and I've caught him several times *looking at the paper!* And Jennie too. I caught Jennie with her hand on it once.

She didn't know I was in the room, and when I asked her in a quiet, a very quiet voice, with the most restrained manner possible, what she was doing with the paper—she turned around as if she had been caught stealing, and looked quite angry—asked me why I should frighten her so!

Then she said that the paper stained everything it touched, that she had found yellow smooches on all my clothes and John's, and she wished we would be more careful!

Did not that sound innocent? But I know she was studying that pattern, and I am determined that nobody shall find it out but myself!

Life is very much more exciting now than it used to be. You see I have something more to expect, to look forward to, to watch. I really do eat better, and am more quiet than I was.

John is so pleased to see me improve! He laughed a little the other day, and said I seemed to be flourishing in spite of my wallpaper.

I turned it off with a laugh. I had no intention of telling him it was *because* of the wallpaper—he would make fun of me. He might even want to take me away.

I don't want to leave now until I have found out. There is a week more, and I think that will be enough.

I'm feeling ever so much better! I don't sleep much at night, for it is so interesting to watch developments; but I sleep a good deal in the daytime.

In the daytime it is tiresome and perplexing.

There are always new shoots on the fungus, and new shades of yellow all over it. I cannot keep count of them, though I have tried conscientiously.

It is the strangest yellow, that wallpaper! It makes me think of all the yellow things I ever saw—not beautiful ones like buttercups, but old foul, bad yellow things.

But there is something else about that paper—the smell! I noticed it the moment we came into the room, but with so much air and sun it was not bad. Now we have had a week of fog and rain, and whether the windows are open or not, the smell is here.

It creeps all over the house.

I find it hovering in the dining room, skulking in the parlor, hiding in the hall, lying in wait for me on the stairs.

It gets into my hair.

Even when I go to ride, if I turn my head suddenly and surprise it—there is that smell!

Such a peculiar odor, too! I have spent hours in trying to analyze it, to find what it smelled like.

It is not bad—at first, and very gentle, but quite the subtlest, most enduring odor I ever met.

In this damp weather it is awful, I wake up in the night and find it hanging over me.

It used to disturb me at first. I thought seriously of burning the house—to reach the smell.

But now I am used to it. The only thing I can think of that it is like is the *color* of the paper! A yellow smell.

There is a very funny mark on this wall, low down, near the mopboard. A streak that runs round the room. It goes behind every piece of furniture, except the bed, a long, straight, even *smooch,* as if it had been rubbed over and over.

I wonder how it was done and who did it, and what they did

it for. Round and round and round—round and round and round—it makes me dizzy!

I really have discovered something at last.

Through watching so much at night, when it changes so, I have finally found out.

The front pattern *does* move—and no wonder! The woman behind shakes it!

Sometimes I think there are a great many women behind, and sometimes only one, and she crawls around fast, and her crawling shakes it all over.

Then in the very bright spots she keeps still, and in the very shady spots she just takes hold of the bars and shakes them hard.

And she is all the time trying to climb through. But nobody could climb through that pattern—it strangles so; I think that is why it has so many heads.

They get through, and then the pattern strangles them off and turns them upside down, and makes their eyes white!

If those heads were covered or taken off it would not be half so bad.

I think that woman gets out in the daytime!

And I'll tell you why—privately—I've seen her!

I can see her out of every one of my windows!

It is the same woman, I know, for she is always creeping, and most women do not creep by daylight.

I see her on the long road under the trees, creeping along, and when a carriage comes she hides under the blackberry vines.

I don't blame her a bit. It must be very humiliating to be caught creeping by daylight!

I always lock the door when I creep by daylight. I can't do it at night, for I know John would suspect something at once.

And John is so queer now, that I don't want to irritate him. I wish he would take another room! Besides, I don't want anybody to get that woman out at night but myself.

I often wonder if I could see her out of all the windows at once.

But, turn as fast as I can, I can only see out of one at one time.

And though I always see her, she *may* be able to creep faster than I can turn!

I have watched her sometimes away off in the open country, creeping as fast as a cloud shadow in a high wind.

If only that top pattern could be gotten off from the under one! I mean to try it, little by little.

I have found out another funny thing, but I shan't tell it this time! It does not do to trust people too much.

There are only two more days to get this paper off, and I believe John is beginning to notice. I don't like the look in his eyes.

And I heard him ask Jennie a lot of professional questions about me. She had a very good report to give.

She said I slept a good deal in the daytime.

John knows I don't sleep very well at night, for all I'm so quiet!

He asked me all sorts of questions, too, and pretended to be very loving and kind.

As if I couldn't see through him!

Still, I don't wonder he acts so, sleeping under this paper for three months.

It only interests me, but I feel sure John and Jennie are secretly affected by it.

Hurrah! This is the last day, but it is enough. John had to stay in town overnight, and won't be out until this evening.

Jennie wanted to sleep with me—the sly thing! but I told her I should undoubtedly rest better for a night all alone.

That was clever, for really I wasn't alone a bit! As soon as it was moonlight and that poor thing began to crawl and shake the pattern, I got up and ran to help her.

I pulled and she shook, I shook and she pulled, and before morning we had peeled off yards of that paper.

A strip about as high as my head and half around the room.

And then when the sun came and that awful pattern began to laugh at me, I declared I would finish it today!

We go away tomorrow, and they are moving all my furniture down again to leave things as they were before.

Jennie looked at the wall in amazement but I told her merrily that I did it out of pure spite at the vicious thing.

She laughed and said she wouldn't mind doing it herself, but I must not get tired.

How she betrayed herself that time!

But I am here, and no person touches this paper but me—not *alive!*

She tried to get me out of the room—it was too patent! But I said it was so quiet and empty and clean now that I believed I would lie down again and sleep all I could; and not to wake me even for dinner—I would call when I woke.

So now she is gone, and the servants are gone, and the things are gone, and there is nothing left but that great bedstead nailed down, with the canvas mattress we found on it.

We shall sleep downstairs tonight, and take the boat home tomorrow.

I quite enjoy the room, now it is bare again.

How those children did tear about there!

This bedstead is fairly gnawed!

But I must get to work.

I have locked the door and thrown the key down into the front path.

I don't want to go out, and I don't want to have anybody come in, till John comes.

I want to astonish him.

I've got a rope up here that even Jennie did not find. If that woman does get out, and tries to get away, I can tie her!

But I forgot I could not reach far without anything to stand on!

This bed will *not* move!

I tried to lift and push it until I was lame, and then I got so angry I bit off a little piece at one corner—but it hurt my teeth.

Then I peeled off all the paper I could reach standing on the floor. It sticks horribly and the pattern just enjoys it! All those strangled heads and bulbous eyes and waddling fungus growths just shriek with derision!

I am getting angry enough to do something desperate. To jump out of the window would be admirable exercise, but the bars are too strong even to try.

Besides I wouldn't do it. Of course not. I know well enough that a step like that is improper and might be misconstrued.

I don't like to *look* out of the windows even—there are so many of those creeping women and they creep so fast.

I wonder if they all come out of that wallpaper as I did?

But I am securely fastened now by my well-hidden rope— you don't get *me* out in the road there!

I suppose I shall have to get back behind the pattern when it comes night, and that is hard!

It is so pleasant to be out in this great room and creep around as I please!

I don't want to go outside. I won't, even if Jennie asks me to.

For outside you have to creep on the ground, and everything is green instead of yellow.

But here I can creep smoothly on the floor, and my shoulder just fits in that long smooch around the wall, so I cannot lose my way.

Why there's John at the door!

It is no use, young man, you can't open it!

How he does call and pound!

Now he's crying for an axe.

It would be a shame to break down that beautiful door!

"John dear!" said I in the gentlest voice, "the key is down by the front steps, under a plantain leaf!"

That silenced him for a few moments.

Then he said—very quietly indeed, "Open the door, my darling!"

"I can't," said I. "The key is down by the front door under a plantain leaf!"

And then I said it again, several times, very gently and slowly, and said it so often that he had to go and see, and he got it of course, and came in. He stopped short by the door.

"What is the matter?" he cried. "For God's sake, what are you doing!"

I kept on creeping just the same, but I looked at him over my shoulder.

"I've got out at last," said I, "in spite of you and Jane. And I've pulled off most of the paper, so you can't put me back!"

Now why should that man have fainted? But he did, and right across my path by the wall, so that I had to creep over him every time!

# The Children, They Laugh So Sweetly

by Charles L. Grant

The rain stopped falling after midnight had passed, and it hangs now in the black, a fog newly formed; the streetlamps grow diffused, the branches grow facets, and puddles on the sidewalk reflect nothing but the night until, an hour later, they glaze over with ice. The lawn shades to white. The leaves stiffen. A twig snaps. On the corner a cat puffs its tail and hisses when the first of the day's winds begins to rattle the trees.

The house, not a large one, sits back from the hedge like an old man in the park—somewhat hunched, grayed by weather, its unlatched storm door flapping unevenly like a hand jumping in fitful sleep. Years past its prime, it watches and welcomes the birds that use it for warmth, and when a light is switched on in a room above the porch, an eye snapping open to stare dimly at the lawn, it seems to shift as if startled by the voices it hears.

Peter lowered his hand from the lamp's switch and put a finger to his lips to prevent Esther from questioning the look on his face. After a moment he sat up and cocked his head, turned it, and listened, and heard only the wind and the drip of a faucet.

"Are you all right?" she whispered.

He rubbed his eyes with a knuckle, scratched his chest, and blinked. "Dreaming, I think." The tone said he wasn't sure. He listened again and tossed the blanket aside. "You didn't turn the water off."

"Hey, not me, I wasn't the last to use it," she said through a yawn.

He didn't argue; it wasn't worth it. He got out of bed and held his breath against the cold, then hurried into the bathroom to turn both handles as far around as they would go. The dripping stopped, and he leaned against the sink for a moment before feeling his way back into the wide hall. Squinting against the bedroom light, he looked left into the spare room and saw nothing but dim furniture shapes and the glowing outlines of windows; to his right was the staircase and another, smaller room whose door was kept closed, the radiator turned off. He had taken a half step toward it when he heard it, when he heard what had broken into his dreams.

"Peter!" Esther called, whispering again.

"Shhhh!" as he ducked back into the room and switched off the light.

Softly, and sweetly.

Through the narrow side window, he could see their lawn and hedge, and the distant trees and grass on the other side of a tall fence that wasn't theirs. All of it was empty, and bristling with frost. A glimmer from a shard of glass or a prowling cat's eyes, but nothing moving that he could see, out there in the dark.

He started when he heard Esther leave the bed, and joined her at the front, the two of them looking over the sloping porch roof to the grass, hedge, road, houses as dark as theirs should have been this time of the morning when, he thought, dreams were the strongest.

"Boy," she said quietly, took his hand, and drew him into the hall to the stairs and down to the landing, left down into the foyer where the streetlight barely reached, where the dry cold gathered.

He opened the front door and checked the porch as he pulled the storm door and locked it, clenching his teeth against the cold and feeling his muscles tighten. Then he followed his wife's explorations through the double parlor, the dining room, back into the kitchen.

"Nothing," he said, and staggered with a moan against the refrigerator when she switched on the light. "God, you could at least warn a guy, huh?"

"So what are you, a vampire or something?" She wore only a yellow T-shirt that reached halfway to her knees, and most of her dark hair was a tumble over her face. She was smiling. "Well?"

"Well what?" He picked his feet up gingerly. "Christ, it's cold! I gotta do something about that damned furnace before we freeze to death come December."

"Well, how'd you do it?"

"Do what? And please, have a heart and turn off the damned light."

She did with a laugh, and settled against his hip when he put his arm around her. "You know . . . the kids."

"Me? I didn't do it. That's what woke me up."

A gust punched at the narrow window over the sink and rattled the back door.

"There," she said, nodding decisively toward the wind as they returned to the stairs. "That's what it was."

"I heard kids. You heard kids."

"At three o'clock in the morning? C'mon, Peter. It's an old house. It makes noises."

He didn't care if it made symphonies or Sousa as long as it didn't do it while he was trying to sleep. It was bad enough the place wasn't as perfect as they had thought when they bought it. Since moving in the June before, they had discovered a hundred hidden defects, each more expensive to repair than the last, each inevitably postponing the new car, the vacation, the interior renovations they had wanted to make to bring the century-old Victorian in line with its elegant neighbors.

"Hey," she said gently in the dark of the bedroom, "don't worry about it, O.K? I think it's neat."

He nodded as he fell asleep wondering what the hell was so great about someone else's children, was awake and eating breakfast before he remembered. Esther was already gone, off to find draperies for the six-foot windows, and, with a bit of luck, locate an inexpensive shop for wallpaper to cover the faded vines and blossoms that made all the rooms seem too old. He cleaned the dishes, put them away, and walked slowly through the first floor, listening to the floorboards, pressing a palm against door-frames, finally pulling on a sweater and going out to the front yard.

A knowing grin then when he realized as he walked over the browning grass that he was searching for footprints, broken branches, betrayals of the kids who had played there the night before. And of course there was nothing he could not blame on the squirrels.

The grin faded, and he stopped at the hedge wall on the property's north side and peered through it. On the other side was the chain-link fence that canted away from him at the top and was strung with barbed wire; beyond the reach of the Memorial Park itself, though the first of the headstones was almost a hundred yards away.

Jesus, he thought with a sharp shake of his head; the sun is out, the sky is blue, and you're walking around hunting for bloody ghosts, for God's sake.

Feeling suddenly exposed and foolish, he returned to the porch steps and thrust his hands in his pockets, looking left down the street. The trees here were nearly as tall as the house and, despite the bright sunlight, somewhat gloomy without their leaves. There was no activity in any of the yards—the kids were in school, the adults off to work. As far as he could tell, he was the only man on the block who didn't have a job.

Esther did by the end of the day, however, and they celebrated that night by ripping a hole in their budget to buy steak
and champagne. A miracle, he said; luck, she corrected. She
had stopped in at the library to see what they had, and started
talking with a woman whose husband turned out to be the edi-
tor of the local paper. Who was also, it turned out, looking for
a secretary to start in two weeks when his old one left to join
the ranks of new mothers.

"A miracle, like I said," Peter told her with a laugh.

"Luck," she insisted. "If I'd gone to the store like I should
have, I never would have met the woman. I was in the right
place at the right time." She emptied her glass and poured herself another. "It has to be luck, Peter, because that would mean
ours is finally changing."

His smile was the best he could give her, while he couldn't
help wondering if that was a crack about his status.

Never mind, he decided when he finally staggered off to
bed; and never mind the next day when he worked in the yard,
raking leaves into the gutters and cutting back the hedge. When
Esther returned from the paint-and-paper store, he strode into
the kitchen feeling damned good.

She was at the sink, the water running, no dishes to clean.

The line of her back told him there was trouble.

"Why did you tell me you'd gone to the school board?" she
asked as she turned to watch him warm his hands with dry
scrubbing.

He licked his lips and almost said that he had, but the dark
expression on her face killed the lie in his throat. "I didn't want
you to worry."

"Worry!" Her right hand became a fist that pushed her hair
back. "Worry? Jesus Christ, Peter, what the hell were you
thinking of?"

A shrug, and he walked slowly into the living room to flop
onto the couch.

"And don't pull that Hamlet act on me, you hear? It doesn't

work anymore." She stood in the doorway, trembling. "I saw that Mrs. Player on Center Street, the woman from the school board you called that time. She asked me when you were going to submit your application. They need substitutes badly, she said. And I could only stand there like a jackass because you told me you'd already done it!"

"I—"

"No!" she said, chopping the air with one hand. "Don't you dare give me that crap about not wanting to teach anymore. I don't want to hear a thing about being burned out and fed up and not caring anymore." She took a step into the room, and he flinched. "We are almost broke, Pete, do you understand that? The money is almost gone. If you don't—"

He waited for the threat, then looked up. She was gone, and there was no sense going after her. Nor was there any sense in feeling sorry for himself. He had played every game in the book, most of them more than once, and his luck had run out.

His legs stretched out under the coffee table; his arms extended along the back of the couch.

It wasn't true that he didn't like teaching anymore; it was everything that had gone with it that had finally worn him down—the students were undisciplined, but the administration seldom backed him; the administration was too busy figuring budgets and manpower to give a damn about education, decent or otherwise; and education became a conveyor belt on which students rode, the teacher machines stamped "passed" on their foreheads, a word half the kids couldn't read.

In the beginning, shortly after they married, Esther had agreed with him, and wasn't dismayed when they moved to Oxrun Station after his last position had been eliminated because of a cut in school funds. There was, after all, a reasonable amount left from his parents' estate, and they had used it to purchase the house on Northland Avenue—investing in their future instead of losing it on rent. But she had also counted on his finding a job to supplement her own, up-until-now temporary income; she had not counted on him being apparently untrained and unfit for anything but standing in front of a class.

He was afraid he would lose her, so he'd lied about his efforts.

"Dumb," he said to the fireplace and hearth. "Really and truly dumb, Peter Hughes."

That night he slept alone, though she was in bed beside him.

The following day he worked in the yard while Esther went to the *Herald* to see what she'd be doing. And when she returned she ignored him, though he could see she had recently been crying.

Dumb, he thought as he raked the leaves hard across the grass; dumb, stupid, idiot, jackass.

And that night he was awakened by an elbow in his side. He pushed at it; it returned; and it was several seconds before he realized she was trying to get him up. He nearly asked her why, until he heard it downstairs—the sweet quiet laughter, the ripple of giggles.

And something else a moment later—the tread of someone small slowly coming up the stairs.

A look at the windows filled with moonlight, a look at the clock on the nightstand. Then he swung his legs over and crept cautiously around the bed, realizing as he reached the door that he didn't have a weapon. He hesitated while Esther watched him, then decided he would simply have to rely on surprise— he could stand against the wall and kick the intruder when he reached the top step.

He moved, then, and he waited, and saw his skin turn to marble in the light of the moon.

But when he finally poked his head around the corner, the stairwell was empty, and the laughter had stopped a long while ago. He considered returning to bed and laughing it off, changed his mind and went downstairs, just in case. The rooms were all empty, doors and windows locked from the inside. The kitchen clock marked four in the morning, but the night felt closer to dawn.

She was asleep by the time he returned, and he wished a

silent curse at the sheet now icy cold, lay staring at the ceiling, wondering about the house and the noises it made.

"The pipes," she said at breakfast. "Air in them, the cold—the wood contracts and expands when the heat escapes at night."

"All figured out, huh?" he said lightly, pleased she was at least speaking to him again.

"Nothing to it."

"No ghosts?"

She gave him a smile and a lift of an eyebrow. "I'd like that, actually, wouldn't you? Some kids maybe murdered here a hundred years ago, trying to find their way back to . . . I don't know . . . wherever kid ghosts are supposed to go."

"Sounds good," he said, "but as I recall, no kids ever lived here. And no one ever died here."

"Jesus, you are no fun, Peter, you know that? You aren't any fun at all anymore." Her coat was on, a woolen cap and mittens. "What are you doing today?"

He shrugged, and she left without giving him a kiss; he sat there for an hour, then dressed in a good suit, and, with a nod to the guilt that filled his stomach with acid, he walked to the board of education office, where he filled out an application for substitute teaching, and on impulse walked the two miles out to Hawksted College and did the same.

The day was cold, staining his cheeks and forehead an angry red, but he didn't mind it once he fell into stride. The snap of the wind, the swift gray of the clouds, the feel and sound of his heels on the pavement forced him to think for the first time without self-pity what it was that had failed him in the classroom, what it was that had made him reach out to the kids, and pull back when he thought he couldn't take it anymore.

He had deserted them, no question about it; he had deserted them and run away.

Not bad, he thought; it might even be true.

Afterward he wandered into the park and stood at the edge of the playing field, watching a gang of youngsters from the grammar school across the street having races with another class. They shrieked, they cheated, they wrestled, they laughed, and he couldn't help noticing how miserable their teachers looked, how they seemed to wish a miracle truck would appear and mow their classes down.

He shuddered and turned away, disgusted at the idea, sickened by the notion he must have looked like that, too, toward the end, before he quit.

When Esther finally returned from the *Herald*, dinner was ready. "I still haven't forgiven you," she said when he told her about his day, about everything but the park. "But thanks for doing the cooking."

"You ought to be getting paid, y'know?" he said. "All the time you're spending at the paper before you're supposed to start working, I mean."

"But they're nice," she told him, helping him clear the table and wash the dishes. "They really care about you, they want to make you feel right at home."

"It's a small town."

The telephone rang before he could answer, and when he returned to help put away the plates, he was grinning.

"What?" she said suspiciously. "You win the lottery or something?"

"Not quite as good; not so bad, either. A second-grade teacher's been in a car accident over in Harley. Nothing serious, she's O.K.," he said hastily to Esther's concern. "A bump on the head and a couple of cuts, but she's taking the rest of the week off. I get to cover."

"Oh, God," she said, and embraced him warmly. "God, Peter, I'm so glad I could bust!"

"Yeah," he said, frowning into her hair. "Yeah, me, too."

"You know, if you impress them," she said hesitantly, "you might be able to find yourself with a permanent job there, not just substituting."

"It crossed my mind," he lied, and was relieved when at last she lifted her face to kiss him. One crisis over; now all he had to do was figure out what to do with the rest of his life.

He was still thinking about it after they'd watched some television, taken a communal and long shower, and she fell asleep before he could reach for her, to cuddle.

There's always the local supermarket, he thought. Unload a few trucks, work the register, maybe even get to be manager of the produce section. It ain't rich, but it's a living. Or a shoe store. The bookstore. With the two of them working, they might even be comfortable.

And when he felt himself scowling at every suggestion made, he couldn't believe he'd jeopardize both his and Esther's future just because of damned pride. Jesus, he was going back to work tomorrow, at what he was trained to do. Why the hell couldn't he see it as a sign or something? Why the goddamned hell couldn't he be as happy as his wife?

He dozed, half-dreaming and not remembering a thing.

He woke to soft silence, turned his head, and saw the snow—large flakes clinging like white spiders to the panes, drifting past the streetlamps to bury the lawn, turn the hedge to a wall, make the black behind it deeper, colder.

And the laughter, just as soft, down in the foyer.

"You hear it?" Esther whispered, nearly frightening him to death. When he nodded and made to rise, she put a firm hand on his shoulder. "My turn. I've always wanted to see what a ghost looked like."

Still; drowsy, and angry at himself, he grunted and watched her shadow leave the room, heard the steps creak under her weight, and heard the laughing continue.

Suddenly the room chilled, and he jumped from the bed and ran out to the hall.

"Esther!"

Giggling behind a hand, from downstairs, from behind him, from the attic above.

"Esther, you see anything?"

The distant rumble of the furnace, and the radiators popping, clanking, hissing their steam.

He was halfway down the steps when the furnace clicked off, and the silence that replaced it made him hold his breath and pause.

"Hey, Esther, knock it off, huh?"

The streetlight from the front was too dim for details, strong enough for shadows, and he waited until his eyes adjusted before moving down to the landing and scanning the foyer.

He wanted to call his wife's name again, but he listened instead.

To the silence.

To the snow.

To the fill of his lungs as he took the last steps and took hold of the doorknob. It was locked, from the inside.

The parlors were empty, the dining room, the kitchen.

It was a trick. It was long past midnight, and she was playing goddamned tricks when she knew damned well he had to get up in the morning and go stand in front of a bunch of empty-brained, unfeeling, goddamned spoiled little brats.

She knew that! Goddamnit, she knew that and she—

Oh, hell, he thought.

"Esther, c'mon, the fun's over."

He hesitated at the cellar door, then flung it open and went down, slapping at the light switch and cursing when it failed. Before he took another step, he grabbed a flashlight from a drawer, tried the lights in all the rooms, and damned the damn fuses.

The fuses were fine.

He couldn't think of anything else then but someone, maybe two or three, throwing a blanket over her head and dragging her from the house. He raced back to the bedroom and dressed as warmly as he could, picked up the telephone to call the police, and stared at the receiver when the dial tone failed.

"Esther!"

All the windows and doors were locked as before—from the inside, never opened.

He searched the closets, the pantry, looked under the couch and chairs, moved standing lamps and hassocks, kicked the rugs and checked the attic. When his voice grew hoarse from calling, he leaned against the kitchen door and looked out at the yard, blinking, nearly weeping, at the snow an inch deep and as smooth as the moonlight that had been there before.

He looked out every window, went out to the porch, and stood at the railing to stare at the street.

Nothing but the snow, falling silently white.

And when his teeth began to chatter, he returned inside, went up the steps to the bedroom, and dropped the flashlight on the floor. Then he sat on the bed and stared out the window. Sooner or later she would tire of the game and come back to him, kid him a little about the neat hiding place she'd found, then listen when he told her how often he had lied. It wasn't, he would say, the system, or the administration, or the parents, or even the lousy pay. It was the kids. It was always the kids—somewhere in there he had started to hate them.

And tomorrow he was going to hate them again. He waited until he felt the cold enter the house, until the snow thickened, the silence deepened, and he knew without reason he wouldn't see her again.

Then he heard the laughter, soft and sweet, filling the house downstairs.

They know, he thought; they know the way kids do, and they don't want me back.

Giggling; quiet running.

"Esther?" he whispered, crushing a pillow to his chest.

They weren't ghosts at all.

They were only his nightmares.

Soft.

And sweet.

And coming up the stairs.

# No Hiding Place

**by Jack L. Chalker**

It was a sleepy little river town, sitting on the silt bed beside the mighty Mississippi. The town of Newtownards, Louisiana, was a waystop for the steamers and barges that plowed the mighty river; it had been a refueling and rest stop on the waterway to New Orleans or up toward Vicksburg since 1850. It was a very small place, and the town hadn't changed much in the century-plus since the first river steamer piled on wood for the long journey north.

The people were a quiet sort, with little ambition and with that sense of peace and tranquillity that only an isolated community atmosphere can give. This isolation gave security of sorts as well, for the town had not been settled by the almost legendary Bayou folk of the surrounding lush, tropical swamplands, but by hardy capitalists who picked their location on the river for profit.

The Bayou people had become more legend than real by the twentieth century. No one alive could remember seeing any of the quiet, backward swamp folk for a long, long time, and even those who claimed experience with the mysterious backwater people were only half believed. Certainly the Bayou's secretive inhabitants were no longer any threat to the community welfare and, at best, were merely the poor people out in the sticks.

A town like Newtownards was a difficult place to keep a secret. The art of gossip had fallen into disuse simply because there was nothing the locals could whisper to each other that wasn't already common knowledge. Crime, too, was a rarity, and the town kept only two local policemen, two old war veterans whose major duty was checking the more deserted areas for hoboes and other itinerants who might be drifting through and looking for a free place to sleep. For anything more serious, a state police barracks ten miles to the south kept watch on several small towns in the swamp, which was a favorite hiding place for escaped fugitives. But since Newtownards had little to offer men on the run, being the most public of places, the only troopers who had visited the place officially came for ceremonial functions.

The town, as did all small communities, had its history, and it was especially colorful. Rackland's Maurauders had ridden through, back when the country was split and Grant was mapping his strategy, and had set up an observation post in the town's one mansion—deserted Hankin House, empty since the founder of the town and builder of his castle had fled, insane. Colonel Rackland's valiant party used the hilltop to look for any signs of Farragut's ships heading up the river toward Vicksburg, and for any signs of Yankee soldiers lurking in the swamps to the west. There, too, they had met the fate that had haunted Hankin House since 1850, when, after only three months in his new home, Josiah Hankin had suddenly gone mad and attempted to kill everyone nearby, while babbling of a horror in the house.

The old juju woman had come after that. She had originally warned Hankin not to build on the knoll, for, she said, a demon lived within the hill and would take all who disturbed its rest. She had not seen the thing, of course. But her grandmother's people, in 1808, had declared the hill a sacred place of worship, where weird, bacchanalian rites had been carried out by ex-slaves who lived in the Bayou. Now, the juju woman had warned, Josiah had paid the price, and so would all others who disturbed the demon who lived in the hill.

Yes, Hankin House was the town's true pride. In an open society, people, being human, still must talk of something, and the locals had talked about the old house for better than a century. The townspeople didn't really *believe* in *Obi* and voodoo demons living in hills, but they remembered, too, that Josiah had been the first, not the last, to meet a strange end.

Colonel Rackland and two of his men had died by fire in that house, without a single part of the house itself being even singed. The lone survivor of his command had come down the hill a white-haired, raving maniac. Fearful townspeople had investigated, but found nothing but three bodies and a still, ever so still, empty house.

The house was vacant, then, when Farragut finally *did* move his force up the Mississippi. It had remained a still, silent, yet expectant spectator while the town wept at the news that at a place called Appomattox the world had ended. The house had slept while pioneers traveled the mighty river in large steamboats, moving beneath the hill on which the house stood.

Then in March of 1872, on that very same day that U.S. Grant was taking the oath of office for his second and tragic presidential term, Philip Cannon bought the house. Cannon had profited from the war, and even more from its aftermath. But his shady past seemed to be so very close behind him that he was always running, running from his past, his shadow, and himself.

He was running west when the ship he was on docked for fuel in Newtownards, and he had seen the mansion sitting majestically above the town. "Fit for a king," Phil Cannon thought, and despite the anxiety of the townspeople, he located the last Hankin relative, paid her off, and the house was his.

Cannon spent lavishly, building up, refurbishing, until the

twenty-two-year-old house looked as if it had been built the day before, a shining monument to Josiah's taste for Gothic architecture and to Phil Cannon's desire to feel like a king.

And Cannon loved it. He became, by virtue of the smell of money, a very big man in Newtownards, and no one asked about his past. People with noble pasts seldom go to live and work in a tiny town in the midst of a swamp.

Then, one day, almost exactly two years after Cannon had moved in, the big man failed to put in an expected appearance with his usual pomp, strutting as he always did with his little saloon-girl on his arm.

It was not just the townspeople's dislike of the unexpected, nor their concern for the legends, that made them immediately investigate. Many had shady dealings with Cannon and they grew panicky at an unscheduled disappearance. So, a group of businessmen walked up the road to Hankin House and knocked. When they received no answer, they tried the door and found it unlocked.

The crystal chandelier Phil Cannon had imported from Spain tinkled as the hot wind blew off the river and through the open door into the main dining room.

They found *her* head, eventually, taken off her slender shoulders as if by a giant razor. They never did find Phil Cannon's.

As was the case when Josiah went mad, the servants were nowhere to be found. There was speculation that the juju people had a firm hold on those servants and that they might have done away with Cannon and his mistress as revenge for some of Cannon's shady dealings with the swamp folk. But no one ever found the servants, and the cleavage was too clean to have been the work of any sword or knife.

And so it was that Hankin House was closed again, and more generations passed as the silent old house looked on. The original panic and talk of a juju hex had caused some townspeople to cry out that the building be razed to the ground. But since

Cannon's will left the old place to his local business syndicate, such talk was quickly suppressed. Besides, by the time talk became action everybody was convinced that the servants and the Bayou people had done the deed.

Hadn't they?

In 1898 the battleship *Maine* sank in Havana harbor, and America for the first time since the War of 1812 went to war a sovereign nation. One of the eager volunteers had been Robert Hornig, a youthful captain with the Fifth Cavalry Brigade. He had fought in Cuba, was wounded, and then returned. He chose as his point of disembarkation both from the war and the military the port of New Orleans, for he was a man with no family save the army. Now that he no longer had even the army, he was a man without a direction—only a discharge and a limp.

When he stopped off on the river trail westward at Newtownards he was immediately struck by the charm and simplicity of the town. He was also fascinated by the old deserted house atop the hill, and this fascination grew when inquiries to the locals brought forth blood-curdling stories.

The house cost him a bit more than he actually had, as all important acquisitions do, but it was worth every penny to Captain Hornig. A lonely man, he loved the old place as a man would love his bride.

After a while, he was no longer alone. An orderly named Murray, who had also faced the test of battle in Cuba, passed through, as much a drifter as the captain had been. Here was the man, thought Hornig, who would at least temper the loneliness and who might also aid in financing the renovation of the house. Although the captain was a crusty sort, the young orderly liked both the man and the town, and assented.

They found Hornig at the bottom of the grand stairway, his body sprawled out on a rug in the entrance hall. Murray's body was in the dining room; he had been shot through the heart with a pistol, a pistol never found. The coroner's verdict of a murder-suicide did not fit all the facts, of course. But what alternatives were there? At least, this time, both victims still retained their heads.

Again the house was shut up and remained so until 1929, when Roger Meredith moved into the house with his wife and daughter. A heavy stock-market investor, he had selected Newtownards and the house carefully as a quiet and peaceful place in which to bring up his child and to escape the hustle and bustle of Wall Street, where his services were no longer required. He was quite a comfortable millionaire and originally a Louisiana boy as well, and so the townspeople offered little protest at his arrival.

When little Carol Meredith was observed—bloody and hysterical, crawling up Main Street not seven weeks after the family had moved in, her face full of buckshot—they said it was another murder-suicide, the last act of a man driven mad by the collapse of the stock market. As usual, the coroner's jury did not bother with details. How could a small man like Meredith ever throw his wife out of the west window? How did he, himself, inflict the merciless blow to the head the doctor stated had killed him? And what of the little girl, lying in the arms of storekeeper Tom Moore, life oozing out of her, who turned her face to his and, with a queer, maniacal smile, whispered as she died: "Daddy shot it!"

World War II came, and passed, and the house remained empty. No longer did fancy riverboats ply the Mississippi at the foot of the hill, but the town remained. Freight traffic had increased, and those ships still needed fuel.

Wars, hot and cold, passed, and generations came and went. The old house sat silently, as always, its mysterious demon undisturbed. Until one day . . .

August was a bad month for Newtownards. It was horribly hot and as humid as the air and the laws of physics would allow. Most people at midday would close their stores and stretch out for a nap while the intolerable heat of the day dissipated. But in the schoolyard, under the shade of a tall, old tree, there was activity.

"I am not yella!" the red-haired, stocky boy of about fourteen yelled to the tall, angular leader of the group of boys, "but nobody's stupid enough to commit suicide, Buzz Murdock!"

The tall, blond-haired teenager towered over the object of derision. "Ya must be, ya half-Yankee!" Buzz Murdock replied haughtily, and not without a deliberate sneer. He was playing to his audience now, the group of young teenage boys who formed the Swamp Rats, a *very* exclusive little club.

Ricky Adherne, the redhead, bristled, his face becoming so red and contorted with anger and rage that his freckles almost faded to invisibility. The "half-Yankee" tag had always stung him. Could he help it if his no-account pa had been from New York?

"Lissen," said Murdock, "we don't allow no chickens in the Rats." The other boys made clucking sounds, like those of a chicken, in support of their leader. "If'n ya caint prove t'us that ya ain't no stupid chicken, ya bettah git along home riaot now!" continued the leader.

"Lissen yuhself!" Adherne snapped back. "I don't mind no test o' bravery, but jumpin' inna rivah with a sacka liam is a shoah way ta diah quick!"

Murdock put on his best sneer. "Hah! Weall wouldn't be so afeared. We's Swamp Rats and ya ain't ouah type. Git along home, kid, afore we beat on ya!"

Adherne saw his opening, and he dived in. "Hah! Big ol' Swamp Rats! If ya *really* wanted a test o' bravery—why, you'n me, Murdock, we'd go upta ol' Hankin House at midniat and sit 'till morn!"

Murdock was in a bind and he knew it. He'd have to go through with this or he would lose face before his followers—*that*, he was smart enough to figure out. But, damn it all, why'd this little punk have to pick Hankin House?

\*   \*   \*

It was 11:22 P.M. when the town policemen Charles "Scully" Wills and Johnny Schmidt got into their patrol car—actually a loaned state police car with a radio connection to the Hawkinston barracks in case of emergencies—to make the rounds for the first time that night. As they drove toward their last checkpoint, Hankin House, Schmidt thought he spied a bluish gleam moving about in one of the old structure's upper windows. But when he blinked and looked again the light was gone. He mentioned his suspicions to his partner, but the older cop had seen nothing; and, when the light failed to reappear, Schmidt told himself he was just tired and seeing things in the night.

The two men made an extra check of the seals on the doors and windows of the old house, though, just to be on the safe side. Nothing human could get by those seals without breaking at least one of them, this they knew.

When all the seals proved to be intact, they left the old, dark place for town and coffee. They'd make their rounds again in about three hours. Both men settled back to another dull, routine night.

It would not be dull or routine.

There was a sound like a hoot-owl, and Ricky Adherne advanced on the little party of boys waiting in the gully near the roadside. Hankin House looked down, grim and foreboding, in the distance.

Murdock was scared, but he dared not show it. Adherne, too, was scared, the sight of the old house by moonlight being even more frightening to him than was his previous all-consuming fear that his mother would check his room and discover he wasn't there. Throughout the evening he had mentally cursed himself for suggesting this stupid expedition, and he'd convinced himself that the Swamp Rats weren't worth the risk. But he still had to go, he knew. His personal honor was at stake. Newtownards was an open town, and he had to live in it, and with himself as well.

The chirping of a cricket chorus and the incessant hum of june bugs flying to and fro in the hot night air were the only sounds as the small party of boys, Murdock and Adherne in the lead, walked up the road to the old manor house. Suddenly they saw headlights turn onto the road and barely jumped into the tall grass by the roadside in time to miss the gaze of Scully and Schmidt as they rode up to the old house. Minutes passed like hours, but no boy made a move. Finally, after an eternity, the car returned and sped back down the hill.

"Man! That was *real* close!" Adherne exclaimed in an excited whisper.

"Shaddup, punk!" called Murdock, who felt like running himself but who, also, had to live in Newtownards.

The old house sat dark and silent as the group reached the tall front steps.

"Now how d'we git in, smaht guy?" Murdock demanded, believing he had discovered a way out of this mess. But Adherne, now pressed on by Murdock's sarcasm and the will to get an unpleasant thing over and done with, was already up on the porch.

"If'n we kin jest git this here crossboahd off'n the doah, we kin git in thisaway," he whispered, not quite understanding why he spoke so low.

Together the frightened boys pried off the wooden crossbar whose nails had been rusted and weakened by weather for better than thirty years. After much tugging the board gave, and one Swamp Rat fell backward, board in hand, with a yelp.

A blue flickering light shone in an upstairs window. Suddenly it froze.

"It's open," one boy whispered huskily.

Murdock swallowed hard and drew up all the courage he could muster. He suddenly pushed ahead of the red-haired boy, who stood statuelike, peering into the black gloom. "Me first, punk," he snapped, but the tall leader wondered why his voice sounded so strange in his ears.

First Murdock, then Adherne, entered the blackness.

The blue light in the upstairs window, unseen by any of the waiting boys encamped below, moved away from the window. And the climax to a strange quest, spanning not one century but more than a score, was close at hand.

## 2

As the small scoutship lifted from the landing grid and rose into the sky above the peculiar red-green surface of the planet men called Conolt IV, a signal flashed in a larger, more formidable, and very alien vessel hiding in the darkness of space. As the tiny Terran scout pulled free of the planet's thick atmosphere, the alien ship's commander gave a crisp order and set out after his prey.

The scoutship pilot, a giant Irishman named Feeny, spotted the dark raider just after leaving radio range of Conolt IV's spaceport. He punched a button on the ship's instrument panel, where myriad dials and switches lay before him.

"Doctor, I'm afraid we've been had," he said, his voice calm and smooth. Intelligence men did not break under pressure and survive.

In the aft compartment, Alei Mofad, a cherubic, balding man in his late sixties who was known as *the* scientific genius of his age, jerked up with a start.

"How far, Feeny?" he asked in a level voice.

"About twelve thousand, Doctor, and closing fast. Too damned fast."

Mofad turned and examined the small cabinet which, aside from the bunk and his own person, was the only other thing in the compartment.

"Feeny, how much time have we got?"

"Ten, twelve minutes at the most. Sorry, Doc. Somebody made one *hell* a slip here."

"Yes, yes, I know, but no use crying over bad security now. I shall require at least fifteen. Can you give that much to me?"

"I can try," the pilot replied dryly, and he began to do more than try. As Mofad worked feverishly to connect his equipment to the ship's power supply, Feeny began trying every maneuver in the book.

The alien spacecraft swung around out of the planetary shadow and shot a tractor beam, its purple glow slicing through the icy darkness of space. Feeny saw the beam only a fraction of a second before it was upon him, and his split-second reflexes urged the tiny scoutship upward, evading the powerful magnetic beam by inches.

The enemy craft swung around again, and for the second time shot out a purple ray from its bow tubes. Again Feeny dodged by inches, banking left and downward as if the two ships were master fencers, with one swordsman now disarmed but yet agile enough and determined enough to avoid his deadly opponent's thrusts.

Feeny knew he could not keep up the game indefinitely, but he was determined to give his illustrious charge as much time as was required. He dodged, banked, dropped up and down, all the time playing for Mofad's precious, essential seconds, while at the same time sending out a distress signal to the cruiser that should have been waiting nearby to pick them up, but was actually a hulk of twisted metal, and loser of an earlier duel with the enemy craft. Twelve minutes passed . . . thirteen . . . fifteen . . . and then the goal was passed.

Eighteen minutes after the game had begun, it ended, when Feeny's lightning reflexes were no longer quite quick enough, and he began to tire. A tractor beam lashed out, enveloping the scoutship in a purple glow, pulling the tiny craft slowly toward the greater ship in the grip of the magnetic field.

"Doctor, they've got us," Feeny called into the ship's intercom. "Are you ready?"

"Yes, Feeny, I'm leaving now," came the physicist's reply, a tinge of sadness in his voice as he thought of the fate to which the faithful pilot had to be abandoned. "Do you want me to do anything, Doc?" Feeny called back.

"You've done enough, but yet you must destroy this machine. You know the detonator." Then, more softly, "Good-bye, Feeny."

Alei Mofad reached up on top of the plasticine cabinet and removed a small box. He stepped into the cabinet then, and vanished.

The two ships collided with a *thunk* which reverberated down the corridor of the smaller ship. Feeny rose from his pilot's chair and began the walk back to the aft compartment, struggling under the excessive gravity taken on when the two ships had linked and began to roll. But he was too slow. The midsection airlock blew open before him, separating him from the precious cargo in the aft compartment. He stopped and stood straight, erect. After all, one died with dignity.

A creature entered the ship, a weird giant thing that could never have been spawned on earth. Humanoid was the closest to Terran that you could get, descriptively, for it stood erect, towering a full seven feet, on two thick, stiff legs. But it wore a chitinous exoskeleton that, as natural body armor, was as strong as sheet metal, yet half-transparent, so that the viewer could get a glimpse of veins, muscle tissue, and even the creature's brain. The two very long arms differed from one another. The right one, which ended in a five-digit hand whose fingers were extremely long and triple-jointed, bore a pistol, aimed at Feeny's head. The left arm, however, ended in a massive set of razor-sharp pincers—the Sirian ceremonial claw, used as a two-fingered hand or used in many Sirian rituals, including the mating ceremony of the species.

Colonel Rifixl Treeg, Hereditary Colonel of Empire Intelligence, fixed one of his stalk-like eyes on Feeny, the other on the door to the aft compartment. There could be no outward expression intelligible to a Terran in that face that resembled the head of a lobster, nor any sound, for the Sirians communicated—it was believed—telepathically. The alien colonel motioned with his pistol for Feeny to move back into the pilot's cabin.

Feeny complied, staring in fascination at his first Sirian. Only a few Terrans, such as those in the original discovery expeditions like Mofad, had *ever* seen them. The Sirians ruled a great stellar empire of allied and vastly different races. They did not fight wars; they directed them.

Feeny decided on a desperate gamble. If he could surprise the Sirian, at least long enough to run to the far wall and throw the generator-feed switches, it was possible that he might be able to blow up the ship.

Treeg watched the Terran captive almost halfheartedly; this was not the prize he was after. As he stepped backward, another member of the Sirian crew entered, partially blocking the colonel's view of Feeny. Feeny saw his chance and dived for the switches. The Sirian who had just entered swung around and fired his pistol at the advancing Feeny. The Terran lurched back with a cry and was instantly consumed by the white-hot pistol fire. Only a burning heap on the control-room floor betrayed the fact that anyone named Feeny had ever existed.

Treeg was annoyed at the killing; he preferred his prisoners alive for interrogation, as his orders specified. There had been talk of late that the old colonel was getting too old for his duties, and this slip would not help his position with the High Command. Still, he was more than annoyed at what he found in the aft compartment—or, rather, what he did not find.

There was a bunk and a plasticine cabinet of dubious purpose. Nothing else. Alei Mofad was not on the ship. Treeg went over to the cabinet and examined it with both eyes. Apparently the only moving part was a small relay on the side which flipped up and down, up and down. Atop the cabinet were two small boxes, each without any writing—just thin little boxes with two buttons, one red and one green: purpose, also unknown.

The law of the survival of the fittest breeds certain characteristics common to all races who struggle to the top, and Treeg
exercised one of those characteristics—he beat his fist in frus-
tration against the compartment wall. He then turned and
stormed out.

In every age there is a special one, a genius who can see beyond the horizon—Copernicus, Edison, Einstein, and the like
being prime examples.

And Alei Mofad.

An explorer and trader in his youth, as he approached middle age, a wealthy and industrious man still full of life, he had
built a great laboratory on the quiet Federation to experiment.
His findings became the cornerstone in the later fight between
his own people, the Trans-Terran Federation, and the other
giant stellar empire he had aided in discovering, the Sirian
League. The Terran-Sirian War of the Empires was a bitter, no-
quarter clash between two equally ruthless and ambitious cen-
ters of power, born out of jealousy and greed and fed on
misunderstanding and hate—too much alike in the way they
thought to ever get along.

And in the midst of the conflict, Alei Mofad broke the fabric of time itself.

His original machine was still in his laboratory on Conolt IV,
along with his notes and specifications. His newer, larger,
model which Terran Command insisted be brought to Terra itself for its first public demonstration had been loaded secretly
on a small scout. Then the doctor and one intelligence man had
attempted to sneak off planet without arousing any curiosity, to
link up with a cruiser off the sixth planet in the system. But
Sirian allies could pass for Terrans, and their spies on Conolt
had blocked the attempt. So Terran Control Center was left
with just one clue, one hope of obtaining the crucial formulae
that would make the Mofad computations on Conolt IV make
sense. Mofad had that in his brain—but he had stated that, if he
could escape, he would somehow place the location at the

Terran test site, Code Louesse 155. They would use the original machine to retrieve it—and, hopefully, Mofad. But, the formulae were hidden in time itself. They knew where, but not
*when*.

For the machines were still imperfect. The day would come
when whole armies would be transported across space and time
to the enemy's heartland in the remote past, then brought up to
the present, an indetectable army of occupation.

Rifixl Treeg, too, had a time machine and the controls to
make use of it. But he knew neither where nor when.

"The physics is quite beyond me," said the Empire's top
physicist. "Mofad is someone centuries ahead of us all. However, the Terran pilot's failure to destroy the cabinet after
Mofad escaped in it gives us more information than you might
suspect, my dear Colonel."

"Terran intelligence knows what's happened, too, by now,
and they have a head start," Treeg replied. "What can we do?
You've already told me you can't duplicate the thing without
Mofad's basic formula, and we can't get the formula without
Mofad. It seems that he's beaten us."

"Pessimism simply will not do in an intelligence officer,
Colonel Treeg. I merely told you that we could not duplicate
the thing; I never said we could not *run* it."

"Ah!" exclaimed the colonel, and then he suddenly drooped
again. "But we still don't know where or when. Terran intelligence at least knows *where*, although, as you tell me, the
thing's too unpredictable for them to know *when*."

"Where is not a problem," replied the physicist. "Obviously
the *where* requires a setting. Since Mofad wasn't there to unset
it, the machine will transport you to the right place, never fear.
Your own intelligence reports show the original test site to be
in the northern and western hemisphere of Terra herself. Since
I credit the doctor with foresight, that's where anyone using the

machine will go. At this point we are even with Terran intelligence. But now we go ahead of them."

Treeg suddenly stood extremely erect, the equivalent of a start in a race that could not physically sit down.

"You see," the scientist continued, "Mofad also had the time *period* set. The machine will follow through there, as well, but not exactly."

Treeg slumped. "Why not exactly, if—"

"Because," the scientist when on in the manner of a professor lecturing a schoolboy, "the machine is imperfect. It will transmit within, roughly, two centuries, I'd say. The disguised control panel here," he said, pointing to a spot on the machine, "is elementary. We can regulate the time sequence much better than could old Mofad, who had to go blind into a two-century span. We could make short jumps in time, with our agent searching the immediate vicinity for traces of Mofad. Since an agent, friend or foe, could appear only minutes after Mofad— even if that agent left days later by our standards—he would have to hide the thing fast. Was there any sort of transcribing equipment missing from the scoutship?"

"Yes," replied Treeg, "a minirecorder. You mean—"

"Precisely. That recorder is somewhere very near the point of emergence, and it contains what we must have. Terran intelligence does not have our present dials, so it will have hundreds of centuries to search. We may yet beat them. Who will you send?"

Treeg was still smarting from the lashing given him by the High Command for allowing Mofad to escape. There had been thoughts all around of retirement.

"Me," he said.

The two Sirians stood by the machine. The physicist began: "The device is based on a geographic point of reference. Mofad in his haste left the two portable units behind, an inexcusable blunder, but one very fortunate from our viewpoint." He handed Treeg a small box that was surprisingly heavy for its three-by-five-inch size and that only contained the red and green buttons which had interested Treeg when he had discovered them.

"This is the portable triggering device. When you want to go, we set the machine, and you step inside. Then you press the green button all the way down, and the machine transforms you into some sort of energy form we don't yet understand and resolidifies you on a preset point determined by the cabinet setting. When you wish to return, you need only return to your exact point of emergence into the other time and place and press the red button down all the way. This will reverse the process. I don't pretend to understand it—this is what we need in the way of Mofad's formulae, that mathematics which will tell us the how of the thing. Let's say that the machine somehow rips the fabric of time and place, which are linked, and that the tear is mended when you reactivate the device, thereby restoring you to your point of origin.

"I advise you to mark your point of emergence on Terra carefully, though. You must return to it exactly or you will remain where and when you are. Are you ready?"

Treeg nodded, and with an effort squeezed his rigid body into the upright cabinet. The scientist examined the control panel. "I have preset it—I think—for the earliest possible time. I will count down. When I say *Now!* you are to press the green button. All right. Five . . . four . . . three . . . two . . . one. . . . *Now!*"

Treeg pressed the button.

The first thought he had was that there had been no sensation whatever. It bothered him; this tampering with time should not be so quiet nor so sudden. But—one moment he was squeezed uncomfortably in that cabinet on Sirius; the next moment he was atop a lonely hillside surrounded by lush, green swamp. Below the hill a large river, glittering in the sunset, flowed its way past the spot. The time was 1808, forty-one

years before a man named Josiah Hankin would found a town
on the flats below, a town he would name after the Belfast
street on which he had been born—Newtownards.

Treeg was overcome by the wildness of the place and by the
idea that he was the first of his race to travel in time. The air,
he noted, was sweet and moist, and it was almost as hot here as
his own native world. He stood there on the hilltop, a grotesque
statue silhouetted in the setting sun, and thought. He had all the
time in the world . . .

He heard a rustling in the undergrowth.

Four men crept through the dense marsh grass, looking not
at the hill and its weird occupant but out at the river. Two
were old-time pirates who had fought with Laffite years before and had then changed occupations to become Bayou
smugglers, finding the new line of work just as profitable but
less risky.

The other two were renegade slaves, who joined the Bayou
settlement as a sanctuary where they could relax, free from the
fear of the law in a society where it was not race, but brains and
muscle, that made a man a man. All four of them loved the art
of smuggling, taking pride in it in the same way as a jeweler
would pride himself in his skillful work.

Treeg had no ears with which to hear the men, and so, oblivious to the danger below, he began walking down the slope toward the base of the hill. He had decided that Mofad would
surely have made traces in the virgin land if this was indeed the
correct time, but he had a duty to perform, and all the time he
would ever need. So he decided to check all the same. In the
military caste society of his birth the first rule taught every
youngling was "Never underestimate your enemy."

"Damn and double that stinkin' Joe Walsh," growled Ned
Harrell as his eyes strained to catch a glimpse of a flatboat on
the great expanse of the river. "If that pig's double-crossed me

I'll—Hey! Did you hear that?" A crash and crackle of under-brush sounded nearby.

Carl, a giant black with a fugitive's reflexes, had already jumped around. Then he screamed. They were looking at a giant demon out of hell come down from his high hill, a demon with the face of a monster and the look of the swamp.

Harrell instinctively grabbed his rifle and shot at the thing in one motion. The bullet struck the Sirian's midsection, a strong point in his body armor, and bounced harmlessly off; but the force of the blast knocked Treeg back, and he grabbed a long vine to keep from crashing to the ground. The initial surprise of the attack wore off almost immediately, and Treeg saw the situation for what it was—he was faced with a bunch of prim-itives, and scared ones at that. Treeg, a born killer trained in his art, charged. Three of the men drew back, but Carl stood his ground. Stopping a few feet away, the Sirian surveyed the Ter-ran who was as big as he.

The big black man charged, and Treeg stepped aside, letting his adversary sail past. The Sirian had spotted Harrell furiously reloading his rifle and wanted to eliminate the threat. Drawing his pistol, Treeg fired. Harrell went up in smoke and flame. The two others ran off, the short black man known as Eliot shout-ing: *"Juju! Juju! Oh, God, we done raised a juju!"* as he stormed through the brush.

Carl had recovered from his missed lunge and, rising to his feet, charged at the back of the monster. He knew he was fac-ing a demon, but he also knew that demons could be wrestled into submission—and Carl was the best wrestler of them all.

The Sirian went down, caught completely off guard. He had forgotten his initial and greatest threat while shooting at the others. Carl pounced on top of him and for a few seconds the two wrestled, the big black man not being able to do much damage to the hard-shelled creature, while Treeg found himself pinned in a viselike grip, not being able to free either claw or hand. They were still in a test of brute strength, a frozen tableau as Carl sat atop the giant creature and strained to keep those arms pinned.

Treeg was virtually helpless if downed, and he had to be able to roll over in order to bring up his claw. He heaved with all his might, at the same time marveling at the strength of this soft Terran ape, as he thought of all Earthmen.

Foam poured from the mouth of the frenzied Carl as he struggled against the giant creature's strength in that death grip. Finally, after a few seconds that seemed to both to pass like hours, Treeg felt a slight slackening as the man tired, and he kicked over to one side. Carl went sprawling over, and Treeg rolled to his right, at the stunned man, claw raised.

Rifixl Treeg had a terrible time bringing himself to his feet again. Rigid, unbending legs propped out, he used his long arms to lift his body semiupright, then grabbed an overhanging vine and pulled himself erect. He then looked down at the cut and bleeding body of Carl, a Terran. He had been more impressed with the courage and skill of this one creature than with any he had encountered before. The primitive should have run away with the rest of his group, yet he had chosen to stay and fight. He had been closer to winning than he knew, for Treeg had been tiring as well, and a mighty blow into the pulpy Sirian face would have penetrated into his brain, bringing instant death.

Treeg resolved not to underestimate these Terrans again. He had often wondered why such seeming weaklings were any threat to the Empire. Then a saying one of his early tutors had drummed into him suddenly came back as he stood there: *Ignorance is not a synonym for stupidity, nor savagery for fear.*

Treeg cast one eye in each direction, looking for a sign of the return of the natives in force. He did not want to be caught off guard again. But he found no signs of any life save the crawling insects and flying birds; so, keeping a watchful eye, the Sirian decapitated the Negro, using the ceremonial claw, in the age-old gesture of respect for the dead of war. He then made his way around the hill, searching for the signs of a more civilized man's presence. He found none and, regretfully, walked back up the hill, back to where a stone marked his point of departure.

From back in the swampy glades, a group of cautious Bayou men and women, attracted by the sounds of a struggle, watched in awe and fear as a great demon stood atop the hill, visible as a fearsome specter in the last fleeting rays of the sun.

And suddenly vanished.

Treeg tumbled out of the time cabinet and onto the floor, unconscious. It was only a split second since he had vanished from the laboratory, but it was plain to the Sirian physicist that the colonel had been through an ordeal. The red blood almost completely covering the claw proved it, and Treeg was carried to the hospital, where Carl's blood was washed off and he was left alone to sleep off his exhaustion.

## 3

Less than two days later, Treeg was ready and able to try again. He had learned a lot about his enemy in his first try. This time, unhampered by the apprehension of transition, the passage to Terra was even easier to take. Yet this time, too, it held a surprise.

Treeg stood in a primitive dwelling made of wood. The size of the room was very large, and it was lavishly furnished. A great, long table divided the room almost into two parts, with chairs stretching endlessly down each side. At the head of the table was a great, padded chair where the master of the house would sit. A long mirror hung on one wall and, overhead, suspended directly above the center of the table, was a massive iron chandelier.

Treeg's first thought was that there had been some sort of mistake. The jump was not more than forty years, he thought, and those primitives of the swamp were surely incapable of making such a dwelling as this. But, of course, forty years brings inevitable change, external as well. The dwelling and the small town below were products of outsiders, who had used the time to carve a slice of civilization from the swamp.

In that time that shrewd old trader Josiah Hankin had built a town and a mansion. He had also been warned not to build on that hill. An old juju woman had prattled about a demon, one her grandmother saw, who lived in the hill and could disappear at a will. But Josiah was a hardheaded man, and he laughed.

It was almost midnight. The servants had retired, the slaves had been locked in their houses. Josiah sat in his study studiously examining the previous month's account books. But as far as Treeg was concerned, the dark house was empty.

The Sirian took a small tube off his wide utility belt, the only clothing he wore. The tube snapped to life, its brilliant blue-white glow illuminating even the darkest corners of the large room. Treeg narrowed the beam after an initial visual scan of the place, and he began his search. Although not conscious of sound himself or capable of fully grasping what it was, he still moved softly and carefully, knowing that the Terrans possessed a certain sense that he did not.

Then, in the most comic of ways, Rifixl Treeg tripped on the edge of the lush Persian carpet at the doorway and hit the floor with a crash, the blue torch flying against a wall.

Josiah jumped at the sound. He had never been quite comfortable in the wilds and was always a little jittery after dark. Cautiously, the old man tiptoed out onto the landing above the grand stairway and looked down into the dark entrance hall. He heard the sound of movement as Treeg dizzily and with great effort hoisted himself back to his feet. Feeling certain that a burglar was in the house, Hankin went back and got out his old flintlock pistol.

In the meantime Treeg, oblivious of discovery, had started his methodical search of the dining-room area, looking for spaces likely to hide a small recorder. He felt certain that the recorder was hidden in an obvious place—a place somewhere in the house, and one where a Terran searcher would be likely to look, since, were it hidden too well, Mofad's own kind would miss the object of their search.

Josiah crept softly down the stairs, loaded gun in hand. The sounds of movement in the dining room continued. Raising his pistol, the old man stepped across the threshold of the room, now lit by a strange blue glow.

Treeg, very near the door, chose that moment to turn around. As he did so, his right arm swung around and hit Hankin hard, sending the old man reeling back into the hallway. The gun fired on contact, but the ball missed its mark and lodged instead in the far wall.

The Sirian walked toward the old man, who was just getting to his feet. The fellow looked up and into the pulpy, grotesque face, screamed, and ran for the front door. Treeg, being slower, did not give chase as the old man sped out the door and down toward the slaves' house, screaming hideously.

Treeg quickly resumed his search. He was certain that he was still too early in time, and so, with only a few more seconds to survey the downstairs layout—and with pursuit probably imminent—he stepped back to the point just behind the great chair that sat at the head of the long table and pressed the button.

Josiah Hankin, driven mad by the horror that had touched him and pursued him, saw monsters in place of bewildered slaves. He grabbed a heavy stick off the ground and started after one of the men, a field hand. The others finally subdued him.

Hankin would live out his life in a New Orleans sanitarium, always babbling a description of the truth that men of 1850 could only accept as the ravings of a maniac.

Private Fetters jumped nervously as Colonel Rackland entered the house. Rackland grinned. A tall, gaunt man with a now-famous blond goatee, he delighted in scaring his men. It kept them on their toes.

"Well, Private," he drawled, "have you seen any signs of those wicked old Yankees yet?"

Fetters relaxed. "No, suh, but ah'm keepin' a shahp lookout, suh."

Rackland smiled again, and went over to the old padded chair that they had uncovered and put back where it rightfully belonged—at the head of the dining room table. The table was ideal for maps and conferences, and the east windows of the room gave an excellent view of the broad expanse of the Mississippi.

Two more men came in—the rest of the observation-post team, one of several Rackland had set up along the riverbank. Rackland walked over to the windows to confer with the new arrivals, and Fetters asked if he could be relieved. This granted, he walked over to the big chair. That saved his life.

Rifixl Treeg appeared between Fetters and the men at the windows, so close to the private that poor Fetters was knocked down. Treeg wanted no surprises and acted by reflex this time, drawing his pistol and firing point-blank at the men at the window.

The wide beam caught all three at once, and each man screamed once, then died from the intense heat. Fetters was only singed slightly, and he saw the creature in the room. One look was enough. Fetters managed to leap up and jump out one of the windows, then ran off, screaming and yelling for help as he raced down the hill toward the town below.

Treeg cursed himself for allowing one to get away, reflecting sourly that that seemed to be all he was doing of late. He made as quick a search as he could, but decided that if this place was being used by these men—seemingly soldiers— Mofad's presence would be marked in some way. Still, he made the rounds of the usual hiding places and then looked over the other downstairs rooms as well. His duty done, Treeg walked back over to the focal point just behind the great chair and pressed the red stud.

She took one look at the creature and fainted, something which puzzled Treeg, who was ever ready to kill but was unused to potential victims dropping unconscious without pain as a precipitant. He decided to kill her while she was out in order to save problems later. Then, despite the fact that head-taking was usually a ceremony of honor, he sliced off the woman's head simply because it seemed the easiest way of killing her.

For once, Treeg allowed himself every luxury of time. He had no reason to believe that anyone else was about, but he kept one eye on the main hall anyway. Lucky for him he did.

Phil Cannon bounced down the stairs, gun in hand. He had watched as the weird creature severed Mary's head cleanly with that claw, but the vision had not driven him mad. Cannon had lived too long and done too much to be scared of any monster that simply was more foul than he. He had accepted Treeg as a reality, probably some sort of unknown animal from the swamps, and he had reached for his .44.

He felt no emotion at Mary's passing. People were things to Phil Cannon; they could be replaced. What mattered was killing the thing in the dining room before it killed him.

Treeg saw movement out of the corner of his eye, drew his pistol, turned, and pulled the trigger. The shot was wide and on a thin beam as well and it missed Cannon, who darted to cover behind the wall partition, completely. Cocking his pistol, Cannon dropped low to the floor, then darted out, firing a volley at Treeg. One shot struck, and though it did Treeg no harm, it had the force to make him drop his searpistol.

Treeg realized that he had no cover and no weapon, and decided immediately that he had to rush the man. He bounded across the dining room and reached out, but Cannon was too fast.

"Com'on, you brute," Phil Cannon whispered, "com'on out where I can get a clear shot with this thing."

Treeg decided to oblige, chancing that the Terran would aim for his midsection. It was a risk, but there was nothing else to do. He charged, and guessed correctly. Cannon fired into the Sirian's chest, to no effect; but Treeg, ready for the blow of the bullet, was able to keep up his charge. Hand and claw reached out for Cannon, picked him up and threw him into the dining room, where the con man landed with a *snap*.

Treeg made certain that the man was dead by severing his head, but as he started to move the body, part of which was on the focal point, he saw people running for the house, attracted by the shots. Treeg decided that this time period was without doubt still much too early for Mofad anyway, and he pressed the stud.

When he arrived back in the Sirian laboratory, he discovered that Phil Cannon's severed head had come along as well.

Cannon's servants, running in the front door in response to the shots, stopped short at the gruesome sight in the dining room. Crossing himself, the butler said: "We'd all bettah git out of heah fast. They's gonna think *we* done it."

So it was that the town investigating committee found two bodies, one head, and were able to place the blame on the servants.

Murray was in the dining room when Treeg appeared. Stunned for a moment by the creature's sudden appearance, he recovered before Treeg could effectively act and ran to a wall, on which a prized pistol sat, ever loaded, the captain's symbol of his life.

Treeg advanced on him, and Murray fired once, the bullet glancing off Treeg and putting yet another hole in the old house's wall.

The Sirian reached out and grabbed for the young ex-orderly, but missed and fell to the floor. Murray, in dodging, was thrown off balance and fell, too, but he retained a grip on his pistol.

Treeg saw the pistol and lashed out his hand, catching the man's arm in an iron grip. They struggled, rolling along the floor, each trying for possession of the pistol. The gun suddenly reversed under Treeg's mighty pressure, and fired. Murray jerked, then was still. Treeg had killed him by forcing the muzzle of his own gun to his side.

Rising, he went immediately to the dining-room doorway, not taking any chances on another Phil Cannon coming down the stairs.

The captain was standing at the head of the stairs. At the sound of the struggle he had painfully gotten up from his bed, where he had been for several days, fighting an old leg wound that had flared anew. At the sight of Treeg he drew back. His bad leg gave out from under him, and he fell headfirst down the grand stairway. When he hit bottom, he lay still, his neck broken in the fall.

Treeg looked down at the body, which was undeniably dead, a bit stunned at this death. It was, at least, the easiest of the lot, and Treeg was glad of that after his tussle with Murray.

This time the search was not interrupted, and Treeg explored the upstairs as well.

The little girl was playing with her doll in a corner of the dining room. She didn't see Treeg, who stood for a second pondering what to do. Younglings meant adults nearby.

Treeg was correct. Meredith walked down the stairs, spotted Treeg, and grabbed his shotgun, which was in the hall in preparation for a day of hunting. He stormed into the room and fired point-blank at Treeg before the slower-moving Sirian could react. The buckshot spread across the room, parts of the shot striking Treeg in the face; others, deflected, hit the little girl in the face as she watched in horror. Treeg blundered about in pain and in rage and lashed out in all directions. Roger Meredith froze as he caught sight of his daughter, bleeding and in shock, inching along the wall. He was thinking only of her when one of Treeg's blows smashed into his head, killing him instantly.

Mrs. Meredith came running in, and all but bumped into Treeg. He grabbed her and threw her hard away from him, doing so with such power that the unfortunate woman was thrown out of the east window to her death.

Treeg didn't see the child, could think only of getting back. The pain bit at him, driving him almost into a frenzy. This allowed little Carol Meredith to back out the dining-room door, out of the house, and to make it to town, where she would bleed to death in a merchant's arms.

Treeg stabbed at the button on the time-distorter unit, but nothing happened. Suddenly, drawing in great gasps of air, racked by nearly intolerable pain, he realized that he was not precisely over the focal point. With effort he stumbled to the place behind the big padded chair and pressed the stud again. Again nothing happened. He panicked. He pressed, and pressed, and pressed. Finally he pushed the red button instead of the green.

It took two weeks in a Sirian hospital to heal the wounds sufficiently for Treeg to continue. Command had all but ordered him to get another man, but Treeg knew that if he chose another in his place, he would be finished—a final failure. The finding of Mofad was no longer a mission with Rifixl Treeg, it was an obsession. To a born warrior retirement would be a living hell—he would commit suicide first.

This time he was very cautious. As soon as he emerged in the darkened house he drew his pistol, prepared to fire on sight. But the dining room was empty, the furniture piled in one corner. Everything was covered with white sheets, and a thick carpet of dust and cobwebs was everywhere. Treeg glanced around in relief. The house was unlived in at this time.

First he checked the traditional spots, and then the rest of the lower floor. For the first time he was completely uninterrupted, but he never let down his guard. Slight pains in his face reminded him to keep vigilant. His pale blue torch flickered as Treeg mounted the grand stairway with effort.

He found a body at the top of the stairs—a fresh one. Treeg, to whom all Terran apes looked alike, knew this one on sight, every feature from the tiny mustache to the potbelly burned indelibly into his brain.

Alei Mofad, in the initial stages of rigor mortis, lay on the landing, dead neither by murder nor suicide, but from a weak heart deprived of its medicine.

Treeg felt a queer thrill run through him. This was it! Even on this mad planet, Terra, he felt, he was still in command of himself.

Mofad had been upstairs, obviously. But had he been going up, or coming down? Coming down, Treeg decided from the angle of the body. Treeg stepped over the body of the scientist, dead in a remote area, remote in time and space—dead many centuries before he would be born. He walked down the second-story corridor.

The master bedroom, in the same dusty condition as the dining room, nonetheless had the look of being used. A big old stuffed chair, the same one that had been in the dining room through many reupholsterings, stood in the middle of the room, a stool resting in front of it. Clearly Mofad had spent his time here, awaiting Terran security, fearful that he would be overlooked and stranded. As Treeg searched the darkened room, his eyes caught the glare of headlights outside.

The police car pulled up and two men stepped out. They checked the front and back doors, and then went back to their car, got in . . . and drove off. Treeg waited a few seconds to make certain of their departure, then resumed his search. It would be midnight shortly, and the moon shone brightly in the window.

Suddenly Treeg glanced out the window again, nervously checking to see if the car would return. After a moment he made out a small group of figures creeping up on the house. Youngling Terrans, he decided. He watched as they moved closer, then up and out of sight underneath him.

Treeg crept out of the bedroom and back over to the stairwell. He watched the front door. After a while, it started to move. This time Rifixl Treeg would not be caught off guard! He switched off his light and melted into the shadows, still watching.

Two young Terrans entered cautiously, even fearfully, each one seeming to urge the other on. They stood for a moment in the hallway, then went into the dining room, where moonlight flooded the interior. They pulled two chairs off the heap, very carefully, and sat down, backs to the wall. In silence, their eyes wide, apprehensive, they gazed at the open door.

Treeg decided that, with the others outside who might run for help, he could wait them out. He relaxed a bit, and leaned against a wall to wait, one eye fixed on the front doorway and the other on the entranceway to the dining room. He wasn't about to run and give the prize away. It was too close!

Hours passed, and Treeg fumed with impatience to get on with his search. But it was evident that for some reason—perhaps religious—those boys, scared as they obviously were, were going to stay the night.

Johnny Schmidt and Scully Wills drove back up to Hankin House. They had gotten bored as usual and decided to give the route a fast, clean check before turning in.

As their headlights reflected against the dark shingle of the house, Schmidt caught sight of a small figure running around the side of the place—a figure he knew.

"Hold up there, Tommy Samuels!" he cried, and the boy, who was more scared of the night than of the police, stopped, turned, and obediently came back to the front. Slowly the other Swamp Rats appeared as well. The game was up, and Tommy was known to be a blabbermouth anyway.

"Now, just what the *hell* are you kids doing up here at this time of night?" the irate officer demanded, and in confused snatches the entire story was told.

"Well," said Schmidt disgustedly to his partner, "we'll have to go in and get them. Let's get it over with." With that the two men mounted the steps and threw open the door.

At that instant a bored and impatient Treeg, curious as to the meaning of the flashes of light outside, chose to risk a peek from his hiding place. So his face was fully outlined in Schmidt's casually aimed flashlight beam.

*"Oh, my God!"* yelled the police officer, who dropped and drew his pistol. Treeg jerked back, but not without sound.

"Did you see what I saw?" Scully whispered huskily.

"I hope not," replied Schmidt, and then a thought struck him. *"The kids!"*

"Buzz Murdock! Ricky Adherne! You two get outa there fast, on the run, when I give the word," Scully shouted. "Then run like hell for town and tell 'em to bring help. We got *something* cornered upstairs."

The two boys ran out, joined their frightened compatriots, and ran down the hill as fast as their legs could carry them. None of them would give a warning! They hadn't seen anything.

"Scully, get out to the car and call the state troopers. Tell 'em we don't know what it is but to get some heavy stuff up here and *fast!*" Scully crept back out the door and ran for the car. There was noise on the second floor, as Treeg retreated to the master bedroom. He knew from the way they reacted that these men were armed professionals, and he wanted a good place both for a stand and for a view of the road.

He set the pistol charge to high intensity and aimed for the patrol car below at which the unfortunate Scully was standing, giving his call for aid to the state-trooper barracks. The beam lashed out from the upper window, exploding the car with a blinding glare and shock wave that was seen and heard in town.

People awoke, looked out, and saw a burning heap in front of Hankin House.

Schmidt was knocked flat by the blast, but quickly picked himself up and stationed himself behind an overturned hall table near the stairs. Whatever was up there he was determined to *keep* up there until reinforcements arrived.

Treeg knew that with only one man downstairs he could get away, but he would return a failure, return to death. Better to make a stand here, he decided, and at least *find* the recorder, if only to destroy it. If the Sirian Empire didn't have it, then at least it would not be used against them.

A small group of villagers ran up the hill. Treeg saw them coming and aimed a shot that exploded the earth just in front of them. Men started screaming. Those unharmed ran back toward town.

Lights went on all over town, including those in the house of National Guard Major Robert Kelsoe, who had two advantages. He had a full view of the old mansion from his bedroom window, and he lived next door to the Guard armory.

Treeg fired a third shot, on wide beam, that cooked swamp grass and vegetation in a five-foot path down the hillside. He did not know where the other Terran man was lurking, but felt that he wouldn't charge without help. And the hilltop shots would discourage anyone coming to help. He continued his search.

Schmidt heard the thing moving furniture around upstairs. He tried to imagine what it was and what it was doing up there, failing on both counts. But he was Newtownards born and bred, and he knew the legends. He knew that he had just seen the demon of Hankin House and that no matter what it was, it was solid.

Major Kelsoe wasted no time in opening the armory. He didn't know what was going on, but he had seen the beams from the house and knew that some sort of power was loose up there. Three of his Guard unit were awaiting him at the armory, and they discussed what they had seen and heard as they broke out submachine guns.

It was eight and a half minutes since Scully had called the state police. Two cars roared into town, having done eighty along the narrow road. They matched Scully's incredible radio report, cut off in midsentence, with what the Guardsmen had seen. The state police corporal looked over at a far rack. *"Hey!"* he exclaimed, "Are those bazookas?"

A few minutes later a cautious group of men, three of them armed with bazookas, crept up the side of the hill to Hankin House.

When they reached the summit and were standing in front of the house, across from the crater left where the patrol car had exploded, Corporal James Watson found his voice and yelled: *"Wills! Schmidt!"*

Schmidt heard the yell and called back, "This is Schmidt in here! Wills was caught in the blast. This thing is unbelievable! It's upstairs moving stuff around at a fearful rate. Come in slowly, and watch it!"

As if on a commando raid, the men zigzagged across the road and up onto the porch, seconds apart.

"Thank God," Schmidt sighed when he saw them. He spotted the bazookas and said, "Get those things ready. The thing's sort of like a big crawfish, I think, and that body armor will be awfully thick on a baby his size. The thing's got to come down this way—maybe we can give it a bellyful."

Treeg was thoroughly frustrated. Not being able to hear anything at all, and not having seen the band of men creep up and into the house, he fancied himself still with only the problem of the lone sentinel below.

Mofad must have hidden the recorder downstairs after all, he thought disgustedly. He'd have to get rid of that pest down there and then have another look.

Quickly Treeg stepped out onto the landing, over Mofad's still body, and started down the stairs, slowly, pistol in hand.

The bazooka shell, designed to penetrate the toughest tank armor, sliced through his body like a hot knife through butter.

The great, alien body toppled headfirst down the stairs and landed with a crash at the feet of the men below, almost exactly where Captain Hornig had lain after his fall.

Colonel Rifixl Treeg, Hereditary Colonel of Empire Intelligence, was dead.

The newsmen had left; the police and Guard had finished their examinations of the building, and the alien body, or what was left of it, had been carted off to Washington, where baffled biologists would almost be driven mad in their unsuccessful attempt to identify the thing. The physicists regretted that the bazooka shell had passed through the curious beltlike container the creature had worn, destroying forever the new science in the ray-pistol power pack and the portable time link.

The excitement was all over, and Hankin House was again boarded up. There was talk of finally tearing the old place down, but in the end the house gave the economy of the tiny town a much-needed boost. The only tourist attraction in the state that drew more year-round visitors was the Latin Quarter of New Orleans.

## 4

A man, Terran, materialized in the hallway, almost on the spot where Rifixl Treeg's body had fallen. He removed a sheet of paperlike material, upon which was written the location of the agreed-upon rendezvous Mofad had established before he had ever left Conolt IV. The slip stated: "LOUESSE 155—EMERGENCY LOCATION IN CASE OF ENEMY ACTION. POINT OF REFERENCE 221."

The agent mounted the stairway, turned at the landing where Mofad's body had lain—he who now was at rest as a John Doe in the potter's field—and went directly into the master bedroom.

The place was a shambles. Treeg had moved everything around, torn down cabinets, mantels, and other such hiding places.

"Now, where the devil would I hide a minirecorder in here if I wanted a place another Terran would probably find but a Sirian probably would not?" That was the problem.

*Where?*

After some exasperating searches the agent crossed his arms, stumped, and surveyed the room. Dammit, Point of Reference 221 in this house was the master bedroom!

The agent suddenly felt tired—he had had a day that spanned twelve centuries. He decided to sit down and think the problem out. Grabbing the overturned master's chair that had once sat at the head of the dining-room table and had, indeed, been Mofad's only comfort, he turned it over and sank down.

*Click.* "The frequency modulation of point seven two betas—"

The man jumped up out of the chair as if he had been shot. But then he smiled, and then he laughed. And then he couldn't stop laughing.

Where was a good place for a Terran to look but a Sirian to overlook? What might a tired Terran do when he reached here: chair and stool set up, inviting . . . but *when you're guarding against a race that was incapable of sitting down!* A simple matter for a genius like Mofad to rig the recorder. Treeg could have torn the chair apart without noticing the tiny minirecorder—but he would never have pressed hard on the seat!

Mofad's voice droned on, telling those precious formulae and figures that would win Terra the war. The Terran agent, still laughing, slit open the seat of the chair and dug into the wooden frame structure which Mofad had built as his recorder's final resting place. Only heavy pressure on the center of the seat would have made it begin playing.

The agent removed the recorder and shut it off. He then walked out of the bedroom, down the stairs, and into the main hallway. He took from his pocket a small control box, on which were two buttons. Pressing the red one, he disappeared.

And the last ghost of Hankin House vanished into time.

# The Right Kind of House

### by Henry Slesar

The automobile that was stopping in front of Aaron Hacker's real estate office had a New York license plate. Aaron didn't need to see the white rectangle to know that its owner was new to the elm-shaded streets of Ivy Corners. It was a red convertible; there was nothing else like it in town.

The man got out of the car.

"Sally," Hacker said to the bored young lady at the only other desk. There was a paperbound book propped in her typewriter, and she was chewing something dreamily.

"Yes, Mr. Hacker?"

"Seems to be a customer. Think we oughta look busy?" He put the question mildly.

"Sure, Mr. Hacker!" She smiled brightly, removed the book, and slipped a blank sheet of paper into the machine. "What shall I type?"

"Anything, anything!" Aaron scowled.

It looked like a customer, all right. The man was heading straight for the glass door, and there was a folded newspaper in his right hand. Aaron described him later as heavy-set. Actually, he was fat. He wore a colorless suit of lightweight material, and the perspiration had soaked clean through the fabric to leave large, damp circles around his arms. He might have been fifty, but he had all his hair, and it was dark and curly. The skin of his face was flushed and hot, but the narrow eyes remained clear and frosty-cold.

He came through the doorway, glanced toward the rattling sound of the office typewriter, and then nodded at Aaron.

"Mr. Hacker?"

"Yes, sir," Aaron smiled. "What can I do for you?"

The fat man waved the newspaper. "I looked you up in the real estate section."

"Yep. Take an ad every week. I use the *Times,* too, now and then. Lot of city people interested in a town like ours. Mr.—"

"Waterbury," the man said. He plucked a white cloth out of his pocket and mopped his face. "Hot today."

"Unusually hot," Aaron answered. "Doesn't often get so hot in our town. Mean temperature's around seventy-eight in the summer. We got the lake, you know. Isn't that right, Sally?" The girl was too absorbed to hear him. "Well. Won't you sit down, Mr. Waterbury?"

"Thank you." The fat man took the proffered chair, and sighed. "I've been driving around. Thought I'd look the place over before I came here. Nice little town."

"Yes, we like it. Cigar?" He opened a box on his desk.

"No, thank you. I really don't have much time, Mr. Hacker. Suppose we get right down to business."

"Suits me, Mr. Waterbury." He looked toward the clacking noise and frowned. *"Sally!"*

"Yes, Mr. Hacker?"

"Cut out the darn racket."

"Yes, Mr. Hacker." She put her hands in her lap, and stared at the meaningless jumble of letters she had drummed on the paper.

"Now, then," Aaron said. "Was there any place in particular you were interested in, Mr. Waterbury?"

"As a matter of fact, yes. There was a house at the edge of

town, across the way from an old building. Don't know what kind of building—deserted."

"Ice-house," Aaron said. "Was it a house with pillars?"

"Yes. That's the place. Do you have it listed? I thought I saw a 'for sale' sign, but I wasn't sure."

Aaron shook his head, and chuckled dryly. "Yep, we got it listed all right." He flipped over a loose-leaf book, and pointed to a typewritten sheet. "You won't be interested for long."

"Why not?"

He turned the book around. "Read it for yourself."

The fat man did so.

AUTHENTIC COLONIAL. 8 rooms, two baths, automatic oil furnace, large porches, trees and shrubbery. Near shopping, schools. $175,000.

"Still interested?"

The man stirred uncomfortably. "Why not? Something wrong with it?"

"Well." Aaron scratched his temple. "If you really like this town, Mr. Waterbury—I mean, if you really want to settle here, I got any number of places that'd suit you better."

"Now, just a minute!" The fat man looked indignant. "What do you call this? I'm asking you about this colonial house. You want to sell it, or don't you?"

"Do I?" Aaron chuckled. "Mister, I've had that property on my hands for five years. There's nothing I'd rather collect a commission only my luck just ain't that good."

"What do you mean?"

"I mean, you won't buy. That's what I mean. I keep the listing on my books just for the sake of old Sadie Grimes. Otherwise, I wouldn't waste the space. Believe me."

"I don't get you."

"Then let me explain." He took out a cigar, but just to roll it in his fingers. "Old Mrs. Grimes put her place up for sale five years ago, when her son died. She gave me the job of selling it. I didn't want the job—no, sir. I told her that to her face. The old place just ain't worth the kind of money she's asking. I mean, heck! The old place ain't even worth *ten* thousand!"

The fat man swallowed. "Fifty? And she wants one-seventy-five?"

"That's right. Don't ask me why. It's a real old house. Oh, I don't mean one of those solid-as-a-rock old houses. I mean *old*. Never been de-termited. Some of the beams will be going in the next couple of years. Basement's full of water half the time. Upper floor leans to the right about nine inches. And the grounds are a mess."

"Then why does she ask so much?"

Aaron shrugged. "Don't ask me. Sentiment, maybe. Been in her family since the Revolution, something like that."

The fat man studied the floor. "That's too bad," he said. "Too bad!" He looked up at Aaron, and smiled sheepishly. "And I kinda liked the place. It was—I don't know how to explain it— the *right* kind of house."

"I know what you mean. It's a friendly old place. A good buy at fifty thousand. But one-seventy-five?" He laughed. "I think I know Sadie's reasoning, though. You see, she doesn't have much money. Her son was supporting her, doing well in the city. Then he died, and she knew that it was sensible to sell. But she couldn't bring herself to part with the old place. So she put a price tag so big that *nobody* would come near it. That eased her conscience." He shook his head sadly. "It's a strange world, ain't it?"

"Yes," Waterbury said distantly.

Then he stood up. "Tell you what, Mr. Hacker. Suppose I drive out to see Mrs. Grimes? Suppose I talk to her about it, get her to change her price."

"You're fooling yourself, Mr. Waterbury. I've been trying for five years."

"Who knows? Maybe if somebody *else* tried—"

Aaron Hacker spread his palms. "Who knows, is right. It's a

strange world, Mr. Waterbury. If you're willing to go to the trouble, I'll be only too happy to lend a hand."

"Good. Then I'll leave now."

"Fine! You just let me ring Sadie Grimes. I'll tell her you're on your way."

Waterbury drove slowly through the quiet streets. The shade trees that lined the avenues cast peaceful dappled shadows on the hood of the convertible. The powerful motor beneath it operated in whispers, so he could hear the fitful chirpings of the birds overhead.

He reached the home of Sadie Grimes without once passing another moving vehicle. He parked his car beside the rotted picket fence that faced the house like a row of disorderly sentries.

The lawn was a jungle of weeds and crabgrass, and the columns that rose from the front porch were entwined with creepers.

There was a hand knocker on the door. He pumped it twice.

The woman who responded was short and plump. Her white hair was vaguely purple in spots, and the lines in her face descended downward toward her small, stubborn chin. She wore a heavy wool cardigan, despite the heat.

"You must be Mr. Waterbury," she said. "Aaron Hacker said you were coming."

"Yes." The fat man smiled. "How do you do, Mrs. Grimes?"

"Well as I can expect. I suppose you want to come in?"

"Awfully hot out here." He chuckled.

"Mm. Well, come in then. I've put some lemonade in the ice-box. Only don't expect me to bargain with you, Mr. Waterbury. I'm not that kind of person."

"Of course not," the man said winningly, and followed her inside.

It was dark and cool. The window shades were opaque, and they had been drawn. They entered a square parlor with heavy, baroque furniture shoved unimaginatively against every wall.

The only color in the room was in the faded hues of the tasseled rug that lay in the center of the bare floor.

The old woman headed straight for a rocker, and sat motionless, her wrinkled hands folded sternly.

"Well?" she said. "If you have anything to say, Mr. Waterbury, I suggest you say it."

The fat man cleared his throat. "Mrs. Grimes, I've just spoken with your real estate agent—"

"I know all that," she snapped. "Aaron's a fool. All the more for letting you come here with the notion of changing my mind. I'm too old for changing my mind, Mr. Waterbury."

"Er—well, I don't know if that was my intention, Mrs. Grimes. I thought we'd just—talk a little."

She leaned back, and the rocker groaned. "Talk's free. Say what you like."

"Yes." He mopped his face again, and shoved the handkerchief only halfway back into his pocket. "Well, let me put it this way, Mrs. Grimes. I'm a businessman—a bachelor. I've worked for a long time, and I've made a fair amount of money. Now I'm ready to retire—preferably, somewhere quiet. I like Ivy Corners. I passed through here some years back, on my way to—er, Albany. I thought, one day, I might like to settle here."

"So?"

"So, when I drove through your town today, and saw this house—I was enthused. It just seemed—right for me."

"I like it too, Mr. Waterbury. That's why I'm asking a fair price for it."

Waterbury blinked. "Fair price? You'll have to admit, Mrs. Grimes, these days a house like this shouldn't cost more than—"

"That's enough!" the old woman cried. "I told you, Mr. Waterbury—I don't want to sit here all day and argue with you. If you won't pay my price, then we can forget all about it."

"But, Mrs. Grimes—"

"Good *day*, Mr. Waterbury!"

She stood up, indicating that he was expected to do the same.

But he didn't. "Wait a moment, Mrs. Grimes," he said, "just a moment. I know it's crazy, but—all right. I'll pay what you want."

She looked at him for a long moment. "Are you sure, Mr. Waterbury?"

"Positive! I've enough money. If that's the only way you'll have it, that's the way it'll be."

She smiled thinly. "I think that lemonade'll be cold enough. I'll bring you some—and then I'll tell you something about this house."

He was mopping his brow when she returned with the tray. He gulped at the frosty yellow beverage greedily.

"This house," she said, easing back in her rocker, "has been in my family since eighteen hundred and two. It was built some fifteen years before that. Every member of the family, except my son, Michael, was born in the bedroom upstairs. I was the only rebel," she added raffishly. "I had new-fangled ideas about hospitals." Her eyes twinkled.

"I know it's not the most solid house in Ivy Corners. After I brought Michael home, there was a flood in the basement, and we never seemed to get it dry since. Aaron tells me there are termites, too, but I've never seen the pesky things. I love the old place, though; you understand."

"Of course," Waterbury said.

"Michael's father died when Michael was nine. It was hard times on us then. I did some needlework, and my own father had left me the small annuity which supports me today. Not in very grand style, but I manage. Michael missed his father, perhaps even more than I. He grew up to be—well, wild is the only word that comes to mind."

The fat man clucked, sympathetically.

"When he graduated from high school, Michael left Ivy Corners and went to the city. Against my wishes, make no mistake.

But he was like so many young men; full of ambition, undirected ambition. I don't know what he did in the city. But he must have been successful—he sent me money regularly." Her eyes clouded. "I didn't see him for nine years."

"And," the man sighed, sadly.

"Yes, it wasn't easy for me. But it was even worse when Michael came home because, when he did, he was in trouble."

"Oh?"

"I didn't know how bad the trouble was. He showed up in the middle of the night, looking thinner and older than I could have believed possible. He had no luggage with him, only a small black suitcase. When I tried to take it from him, he almost struck me. Struck *me*—his own mother!

"I put him to bed myself, as if he was a little boy again. I could hear him crying out during the night.

"The next day, he told me to leave the house. Just for a few hours—he wanted to do something, he said. He didn't explain what. But when I returned that evening, I noticed that the little black suitcase was gone."

The fat man's eyes widened over the lemonade glass.

"What did it mean?" he asked.

"I didn't know then. But I found out soon—too terribly soon. That night, a man came to our house. I don't even know how he got in. I first knew when I heard voices in Michael's room. I went to the door, and tried to listen, tried to find out what sort of trouble my boy was in. But I heard only shouts and threats, and then . . ."

She paused, and her shoulders sagged.

"And a shot," she continued, "a gunshot. When I went into the room. I found the bedroom window open, and the stranger gone. And Michael—he was on the floor. He was dead."

The chair creaked.

"That was five years ago," she said. "Five long years. It was a while before I realized what had happened. The police told me the story. Michael and this other man had been involved in a crime, a serious crime. They had stolen many, many thousands of dollars.

"Michael had taken that money, and run off with it, wanting to keep it all for himself. He hid it somewhere in this house—to this very day I don't know where. Then the other man came looking for my son, came to collect his share. When he found the money gone, he—he killed my boy."

She looked up. "That's when I put the house up for sale, at $175,000. I knew that, someday, my son's killer would return. Someday, he would want this house at any price. All I had to do was wait until I found the man willing to pay much too much for an old lady's house."

She rocked gently.

Waterbury put down the empty glass and licked his lips, his eyes no longer focusing, his head rolling loosely on his shoulders.

*"Ugh!"* he said. "This lemonade is bitter."

# The Cat Jumps

## by Elizabeth Bowen

After the Bentley murder, Rose Hill stood empty two years. Lawns mounted to meadows, white paint peeled from the balconies; the sun, looking more constantly, less fearfully, in than sightseers' eyes through the naked windows, bleached the floral wallpapers. The week after the execution Harold Bentley's legatees had placed the house on the books of the principal agents, London and local. But though sunny, modern and convenient, though so delightfully situated over the Thames valley (above flood level), within easy reach of a golf course, Rose Hill, while frequently viewed, remained unpurchased. Dreadful associations apart, the privacy of the place had been violated; with its terrace garden, lily-pond, and pergola cheerfully rose-encrusted, the public had been made too familiar. On the domestic scene, too many eyes had burnt the impression of their horror. Moreover, that pearly bathroom, bedroom with wide outlook over a loop of the Thames . . . "The Rose Hill Horror": headlines flashed up at the very sound of the name. "Oh *no*, dear!" many wives had exclaimed, drawing their husbands from the gate. "Come away!" they urged, crumpling the agent's order to view as though the house were advancing on them. And husbands came away—with a backward glance at the garage. Funny to think: a chap who was hanged had kept his car there.

The Harold Wrights, however, were not deterred. They had light, bright, shadowless, thoroughly disinfected minds. They believed that they disbelieved in most things but were unprejudiced; they enjoyed frank discussions. They dreaded nothing but inhibitions: they had no inhibitions. They were pious agnostics, earnest for social reform; they explained everything to their children and were annoyed to find their children could not sleep at nights because they thought there was a complex under the bed. They knew all crime to be pathological, and read their murders only in scientific books. They had Vita Glass put into all their windows. No family, in fact, could have been more unlike the mistaken Harold Bentleys.

Rose Hill, from the first glance, suited the Wrights admirably. They were in search of a cheerful weekend house with a nice atmosphere where their friends could join them for frank discussions, and their own and their friends' children "run wild" during the summer months. Harold Wright, who had a good head, got the agent to knock six hundred off the quoted price of the house. "The unfortunate affair," he murmured. Jocelyn commended his inspiration. Otherwise, they did not give the Bentleys another thought.

The Wrights had the floral wallpapers all stripped off and the walls cream-washed; they removed some disagreeably thick pink shades from the electricity, and had the paint renewed inside and out. (The front of the house was bracketed over with balconies, like an overmantel.) Their bedroom mantelpiece, stained by the late Mrs. Bentley's cosmetics, had to be scrubbed with chemicals. Also, they had removed from the rock-garden Mrs. Bentley's little dog's memorial tablet, with a quotation on it from "Indian Love Lyrics." Jocelyn Wright, looking into the unfortunate bath, *the* bath, so square and opulent with its surround of nacreous titles, said, laughing lightly, she supposed anyone *else* would have had that bath changed.

"Not that that would be possible," she added; "the bath's built in. . . . I've always wanted a built-in bath."

Harold and Jocelyn turned from the bath to look down at the cheerful river shimmering under a spring haze. All the way down the slope cherry trees were in blossom. Life should be simplified for the Wrights—they were fortunate in their mentality.

After an experimentary week-end, without guests or children, only one thing troubled them: a resolute stuffiness, up-stairs and down—due, presumably, to the house's having been so long shut up—a smell of unsavory habitation, of rich ciga-rette smoke stale in the folds of unaired curtains, of scent spilled on unbrushed carpets; an alcoholic smell—persistent in their perhaps too sensitive nostrils after days of airing, doors and windows open, in rooms drenched thoroughly with sun and wind. They told each other it came from the parquet—they didn't like it, somehow. They had the parquet taken up—at great expense—and put down plain oak floors.

In their practical way the Wrights now set out to expel, live out, live down, almost (had the word had place in their vocab-ulary) to "lay" the Bentleys. Deferred by trouble over the par-quet, their occupation of Rose Hill (which should have dated from mid-April) did not begin till the end of May. Throughout a week Jocelyn had motored from town daily, so that the final installation of themselves and the children was able to coincide with their first week-end party—they asked down five of their friends to warm the house.

That first Friday, everything was auspicious; afternoon sky blue as the garden irises; later, a full moon pendant over the river; a night so warm that, after midnight, their enlightened friends, in pyjamas, could run on the blanched lawns in a state of high though rational excitement. Jane, John and Janet, their admirably spaced-out children, kept awake by the moonlight, hailed their elders out of the nursery skylight. Jocelyn waved to them: they never had been repressed.

The girl Muriel Barker was found looking up the terraces at the house a shade doubtfully. "You know," she said, "I do rather wonder they don't feel . . . *sometimes* . . . You know what I mean?"

"No," replied her companion, a young scientist.

Muriel sighed. "No one would mind if it had been just a short, sharp shooting. But it was so . . . prolonged. It went on all over the house. Do you remember?" she said timidly.

"No," replied Mr. Cartaret; "it didn't interest me."

"Oh, nor me either!" agreed Muriel quickly, but added: "How he must have hated her! . . ."

The scientist, sleepy, yawned frankly and referred her to Krafft Ebing. But Muriel went to bed with *Alice in Wonderland*; she went to sleep with the lights on. She was not, as Jocelyn realized later, the sort of girl to have asked at all.

Next morning was overcast; in the afternoon it rained, suddenly and heavily, interrupting, for some, tennis, for others a pleasant discussion, in a punt, on marriage under the Soviet. Defeated, they all rushed in. Jocelyn went round from room to room, shutting tightly the rain-lashed casements along the front of the house: these continued to rattle; the balconies creaked. An early dusk set in; an oppressive, almost visible moisture, up from the darkening river, pressed on the panes like a presence and slid through the house. The party gathered in the library, round an expansive but thinly burning fire. Harold circulated photographs of modern architecture; they discussed these tendencies. Then Mrs. Monkhouse, sniffing, exclaimed: "Who uses 'Trèfle Incarnat'?"

"Now *who*ever would—" her hostess began scornfully. Then from the hall came a howl, a scuffle, a thin shriek. They too sat still in the dusky library. Mr. Cartaret laughed out loud. Harold Wright, indignantly throwing open the door, revealed Jane and John rolling at the foot of the stairs biting each other, their faces dark with uninhibited passion. Bumping alternate heads against the foot of the banisters, they shrieked in concord.

"Extraordinary," said Harold; "they've never done that before. They have always understood each other so well."

"I wouldn't do that," advised Jocelyn, raising her voice slightly; "you'll hurt your teeth. Other teeth won't grow at once, you know."

"You should let them find that out for themselves," disapproved Edward Cartaret, taking up the *New Statesman*. Harold, in perplexity, shut the door on his children, who soon stunned each other to silence.

Meanwhile, Sara and Talbot Monkhouse, Muriel Barker and Theodora Smith had drawn together over the fire in a tight little knot. Their voices twanged with excitement. By that shock just now, something seemed to have been released. Even Cartaret gave them half his attention. They were discussing *crime passionel*.

"Of course, if that's what they really *want* to discuss . . ." thought Jocelyn. But it did seem unfortunate. Partly from an innocent desire to annoy her visitors, partly because the room felt awful—you would have thought fifty people had been there for a week—she went across and opened one of the windows, admitting a pounce of damp wind. They all turned, started, to hear rain crash on the lead of an upstairs balcony. Muriel's voice was left in forlorn solo: "Dragged herself . . . whining 'Harold' . . ."

Harold Wright looked remarkably conscious. Jocelyn said brightly, "Whatever *are* you talking about?" But unfortunately Harold, on almost the same breath, suggested: "Let's leave that family alone, shall we?" Their friends all felt they might not be asked again. Though they did feel, plaintively, that they had been being natural. However, they disowned Muriel, who, getting up abruptly, said she thought she'd like to go for a walk in the rain before dinner. Nobody accompanied her.

Later, overtaking Mrs. Monkhouse on the stairs, Muriel confided: absolutely, she could not stand Edward Cartaret. She could hardly bear to be in the room with him. He seemed

so . . . cruel. Cold-blooded? No, she meant cruel. Sara
Monkhouse, going into Jocelyn's room for a chat (at her entrance Jocelyn started violently), told Jocelyn that Muriel could
not stand Edward, could hardly bear to be in a room with him.
"Pity," said Jocelyn; "I had thought they might do for each
other." Jocelyn and Sara agreed that Muriel was unrealized:
what she ought to have was a baby. But when Sara, dressing,
told Talbot Monkhouse that Muriel could not stand Edward,
and Talbot said Muriel was unrealized, Sara was furious. The
Monkhouses, who never did quarrel, quarreled bitterly and
were late for dinner. They would have been later if the meal itself had not been delayed by an outburst of sex-antagonism between the nice Jacksons, a couple imported from London to run
the house. Mrs. Jackson, putting everything in the oven, had
locked herself into her room.

"Curious," said Harold, "the Jacksons' relations to each
other always seemed so modern. They have the most intelligent
discussions."

Theodora said she had been re-reading Shakespeare—this
brought them point-blank up against Othello. Harold, with ti-
tanic force, wrenched round the conversation to Relativity;
about this no one seemed to have anything to say but Edward
Cartaret. And Muriel, who by some mischance had again been
placed beside him, sat deathly, turning down her dark-rimmed
eyes. In fact, on the intelligent, sharp-featured faces all round
the table, something, perhaps simply a clearness, seemed to be
lacking, as though these were wax faces for one fatal instant
exposed to a furnace. Voices came out from some dark interi-
ority; in each conversational interchange a mutual vote of no
confidence was implicit. You would have said that each personality had been attacked by some kind of decomposition.

"No moon tonight," complained Sara Monkhouse. Never
mind, they would have a cozy evening, they would play paper
games, Jocelyn promised.

"If you can see," said Harold. "Something seems to be going wrong with the light."

Did Harold think so? They had all noticed the light seemed to be losing quality, as though a film, smoke-like, were creeping over the bulbs. The light, thinning, darkening, seemed to contract round each lamp into a blurred aura. They had noticed, but, each with a proper dread of his own subjectivity, had not spoken.

"Funny stuff," Harold said, "electricity."

Mr. Cartaret could not agree with him.

Though it was late, though they yawned and would not play paper games, they were reluctant to go to bed. You would have supposed a delightful evening. Jocelyn was not gratified.

The library stools, rugs and divans were strewn with Krafft Ebing, Freud, Forel, Weiniger and the heterosexual volume of Havelock Ellis. (Harold had thought it right to install his reference library; his friends hated to discuss without basis.) The volumes were pressed open with paper-knives and small pieces of modern statuary; stooping from one to another, purposeful as a bee, Edward Cartaret read extracts aloud to Harold, to Talbot Monkhouse and to Theodora Smith, who stitched *gros point* with resolution. At the far end of the library, under a sallow drip from a group of electric candles, Mrs. Monkhouse and Miss Barker shared an ottoman, spines pressed rigid against the wall. Tensely, one spoke, one listened.

"And these," thought Jocelyn, leaning back with her eyes shut between the two groups, "are friends I liked to have in my life. Pellucid, sane . . ."

It was remarkable how much Muriel knew. Sara, very much shocked, edged up till their thighs touched. You would have thought the Harold Bentleys had been Muriel's relatives. Surely, Sara attempted, in one's large, bright world one did not think of these things? Practically, they did not exist! Surely Muriel should not. . . . But Muriel looked at her strangely.

"Did you know," she said, "that one of Mrs. Bentley's hands was found in the library?"

Sara, smiling a little awkwardly, licked her lips. "Oh," she said.

"But the fingers were in the dining room. He began there."

"Why isn't he in Broadmoor?"

"That defence failed. He didn't really subscribe to it. He said having done what he wanted was worth anything."

"Oh!"

"Yes, he was nearly lynched. . . . She dragged herself upstairs. She couldn't lock any doors—naturally. One maid, her maid, got shut into the house with them; he'd sent all the others away. For a long time everything seemed to quiet: the maid crept out and saw Harold Bentley sitting half-way upstairs, finishing a cigarette. All the lights were full on. He nodded to her and dropped the cigarette through the banisters. Then she saw the . . . state of the hall. He went upstairs after Mrs. Bentley, saying: 'Lucinda!' He looked into room after room, whistling, then he said, 'Here we are,' and shut a door after him.

"The maid fainted. When she came to it was still going on, upstairs. . . . Harold Bentley had locked all the garden doors, there were locks even on the french windows. The maid couldn't get out. Everything she touched was . . . sticky. At last she broke a pane and got through. As she ran down the garden—the lights were on all over the house—she saw Harold Bentley moving about in the bathroom. She fell right over the edge of a terrace and one of the tradesmen picked her up next day.

"Doesn't it seem odd, Sara, to think of Jocelyn in that bath?"

Finishing her recital, Muriel turned on Sara an ecstatic and brooding look that made her almost beautiful. Sara fumbled with a cigarette; match after match failed her. "Muriel, you should see a specialist."

Muriel held out her hand for a cigarette. "He put her heart in her hat-box. He said it belonged there."

"You had no right to come here. It was most unfair to Jocelyn. Most . . . indelicate."

Muriel, to whom the word was, properly, unfamiliar, eyed incredulously Sara's lips.

"How dared you come?"

"I thought I might like it. I thought I ought to fulfill myself. I'd never had any experience of these things."

*"Muriel! . . ."*

"Besides, I wanted to meet Edward Cartaret. Several people said we were made for each other. Now, of course, I shall never marry. Look what comes of it. . . . I must say, Sara, I wouldn't be you or Jocelyn. Shut up all night with a man all alone—I don't know how you dare sleep. I've arranged to sleep with Theodora, and we shall barricade the door. I noticed something about Edward Cartaret the moment I arrived; a kind of insane glitter. He is utterly pathological. He's got instruments in his room, in that black bag. Yes, I looked. Did you notice the way he went on and on about cutting up that cat, and the way Talbot and Harold listened?"

Sara, looking furtively round the room, saw Mr. Cartaret making passes over the head of Theodora Smith with a paper-knife. Both appeared to laugh heartily, but in silence.

"Here we are," said Harold, showing his teeth, smiling.

He stood over Muriel with a siphon in one hand, glass in the other.

At this point Jocelyn, rising, said she, for one, intended to go to bed.


Jocelyn's bedroom curtains swelled a little over the noisy window. The room was stuffy and—insupportable, so that she did not know where to turn. The house, fingered outwardly by the wind that dragged unceasingly past the walls, was, within, a solid silence: silence heavy as flesh. Jocelyn dropped her wrap to the floor, then watched how its feathered edges crept a little—a draught came in under her bathroom door.

Jocelyn turned in despair and hostility from the strained, pale woman looking at her room from her oblong glass. She said aloud: "There *is* no fear," then within herself heard this taken up: "But the death fear, that one is not there to relate! If the spirit, dismembered in agony, dies before the body! If the spirit, in the whole knowledge of its dissolution, drags from chamber to chamber, drops from plane to plane of awareness (as from knife to knife down an oubliette) shedding, receiving agony! Till, long afterward, death with its little pain is established in the indifferent body." There was no comfort: death (now at every turn and instant claiming her) was in its every possible manifestation violent death: ultimately she was to be given up to terror.

Undressing, shocked by the iteration of her reflected movements, she flung a towel over the glass. With what desperate eyes of appeal, at Sara's door, she and Sara had looked at each other, clung with their looks—and parted. She could have sworn she heard Sara's bolt slide softly to. But what then, subsequently, of Talbot? And what—she eyed her own bolt, so bright (and for the late Mrs. Bentley so ineffective)—what of Harold?

"It's atavistic!" she said aloud, in the dark-lit room, and, kicking away her slippers, got into bed. She took *Erewbon* from the rack, but lay rigid, listening. As though snatched by a movement, the towel slipped from the mirror beyond her bedend. She faced the two eyes of an animal in extremity, eyes black, mindless. The clock struck two: she had been waiting an hour.

On the floor her feathered wrap shivered again all over. She heard the other door of the bathroom very stealthily open, then shut. Harold moved in softly, heavily, knocked against the side of the bath and stood still. He was quietly whistling.

"Why didn't I understand? He must always have hated me. It's tonight he's been waiting for. . . . *He wanted this house.* His look, as we went upstairs . . ."

She shrieked: "Harold!"

Harold, so softly whistling, remained behind the imperturbable door, remained quite still. . . . "He's *listening* for me. . . ." One pin-point of hope at the tunnel end: to get to Sara, to Theodora, to Muriel. Unmasked, incautious, with a long tearing sound of displaced air, Jocelyn leapt from bed to the door.

But her door had been locked from the outside.

With a strange, rueful smile, like an actress, Jocelyn, skirting the foot of the two beds, approached the door of the bathroom. "At least I have still . . . my feet." For, for some time, the heavy body of Mrs. Bentley, tenacious of life, had been dragging itself from room to room. *"Harold!"* she said to the silence, face close to the door.

The door opened on Harold, looking more dreadfully at her than she had imagined. With a quick, vague movement he roused himself from his meditation. Therein he had assumed the entire burden of Harold Bentley. Forces he did not know of assembling darkly, he had faced for untold ages the imperturbable door to his wife's room. She would be there, densely, smotheringly there. She lay like a great cat, always, over the mouth of his life.

The Harolds, superimposed on each other, stood searching the bedroom strangely. Taking a step forward, shutting the door behind him:

"Here we are," said Harold.

Jocelyn went down heavily. Harold watched.

Harold Wright was appalled. Jocelyn had fainted: Jocelyn never had fainted before. He shook, he fanned, he applied restoratives. His perplexed thoughts fled to Sara—oh, Sara, certainly. "Hi!" he cried. "Sara!" and successively fled from each to each of the locked passage doors. There was no way out.

Across the passage a door throbbed to the maniac drumming

of Sara Monkhouse. She had been locked in. For Talbot, ago-
nized with solicitude, it was equally impossible to emerge from
his dressing-room. Farther down the passage Edward Cartaret,
interested by this nocturnal manifestation, wrenched and rattled his door-handle in vain.

Muriel, on her way through the house to Theodora's bedroom, had turned all the keys on the outside, impartially. She
did not know which door was Edward Cartaret's. Muriel was a
woman who took no chances.

# The House In Bel Aire

## by Margaret St. Clair

A solid gold toilet seat is unsettling to the mind. Alfred Gluckshoffer, proprietor of the Round the Clock Plumbing Company, raised and lowered the lid several times experimentally and decided that it, too, was gold. It looked like gold, it felt like gold: Gluckshoffer, whose brother-in-law Milt was a salesman for a firm of manufacturing jewelers, and who had heard Milt talking about carats and alloys as long as he had known him, was sure it *was* gold. About fourteen carat.

From the doorway the elderly party in the dusty dress suit cleared his throat. It was not a menacing sound, but Alfred jumped. Hastily he picked up his screwdriver and began prying at the valve in the float again.

"Oh, it's a genuine stone," Milt said later that day. "They cut the synthetics out of a boule, see, and they always show the curved lines. Yours has a good color, too. The deeper the color in sapphire, the more valuable, and this one is nearly true cornflower blue. A beauty. Worth maybe four or five hundred. Where'd you get it, Al?"

Gluckshoffer decided to be frank. "Out of that house I was telling you about. The one where they called me to fix the can in the middle of the night. I dropped my pliers under the washbasin, and when I got down to pick them up, I found it. There was a sort of patch of inlaid work over the tub, wire and stone and tile and stuff, and I guess it must have fallen out of that."

Milt stuck his hands in his pockets and began to walk up and down the shop. Cupidity was coating his features with a dreamy, romantic glaze. "Think you could find the house again, Al?" he asked.

"I don't know. Like I told you, they called for me in a car with all the blinds down, and before I got out they tied a cloth over my eyes. I couldn't see a thing. There was a swimming pool on the left as we went in—I could tell by the way it echoed—and when I was getting out of the car I brushed up against a big tall hedge. Oh, yes, and from the way the streets felt, I think it was out in Bel Aire."

Milt sagged. "A house with a hedge and a swimming pool in Bel Aire. That's about like looking for a girl with brown eyes."

"Oh, I don't know," Gluckshoffer said perversely. "I might be able to tell it if I ran across it again. There was a kind of funny feel to the place, Milt. Sleepy. Dead. Why? Why're you so keen on locating it?"

"Don't be a dope," Milt said. "You want to be a plumber all your life?"

They located the house on the fifth night. It stood by itself on what must have been nearly two acres of ground, a whitely glimmering bulk, lightless and somnolent.

"Looks like there's nobody home," Milt said as he brought the car to a noiseless halt. "You oughtn't to have any trouble, Al."

Gluckshoffer snorted softly. "There's at least two people on the place," he whispered, "the chauffeur and the old geezer in the dress suit that called for me that night. Remember what you promised, Milt, about coming in for me if I'm not back in forty-five minutes. After all, this was your idea. And don't forget about honking twice if a patrol car comes by, either." His tone, though subdued, was fierce.

"Oh, sure," Milt said easily. "Don't worry about it. I won't forget."

Al Gluckshoffer got out of the car and began to worm his way through the pale green leaves of a tall pittosporum hedge. As he padded past the swimming pool (on the left, as he had remembered it) in his tennis shoes, he found himself swallowing a yawn.

This was the darnedest place. As he'd told Milt, there were two people at home—probably more, since you wouldn't keep a chauffeur unless there was somebody for him to drive—and the old party in the dress suit must sleep in the house because he'd said something to Al about the noise of the can having awakened him. But the feel in the air was so sleepy and dead that you'd think everybody on the place had been asleep for the last hundred years.

At the back of the house a window looked promising. Al tried it and found it unlocked. Stifling a yawn, and then another one, he raised the window and slipped inside.

He went into a lavatory on the ground floor first. He had unscrewed the gold faucets on the washbasin and pried eight or ten stones out of the mosaic on the wall before it occurred to him that he was wasting his time. Would people in a house like this put their best stuff in the cans. Obviously not. The place to look for the hot stuff—the really *hot* hot stuff—would be in the bedrooms upstairs. Palladium-backed clothes brushes. Mirrors set with big diamonds all around the edges. He was a dope not to have thought of it before.

Al wrapped the faucets carefully in the old rags he had brought to muffle their chinking and put them in his little satchel. Noiselessly as a shadow, he stole up the stair.

In the upper hall he hesitated. His idea about the bedrooms was all very well, but it wouldn't do to pick one where the old geezer in the dress suit, say, was asleep.

* * *

The moonlight slanting through the big windows in the hall
and falling on the door to his right put an end to Al's difficulties. There were cobwebs thick between the door itself and the
jamb, cobwebs all over the frame. A room like that must be
perfectly safe. There couldn't be anybody in a room like that.
Softly he turned the knob.

The bed, swathed in shimmering gauze, was at one end of
the room. Al paid no attention to it. His eyes were fixed on the
dressing table where, even in the subdued light, he could make
out jewelry—earrings, rings, tiara, bracelets—lying in a corus-
cating heap. The pendants at the corners of the tiara were
teardrop-shaped things, big as bantam's eggs, and the earrings
and bracelets were set all over with flashing gems.

Al licked his lips. He put out a skeptical hand toward the tiara
and touched the pendants very cautiously. They were cold, and
from the motion his hand imported to them, they started to swing
back and forth and give out rays of colored light.

From sheer nervous excitement he was on the edge of bursting
into tears or something. The stones in the bracelets seemed to be
square-cut diamonds, and the pendants on the tiara surpassed
anything he had ever imagined. They made him feel like getting
down and kowtowing in a paroxysm of unworthiness. He con-
trolled himself and began to put the jewels away in his bag.

The earrings were following the bracelets into custody when
there was a slight creak from the bed. Al turned to stone. In
very much less than a second (nervous impulses, being electri-
cal in origin, move at the speed of light, which is 186,000
m.p.s.), he had decided that the jewelry was a trap, that the trap
was being sprung, and that he was hauling tail out. He began
backing toward the door. There was another creak from the
bed. This time it was accompanied by a wonderful, a glorious,
flash of prismatic light.

Al Gluckshoffer faltered, torn cruelly between cupidity and
fear. If it *wasn't* a trap, the biggest diamond in the whole world

must be hanging around the throat, or otherwise depending from the person, or whoever was sleeping in the bed. Indecision almost made him groan. Then he made up his mind and, the sweat starting out on his forehead, tiptoed in the direction of the flash of light.

The beauty of the girl lying on the bed in the moonlight was so extreme that he forgot all about the necklace which clasped her throat. He stared down at her for an instant. Then he put his bag on the floor, knelt beside the bed and drew the curtains back. He leaned forward and kissed her on the lips.

His heart was beating like a hammer. Slowly her shadowy lids opened and she looked into his eyes. A faint, joyous smile began to curve her lips.

The expression was succeeded almost instantly by a look of regal rage. "By the scepter of Mab," the girl said, sitting up in bed and glaring at him, "you are not His Highness at all! In fact, I perceive clearly from your attitude and bearing that you are not *any* Highness. You are some low creature who has no proper business of any sort in the palace. You are Another One."

With the words, she pressed a button beside her bed. While Al cowered back, there was a clamor as strident as that of a burglar alarm, and then the elderly party in the dress suit came in, yawning and rubbing his eyes.

"He awakened me in the proper way," the girl said, gesturing in Al's direction, "but he is by no means the proper person."

"So I see, Your Highness," the old gent said with a bow. "I believe—" He peered closely at Gluckshoffer, who pushed himself hard against the wall and tried to pretend that he wasn't there. "I believe he is the plumber whom I called in last week to repair the lavatory. I am sorry. What disposition does Your Highness wish me to make of him?"

"Use the transformation machine to make him into something," the princess said, turning around and punching at the pillows on her bed. They were embroidered with a little crown.

"What would Your Highness suggest?"

"Anything you like," the princess replied. The pillows arranged to her satisfaction, she lay back on them once more. "Something appropriate, of course. Frankly, Norfreet, I'm getting tired of being waked once or twice a year by some incompetent idiot who has no legitimate business in the palace in the first place. The next bungler who wakes me up, I want you to turn into a mouse and give to the cat next door to play with. Good night." Delicately she closed her eyes.

"Good night, Your Highness," the chamberlain replied with another low bow. He turned to Al, who had been listening to this talk of transformations with a comforting sense of its impossibility, and fixed him with a hypnotic gaze. "Come with me," he said sternly. "Before I transform you, you must repair the damage you have done."

Some twenty minutes later, the chamberlain gave the solid brass cuspidor which had been Al Gluckshoffer a contemptuous shove with his foot. He ought to take the thing up to the attic and leave it, but he was getting dreadfully sleepy. He needed his rest at his age. Some other time.

He got into bed, his joints creaking. Her Highness was right; there were altogether too many intruders in the palace these days. They needed to be shown their place, made an example of. The next person who woke him up was going to be the object of something special in the way of transformations. Norfreet began to snore.

And on the other side of the pittosporum hedge, Milt looked at his watch and decided that it was time to go in and see what had happened to Al. He started to worm his way through the hedge.

# The School Friend

## by Robert Aickman

*To be taken advantage of is every woman's secret wish.*
—PRINCESS ELIZABETH BIBESCO

It would be false modesty to deny that Sally Tessler and I were the bright girls of the school. Later it was understood that I went more and more swiftly to the bad; but Sally continued being bright for some considerable time. Like many males, but few females, even among those inclined to scholarship, Sally combined a true love for the Classics, the ancient ones, with an insight into mathematics which, to the small degree that I was interested, seemed to me almost magical. She won three scholarships, two gold medals, and a sojourn among the Hellenes with all expenses paid. Before she had graduated, she had published a little book of popular mathematics which, I understood, made her a surprising sum of money. Later she edited several lesser Latin authors, published in editions so small that they can have brought her nothing but inner satisfaction.

The foundations of all this erudition had almost certainly been laid in Sally's earliest childhood. The tale went that Dr. Tessler had once been the victim of some serious injustice, or considered that he had: certainly it seemed to be sure that, as his neighbors put it, he "never went out." Sally herself once told me that she not only could remember nothing of her mother but had never come across any trace or record of her.

From the very beginning Sally had been brought up, it was said, by her father alone. Rumor suggested that Dr. Tessler's regimen was threefold: reading, domestic drudgery, and obedience. I deduced that he used the last to enforce the two first: when Sally was not scrubbing the floor or washing up, she was studying Vergil and Euclid. Even then I suspected that the doctor's ways of making his will felt would not have borne examination by the other parents. Certainly, however, when Sally first appeared at school, she had much more than a grounding in almost every subject taught, and in several which were not taught. Sally, therefore, was from the first a considerable irritant to the mistresses. She was always two years or more below the average age of her form. She had a real technique of acquiring knowledge. She respected learning in her preceptors, and detected its absence. . . . I once tried to find out in what subject Dr. Tessler had obtained his doctorate. I failed; but, of course, one then expected a German to be a doctor.

It was the first school Sally had attended. I was a member of the form to which she was originally assigned but in which she remained for less than a week, so eclipsing to the rest of us was her mass of information. She was thirteen years and five months old at the time, nearly a year younger than I. (I owe it to myself to say that I was promoted at the end of the term and thereafter more or less kept pace with the prodigy, although this, perhaps, was for special reasons.) Her hair was remarkably beautiful; a perfect light blonde and lustrous with brushing, although cut short and done in no particular way, indeed usually very untidy. She had dark eyes, a pale skin, a large distinguished nose, and a larger mouth. She had also a slim but precocious figure, which later put me in mind of Tessa in "The Constant Nymph." For better or for worse, there was no school uniform, and Sally invariably appeared in a dark-blue dress of foreign aspect and extreme simplicity, which nonetheless distinctly became her looks. As she grew, she seemed to wear later editions of the same dress, new and enlarged, like certain publications.

Sally, in fact, was beautiful; but one would be unlikely ever to meet another so lovely who was so entirely and genuinely unaware of the fact and of its implications. And, of course, her casualness about her appearance, and her simple clothes, added to her charm. Her disposition seemed kindly and easy-going in the extreme, and her voice was lazy to drawling. But Sally nonetheless seemed to live only in order to work, and although I was, I think, her closest friend (it was the urge to keep up with her which explained much of my own progress in the school), I learnt very little about her. She seemed to have no pocket money at all: as this amounted to a social deficiency of the vastest magnitude, and as my parents could afford to be and were generous, I regularly shared with her. She accepted the arrangement simply and warmly. In return she gave me frequent little presents of books: a copy of Goethe's *Faust* in the original language and bound in somewhat discouraging brown leather, and an edition of Petronius, with some remarkable drawings. . . . Much later, when in need of money for a friend, I took the *Faust,* in no hopeful spirit, to Sotheby's. It proved to be a rebound first edition . . .

But it was a conversation about the illustrations in the Petronius (I was able to construe Latin fairly well for a girl, but the italics and long *s*'s daunted me) which led me to the discovery that Sally knew more than any of us about the subject illustrated. Despite her startling range of information she seemed then, and certainly for long after, completely disinterested in any personal way. It was as if she discoursed, in the gentlest, sweetest manner, about some distant far off thing, or, to use a comparison absurdly hackneyed but here appropriate, about botany. It was an ordinary enough school, and sex was a preoccupation among us. Sally's attitude was surprisingly new and unusual. In the end she did ask me not to tell the others what she had just told me.

"As if I would," I replied challengingly, but still musingly.

And in fact I didn't tell anyone until considerably later, when I found that I had learned from Sally things which no one else at all seemed to know, things which I sometimes think have in themselves influenced my life, so to say, not a little. Once I tried to work out how old Sally was at the time of this conversation. I think she could hardly have been more than fifteen.

In the end Sally won her university scholarship, and I just failed, but won the school's English Essay Prize and also the Good Conduct Medal, which I deemed (and still deem) in the nature of a stigma, but believed, consolingly, to be awarded more to my prosperous father than to me. Sally's conduct was in any case much better than mine, being indeed irreproachable. I had entered for the scholarship with the intention of forcing the examiners, in the unlikely event of my winning it, to bestow it upon Sally, who really needed it. When this doubtless impracticable scheme proved unnecessary, Sally and I parted company, she to her triumphs of the intellect, I to my lesser achievements. We corresponded intermittently, but decreasingly as our areas of common interest diminished. Ultimately, for a very considerable time, I lost sight of her altogether, although occasionally over the years I used to see reviews of her learned books and encounter references to her in leading articles about the Classical Association and similar indispensable bodies. I took it for granted that by now we should have difficulty in communicating at all. I observed that Sally did not marry. One couldn't wonder, I foolishly and unkindly drifted into supposing . . .

When I was forty-one, two things happened which have a bearing on this narrative. The first was that a catastrophe befell me which led to my again taking up residence with my parents. Details are superfluous. The second thing was the death of Dr. Tessler.

I should probably have heard of Dr. Tessler's death in any

case, for my parents, who, like me and the rest of the neighbors, had never set eyes upon him, had always regarded him with mild curiosity. As it was, the first I knew of it was when I saw the funeral. I was shopping on behalf of my mother and reflecting upon the vileness of things when I observed old Mr. Orbit remove his hat, in which he always served, and briefly sink his head in prayer. Between the aggregations of "Shredded Wheat" in the window, I saw the passing shape of a very old-fashioned and therefore very ornate horse-drawn hearse. It bore a coffin covered in a pall of worn purple velvet, but there seemed to be no mourners at all.

"Didn't think never to see a 'orse 'earse again, Mr. Orbit," remarked old Mrs. Rind, who was ahead of me in the queue.

"Pauper funeral, I expect," said her friend old Mrs. Edge.

"No such thing no more," said Mr. Orbit quite sharply, and replacing his hat. "That's Dr. Tessler's funeral. Don't suppose 'e 'ad no family come to look after things."

I believe the three white heads then got together and began to whisper; but, on hearing the name, I had made toward the door. I looked out. The huge ancient hearse, complete with the vast black plumes, looked much too big for the narrow autumnal street. It put me in mind of how toys are often so grossly out of scale with one another. I could now see that instead of mourners, a group of urchins, shadowy in the fading light, ran behind the bier, shrieking and jeering: a most regrettable scene in a well-conducted township.

For the first time in months, if not years, I wondered about Sally.

Three days later she appeared without warning at my parents' front door. It was I who opened it.

"Hallo, Mel."

One hears of people who after many years take up a conversation as if the same number of hours had passed. This was a case in point. Sally, moreover, looked almost wholly unchanged. Possibly her lustrous hair was one half-shade darker, but it was still short and wild. Her lovely white skin was un-wrinkled. Her large mouth smiled sweetly but, as always, somewhat absently. She was dressed in the most ordinary clothes but still managed to look like anything but a don or a dominie: although neither did she look like a woman of the world. It was, I reflected, hard to decide what she did look like.

"Hallo, Sally."

I kissed her and began to condole.

"Father really died before I was born. You know that."

"I have heard something." I should not have been sorry to hear more; but Sally threw off her coat, sank down before the fire, and said:

"I've read all your books. I loved them. I should have writ-ten."

"Thank you," I said. "I wish there were more who felt like you."

"You're an artist, Mel. You can't expect to be a success at the same time." She was warming her white hands. I was not sure that I was an artist, but it was nice to be told.

There was a circle of leather-covered armchairs round the fire. I sat down beside her. "I've read about you often in the *Times Lit*," I said, "but that's all. For years. Much too long."

"I'm glad you're still living here," she replied.

"Not *still*. Again."

"Oh?" She smiled in her gentle, absent way.

"Following a session in the frying pan, and another one in the fire . . . I'm sure you've been conducting yourself more sensibly." I was still fishing.

But all she said was, "Anyway I'm still glad you're living here."

"Can't say *I* am. But why in particular?"

"Silly Mel! Because I'm going to live here too."

I had never even thought of it.

I could not resist a direct question.

"Who told you your father was ill?"

"A friend. I've come all the way from Asia Minor. I've been looking at potsherds." She was remarkably untanned for one who had been living under the sun; but her skin was of the kind which does not tan readily.

"It will be lovely to have you about again. Lovely, Sally. But what will you do here?"

"What do *you* do?"

"I write . . . In other ways my life is rather over, I feel."

"*I* write too. Sometimes. At least I edit . . . And I don't think my life, properly speaking, has ever begun."

I had spoken in self-pity, although I had not wholly meant to do so. The tone of her reply I found it impossible to define. Certainly, I thought with slight malice, certainly she does look absurdly virginal.

A week later a van arrived at Dr. Tessler's house, containing a great number of books, a few packed trunks, and little else; and Sally moved in. She offered no further explanation for this gesture of semiretirement from the gay world (for we lived about forty miles from London, too many for urban participation, too few for rural self-sufficiency); but it occurred to me that Sally's resources were doubtless not so large that she could disregard an opportunity to live rent free, although I had no idea whether the house was freehold, and there was no mention even of a will. Sally was and always had been so vague about practicalities that I was a little worried about these matters; but she declined ideas of help. There was no doubt that if she were to offer the house for sale, she could not expect from the proceeds an income big enough to enable her to live elsewhere; and I could imagine that she shrank from the bother and uncertainty of letting.

I heard about the contents of the van from Mr. Ditch, the remover; and it was, in fact, not until she had been in residence for about ten days that Sally sent me an invitation. During this time, and after she had refused my help with her affairs, I had thought it best to leave her alone. Now, although the house which I must thenceforth think of as hers, stood only about a quarter of a mile from the house of my parents, she sent me a postcard. It was a picture postcard of Mitylene. She asked me to tea.

The way was through the avenues and round the corners of a mid-nineteenth-century housing estate for merchants and professional men. My parents' house was intended for the former; Sally's for the latter. It stood, in fact, at the very end of a cul-de-sac; even now the house opposite bore the plate of a dentist.

I had often stared at the house during Dr. Tessler's occupancy and before I knew Sally; but not until that day did I enter it. The outside looked much as it had ever done. The house was built in a gray brick so depressing that one speculated how anyone could ever come to choose it (as many once did, however, throughout the Home Counties). To the right of the front door (approached by twelve steps, with blue and white tessellated risers) protruded a greatly disproportionate obtuse-angled bay window: it resembled the thrusting nose on a gray and wrinkled face. This bay window served the basement, the ground floor, and the first floor: between the two latter ran a dull red string course "in an acanthus pattern," like a chaplet round the temples of a dowager. From the second floor window it might have been possible to step onto the top of the projecting bay, the better to view the surgery opposite, had not the second floor window been barred, doubtless as protection for a nursery. The wooden gate had fallen from its hinges and had to be lifted open and shut. It was startlingly heavy.

The bell was in order.

Sally was, of course, alone in the house.

Immediately she opened the door (which included two large tracts of colored glass), I apprehended a change in her, essentially the first change in all the time I had known her, for the woman who had come to my parents' house a fortnight or three weeks before had seemed to me very much the girl who had joined my class when we were both children. But now there was a difference . . .

In the first place she looked different. Previously there had always been a distinction about her appearance, however inexpensive her clothes. Now she wore a fawn jumper which needed washing and stained, creaseless gray slacks. When a woman wears trousers, they need to be smart. These were slacks indeed. Sally's hair was not so much picturesquely untidy as in the past, but, more truly, in bad need of trimming. She wore distasteful sandals. And her expression had altered.

"Hallo, Mel. Do you mind sitting down and waiting for the kettle to boil?" She showed me into the ground floor room (although to make possible the basement, it was cocked high in the air) with the bay window. "Just throw your coat on a chair." She bustled precipitately away. It occurred to me that Sally's culinary aplomb had diminished since her busy childhood of legend.

The room was horrible. I had expected eccentricity, discomfort, bookworminess, even perhaps the slightly macabre. But the room was entirely commonplace and in the most unpleasing fashion. The furniture had probably been mass-produced in the early twenties. It was of the kind which it is impossible, by any expenditure of time and polish, to keep in good order. The carpet was dingy jazz. There were soulless little pictures in gilt frames. There were dreadful modern knickknacks. There was a wireless set, obviously long broken . . . For the time of year, the rickety smoky fire offered none too much heat. Rejecting Sally's invitation, I drew my coat about me.

There was nothing to read except a prewar copy of "Tit-Bits," which I found on the floor under the lumpy settee. Like Sally's jumper, the dense lace curtains could have done with a wash. But before long Sally appeared with tea: six uniform pink cakes from the nearest shop and a flavorless liquid full of floating "strangers." The crockery accorded with the other appurtenances.

I asked Sally whether she had started work of any kind.

"Not yet," she replied, a little dourly. "I've got to get things going in the house first."

"I suppose your father left things in a mess?"

She looked at me sharply. "Father never went out of his library."

She seemed to suppose that I knew more than I did. Looking around me, I found it hard to visualize a "library." I changed the subject.

"Aren't you going to find it rather a big house for one?"

It seemed a harmless, though uninspired, question. But Sally, instead of answering, simply sat staring before her. Although it was more as if she stared within her at some unpleasant thought.

I believe in acting upon impulse. "Sally," I said, "I've got an idea. Why don't you sell this house, which *is* much too big for you and come and live with me? We've plenty of room, and my father is the soul of generosity."

She only shook her head. "Thank you, Mel. No." She still seemed absorbed by her own thoughts, disagreeable thoughts.

"You remember what you said the other day. About being glad I was living here. I'm likely to go on living here. I'd love to have you with me, Sally. Please think about it."

She put down her ugly little teaplate on the ugly little table. She had taken a single small bite out of her pink cake. She stretched out her hand toward me, very tentatively, not nearly touching me. She gulped slightly. "Mel—"

I moved to take her hand, but she drew it back. Suddenly she shook her head violently. Then she began to talk about her work.

She did not resume eating or drinking; and indeed both the cakes and tea, which every now and then she pressed upon me in a casual way more like her former manner, were remarkably unappetizing. But she talked interestingly and familiarly for about half an hour—about indifferent matters. Then she said, "Forgive me, Mel. But I must be getting on."

She rose. Of course I rose too. Then I hesitated.

"Sally . . . Please think about it. I'd like it so much. Please."

"Thank you, Mel. I'll think about it."

"Promise?"

"Promise . . . Thank you for coming to see me."

"I want to see much more of you."

She stood in the open front door. In the dusk she looked inexplicably harassed and woebegone.

"Come and see me whenever you want. Come to tea tomorrow and stay to dinner." Anything to get her out of that horrible, horrible house.

But, as before, she only said, "I'll think about it."

Walking home it seemed to me that she could only have invited me out of obligation. I was much hurt and much frightened by the change in her. As I reached my own gate it struck me that the biggest change of all was that she had never once smiled.

When five or six days later I had neither seen nor heard from Sally, I wrote asking her to visit me. For several days she did not reply at all: then she sent me another picture postcard this time of some ancient bust in a museum, informing me that she would love to come when she had a little more time. I noticed that she had made a slight error in my address, which she had hastily and imperfectly corrected. The postman, of course, knew me. I could well imagine that there was much to do in Sally's house. Indeed, it was a house of the kind in which the work is never either satisfying or complete: an ever-open mouth of a house. But, despite the tales of her childhood, I could not imagine the Sally I knew doing it . . . I could not imagine what she was doing, and I admit that I did want to know.

Some time after that I came across Sally in the International

Stores. It was not a shop I usually patronized, but Mr. Orbit was out of my father's particular pickles. I could not help wondering whether Sally did not remember perfectly well that it was a shop in which I was seldom found.

She was there when I entered. She was wearing the same grimy slacks and this time a white blouse which was worse than her former jumper, being plainly filthy. Against the autumn she wore a blue raincoat which I believed to be the same she had worn to school. She looked positively unkempt and far from well. She was nervously shoving a little heap of dark blue bags and gaudy packets into a very ancient holdall. Although the shop was fairly full, no one else was waiting to be served at the part of the counter where Sally stood. I walked up to her.

"Good morning, Sally."

She clutched the ugly holdall to her, as if I were about to snatch it. Then at once she became ostentatiously relaxed.

"Don't look at me like that," she said. There was an upsetting little rasp in her voice. "After all, Mel, you're not my mother." Then she walked out of the shop.

"Your change, miss," cried the International Stores shopman after her.

But she was gone. The other women in the shop watched her go as if she were the town tart. Then they closed up along the section of the counter where she had been standing.

"Poor thing," said the shopman unexpectedly. He was young. The other women looked at him malevolently and gave their orders with conscious briskness.

Then came Sally's accident.

By this time there could be no doubt that something was much wrong with her; but I had always been very nearly her only friend in the town, and her behavior to me made it difficult for me to help. It was not that I lacked will or, I think, courage, but that I was unable to decide how to set about the task. I was still thinking about it when Sally was run over. I imagine that her trouble, whatever it was, had affected her ordinary judgment. Apparently she stepped right under a lorry in the High Street, having just visited the post office. I learned shortly afterward that she refused to have letters delivered at her house but insisted upon them being left *Poste Restante*.

When she had been taken to the Cottage Hospital, the matron, Miss Garvice, sent for me. Everyone knew that I was Sally's friend.

"Do you know who is her next of kin?"

"I doubt whether she has such a thing in this country."

"Friends?"

"Only me that I know of." I had always wondered about the mysterious informant of Dr. Tessler's passing.

Miss Garvice considered for a moment.

"I'm worried about her house. Strictly speaking, in all the circumstances, I suppose I ought to tell the police and ask them to keep an eye on it. But I am sure she would prefer me to ask you."

From her tone I rather supposed that Miss Garvice knew nothing of the recent changes in Sally. Or perhaps she thought it best to ignore them.

"As you live so close, I wonder if it would be too much to ask you just to look in every now and then? Perhaps daily might be best?"

I think I accepted mainly because I suspected that something in Sally's life might need, for Sally's sake, to be kept from the wrong people.

"Here are her keys."

It was a numerous assembly for such a commonplace establishment as Sally's.

"I'll do it as I say, Miss Garvice. But how long do you think it will be?"

"Hard to say. But I don't think Sally's going to die."

One trouble was that I felt compelled to face the assignment unaided because I knew no one in the town who seemed likely

to regard Sally's predicament with the sensitiveness and delicacy—and indeed love—which I suspected were essential.
There was also a dilemma about whether or not I should explore the house. Doubtless I had no right; but to do so might,
on the other hand, possibly be regarded as in Sally's "higher interests." I must acknowledge, nonetheless, that my decision to
proceed was considerably inspired by curiosity. This did not
mean that I should involve others in whatever might be disclosed. Even that odious sitting room would do Sally's reputation no good . . .

Miss Garvice had concluded by suggesting that I perhaps
ought to pay my first visit at once. I went home to lunch. Then
I set out.

Among the first things I discovered were that Sally kept
every single door in the house locked: and that the remains of
the tea I had taken with her weeks before still lingered in the
sitting room; not, mercifully, the food, but the plates, and cups,
and genteel little knives, and the teapot with leaves and liquor
at the bottom of it.

Giving on to the passage from the front door was a room adjoining the sitting room and corresponding to it at the back of
the house. Presumably one of these rooms was intended by the
builder (the house was not of a kind to have had an architect)
for use as a dining room, the other as a drawing room. I went
through the keys. They were big keys, the doors and locks
being pretentiously oversized. In the end the door opened. I noticed a stale cold smell. The room appeared to be in complete
darkness. Possibly Dr. Tessler's library?

I groped round the inside of the door frame for an electric
light switch but could find nothing. I took another half step inside. The room seemed blacker than ever and the stale cold
smell somewhat stronger. I decided to defer exploration until
later.

I shut the door and went upstairs. The ground floor rooms
were high, which made the stairs many and steep.

On the first floor were two rooms corresponding in plan to the two rooms below. It could be called neither an imaginative design, nor a convenient one. I tried the front room first, again going through the rigmarole with the keys. The room was in a dilapidated condition and contained nothing but a considerable mass of papers. They appeared once to have been stacked on the bare floor; but the stacks had long since fallen over, and their component elements accumulated a deep top-dressing of flaky black particles. The grime was of that ultimate kind which seems to have an actually greasy consistency: the idea of further investigating those neglected masses of scroll and manuscript made me shudder.

The back room was a bedroom, presumably Sally's. All the curtains were drawn, and I had to turn on the light. It contained what must truly be termed, in the worn phrase, "a few sticks of furniture," all in the same period as the pieces in the sitting room, though more exiguous and spidery-looking. The inflated size and height of the room, the heavy plaster cornice and even heavier plaster rose in the center of the cracked ceiling emphasized the sparseness of the anachronistic furnishing. There was, however, a more modern double-divan bed, very low on the floor and looking as if it had been slept in but not remade for weeks. Someone seemed to have arisen rather suddenly, as at an alarm clock. I tried to pull open a drawer in the rickety dressing table. It squeaked and stuck and proved to contain some pathetic-looking underclothes of Sally's. The long curtains were very heavy and dark green.

It was a depressing investigation, but I persisted.

The second floor gave the appearance of having been originally one room, reached from a small landing. There was marked evidence of unskilled cuttings and bodgings; aimed, it was clear, at partitioning off this single vast room in order to form a bathroom and lavatory and a passage giving access thereto. Could the house have been originally built without these necessary amenities? Anything seemed possible. I remembered the chestnut about the architect who forgot the staircase.

But there was something here which I found not only squalid but vaguely frightening. The original door, giving from the small landing into the one room, showed every sign of having been forcibly burst open, and from the inside (characteristically, it had been hung to open outward). The damage was seemingly not recent (although it is not easy to date such a thing); but the shattered door still hung dejectedly outward from its weighty lower hinge only and, in fact, made it almost impossible to enter the room at all. Gingerly I forced it a little more forward. The ripped woodwork of the heavy door shrieked piercingly as I dragged at it. I looked in. The room, such as it had ever been, had been finally wrecked by the introduction of the batten partition which separated it from the bathroom and was covered with blistered dark brown varnish. The only contents were a few decaying toys. The nursery, as I remembered from the exterior prospect. Through the gap between the sloping door and its frame I looked at the barred windows. Like everything else in the house, the bars seemed very heavy. I looked again at the toys. I observed that *all* of them seemed to be woolly animals. They were rotted with moth and mold, but not so much so as to conceal the fact that at least some of them appeared also to have been mutilated. There were the decomposing leg of a teddy bear, inches away from the main torso; the severed head of a fanciful stuffed bird. It was as unpleasant a scene as every other in the house.

What had Sally been doing all day? As I had suspected, clearly not cleaning the house. There remained the kitchen quarters; and, of course, the late doctor's library.

There were odd scraps of food about the basement and signs of recent though sketchy cooking. I was almost surprised to discover that Sally had not lived on air. In general, however, the basement suggested nothing more unusual than the familiar feeling of wonder at the combined magnitude and cumbrousness of cooking operations in the homes of our middle class great-grandfathers.

I looked round for a candle with which to illumine the library. I even opened various drawers, bins, and cupboards. It seemed that there were no candles. In any case, I thought, shivering slightly in the descending dusk, the library was probably a job for more than a single candle. Next time I would provide myself with my father's imposing flashlamp.

There seemed nothing more to be done. I had not even taken off my coat. I had discovered little which was calculated to solve the mystery. Could Sally be doping herself? It really seemed a theory. I turned off the kitchen light, ascended to the ground floor, and, shutting the front door, descended again to the garden. I eyed the collapsed front gate with new suspicion. Some time later I realized that I had relocked none of the inside doors.

Next morning I called at the Cottage Hospital.

"In a way," said Miss Garvice, "she's much better. Quite surprisingly so."

"Can I see her?"

"I am afraid not. She's unfortunately had a very restless night." Miss Garvice was sitting at her desk with a large yellow cat in her lap. As she spoke, the cat gazed up into her face with a look of complacement interrogation.

"Not pain?"

"Not exactly, I think." Miss Garvice turned the cat's head downward toward her knee. She paused before saying: "She's been weeping all night. And talking too. More hysterical than delirious. In the end we had to move her out of the big ward."

"What does she say?"

"It wouldn't be fair to our patients if we repeated what they say when they're not themselves."

"I suppose not. Still—"

"I admit that I cannot at all understand what's the matter with her. With her mind, I mean, of course."

"She's suffering from shock."

"Yes . . . But when I said 'mind,' I should perhaps have said 'emotions.'" The cat jumped from Miss Garvice's lap to the floor. It began to rub itself against my stockings. Miss Garvice followed it with her eyes. "Were you able to get to her house?"

"I looked in for a few minutes."

Miss Garvice wanted to question me; but she stopped herself and only asked, "Everything in order?"

"As far as I could see."

"I wonder if you would collect together a few things and bring them when you next come. I am sure I can leave it to you."

"I'll see what I can do." Remembering the house, I wondered what I *could* do. I rose. "I'll look in tomorrow, if I may." The cat followed me to the door purring. "Perhaps I shall be able to see Sally then."

Miss Garvice only nodded.

The truth was that I could not rest until I had investigated that back room. I was afraid, of course, but much more curious. Even my fear, I felt, perhaps wrongly, was more fear of the unknown than of anything I imagined myself likely in fact to find. Had there been a sympathetic friend available, I should have been glad of his company (it was a job for a man, or for no one). As it was, loyalty to Sally sent me, as before, alone.

During the morning it had become more and more overcast. In the middle of lunch it began to rain. Throughout the afternoon it rained more and more heavily. My mother said I was mad to go out, but I donned a pair of heavy walking shoes and my riding mackintosh. I had borrowed my father's flashlamp before he left that morning for his business.

I first entered the sitting room, where I took off my mackintosh and saturated beret. It would perhaps have been more sensible to hang the dripping object in the lower regions; but I think I felt it was wise not to leave them too far from the front door. I stood for a time in front of the mirror combing my matted hair. The light was fading fast, and it was difficult to see very much. The gusty wind hurled the rain against the big bay window, down which it descended like a ripping membrane of wax, distorting what little prospect remained outside. The window frame leaked copiously, making little pools on the floor.

I pulled up the collar of my sweater, took the flashlamp, and entered the back room. Almost at once in the beam of light, I found the switch. It was placed at the normal height, but about three feet from the doorway: as if the intention were precisely to make it impossible for the light to be switched on—or off—from the door. I turned it on.

I had speculated extensively, but the discovery still surprised me. Within the original walls had been laid three courses of stonework, which continued overhead to form an arched vault under the ceiling. The gray stones had been unskillfully laid, and the vault in particular looked likely to collapse. The inside of the door was reinforced with a single sheet of iron. There remained no window at all. A crude system of electric lighting had been installed, but there seemed provision for neither heating nor ventilation. Conceivably the room was intended for use in air raids; it had palpably been in existence for some time. But in that case it was hard to see why it should still be inhabited as it so plainly was . . .

For within the dismal place were many rough wooden shelves laden with crumbling brown books; several battered wooden armchairs; a large desk covered with papers; and a camp bed, showing, like the bed upstairs, signs of recent occupancy. Most curious of all were a small ashtray by the bedside choked with cigarette ends, and an empty coffee cup. I lifted the pillow; underneath it were Sally's pajamas, not folded, but stuffed away out of sight. It was difficult to resist the unpleasant idea that she had begun by sleeping in the room upstairs but for some reason had moved down to this stagnant cavern; which, moreover, she had stated that her father had never left.

I liked to think of myself as more imaginative than sensible. I had, for example, conceived it as possible that Dr. Tessler had been stark raving mad, and that the room he never left would prove to be padded. But no more like a prison. It seemed impossible that all through her childhood Sally's father had been under some kind of duress. The room also—and horribly—resembled a tomb. Could the doctor have been one of those visionaries who are given to brooding upon The End and to decking themselves with the symbols of mortality, like Donne with his shroud? It was difficult to believe in Sally emulating her father in this ... For some time, I think, I fought off the most probable solution, carefully giving weight to every other suggestion which my mind could muster up. In the end I faced the fact that more than an oubliette or a grave, the place resembled a fortress; and the suggestion that there was something in the house against which protection was necessary, was imperative. The locked doors, the scene of ruin on the second floor, Sally's behavior. I had known it all the time.

I turned off the bleak light, hanging by its kinked flex. As I locked the library door, I wondered upon the unknown troubles which might have followed my failure of yesterday to leave the house as I had found it. I walked the few steps down the passage from the library to the sitting room, at once preoccupied and alert. But, for my peace of mind, neither preoccupied nor alert enough. Because, although only for a moment, a second, a gleam, when in that almost vanished light I reentered the sitting room, I saw him.

As if, for my benefit, to make the most of the little light, he stood right up in the big bay window. The view he presented to me was what I should call three-quarters back. But I could see a fraction of the outline of his face; entirely white (a thing which has to be seen to be believed) and with the skin drawn tight over the bones as by a tourniquet. There was a suggestion of wispy hair. I think he wore black; a garment, I thought, like a frock coat. He stood stooped and shadowy, except for the glimpse of white face. Of course I could not see his eyes. Needless to say, he was gone almost as soon as I beheld him; but it would be inexact to say that he went quite immediately. I had a scintilla of time in which to blink. I thought at first that dead or alive, it was Dr. Tessler; but immediately afterward I thought not.

That evening I tried to take my father into my confidence. I had always considered him the kindest of men, but one from whom I had been carried far out to sea. Now I was interested, as often with people, by the unexpectedness of his response. After I had finished my story (although I did not tell him every-thing), to which he listened carefully, sometimes putting an in-telligent question about a point I had failed to illuminate, he said, "If you want my opinion, I'll give it to you."

"Please."

"It's simple enough. The whole affair is no business of yours." He smiled to take the sting out of the words, but un-derneath he seemed unusually serious.

"I'm fond of Sally. Besides, Miss Garvice asked me."

"Miss Garvice asked you to look in and see if there was any post; not to poke and pry about the house."

It was undoubtedly my weak point. But neither was it an al-together strong one for him. "Sally wouldn't let the postman deliver," I countered. "She was collecting her letters from the post office at the time she was run over. I can't imagine why."

"Don't try," said my father.

"But," I said, "what I saw? Even if I *had* no right to go all over the house."

"Mel," said my father, "you're supposed to write novels. Haven't you noticed by this time that everyone's lives are full of things you can't understand? The exceptional thing is the thing you *can* understand. I remember a man I knew when I

was first in London . . ." He broke off. "But fortunately we
don't *have* to understand. And for that reason we've no right to
scrutinize other people's lives too closely."

Completely baffled, I said nothing.

My father patted me on the shoulder. "You can fancy you see
things when the light's not very good, you know. Particularly
an artistic girl like you, Mel."

Even by my parent I still liked occasionally to be called a
girl.

When I went up to bed it struck me that again something had
been forgotten. This time it was Sally's "few things."


Naturally it was the first matter Miss Garvice mentioned.

"I'm very sorry. I forgot. I think it must have been the rain,"
I continued, excusing myself like an adolescent to authority.

Miss Garvice very slightly clucked her tongue. But her mind
was on something else. She went to the door of her room.

"Serena!"

"Yes, Miss Garvice?"

"See that I'm not disturbed for a few minutes, will you
please? I'll call you again."

"Yes, Miss Garvice." Serena disappeared, mousily shutting
the door.

"I want to tell you something in confidence."

I smiled. Confidences preannounced are seldom worthwhile.

"You know our routine here. We've been making various
tests on Sally. One of them roused our suspicion." Miss Garvice scraped a Swan vesta on the composition striker which
stood on her desk. For the moment she had forgotten the relative cigarette. "Did you know that Sally was pregnant?"

"No," I replied. But it might provide an explanation. Of a
few things.

"Normally, of course, I shouldn't tell you. Or anyone else.
But Sally is in such a hysterical state. And you say you know
of no relatives?"

"None. What can I do?"

"I wonder if you would consider having her to stay with you? Not at once, of course. When we discharge her. Sally's going to need a friend."

"She won't come. Or she wouldn't. I've already pressed her."

Miss Garvice now was puffing away like a traction engine. "Why did you do that?"

"I'm afraid that's my business."

"You don't know who the father is?"

I said nothing.

"It's not as if Sally were a young girl. To be perfectly frank, there are things about her condition which I don't like."

It was my turn for a question.

"What about the accident? Hasn't that affected matters?"

"Strangely enough, no. Although it's nothing less than a miracle. Of one kind or the other," said Miss Garvice, trying to look broadminded.

I felt that we were unlikely to make further progress. Assuring Miss Garvice that in due course I should invite Sally once more, I asked again if I could see her.

"I am sorry. But it's out of the question for Sally to see anyone."

I was glad that Miss Garvice did not revert to the subject of Sally's few things, although, despite everything, I felt guilty for having forgotten them. Particularly because I had no wish to go back for them. It was out of the question even to think of explaining my real reasons to Miss Garvice, and loyalty to Sally continued to weigh heavily with me; but something must be devised. Moreover I must not take any step which might lead to someone else being sent to Sally's house. The best I could think of was to assemble some of my own "things" and say they were Sally's. It would be for Sally to accept the substitution.

But the question which struck me next morning was whether

the contamination in Sally's house could be brought to an end by steps taken in the house itself; or whether it could have influence outside. Sally's mysterious restlessness, as reported by Miss Garvice, was far from reassuring; but on the whole I inclined to see it as an aftermath or revulsion. (Sally's pregnancy I refused at this point to consider at all.) It was impossible to doubt that immediate action of some kind was vital. Exorcism? Or, conceivably, arson? I doubt whether I am one to whom the former would ever strongly appeal: certainly not as a means of routing something so apparently sensible to feeling as to sight. The latter, on the other hand, might well be defeated (apart from other difficulties) by that stone strongbox of a library. Flight? I considered it long and seriously. But still it seemed that my strongest motive in the whole affair was pity for Sally. So I stayed.

I did not visit the hospital that morning, from complete perplexity as to what there to do or say; but instead, during the afternoon, wandered back to the house. Despite my horror of the place, I thought that I might hit upon something able to suggest a course of action. I would look more closely at those grimy papers and even at the books in the library. The idea of burning the place down was still by no means out of my mind. I would further ponder the inflammability of the house and the degree of risk to the neighbors . . . All the time, of course, I was completely miscalculating my own strength and what was happening to me.

But as I hoisted the fallen gate, my nerve suddenly left me; again, something which had never happened to me before, either in the course of these events or at any previous time, I felt very sick. I was much afraid lest I faint. My body felt simultaneously tense and insubstantial.

Then I became aware that Mr. Orbit's delivery boy was staring at me from the gate of the dentist's house opposite. I must have presented a queer spectacle because the boy seemed to be standing petrified. His mouth, I saw, was wide open. I knew the boy quite well. It was essential for all kinds of reasons that I conduct myself suitably. The boy stood, in fact, for public opinion. I took a couple of deep breaths, produced the weighty bunch of keys from my handbag and ascended the steps as steadily as possible.

Inside the house, I made straight for the basement, with a view to a glass of water. With Mr. Orbit's boy no longer gaping at me, I felt worse than ever; so that, even before I could look for a tumbler or reach the tap, I had to sink upon one of the two battered kitchen chairs. All my hair was damp, and my clothes felt unbearably heavy.

Then I became aware that steps were descending the basement staircase.

I completed my sequence of new experiences by fainting indeed.

I came round to the noise of an animal; a snuffling, grunting cry, which seemed to come, with much persistence, from the floor above. I seemed to listen to it for some time, even trying, though failing, to identify what animal it was; before recovering more fully and realizing that Sally was leaning back against the dresser and staring at me.

"Sally! It was you."

"Who did you think it was? It's my house."

She no longer wore the stained gray slacks but was dressed in a very curious way about which I do not think it fair to say more. In other ways also, the change in her had become complete: her eyes had a repulsive lifelessness; the bone structure of her face, previously so fine, had altered unbelievably. There was an unpleasant croak in her voice, precisely as if her larynx had lost flexibility.

"Will you please return my keys?"

I even had difficulty in understanding what she said, although doubtless my shaky condition did not help. Very foolishly, I rose to my feet while Sally glared at me with her changed eyes. I had been lying on the stone floor. There was a bad pain in the back of my head and neck.

"Glad to see you're better, Sally. I didn't expect you'd be about for some time yet." My words were incredibly foolish.

She said nothing but only stretched out her hand. It too was changed: it had become gray and bony, with protruding knotted veins.

I handed her the big bunch of keys. I wondered how she had entered the house without them. The animal wailing above continued without intermission. To it now seemed to be added a noise which struck me as resembling that of a pig scrabbling. Involuntarily I glanced upward to the ceiling.

Sally snatched the keys, snatched them gently and softly, not violently, then cast her unblinking eyes upwards in parody of mine and emitted an almost deafening shriek of laughter.

"Do you love children, Mel? Would you like to see my baby?"

Truly it was the last straw; and I do not know quite how I behaved.

Now Sally seemed filled with terrible pride. "Let me tell you, Mel," she said, "that it's possible for a child to be born in a manner you'd never dream of."

I had begun to shudder again, but Sally clutched hold of me with her gray hand and began to drag me up the basement stairs.

"Will you be godmother? Come and see your godchild, Mel."

The noise was coming from the library. I clung to the top of the basement baluster. Distraught as I was, I now realized that the scrabbling sound was connected with the tearing to pieces of Dr. Tessler's books. But it was the wheezy, throaty cry of the creature which most turned my heart and sinews to water.

Or to steel. Because as Sally tugged at me, trying to pull me away from the baluster and into the library, I suddenly realized that she had no strength at all. Whatever else had happened to her, she was weak as a wraith.

I dragged myself free from her, let go of the baluster, and made toward the front door. Sally began to scratch my face and neck, but I made a quite capable job of defending myself. Sally then began to call out in her unnatural voice: she was trying to summon the creature into the passage. She scraped and tore at me, while panting out a stream of dreadful endearments to the thing in the library.

In the end, I found that my hands were about her throat, which was bare despite the cold weather. I could stand no more of that wrecked voice. Immediately she began to kick; and the shoes she was wearing seemed to have metal toes. I had the final awful fancy that she had acquired iron feet. Then I threw her from me on the floor of the passage and fled from the house.

It was now dark, somehow darker outside the house than inside it, and I found that I still had strength enough to run all the way home.

I went away for a fortnight, although on general grounds it was the last thing I had wanted to do. At the end of that time, and with Christmas drawing near, I returned to my parents' house; I was not going to permit Sally to upset my plan for a present way of life.

At intervals through the winter I peered at Sally's house from the corner of the cul-de-sac in which it stood, but never saw a sign of occupancy or change.

I had learned from Miss Garvice that Sally had simply "disappeared" from the Cottage Hospital.

"Disappeared?"

"Long before she was due for discharge, I need hardly say."

"How did it happen?"

"The night nurse was going her rounds and noticed that the bed was empty."

Miss Garvice was regarding me as if I were a material witness. Had we been in Miss Garvice's room at the hospital, Serena would have been asked to see that we were not disturbed.

*   *   *

Sally had not been back long enough to be much noticed in the town; and I observed that soon no one mentioned her at all.

Then, one day between Easter and Whitsun, I found she was at the front door.

"Hallo, Mel."

Again she was taking up the conversation. She was as until last autumn she had always been; with that strange, imperishable, untended prettiness of hers and her sweet absent smile. She wore a white dress.

"Sally!" What could one say?

Our eyes met. She saw that she would have to come straight to the point.

"I've sold my house."

I kept my head. "I said it was too big for you. Come in."

She entered.

"I've bought a villa. In the Cyclades."

"For your work?"

She nodded. "The house fetched a price of course. And my father left me more than I expected."

I said something banal.

Already she was lying on the big sofa and looking at me over the arm. "Mel, I should like you to come and stay with me. For a long time. As long as you can. You're a free agent, and you can't want to stay here."

Psychologists, I recollected, have ascertained that the comparative inferiority of women in contexts described as purely intellectual is attributable to the greater discouragement and repression of their curiosity when children.

"Thank you, Sally. But I'm quite happy here, you know."

"You're *not*. Are you, Mel?"

"No. I'm not."

"Well then?"

One day I shall probably go.

# Ladies in Waiting

## by Hugh B. Cave

$\mathcal{H}$alper, the village real-estate man, said with a squint, "You're the same people looked at that place back in April, aren't you? Sure you are. The ones got caught in that freak snowstorm and spent the night there. Mr. and Mrs. Wilkes, is it?"

"Wilkins," Norman corrected, frowning at a photograph on the wall of the old man's dingy office: a yellowed, fly-spotted picture of the house itself, in all its decay and drabness.

"And you want to look at it again?"

"Yes!" Linda exclaimed.

Both men looked at her sharply because of her vehemence. Norman, her husband, was alarmed anew by the eagerness that suddenly flamed in her lovely brown eyes and as suddenly was replaced by a look of guilt. Yes—unmistakably a look of guilt.

"I mean," she stammered, "we still want a big old house that we can do over, Mr. Halper. We've never stopped looking. And we keep thinking the Creighton place just might do."

*You* keep thinking it might do, Norman silently corrected. He himself had intensely disliked the place when Halper showed it to them four months ago. The sharp edge of his abhorrence was not even blunted, and time would never dull his remembrance of that shocking expression on Linda's face.

When he stepped through that hundred-seventy-year-old door-way again, he would hate and fear the house as much as before, he was certain.

Would he again see that look on his wife's face? God forbid!

"Well," Halper said, "there's no need for me to go along with you this time, I guess. I'll just ask you to return the key when you're through, same as you did before."

Norman accepted the tagged key from him and walked un-happily out to the car.

It was four miles from the village to the house. One mile of narrow blacktop, three of a dirt road that seemed forlorn and forgotten even in this neglected part of New England. At three in the afternoon of an awesomely hot August day the car made the only sound in a deep green silence. The sun's heat had robbed even birds and insects of their voices.

Norman was silent too—with apprehension. Beside him his adored wife of less than two years leaned forward to peer through the windshield for the first glimpse of their destina-tion, seeming to have forgotten he existed. Only the house now mattered.

And there it was.

Nothing had changed. It was big and ugly, with a sagging front piazza and too few windows. It was old. It was gray be-cause almost all its white paint had weathered away. According to old Halper the Creightons had lived here for generations, having come here from Salem, where one of their women in the days of witchcraft madness had been hanged for practicing demonolatry. A likely story.

As he stopped the car by the piazza steps, Norman glanced at the girl beside him. His beloved. His childhood sweetheart. Why in God's name was she eager to come here again? She had not been so in the beginning. For days after that harrowing ordeal she had been depressed, unwilling even to talk about it.

But then, weeks later, the change. Ah, yes, the change! So subtle at first, or at least as subtle as her unsophisticated nature could contrive. "Norm . . . do you remember that old house we were snowbound in? Do you suppose we might have liked it if things had been different? . . ."

Then not so subtle. "Norm, can we look at the Creighton place again? Please? Norm?"

As he fumbled the key into the lock, he reached for her hand. "Are you all right, hon?"

"Of course!" The same tone of voice she had used in Halper's shabby office. Impatient. Critical. *Don't ask silly questions!*

With a premonition of disaster he pushed the old door open.

It was the same.

Furnished, Halper had called it, trying to be facetious. There were dusty ruins of furniture and carpets and—yes—someone or something was using them; that the house had *not* been empty for eight years, as Halper claimed. Now the feeling returned as Norman trailed his wife through the downstairs rooms and up the staircase to the bed chambers above. But the feeling was strong! He wanted desperately to seize her hand again and shout, "No, no, darling! Come out of here!"

Upstairs, when she halted in the big front bedroom, turning slowly to look about her, he said helplessly, "Hon, please— what is it? What do you *want?*"

No answer. He had ceased to exist. She even bumped into him as she went past to sit on the old four-poster with its mildewed mattress. And, seated there, she stared emptily into space as she had done before.

He went to her and took her hands. "Linda, for God's sake! What *is* it with this place?"

She looked up and smiled at him. "I'm all right. Don't worry, darling."

There had been an old blanket on the bed when they entered this room before. He had thought of wrapping her in it because she was shivering, the house was frigid, and with the car trapped in deepening snow they would have to spend the night here. But the blanket reeked with age and she had cringed from the touch of it.

Then—"Wait," he had said with a flash of inspiration. "Maybe if I could jam this under a tire! . . . Come on. It's at least worth a try."

"I'm cold, Norm. Let me stay here."

"You'll be all right? Not scared?"

"Better scared than frozen."

"Well . . . I won't be long."

How long was he gone? Ten minutes? Twenty? Twice the car had seemed about to pull free from the snow's mushy grip. Twice the wheel had spun the sodden blanket out from under and sent it flying through space like a huge yellow bird, and he'd been forced to go groping after it with the frigid wind lashing his half-frozen face. Say twenty minutes; certainly no longer. Then, giving it up as a bad job, he had trudged despondently back to the house and climbed the stairs again to that front bedroom.

And there she sat on the bed, as she was sitting now. White as the snow itself. Wide-eyed. Staring at or into something that only she could see.

"Linda! What's wrong?"

"Nothing. Nothing . . ."

He grasped her shoulders. "Look at me! Stop staring like that! What's happened?"

"I thought I heard something. Saw something."

"Saw *what?*"

"I don't know. I don't . . . remember."

Lifting her from the bed, he put his arms about her and glowered defiantly at the empty doorway. Strange. A paper-thin layer of mist or smoke moved along the floor there, drifting out into the hall. And there were floating shapes of the same darkish stuff trapped in the room's corners, as though left behind when the chamber emptied itself of a larger mass. Or was he imagining these things? One moment they seemed to be there; a moment later they were gone.

And was he also imagining the odor? It had not been present in the musty air of this room before; it certainly seemed to be now, unless his senses were playing tricks on him. A peculiarly robust smell, unquestionably male. But now it was fading.

Never mind. There *was* someone in this house, by God! He had felt an alien presence when Halper was here; even more so after the agent's departure. Someone, something, following them about, watching them.

The back of Linda's dress was unzipped, he realized then. His hands, pressing her to him, suddenly found themselves inside the garment, on her body. And her body was cold. Colder than the snow he had struggled with outside. Cold and clammy.

The zipper. He fumbled for it, found it drawn all the way down. What in God's name had she tried to do? This was his wife, who loved him. This was the girl who only a few weeks ago, at the club, had savagely slapped the face of the town's richest, handsomest playboy for daring to hint at a mate-swapping arrangement. Slowly he drew the zipper up again, then held her at arm's length and looked again at her face.

She seemed unaware he had touched her. Or that he even existed. She was entirely alone, still gazing into that secret world in which he had no place.

The rest of that night had seemed endless, Linda lying on the bed, he sitting beside her waiting for daylight. She seemed to sleep some of the time; at other times, though she said nothing even when spoken to, he sensed she was as wide awake as he. About four o'clock the wind died and the snow stopped its wet slapping of the windowpanes. No dawn had ever been more welcome, even though he was still unable to free the car and they both had to walk to the village to send a tow truck for it.

And now he had let her persuade him to come back here. He must be insane.

"Norman?"

She sat there on the bed, the same bed, but at least she was looking *at* him now, not through him into that secret world of hers. "Norman, you do like this house a little, don't you?"

"If you mean could I ever seriously think of living here—" Emphatically he shook his head. "My God, no! It gives me the horrors!"

"It's really a lovely old house, Norman. We could work on it little by little. Do you think I'm crazy?"

"If you can even imagine living in this mausoleum, I *know* you're crazy. My God, woman, you were nearly frightened out of your wits here. In this very room, too."

"Was I, Norman? Really?"

"Yes, you were! If I live to be a hundred, I'll never stop seeing that look on your face."

"What kind of look was it, Norman?"

"I don't know. That's just it—I don't know! What in heaven's name *were* you seeing when I walked back in here after my session with the car? What was that mist? That smell?"

Smiling, she reached for his hands. "I don't remember any mist or smell, Norman. I was just a little frightened. I told you—I thought I heard something."

"You *saw* something too, you said."

"Did I say that? I've forgotten." Still smiling, she looked around the room—at the garden of faded roses on shreds of time-stained wallpaper; at the shabby bureau with its solitary broken cut-glass vase. "Old Mr. Halper was to blame for what happened, Norman. His talk of demons."

"Halper didn't do that much talking, Linda."

"Well, he told us about the woman who was hanged in Salem. I can see now, of course, that he threw that out as bait, because I had told him you write mystery novels. He probably pictured you sitting in some sort of Dracula cape, scratching out your books with a quill, by lamplight, and thought this would be a marvelous setting for it." Her soft laugh was a welcome sound, reminding Norman he loved this girl and she loved him—that their life together, except for her inexplicable interest in this house, was full of gentleness and caring.

But he could not let her win this debate. "Linda, listen. If this is such a fine old house, why has it been empty for eight years?"

"Well, Mr. Halper explained that, Norman."

"Did he? I don't seem to recall any explanation."

"He said that last person to live here was a woman who died eight years ago at ninety-three. Her married name was Stanhope, I think he said, but she was a Creighton—she even had the same given name, Prudence, as the woman hanged in Salem for worshipping demons. And when she passed away there was some legal question about the property because her husband had died some years before in an asylum, leaving no will."

Norman reluctantly nodded. The truth was, he hadn't paid much attention to the real-estate man's talk, but he did recall the remark that the last man of the house had been committed to an asylum for the insane. Probably from having lived in such a gloomy old house for so long, he had thought at the time.

Annoyed with himself for having lost the debate—at least, for not having won it—he turned from the bed and walked to a window, where he stood gazing down at the yard. Right down there, four months ago, was where he had struggled to free the car. Frowning at the spot now, he suddenly said aloud, "Wait. That's damn queer."

"What is, dear?" Linda said from the bed.

"I've always thought we left the car in a low spot that night. A spot where the snow must have drifted extra deep, I mean. But we didn't. We were in the highest part of the yard."

"Perhaps the ground is soft there."

"Uh-uh. It's rocky."

"Then it might have been slippery?"

"Well, I suppose—" Suddenly he pressed closer to the window glass. "Oh, damn! We've got a flat."

"What, Norman?"

"A flat! Those are new tires, too. We must have picked up a nail on our way into this stupid place." Striding back to the bed, he caught her hand. "Come on. I'm not leaving you here this time!"

She did not protest. Obediently she followed him downstairs and along the lower hall to the front door. On the piazza she hesitated briefly, glancing back in what seemed to be a moment of panic, but when he again grasped her hand, she meekly went with him down the steps and out to the car.

The left front tire was the flat one. Hunkering down beside it, he searched for the culprit nail but failed to find any. It was underneath, no doubt. Things like flat tires always annoyed him; in a properly organized world they wouldn't happen. Of course, in such a world there would not be the kind of road one had to travel to reach this place, nor would there be such an impossible house to begin with.

Muttering to himself, he opened the trunk, extracted jack, tools, and spare, and went to work.

Strange. There was no nail in the offending tire. No cut or bruise, either. The tire must have been badly made. The thought did not improve his mood as, on his knees, he wrestled the spare into place.

Then when he lowered the jack, the spare gently flattened under the car's weight and he knelt there staring at it in disbelief. "What the hell . . ." Nothing like this had *ever* happened to him before.

He jacked the car up again, took the spare off and examined it. No nail, no break, no bruise. It was a new tire, like the others. Newer, because never yet used. He had a repair kit for tubeless tires in the trunk, he recalled—bought one day on an impulse. "Repair a puncture in minutes without even taking the tire off the car." But how could you repair a puncture that wasn't there?

"Linda, this is crazy. We'll have to walk back to town as we did before." He turned his head. "Linda?"

She was not there.

He lurched to his feet. "Linda! Where are you?" How long had she been gone? He must have been working on the car for fifteen or twenty minutes. She hadn't spoken in that time, he suddenly realized. Had she slipped back into the house the moment he became absorbed in his task? She knew well enough how intensely he concentrated on such things. How when he was writing, for instance, she could walk through the room without his even knowing it.

"Linda, for God's sake—no!" Hoarsely shouting her name, he stumbled toward the house. The door clattered open when he flung himself against it, and the sound filled his ears as he staggered down the hall. But now the hall was not just an ancient, dusty corridor; it was a dim tunnel filled with premature darkness and strange whisperings.

He knew where she must be. In that cursed room at the top of the stairs where he had seen the look on her face four months ago, and where she had tried so cunningly to conceal the truth from him this time. But the room was hard to reach now. A swirling mist choked the staircase, repeatedly causing him to stumble. Things resembling hands darted out of it to clutch at him and hold him back.

He stopped in confusion, and the hands nudged him forward again. Their owner was playing a game with him, he realized, mocking his frantic efforts to reach the bedroom yet at the same time seductively urging him to try even harder. And the whisperings made words, or seemed to. "Come Norman . . . sweet Norman . . . come come come. . . ."

In the upstairs hall, too, the swirling mist challenged him, deepening into a moving mass that hid the door of the room. But he needed no compass to find that door. Gasping and cursing—"Damn you, leave me alone! Get out of my way!" He struggled to it and found it open as Linda and he had left it. Hands outthrust, he groped his way over the threshold.

The alien presence here was stronger. The sense of being confronted by some unseen creature was all but overwhelming. Yet the assault upon him was less violent now that he had reached the room. The hands groping for him in the eerie darkness were even gentle, caressing. They clung with a velvet softness that was strangely pleasurable, and there was something voluptuously female about them, even to a faint but pervasive female odor.

An *odor*, not a perfume. A body scent, druglike in its effect upon his senses. Bewildered, he ceased his struggle for a moment to see what would happen. The whispering became an invitation, a promise of incredible delights. But he allowed himself only a moment of listening and then, shouting Linda's name, hurled himself at the bed again. This time he was able to reach it.

But she was not now sitting there staring into that secret world of hers, as he had expected. The bed was empty and the seductive voice in the darkness softly laughed at his dismay. "Come Norman . . . sweet Norman . . . come come come. . . ."

He felt himself taken from behind by the shoulders, turned and ever so gently pushed. He fell floating onto the old mattress, half-heartedly thrusting up his arms to keep the advancing shadow-form from possessing him. But it flowed down over him, onto him, into him, despite his feeble resistance, and the female smell tantalized his senses again, destroying his will to resist.

As he ceased struggling he heard a sound of rusty hinges creaking in that part of the room's dimness where the door was, and then a soft thud. The door had been closed. But he did not cry out. He felt no alarm. It was good to be here on the bed, luxuriating in this sensuous, caressing softness. As he became quiescent it flowed over him with unrestrained indulgence, touching and stroking him to heights of ecstasy.

Now the unseen hands, having opened his shirt, slowly and seductively glided down his body to his belt. . . .

He heard a new sound then. For a moment it bewildered him because, though coming through the ancient wall behind him, from the adjoining bedroom, it placed him at once in his own bedroom at home. Linda and he had joked about it often, as true lovers could—the explosive little syllables to which she always gave voice when making love.

So she was content, too. Good. Everything was straightforward and aboveboard, then. After all, as that fellow at the club had suggested, mate-swapping was an in thing in this year of our Lord 1975 . . . wasn't it? All kinds of people did it.

He must buy this house, as Linda has insisted. Of course. She was absolutely right. With a sigh of happiness he closed his eyes and relaxed, no longer made reluctant by a feeling of guilt.

But—something was wrong. Distinctly, now, he felt not two hands caressing him, but more. And were they hands? They suddenly seemed cold, clammy, frighteningly eager.

Opening his eyes, he was startled to find that the misty darkness had dissolved and he could see. Perhaps the seeing came with total surrender, or with the final abandonment of his guilt feeling. He lay on his back, naked, with his nameless partner half beside him, half on him. He saw her scaly, misshapen breasts overflowing his chest and her monstrous, demonic face swaying in space above his own. And as he screamed, he saw that she did have more than two hands: she had a whole writhing mass of them at the ends of long, searching tentacles.

The last thing he saw before his scream became that of a madman was a row of three others like her squatting by the wall, their tentacles restlessly reaching toward him as they impatiently awaited their turn.

# The Haunting of Shawley Rectory

## by Ruth Rendell

I don't believe in the supernatural, but just the same I wouldn't live in Shawley Rectory.

That was what I had been thinking and what Gordon Scott said to me when we heard we were to have a new Rector at St. Mary's. Our wives gave us quizzical looks.

"Not very logical," said Eleanor, my wife.

"What I mean is," said Gordon, "that however certain you might be that ghosts don't exist, if you lived in a place that was reputedly haunted you wouldn't be able to help wondering every time you heard a stair creak. All the normal sounds of an old house would take on a different significance."

I agreed with him. It wouldn't be very pleasant feeling uneasy every time one was alone in one's own home at night.

"Personally," said Patsy Scott, "I've always believed there are no ghosts in the Rectory that a good central-heating system wouldn't get rid of."

We laughed at that, but Eleanor said, "You can't just dismiss it like that. The Cobworths heard and felt things even if they didn't actually see anything. And so did the Bucklands before them. And you won't find anyone more level-headed than Kate Cobworth."

Patsy shrugged. "The Loys didn't even hear or feel anything. They'd heard the stories, they *expected* to hear the footsteps and the carriage wheels. Diana Loy told me. And Diana was quite a nervy highly strung sort of person. But absolutely nothing happened while they were there."

"Well, maybe the Church of England or whoever's responsible will install central heating for the new parson," I said, "and we'll see if your theory's right, Patsy."

Eleanor and I went home after that. We went on foot because our house is only about a quarter of a mile up Shawley Lane. On the way we stopped in front of the Rectory which is about a hundred yards along. We stood and looked over the gate.

I may as well describe the Rectory to you before I get on with this story. The date of it is around 1760 and it's built of pale dun-colored brick with plain classical windows and a front door in the middle with a pediment over it. It's a big house with three reception rooms, six bedrooms, two kitchens, and two staircases—and one poky little bathroom made by having converted a linen closet. The house is a bit stark to look at, a bit forbidding; it seems to stare straight back at you, but the trees round it are pretty enough and so are the stables on the left-hand side with a clock in their gable and a weathervane on top. Tom Cobworth, the last Rector, kept his old Morris in there. The garden is huge, a wilderness that no one could keep tidy these days—eight acres of it including the glebe.

It was years since I had been inside the Rectory. I remember wondering if the interior was as shabby and in need of paint as the outside. The windows had that black, blank, hazy look of windows at which no curtains hang and which no one has cleaned for months or even years.

"Who exactly does it *belong* to?" said Eleanor.

"Lazarus College, Oxford," I said. "Tom was a Fellow of Lazarus."

"And what about this new man?"

"I don't know," I said. "I think all that system of livings has changed but I'm pretty vague about it."

I'm not a churchgoer, not religious at all really. Perhaps that was why I hadn't got to know the Cobworths all that well. I used to feel a bit uneasy in Tom's company, I used to have the feeling he might suddenly round on me and demand to know why he never saw me in church. Eleanor had no such inhibitions with Kate. They were friends, close friends, and Eleanor had missed her after Tom died suddenly of a heart attack and she had had to leave the Rectory. She had gone back to her people up north, taking her fifteen-year-old daughter Louise with her.

Kate is a practical down-to-earth Yorkshirewoman. She had been a nurse—a ward sister, I believe—before her marriage. When Tom got the living of Shawley she several times met Mrs. Buckland, the wife of the retiring incumbent, and from her learned to expect what Mrs. Buckland called "manifestations."

"I couldn't believe she was actually saying it," Kate had said to Eleanor. "I thought I was dreaming and then I thought she was mad. I mean really psychotic, mentally ill. Ghosts! I ask you—people believing things like that in this day and age. And then we moved in and I heard them too."

The crunch of carriage wheels on the gravel drive when there was no carriage or any kind of vehicle to be seen. Doors closing softly when no doors had been left open. Footsteps crossing the landing and going downstairs, crossing the hall, then the front door opening softly and closing softly.

"But how could you bear it?" Eleanor said. "Weren't you afraid? Weren't you terrified?"

"We got used to it. We had to, you see. It wasn't as if we could sell the house and buy another. Besides, I love Shawley—I loved it from the first moment I set foot in the village. After the harshness of the north, Dorset is so gentle and mild and pretty. The doors closing and the footsteps and the wheels on the drive—they didn't do us any harm. And we had each other, we weren't alone. You can get used to anything—to ghosts as much as to damp and woodworm and dry rot. There's all that in the Rectory too and I found it much more trying!"

The Bucklands, apparently, had got used to it too. Thirty years he had been Rector of the parish, thirty years they had lived there with the wheels and the footsteps, and had brought up their son and daughter there. No harm had come to them; they slept soundly, and their grownup children used to joke about their haunted house.

"Nobody ever seems to *see* anything," I said to Eleanor as we walked home. "And no one ever comes up with a story, a sort of background to all this walking about and banging and crunching. Is there supposed to have been a murder there or some other sort of violent death?"

She said she didn't know, Kate had never said. The sound of the wheels, the closing of the doors, always took place at about nine in the evening, followed by the footsteps and the opening and closing of the front door. After that there was silence, and it hadn't happened every evening by any means. The only other thing was that Kate had never cared to use the big drawing room in the evenings. She and Tom and Louise had always stayed in the dining room or the morning room.

They did use the drawing room in the daytime—it was just that in the evenings the room felt strange to her, chilly even in summer, and indefinably hostile. Once she had had to go in there at ten thirty. She needed her reading glasses which she had left in the drawing room during the afternoon. She ran into the room and ran out again. She hadn't looked about her, just rushed in, keeping her eyes fixed on the eyeglass case on the mantelpiece. The icy hostility in that room had really frightened her, and that had been the only time she had felt dislike and fear of Shawley Rectory.

Of course one doesn't have to find explanations for an icy

hostility. It's much more easily understood as being the prod-
uct of tension and fear than aural phenomena are. I didn't have
much faith in Kate's feelings about the drawing room. I
thought with a kind of admiration of Jack and Diana Loy, that
elderly couple who had rented the Rectory for a year after
Kate's departure, had been primed with stories of hauntings by
Kate, yet had neither heard nor felt a thing. As far as I know,
they had used that drawing room constantly. Often, when I had
passed the gate in their time, I had seen lights in the drawing-
room windows, at nine, at ten thirty, and even at midnight.

The Loys had been gone three months. When Lazarus had
first offered the Rectory for rent, the idea had been that Shawley should do without a clergyman of its own. I think this must
have been the Church economizing—nothing to do certainly
with ghosts. The services at St. Mary's were to be undertaken
by the Vicar of the next parish, Mr. Hartley—Whether he
found this too much for him in conjunction with the duties of
his own parish or whether the powers-that-be in affairs Angli-
can had second thoughts, I can't say; but on the departure of
the Loys it was decided there should be an incumbent to re-
place Tom.

The first hint of this we had from local gossip; next the facts
appeared in our monthly news sheet, the *Shawley Post*.
Couched in its customary parish magazine journalese it said:
"Shawley residents all extend a hearty welcome to their new
Rector, the Reverend Stephen Galton, whose coming to the
parish with his charming wife will fill a long-felt need."

"He's very young," said Eleanor a few days after our discussion of haunting with the Scotts. "Under thirty."

"That won't bother me," I said. "I don't intend to be
preached at by him. Anyway, why not? Out of the mouths of
babes and sucklings," I said, "hast Thou ordained strength."

"Hark at the devil quoting scripture," said Eleanor. "They
say his wife's only twenty-three."

I thought she must have met them; she knew so much. But no.

"It's just what's being said. Patsy got it from Judy Lawrence. Judy said they're moving in next month and her mother's coming with them."

"Who, Judy's?"

"Don't be silly," said my wife. "Mrs. Galton's mother, the Rector's mother-in-law. She's coming to live with them."

Move in they did. And out again two days later.

The first we knew that something had gone very wrong for the Galtons was when I was out for my usual evening walk with our Irish setter Liam. We were coming back past the cottage that belongs to Charlie Lawrence (who is by way of being Shawley's squire) and which he keeps for the occupation of his gardener when he is lucky enough to have a gardener. At that time, last June, he hadn't had a gardener for at least six months, and the cottage should have been empty. As I approached, however, I saw a woman's face, young, fair, very pretty, at one of the upstairs windows.

I rounded the hedge and Liam began an insane barking, for just inside the cottage gate, on the drive, peering in under the hood of an aged Wolseley, was a tall young man wearing a tweed sports jacket over one of those black-top things the clergy wear, and a clerical collar.

"Good evening," I said. "Shut up, Liam, will you?"

"Good evening," he said in a quiet, abstracted sort of way.

I told Eleanor. She couldn't account for the Galtons occupying Charlie Lawrence's gardener's cottage instead of Shawley Rectory, their proper abode. But Patsy Scott could. She came round on the following morning with a punnet of strawberries for us. The Scotts grow the best strawberries for miles around.

"They've been driven out by the ghosts," she said. "Can you credit it? A clergyman of the Church of England! An educated man! They were in that place not forty-eight hours before they were screaming to Charlie Lawrence to find them somewhere else to go."

I asked her if she was sure it wasn't just the damp and the dry rot.

"Look, you know me. *I* don't believe the Rectory's haunted or anywhere *can* be haunted, come to that. I'm telling you what Mrs. Galton told me. She came in to us on Thursday morning and said did I think there was anyone in Shawley had a house or a cottage to rent because they couldn't stick the Rectory another night. I asked her what was wrong. And she said she knew it sounded crazy—it did too, she was right there—she knew it sounded mad, but they'd been terrified out of their lives by what they'd heard and seen since they moved in."

"*Seen?*" I said. "She actually claims to have seen something?"

"She said her mother did. She said her mother saw something in the drawing room the first evening they were there. They'd already heard the carriage wheels and the doors closing and the footsteps and all that. The second evening no one dared go in the drawing room. They heard all the sounds again and Mrs. Grainger—that's the mother—heard voices in the drawing room, and it was then that they decided they couldn't stand it, they'd have to get out."

"I don't believe it!" I said. "I don't believe any of it. The woman's a psychopath, she's playing some sort of ghastly joke."

"Just as Kate was and the Bucklands," said Eleanor quietly.

Patsy ignored her and turned to me. "I feel just like you. It's awful, but what can you do? These stories grow and they sort of infect people and the more suggestible the people are, the worse the infection. Charlie and Judy are furious, they don't want it getting in the papers that Shawley Rectory is haunted. Think of all the people we shall get coming in cars on Sundays and gawping over the gates. But they had to let them have the cottage in common humanity. Mrs. Grainger was hysterical and poor little Mrs. Galton wasn't much better. Who told them to expect all those horrors? That's what I'd like to know."

"What does Gordon say?" I said.

"He's keeping an open mind, but he says he'd like to spend an evening there."

In spite of the Lawrences' fury, the haunting of Shawley Rectory did get quite a lot of publicity. There was a sensational story about it in one of the popular Sundays and then Stephen Galton's mother-in-law went on television. Western TV interviewed her on a local news program. I hadn't ever seen Mrs. Grainger in the flesh and her youthful appearance rather surprised me. She looked no more than 35, though she must be into her forties.

The interviewer asked her if she had ever heard any stories of ghosts at Shawley Rectory before she went there and she said she hadn't. Did she believe in ghosts? Now she did. What had happened, asked the interviewer, after they had moved in?

It had started at nine o'clock, she said, at nine on their first evening. She and her daughter were sitting in the bigger of the two kitchens, having a cup of coffee. They had been moving in all day, unpacking, putting things away. They heard two doors close upstairs, then footsteps coming down the main staircase. She had thought it was her son-in-law, except that it couldn't have been because as the footsteps died away he came in through the door from the back kitchen. They couldn't understand what it had been, but they weren't frightened. Not then.

"We were all planning on going to bed early," said Mrs. Grainger. She was very articulate, very much at her ease in front of the cameras. "Just about half-past ten I had to go into the big room they call the drawing room. The removal men had put some of our boxes in there and my radio was in one of them. I wanted to listen to my radio in bed. I opened the drawing-room door and put my hand to the light switch. I didn't put the light on. The moon was quite bright that night and it was shining into the room.

"There were two people, two figures, I don't know what to call them, between the windows. One of them, the girl, was lying huddled on the floor. The other figure, an older woman, was bending over her. She stood up when I opened the door and looked at me. I knew I wasn't seeing real people, I don't know how but I knew that. I remember I couldn't move my hand to switch the light on. I was frozen, just staring at that pale tragic face while it stared back at me. I did manage at last to back out and close the door, and I got back to my daughter and my son-in-law in the kitchen and I—well, I collapsed. It was the most terrifying experience of my life."

Yet you stayed a night and a day and another night in the Rectory? said the interviewer. Yes, well, her daughter and her son-in-law had persuaded her it had been some sort of hallucination, the consequence of being overtired. Not that she had ever really believed that. The night had been quiet and so had the next day until nine in the evening when they were all this time in the morning room and they had heard a car drive up to the front door. They had all heard it, wheels crunching on the gravel, the sound of the engine, the brakes going on. Then had followed the closing of the doors upstairs and the footsteps, the opening and closing of the front door.

Yes, they had been very frightened, or she and her daughter had. Her son-in-law had made a thorough search of the whole house but found nothing, seen or heard no one. At ten thirty they had all gone into the hall and listened outside the drawing-room door and she and her daughter had heard voices from inside the room, women's voices. Stephen had wanted to go in, but they had stopped him, they had been so frightened.

Now the interesting thing was that there had been something in the *Sunday Express* account about the Rectory being haunted by the ghosts of two women. The story quoted someone it described as a "local antiquarian," a man named Joseph Lamb, whom I had heard of but never met. Lamb had told the *Express* there was an old tradition that the ghosts were of a mother and her daughter and that the mother had killed the daughter in the drawing room.

"I never heard any of that before," I said to Gordon Scott, "and I'm sure Kate Cobworth hadn't. Who is this Joseph Lamb?"

"He's a nice chap," said Gordon. "And he's supposed to know more of local history than anyone else around. I'll ask him over and you can come and meet him if you like."

Joseph Lamb lives in a rather fine Jacobean house in a hamlet—you could hardly call it a village—about a mile to the north of Shawley. I had often admired it without knowing who lived there. The Scotts asked him and his wife to dinner shortly after Mrs. Grainger's appearance on television, and after dinner we got him onto the subject of the hauntings. Lamb wasn't at all unwilling to enlighten us. He's a man of about 60 and he said he first heard the story of the two women from his nurse when he was a little boy. Not a very suitable subject with which to regale a seven-year-old, he said.

"These two are supposed to have lived in the Rectory at one time," he said. "The story is that the mother had a lover or a man friend or whatever, and the daughter took him away from her. When the daughter confessed it, the mother killed her in a jealous rage."

It was Eleanor who objected to this. "But surely if they lived in the Rectory they must have been the wife and daughter of a Rector. I don't really see how in those circumstances the mother could have had a lover or the daughter could steal him away."

"No, it doesn't sound much like what we've come to think of as the domestic life of the English country parson, does it?" said Lamb. "And the strange thing is, although my nanny used to swear by the story and I heard it later from someone who worked at the Rectory, I haven't been able to find any trace of these women in the Rectory's history. It's not hard to research, you see, because only the Rectors of Shawley had ever lived there until the Loys rented it, and the Rectors' names are all up on that plaque in the church from 1380 onwards. There was another house on the site before this present one, of course, and parts of the older building are incorporated in the newer.

"My nanny used to say that the elder lady hadn't got a husband, he had presumably died. She was supposed to be forty years old and the girl nineteen. Well, I tracked back through the families of the various Rectors and I found a good many cases where the Rectors had predeceased their wives. But none of them fitted my nanny's story. They were either too old—one was much too young—or their daughters were too old or they had no daughters."

"It's a pity Mrs. Grainger didn't tell us what kind of clothes her ghosts were wearing," said Patsy with sarcasm. "You could have pinpointed the date then, couldn't you?"

"You mean that if the lady had had a steeple hat on she'd be medieval or around 1850 if she was wearing a crinoline?"

"Something like that," said Patsy.

At this point Gordon repeated his wish to spend an evening in the Rectory. "I think I'll write to the Master of Lazarus and ask permission," he said.

Very soon after we heard that the Rectory was to be sold. Notice boards appeared by the front gate and at the corner where the glebe abutted Shawley Lane, announcing that the house would go up for auction on October 30th. Patsy, who always seems to know everything, told us that a reserve price of £60,000 had been put on it.

"Not as much as I'd have expected," she said. "It must be the ghosts keeping the price down."

"Whoever buys it will have to spend another ten thousand on it," said Eleanor.

"And central heating will be a priority."

Whatever was keeping the price down—ghosts, cold, or dry rot—there were plenty of people anxious to view the house and land with, I supposed, an idea of buying it. I could hardly be at work in my garden or out with Liam without a car stopping and the driver asking me the way to the Rectory. Gordon and Patsy got quite irritable about what they described as "crowds milling about" in the lane and trippers everywhere, waving orders to view.

The estate agents handling the sale were a firm called Curlew, Pond and Co. Gordon didn't bother with the Master of Lazarus but managed to get the key from Graham Curlew, whom he knew quite well, and permission to spend an evening in the Rectory. Curlew didn't like the idea of anyone staying the night, but Gordon didn't want to do that anyway; no one had ever heard or seen anything after ten thirty. He asked me if I'd go with him. Patsy wouldn't—she thought it was all too adolescent and stupid.

"Of course I will," I said. "As long as you'll agree to our taking some sort of heating arrangement with us and brandy in case of need."

By then it was the beginning of October and the evenings were turning cool. The day on which we decided to have our vigil happened also to be the one on which Stephen Galton and his wife moved out of Charlie Lawrence's cottage and left Shawley for good. According to the *Shawley Post*, he had got a living in Manchester. Mrs. Grainger had gone back to her own home in London from where she had written an article about the Rectory for *Psychic News*.

Patsy shrieked with laughter to see the two of us setting forth with our oil stove, a dozen candles, two torches, and half a bottle of Courvoisier. She did well to laugh, her amusement wasn't misplaced. We crossed the lane and opened the Rectory gate and went up the gravel drive on which those spirit wheels had so often been heard to crunch. It was seven o'clock in the evening and still light. The day had been fine and the sky was red with the aftermath of a spectacular sunset.

I unlocked the front door and in we went.

The first thing I did was put a match to one of the candles

because it wasn't at all light inside. We walked down the passage to the kitchens, I carrying the candle and Gordon shining one of the torches across the walls. The place was a mess. I suppose it hadn't had anything done to it, not even a cleaning, since the Loys moved out. It smelled damp and there was even fungus growing in patches on the kitchen walls. And it was extremely cold. There was a kind of deathly chill in the air, far more of a chill than one would have expected on a warm day in October. That kitchen had the feel you get when you open the door of a refrigerator that hasn't been kept too clean and is in need of defrosting.

We put our stuff down on a kitchen table someone had left behind and made our way up the back stairs. All the bedroom doors were open and we closed them. The upstairs had a neglected, dreary feel but it was less cold. We went down the main staircase, a rather fine curving affair with elegant banisters and carved newel posts, and entered the drawing room. It was empty, palely lit by the evening light from two windows. On the mantelpiece was a glass jar with greenish water in it, a half-burnt candle in a saucer, and a screwed-up paper table napkin. We had decided not to remain in this room but to open the door and look in at ten thirty; so accordingly we returned to the kitchen, fetched out candles and torches and brandy, and settled down in the morning room, which was at the front of the house, on the other side of the front door.

Curlew had told Gordon there were a couple of deckchairs in this room. We found them resting against the wall and we put them up. We lit our oil stove and a second candle, and we set one candle on the window sill and one on the floor between us. It was still and silent and cold. The dark closed in fairly rapidly, the red fading from the sky which became a deep hard blue, then indigo.

We sat and talked. It was about the haunting that we talked, collating the various pieces of evidence, assessing the times this or that was supposed to happen and making sure we both knew the sequence in which things happened. We were both wearing watches and I remember that we constantly checked the time. At half-past eight we again opened the drawing-room door and looked inside. The moon had come up and was shining through the windows as it had shone for Mrs. Grainger.

Gordon went upstairs with a torch and checked that all the doors remained closed and then we both looked into the other large downstairs room, the dining room, I suppose. Here a fanlight in one of the windows was open. That accounted for some of the feeling of cold and damp, Gordon said. The window must have been opened by some prospective buyer, viewing the place. We closed it and went back into the morning room to wait.

The silence was absolute. We didn't talk any more. We waited, watching the candles and the glow of the stove which had taken some of the chill from the air. Outside it was pitch-dark. The hands of our watches slowly approached nine.

At three minutes to nine we heard the noise.

Not wheels or doors closing or a tread on the stairs but a faint, dainty, pattering sound. It was very faint, it was distant, it was on the ground floor. It was as if made by something less than human, lighter than that, tiptoeing. I had never thought about this moment beyond telling myself that if anything did happen, if there was a manifestation, it would be enormously interesting. It had never occurred to me even once that I should be so dreadfully, so hideously, afraid.

I didn't look at Gordon, I couldn't. I couldn't move either. The pattering feet were less faint now, were coming closer. I felt myself go white, the blood all drawn in from the surface of my skin, as I was gripped by that awful primitive terror that has nothing to do with reason or with knowing what you believe in and what you don't.

Gordon got to his feet and stood there looking at the door. And then I couldn't stand it any more. I jumped up and threw open the door, holding the candle aloft—and looked into a pair of brilliant, golden-green eyes, staring steadily back at me about a foot from the ground.

"My God," said Gordon. "My God, it's Lawrences' cat. It must have got in through the window."

He bent down and picked up the cat, a soft, stout, marmalade-colored creature. I felt sick at the anticlimax. The time was exactly nine o'clock. With the cat draped over his arm, Gordon went back into the morning room and I followed him. We didn't sit down. We stood waiting for the wheels and the closing of the doors.

Nothing happened.

I have no business to keep you in suspense any longer, for the fact is that after that business with the cat nothing happened at all. At nine fifteen we sat down in our deckchairs. The cat lay on the floor beside the oil stove and went to sleep. Twice we heard a car pass along Shawley Lane, a remotely distant sound, but we heard nothing else.

"Feel like a spot of brandy?" said Gordon.

"Why not?" I said.

So we each had a nip of brandy and at ten we had another look in the drawing room. By then we were both feeling bored and quite sure that since nothing had happened at nine nothing would happen at ten thirty either. Of course we stayed till ten thirty and for half an hour after that, and then we decamped. We put the cat over the wall into Lawrences' ground and went back to Gordon's house where Patsy awaited us, smiling cynically.

I had had quite enough of the Rectory but that wasn't true of Gorton. He said it was well-known that the phenomena didn't take place every night; we had simply struck an off-night, and he was going back on his own. He did too, half a dozen times between then and the 30th, even going so far as to have (rather unethically) a key cut from the one Curlew had lent him. Patsy would never go with him, though he tried hard to persuade her.

But in all those visits he never saw or heard anything. And the effect on him was to make him as great a skeptic as Patsy.

"I've a good mind to make an offer for the Rectory myself," he said. "It's a fine house and I've got quite attached to it."

"You're not serious," I said.

"I'm perfectly serious. I'll go to the auction with a view to buying it if I can get Patsy to agree."

But Patsy preferred her own house and, very reluctantly, Gordon had to give up the idea. The Rectory was sold for £62,000 to an American woman, a friend of Judy Lawrence. About a month after the sale the builders moved in. Eleanor used to get progress reports from Patsy, how they had re-wired and treated the whole place for woodworm and painted and re-laid floors. The central-heating engineers came too, much to Patsy's satisfaction.

We met Carol Marcus, the Rectory's new owner, when we were asked round to the Hall for drinks one Sunday morning. She was staying there with the Lawrences until such time as the improvements and decorations to the Rectory were complete. We were introduced by Judy to a very pretty, well-dressed woman in young middle age. I asked her when she expected to move in. April, she hoped, as soon as the builders had finished the two extra bathrooms. She had heard rumors that the Rectory was supposed to be haunted and these had amused her very much. A haunted house in the English countryside! It was too good to be true.

"It's all nonsense, you know," said Gordon, who had joined us. "It's all purely imaginary." And he went on to tell her of his own experiences in the house during October—or his non-experiences, I should say.

"Well, for goodness' sake, I didn't *believe* it!" she said, and she laughed and went on to say how much she loved the house and wanted to make it a real home for her children to come to. She had three, she said, all in their teens, two boys away at school and a girl a bit older.

That was the only time I ever talked to her and I remember thinking she would be a welcome addition to the neighborhood. A nice woman. Serene is the word that best described her. There was a man friend of hers there too. I didn't catch his surname but she called him Guy. He was staying at one of the local hotels, to be near her presumably.

"I should think those two would get married, wouldn't you?" said Eleanor on the way home. "Judy told me she's waiting to get her divorce."

Later that day I took Liam for a walk along Shawley Lane and when I came to the Rectory I found the gate open. So I walked up the gravel drive and looked through the drawing-room window at the new woodblock floor and ivory-painted walls and radiators. The place was swiftly being transformed. It was no longer sinister or grim. I walked round the back and peered in at the splendidly fitted kitchens, one a laundry now, and wondered what on earth had made sensible women like Mrs. Buckland and Kate spread such vulgar tales and the Galtons panic. What had come over them? I could only imagine that they felt a need to attract attention to themselves which they perhaps could do in no other way.

I whistled for Liam and strolled down to the gate and looked back at the Rectory. It stared back at me. Is it hindsight that makes me say this or did I really feel it then? I think I did feel it, that the house stared at me with a kind of steady insolence.

Carol Marcus moved in three weeks ago, on a sunny day in the middle of April. Two nights later, just before eleven, there came a sustained ringing at Gordon's front door as if someone were leaning on the bell. Gordon went to the door. Carol Marcus stood outside, absolutely calm but deathly white.

She said to him, "May I use your phone, please? Mine isn't in yet and I have to call the police. I just shot my daughter."

She took a step forward and crumpled in a heap on the threshold.

Gordon picked her up and carried her into the house and

Patsy gave her brandy, and then he went across the road to the Rectory. There were lights on all over the house; the front door was open and light was streaming out onto the drive and the little Citroen Diane that was parked there.

He went into the house. The drawing-room door was open and he walked in there and saw a young girl lying on the carpet between the windows. She was dead. There was blood from a bullet wound on the front of her dress, and on a low round table lay the small automatic that Carol Marcus had used.

In the meantime Patsy had been the unwilling listener to a confession. Carol Marcus told her that the girl, who was 19, had unexpectedly driven down from London, arriving at the Rectory at nine o'clock. She had had a drink and something to eat and then said she had something to tell her mother, that was why she had come down. While in London she had been seeing a lot of the man called Guy and now they found that they were in love with each other. She knew it would hurt her mother, but she wanted to tell her at once, she wanted to be honest about it.

Carol Marcus told Patsy she felt nothing, no shock, no hatred or resentment, no jealousy. It was as if she were impelled by some external force to do what she did—take the gun she always kept with her from a drawer in the writing desk and kill her daughter.

At this point Gordon came back and they phoned the police. Within a quarter of an hour the police were at the house. They arrested Carol Marcus and took her away and now she is on remand, awaiting trial on a charge of murder.

So what is the explanation of all this? Or does there, in fact, have to be an explanation? Eleanor and I were so shocked by what had happened, and awed too, that for a while we were somehow wary of talking about it even to each other. Then Eleanor said, "It's as if all this time the coming event cast its shadow before it."

I nodded, yet it didn't seem quite that to me. It was more that the Rectory was waiting for the right people to come along, the people who would *fit* its still un-played scenario, the woman of 40, the daughter of 19, the lover. And only to those who approximated these characters could it show shadows and whispers of the drama; the closer the approximation, the clearer the sounds and signs.

The Loys were old and childless, so they saw nothing. Nor did Gordon and I—we were of the wrong sex. But the Bucklands who had a daughter heard and felt things, and so did Kate, though she was too old for the tragic leading role and her adolescent girl too young for victim. The Galtons had been nearly right—had Mrs. Grainger once hoped the young Rector would marry her before he showed his preference for her daughter? —but the women had been a few years too senior for the parts. Even so, they had come closer to participation than those before them.

All this is very fanciful and I haven't mentioned a word of it to Gordon and Patsy. They wouldn't listen if I did. They persist in seeing the events of three weeks ago as no more than a sordid murder, a crime of jealousy committed by someone whose mind was disturbed.

But I haven't been able to keep from asking myself what would have happened if Gordon had bought the Rectory when he talked of doing so. Patsy will be 40 this year. I don't think I've mentioned that she has a daughter by her first marriage who is away at the university and going on 19 now, a girl that they say is extravagantly fond of Gordon.

He is talking once more of buying, since Carol Marcus, whatever may become of her, will hardly keep the place now. The play is played out, but need that mean there will never be a repeat performance . . . ?

# Teeth Marks

## by Edward Bryant

M y favorite vantage has always been the circular window at the end of the playroom. It is cut from the old-fashioned glass installed by Frank Alessi's father. As a young man, he built this house with his own hands. The slight distortions in the pane create a rainbow sheen when the light is proper. I enjoy the view so much more than those seen through the standard rectangular windows on the other floors, the panes regularly smashed by the enthusiasms of the younger Alessis through the years and duly replaced. The circular window is set halfway between the hardwood floor and the peak of the gabled ceiling, low enough that I can watch the outside world from a chair.

Watching window scenes with slight distortions and enhanced colors satisfies my need for stimulation, since I don't read, nor go out to films, nor do I ever turn on the cold television console in the study. Sometimes I see jays quarreling with magpies, robins descending for meals on the unkempt lawn, ducks in the autumn and spring. I see the clouds form and roil through a series of shapes. The scene is hardly static, though it might seem such to a less patient observer. Patience must be my most obvious virtue, fixed here as I am on this eternal cutting edge of the present.

I possess my minor powers, but complete foreknowledge is

not numbered among them. Long since taking up residence here, I've explored the dimensions of the house. Now I spend the bulk of my time in what I consider the most comfortable room in the house. I haunt the old-fashioned circular window, and I wait.

Frank Alessi took a certain bitter pleasure in driving his own car. All the years he'd had a staff and driver, he had forgotten the autonomous freedoms of the road. The feel of the wheel in his hands was a little heady. Any time he wanted, any time at all, he could twist the steering wheel a few degrees and direct the Ford into the path of a Trailways bus or a logging truck. It was his decision, reaffirmed from minute to minute on the winding mountain highway, his alone. He glanced at the girl beside him, not hearing what she was saying. She wouldn't be smiling so animatedly if she knew he was chilling his mind with an image of impalement on a bridge railing.

Her name was Sally Lakey, and he couldn't help thinking of her as a girl even though she'd told him at least three times that she had celebrated her twentieth birthday the week before.

" . . . *that* Alessi?" she said.

He nodded and half smiled.

"Yeah, really?" She cocked her head like some tropical bird and stared from large dark eyes.

Alessi nodded again and didn't smile.

"That's really something. Yeah, I recognize you from the papers now. You're you." She giggled. "I even saw you last spring. In the campaign."

"The campaign," he repeated.

Lakey said apologetically, "Well, actually I didn't watch you much. What it comes down to is that I'm pretty apolitical, you know?"

Alessi forced another half-smile. "I could have used your vote."

"I wasn't registered."

Alessi shrugged mentally and returned his attention to the awesome drop-offs that tugged at the car on Lakey's side. Gravel and raw rock gave way to forest and then to valley floor. Much of the valley was cleared and quilted with irrigated squares. It's a much tamer country than when I left, Alessi thought.

"I'm really sorry I didn't vote."

"What?" Distracted, Alessi swerved slightly to avoid two fist-sized rocks that had rolled onto the right-hand lane probably during the night.

"I think you're a nice man. I said I'm sorry I didn't vote."

"It's a little late for that." Alessi envenomed the words. He heard the tone of pettiness, recognized it, said the words anyway.

"Don't blame me, Mr. Alessi," she said. "Really, I'm not stupid. You can't blame me for losing . . . Senator."

I'm being reproached, he thought, by a drop-out, wet-behind-the-ears girl. Me, a fifty-seven-year-old man. A fifty-seven-year-old unemployable. God damn it! The rage he thought he'd exorcised in San Francisco rose up again. He thought the rim of the steering wheel would shatter under his fingers into jagged, slashing shards.

Lakey must have seen something in his eyes. She moved back across the front seat and wedged herself uneasily into the juncture of bench seat and door. "You, uh, all right?"

"Yes," said Alessi. He willed the muscles cording his neck to relax, with little effect. "I am very sorry I snapped at you, Sally."

"It's okay." But she looked dubious of the sincerity of his apology.

They rode in silence for another few miles. She'll talk, thought Alessi. Sooner or later.

Sooner. "How soon?"

"Before we get to the house? Not long. The turn-off's another few miles." And what the hell, he asked himself, are you doing taking a kid little better than a third your age to the half-remembered refuge where you're going to whimper, crawl in and pull the hole in after you? It's perhaps the worst time in your life and you're acting the part of a horny old man. You've known her a grand total of eight hours. No, he answered himself. More than that. She reminds me—He tensed. She asked me if she could come along. Remember? She asked me.

I see the dark-blue sedan turn into the semicircular driveway and slide between the pines toward the house. Tires crunch on drifted cones and dead leaves; the crisp sound rises toward me. I stretch to watch as the auto nears the porch and passes below the angle of my sight. The engine dies. I hear a car door slam. Another one. For some reason it had not occurred to me that Frank might bring another person.

The equations of the house must be altered.

They stood silently for a while, looking up at the house. It was a large house, set in scale by the towering mountains beyond. Wind hissed in the pine needles; otherwise the only sound was the broken buzz of a logging truck down-shifting far below on the highway.

"It's lovely," Lakey said.

"That's the original building." Alessi pointed. "My father put it together in the years before the First World War. The additions were constructed over a period of decades."

"It must have twenty rooms."

"Ought to have been a hotel," said Alessi. "Never was. Dad liked baronial space. Some of the rooms are sealed off, never used."

"What's that?" Lakey stabbed a finger at the third floor. "The thing that looks like a porthole."

"Old glass, my favorite window when I was a kid. Behind it is a room that's been used variously as a nursery, playroom and guest room."

Lakey stared at the glass. "I thought I saw something move."

"Probably a tree shadow, or maybe a squirrel's gotten in. It wasn't the caretaker—I phoned ahead last night; he's in bed with his arthritis. Nobody else has been in the house in close to twenty years."

"I did see something," she said stubbornly.

"It isn't haunted."

She looked at him with a serious face. "How do you know?"

"No one ever died in there."

Lakey shivered. "I'm cold."

"We're at seven thousand feet." He took a key from an inside pocket of his coat. "Come in and I'll make a fire."

"Will you check the house first?"

"Better than that," he said, "*we* will check the house."

The buzz of voices drifts to the window. I am loath to leave my position behind the glass. Steps, one set heavier, one lighter, sound on the front walk. Time seems suspended as I wait for the sound of a key inserted into the latch. I anticipate the door opening. Not wanting to surprise the pair, I settle back.

Though they explored the old house together, Lakey kept forging ahead as though to assert her courage. Fine, thought Alessi. If there is something lurking in a closet, let it jump out and get *her.* The thought was only whimsical; he was a rational man.

Something did jump out of a closet at her—or at least it seemed to. Lakey opened the door at the far end of a second-floor bedroom and recoiled. A stack of photographs, loose and in albums displaced from precarious balance on the top shelf, cascaded to her feet. A plume of fine dust rose.

"There's always avalanche danger in the mountains," said Alessi.

She stopped coughing. "Very funny." Lakey knelt and picked up a sheaf of pictures. "Your family?"

Alessi studied the photographs over her shoulder. "Family, friends, holidays, vacation shots. Everyone in the family had a camera.""

"You too?"

He took the corner of a glossy landscape between thumb and forefinger. "At one time I wanted to be a Stieglitz or a Cartier-Bresson, or even a Mathew Brady. Do you see the fuzz of smoke?"

She examined the photograph closely. "No."

"That's supposed to be a forest fire. I was not a good photographer. Photographs capture the present, and that in turn immediately becomes the past. My father insistently directed me to the future."

Lakey riffled through the pictures and stopped at one portrait. Except for his dress, the man might have doubled for Alessi. His gray hair was cut somewhat more severely than the Senator's. He sat stiffly upright behind a wooden desk, staring directly at the camera.

Alessi answered the unspoken question. "My father."

"He looks very distinguished," said Lakey. Her gaze flickered up to meet his. "So do you."

"He wanted something more of a dynasty than what he got. But he tried to mold one; he really did. Every inch a mover and shaker," Alessi said sardonically. "He stayed here in the mountains and raped a fortune."

"Raped?" she said.

"Reaped. Raped. No difference. The timber went for progress and, at the time, nobody objected. My father taught me about power and I learned the lessons well. When he deemed me prepared, he sent me out to amass my own fortune in power—political, not oil or uranium. I went to the legislature and then to Washington. Now I'm home again."

"Home," she said, softening his word. "I think maybe you're

leaving out some things." He didn't answer. She stopped at another picture. "Is this your mother?"

"No." He stared at the sharp features for several seconds. "That is Mrs. Norrinssen, an ironbound, more-Swedish-than-thou, pagan lady who came out here from someplace in the Dakotas. My father hired her to—take care of me in lieu of my mother."

Lakey registered his hesitation, then said uncertainly, "What happened to your mother?"

Alessi silently sorted through the remainder of the photographs. Toward the bottom of the stack, he found what he was looking for and extracted it. A slender woman, short-haired and of extraordinary beauty, stared past the camera; or perhaps *through* the camera. Her eyes had a distant, unfocused quality. She stood in a stand of dark spruce, her hands folded.

"It's such a moody picture," said Lakey.

The pines loomed above Alessi's mother, conical bodies appearing to converge in the upper portion of the grainy print. "I took that," said Alessi. "She didn't know. It was the last picture anyone took of her."

"She . . . died?"

"Not exactly. I suppose so. No one knows."

"I don't understand," said Lakey.

"She was a brilliant, lonely, unhappy lady," said Alessi. "My father brought her out here from Florida. She hated it. The mountains oppressed her; the winters depressed her. Every year she retreated further into herself. My father tried to bring her out of it, but he treated her like a child. She resisted his pressures. Nothing seemed to work." He lapsed again into silence.

Finally Lakey said, "What happened to her?"

"It was after Mrs. Norrinssen had been here for two years. My mother's emotional state had been steadily deteriorating. Mrs. Norrinssen was the only one who could talk with her, or perhaps the only one with whom my mother would talk. One autumn day—it was in October. My mother got up before everyone else and walked out into the woods. That was that."

"That can't be all," said Lakey. "Didn't anyone look?"

"Of course we looked. My father hired trackers and dogs and the sheriff brought in his searchers. They trailed her deep into the pine forest and then lost her. They spent weeks. Then the snows increased and they gave up. There's a stone out behind the house in a grove, but no one's buried under it."

"Jesus," Lakey said softly. She put her arms around Alessi and gave him a slow, warm hug. The rest of the photographs fluttered to the hardwood floor.

I wait, I wait. I see no necessity of movement, not for now. I am patient. No longer do I go to the round window. My vigil is being rewarded. There is no reason to watch the unknowing birds, the forest, the road. The clouds have no message for me today.

I hear footsteps on the stair, and that is message enough.

"Most of the attic," said Alessi, "was converted into a nursery for me. My father always looked forward. He believed in constant renovation. As I became older, the nursery evolved to a playroom, though it was still the room where I slept. After my father died, I moved back here with my family for a few years. This was Connie's room."

"Your wife or your—"

"Daughter. For whatever reason, she preferred this to all the other rooms."

They stood just inside the doorway. The playroom extended most of the length of the house. Alessi imagined he could see the straight, carefully crafted lines of construction curving toward one another in perspective. Three dormer windows were spaced evenly along the eastern pitch of the ceiling. The round window allowed light to enter at the far end.

"It's huge," said Lakey.

"It outscales children. It was an adventure to live here. Sometimes it was very easy for me to imagine I was playing in a jungle or on a sea, or across a trackless Arctic waste."

"Wasn't it scary?"

"My father didn't allow that," said Alessi. Nor did I later on, he thought.

Lakey marveled. "The furnishings are incredible." The canopied bed, the dressers and vanity, the shelves and chairs, all were obviously products of the finest woodcraft. "Not a piece of plastic in all this." She laughed. "I love it." In her denim jeans and Pendleton shirt, she pirouetted. She stopped in front of a set of walnut shelves. "Are the dolls your daughter's?"

Alessi nodded. "My father was not what you would call a liberated man. Connie collected them all during her childhood." He carefully picked up a figure with a silk nineteenth-century dress and china head.

Lakey eagerly moved from object to object like a butterfly sampling flowers. "That horse! I always wanted one."

"My father made it for me. It's probably the most exactingly carpentered hobbyhorse made."

Lakey gingerly seated herself on the horse. Her feet barely touched the floor. "It's so big." She rocked back and forth, leaning against the leather reins. Not a joint squeaked.

Alessi said, "He scaled it so it would be a child's horse, not a pony. You might call these training toys for small adults."

The woman let the horse rock to a stop. She dismounted and slowly approached a tubular steel construction. A six-foot horizontal ladder connected the top rungs of two vertical four-foot ladders. "What on earth is this?"

Alessi was silent for a few seconds. "That is a climbing toy for three- and four-year-olds."

"But it's too big," said Lakey. "Too high."

"Not," said Alessi, "with your toes on one rung and your fingers on the next—just barely."

"It's impossible."

Alessi shook his head. "Not quite; just terrifying."

"But why?" she said. "Did you do this for fun?"

"Dad told me to. When I balked, he struck me. When he had to, my father never discounted the effect of force."

Lakey looked disconcerted. She turned away from the skeletal bridge toward a low table shoved back against the wall.

"Once there was a huge map of fairyland on the wall above the table," said Alessi. "Mrs. Norrinssen gave it to me. I can remember the illustrations, the ogres and frost giants and fairy castles. In a rage one night, my father ripped it to pieces."

Lakey knelt before the table so she could look on a level with the stuffed animals. "It's a whole zoo!" She reached out to touch the plush hides.

"More than a zoo," said Alessi. "A complete bestiary. Some of those critters don't exist. See the unicorn on the end?"

Lakey's attention was elsewhere. "The bear," she said, greedily reaching like a small child. "He's beautiful. I had one like him when I was little." She gathered the stuffed bear into her arms and hugged it. The creature was almost half her size. "What's his name? I called mine Bear. Is he yours?"

Alessi nodded. "And my daughter's. His name is Bear too. Mrs. Norrinssen made him."

She traced her finger along the bear's head, over his ears, down across the snout. Bear's hide was virtually seamless, sewn out of some rich pile fabric. After all the years, Bear's eyes were still black and shiny.

"The eyes came from the same glazier who cut the round window. Good nineteenth-century glass."

"This is wild," said Lakey. She touched the teeth.

"I don't really know whether it was Mrs. Norrinssen's idea or my father's," said Alessi. "A hunter supplied them. They're real. Mrs. Norrinssen drilled small holes toward the back of each tooth; they're secured inside the lining." Bear's mouth was lined with black leather, pliable to Lakey's questing finger. "Don't let him bite you."

"Most bears' mouths are closed," said Lakey.

"Yes."

"It didn't stop my Bear from talking to me."

"Mine didn't have to overcome that barrier." Alessi suddenly listened to what he was saying. Fifty-seven years old. He smiled self-consciously.

They stood silently for a few seconds; Lakey continued to hug the bear. "It's getting dark," she said. The sun had set while they explored the house. The outlines of solid shapes in the playroom had begun to blur with twilight. Doll faces shone almost luminously in the dusk.

"We'll get the luggage out of the car," said Alessi.

"Could I stay up here?"

"You mean tonight?" She nodded. "I see no reason why not," he said. He thought, did I really plan this?

Lakey stepped closer. "What about you?"

I watch them both. Frank Alessi very much resembles his father: distinguished. He looks harried, worn, but that is understandable. Some information I comprehend without knowing why. Some perceptions I don't have to puzzle over. I know that I see.

The woman is in her early twenties. She has mobile features, a smiling, open face. She is quick to react. Her eyes are as dark as her black hair. They dart back and forth in their sockets, her gaze lighting upon nearly everything in the room but rarely dwelling. Her speech is rapid with a hint of eastern nasality. Except for her manner of speaking, she reminds me of a dear memory.

For a moment I see four people standing in the playroom. Two are reflections in the broad, hand-silvered mirror above the vanity across the room. Two people are real. They hesitantly approach each other, a step at a time. Their arms extend, hands touch, fingers plait. Certainly at this time, in this place, they have found each other. The mirror images are inexact, but I think only I see that. The couple in the mirror seem to belong to another time. And, of course, I am there in the mirror too—though no one notices me.

"That's, uh, very gratifying to my ego," said Alessi. "But do you know how old I am?"

Lakey nodded. The semi darkness deepened. "I have some idea."

"I'm old enough to—"

"—be my father. I know." She said lightly, "So?"

"So. . . ." He took his hands away from hers. In the early night the dolls seemed to watch them. The shiny button eyes of Bear and the other animals appeared turned toward the human pair.

"Yes," she said. "I think it's a good idea." She took his hand again. "Come on, we'll get the stuff out of the car. It's been a long day."

Day, Alessi thought. Long week, long month, longer campaign. A lifetime. The headlines flashed in his mind, television commentaries replayed. It all stung like acid corroding what had been cold, shining and clean. Old, old, old, like soldiers and gunfighters. How had he missed being cleanly shot? Enough had seemed to want that. To fade . . . "I *am* a little bushed," he said. He followed Lakey out toward the stairs.

Frank Alessi's father was forceful in his ideal. That lent the foundation to that time and this place. Strength was virtue. "Fair is fair," he would say, but the fairness was all his. Such power takes time to dissipate. Mrs. Norrinssen stood up to that force; everyone else eventually fled.

"Witchy bitch!" he would storm. She only stared back at him from calm, glacial eyes until he sputtered and snorted and came to rest like a great, sulky, but now gentled beast. Mrs. Norrinssen was a woman of extraordinary powers and she tapped ancient reserves.

Structure persists. I am part of it. That is my purpose and I cannot turn aside. Now I wait in the newly inhabited house. Again I hear the positive, metallic sounds of automobile doors and a trunk lid opening and closing. I hear the voices and the footsteps and appreciate the human touch they lend.

She stretched slowly. "What time is it?"

"Almost ten," said Alessi.

"I saw you check your watch. I thought you'd be asleep. Not enough exercise?"

She giggled and Alessi was surprised to find the sound did not offend him as it had earlier in the day. He rolled back toward her and lightly kissed her lips. "Plenty of exercise."

"You were really nice."

Fingertips touched his face, exploring cheekbones, mouth corners, the stubble on the jowl line. That made him slightly nervous; his body was still tight. Tennis, handball, swimming, it all helped. Reasonably tight. Only slight concessions to slackness. But after all, he *was*—Shut up, he told himself.

"I feel very comfortable with you," she said.

Don't talk, he thought. Don't spoil it.

Lakey pressed close. "Say something."

No.

"Are you nervous?"

"No," Alessi said. "Of course not."

"I guess I did read about the divorce," said Lakey. "It was in a picture magazine in my gynecologist's office."

"There isn't much to say. Marge couldn't take the heat. She got out. I can't blame her." But silently he denied that. The Watergate people—*their* wives stood by. All the accumulated years. . . . Betrayal is so goddamned nasty. Wish her well in Santa Fe?

"Tell me about your daughter," said Lakey.

"Connie—why her?"

"You've talked about everyone else. You haven't said a thing about Connie except to say she slept in this room." She paused. "In this bed?"

"We both did," said Alessi, "at different times."

"The stuff about the divorce didn't really mention her, at least not that I remember. Where is she?"

"I truly don't know."

Lakey's voice sounded peculiar. "She disappeared, uh, just like—"

"No. She left." Silently: she left me. Just like—

"You haven't heard from her? Nothing?"

"Not in several years. It was her choice; we didn't set detectives on her. The last we heard, she was living in the street in some backwater college town in Colorado."

"I mean, you didn't try—"

"It was her choice." She always said I didn't *allow* her any choice, he thought. Maybe. But I tried to handle her as my father handled me. And *I* turned out—

"What was she like?"

Alessi caressed her long smooth hair; static electricity snapped and flashed. "Independent, intelligent, lovely. I supposed fathers tend to be biased."

"How old is she?"

"Connie was about your age when she left." He realized he had answered the question in the past tense.

"You're not so old yourself," said Lakey, touching him strategically. "Not old at all."


Moonlight floods through the dormer panes; beyond the round window I see starlight fleck the sky. I am very quiet, though I need not be. The couple under the quilted coverlet are enthralled in their passion. I cannot question their motives yet. Love? I doubt it. Affection? I would approve of that. Physical attraction, craving for bodily contact, psychic tension?

I move to my window in the end of the playroom, leaving the love-making behind. The aesthetics of the bed are not as pleasing as the placid starfield. It may be that I am accustomed to somewhat more stately cycles and pulsings.

Perhaps it is the crowding of the house, the apprehension that more than one human body dwells within it, that causes me now to feel a loneliness. I wonder where Mrs. Norrinssen settled after the untimely death of her employer. "A bad bargain," he said somberly time after time. "Very bad indeed." And she only smiled back, never maliciously or with humor, but patiently. She had given him what he wanted. "But still a bargain," she said.

I am aware of the sounds subsiding from the canopied bed. I wonder if both now will abandon themselves to dreams and to sleep. A shadow dips silently past the window, a nighthawk. Faintly I hear the cries of hunting birds.


He came awake suddenly with teeth worrying his guilty soul. Connie glared at him from dark eyes swollen from crying and fury. She shook long black hair back from her shoulders. ". . . drove her through the one breakdown and into another." He dimly heard the words. "She's out of it, and good for her. No more campaigns. You won't do the same to me, you son of a bitch." Bitter smile. "Or I should say, you son of a bastard."

"I can't change these things. I'm just trying—" Alessi realized he was shaking in the darkness.

"What's wrong, now what's wrong?" said Connie.

Alessi cried out once, low.

"Baby, what is it?"

He saw Lakey's face in the pooled moonlight. "You." He reached out to touch her cheek and grazed her nose.

"Me," she said. "Who else?"

"Jesus," Alessi said. "Oh God."

"Bad dream?"

Orientation slowly settled in. "A nightmare." He shook his head violently.

"Tell me about it?"

"I can't remember."

"So don't tell me if you don't want to." She gathered him close, blotting the sweat on his sternum with the sheet.

He said dreamily, "You always plan to make it up, but after a while it's too late."

"What's too late?"

Alessi didn't answer. He lay rigid beside her.

I see them in the gilt-framed mirror and I see them in bed. I feel both a terrible sympathy for her and an equally terrible love for him. For as long as I can recall, I've husbanded proprietary feelings about this house and those in it.

Frank Alessi makes me understand. I remember the woman's touch and cherish that feeling, though I simultaneously realize her touch was yet another's. I also remember Frank's embrace. I have touched all of them.

I love all these people. That terrifies me.

I want to tell him, you *can* change things, Frank.

Sometime after midnight he awoke again. The night had encroached; moonlight now filled less than a quarter of the playroom. Alessi lay still, staring at shadow patterns. He heard Lakey's soft, regular breathing beside him.

He lay without moving for what seemed to be hours. When he checked his watch only minutes had passed. Recumbent, he waited, assuming that for which he waited was sleep.

Sleep had started to settle about Alessi when he thought he detected a movement across the room. Part vague movement, part snatch of sound, it was *something*. Switching on the bed-table lamp, Alessi saw nothing. He held his breath for long seconds and listened. Still nothing. The room held only its usual complement of inhabitants: dolls, toys, stuffed creatures. Bear stared back at him. The furniture was all familiar. Everything was in its place, natural. He felt his pulse speeding. He turned off the light and settled back against the pillow.

It's one o'clock in the soul, he thought. Not quite Fitzgerald, but it will do. He remembered Lakey in the car that afternoon asking why he had cut and run. That wasn't the exact phraseology, but it was close enough. So what if he had been forced out of office? He still could have found some kind of political employment. Alessi had not told her about all the records unsubpoenaed as well as subpoenaed—at first. Then, perversely, he had started to catalog the sordid details the investigating committees had decided not to use. After a while she had turned her head back toward the clean mountain scenery. He continued the list. Finally she had told him to shut up. She turned back toward him gravely, had told him it was all right— she had forgiven him. It had been simple and sincere.

I don't need easy forgiveness, he thought. Nor would *I* forgive. That afternoon he had lashed out at her. "Damn it, what do you know about these things—about responsibility and power? You're a hippy—or whatever hippies are called now. Did you ever make a single solitary decision that put you on the line? Made you a target for second-guessing, carping analysis, sniping, unabashed viciousness?" The overtaut spring wound down.

Lakey visibly winced; muscles tightened around her mouth. "Yes," she said.

"So tell me."

She stared back at him like a small surprised animal. "I've been traveling a long time. Before I left, I was pregnant." Her voice flattened; Alessi strained to hear the words. "They told me it should have been a daughter."

He focused his attention back on the road. There was nothing to say. He knew about exigencies. He could approve.

"None of them wanted me to do it. They made it more than it really was. When I left, my parents told me they would never speak to me again. They haven't."

Alessi frowned.

"I loved them."

Alessi heard her mumble, make tiny incoherent sounds. She shifted in her sleep in a series of irregular movements. Her voice raised slightly in volume. The words still were unintelligible. Alessi recognized the tenor; she was dreaming of fearful things. He stared intently: his vision blurred.

Gently he gathered Connie into his arms and stroked her hair. "I will make it right for you. I know, I know . . . I can."

"No," she said, the word sliding into a moan. Sharply, "No."

"I am your father."

But she ignored him.


I hear more than I can see. I hear the woman come fully awake, her moans sliding raggedly up the register to screams; pain—not love; shock—not passion. I would rather not listen, but I have no choice. So I hear the desperation of a body whose limbs are trapped between strangling linens and savage lover. I hear the endless, pounding slap of flesh against meat. Finally I hear the words, the words, the cruel words and the ineffectual. Worst of all, I hear the cries. I hear them in sadness.

Earlier I could not object. But now he couples with her not out of love, not from affection, but to force her. No desire, no lust, no desperate pleasure save inarticulate power.

Finally she somehow frees herself and scrambles off the bed. She stumbles through the unfamiliar room and slams against the wall beside the door. Only her head intrudes into the moonlight, her mouth is set in a rigid, silent oval. The wet blackness around her eyes is more than shadow. She says nothing. She fumbles for the door, claws the knob, is gone. He does not pursue her.

I hear the sound of the woman's stumbling steps. I hear her pound on the doors of the car Alessi habitually locks. The sounds of her flight diminish in the night. She will be safer with the beasts of the mountain.


Alessi endlessly slammed his fist into the bloody pillow. His body shook until the inarticulate rage began to burn away. Then he got up from the bed and crossed the playroom to the great baroque mirror.

"This time could have been different," he said. "I wanted it to be."

His eyes adjusted to the darkness. A thin sliver of moonlight striped the ceiling. Alessi confronted the creature in the mirror. He raised his hands in fists and battered them against unyielding glass, smashed them against the mirror until the surface fragmented into glittering shards. He presented his wrists, repeating in endless rote, "Different, this time, different. . . ."

Then he sensed what lay behind him in the dark. Alessi swung around, blood arcing. Time overcame him. The warm, coppery smell rose up in the room.

Perhaps the house now is haunted; that I cannot say. My own role is ended. Again I am alone; and now lonely. This morning I have not looked through the round window. The carrion crows are inside my mind picking at the bones of memories.

I watch Frank Alessi across the stained floor of the playroom.

The house is quiet; I'm sure that will not continue. The woman will have reached the highway and surely has been found by now. She will tell her story and then the people will come.

For a time the house will be inhabited by many voices and many bodies. The people will look at Frank Alessi and his wrists and his blood. They will remark upon the shattered mirror. They may even note the toys, note me; wonder at the degree of the past preserved here in the house. I doubt they can detect the pain in my old-fashioned eyes.

They will search for answers.

But they can only question why Frank came here, and why he did what he did. They cannot see the marks left by the teeth of the past. Only the blood.

# Dark Winner

## by William F. Nolan

NOTE: The following is an edited transcript of a taped conversation between Mrs. Franklin Evans, resident of Woodland Hills, California, and Lieutenant Harry W. Lyle of the Kansas City Police Department.

Transcript is dated July 12, 1975, K.C., Missouri.

LYLE: . . . and if you want us to help you, we'll have to know everything. When did you arrive here, Mrs. Evans?

MRS. EVANS: We just got in this morning. A stopover on our trip from New York back to California. We were at the airport when Frank suddenly got this idea about his past.

LYLE: What idea?

MRS. E: About visiting his old neighborhood . . . the school he went to . . . the house where he grew up . . . He hadn't been back here in twenty-five years.

LYLE: So you and your husband planned this . . . nostalgic tour?

MRS. E: Not *planned*. It was very abrupt . . . Frank seemed . . . suddenly . . . *possessed* by the idea.

LYLE:    So what happened?

MRS. E:    We took a cab out to Flora Avenue . . . to Thirty-first . . . and we visited his old grade school. St. Vincent's Academy. The neighborhood is . . . well, I guess you know it's a slum area now . . . and the school is closed down, locked. But Frank found an open window . . . climbed inside . . .

LYLE:    While you waited?

MRS. E:    Yes—in the cab. When Frank came out he was all . . . upset . . . Said that he . . . Well, this sounds . . .

LYLE:    Go on, please.

MRS. E:    He said he felt . . . very *close* to his childhood while he was in there. He was ashen-faced. His hands were trembling.

LYLE:    What did you do then?

MRS. E:    We had the cab take us up Thirty-first to the Isis Theater. The movie house at Thirty-first and Troost where Frank used to attend those Saturday horror shows they had for kids. Each week a new one . . . Frankenstein . . . Dracula . . . you know the kind I mean.

LYLE:    I know.

MRS. E:    It's a porno place now . . . but Frank bought a ticket anyway . . . went inside alone. Said he wanted to go into the balcony, find his old seat . . . see if things had changed . . .

LYLE:   And?

MRS. E:   He came out looking very shaken . . . saying it had happened again.

LYLE:   *What* had happened again?

MRS. E:   The feeling about being close to his past . . . to his childhood . . . As if he could—

LYLE:   Could what, Mrs. Evans?

MRS. E:   . . . step over the line dividing past and present . . . step back into his childhood. That's the feeling he said he had.

LYLE:   Where did you go from the Isis?

MRS. E:   Frank paid off the cab . . . said he wanted to walk to his old block . . . the one he grew up on . . . Thirty-third and Forest. So we walked down Troost to Thirty-third . . . past strip joints and hamburger stands . . . I was nervous . . . we didn't . . . belong here . . . Anyway, we got to Thirty-third and walked down the hill from Troost to Forest . . . and on the way Frank told me how much he'd hated being small, being a child . . . that he could hardly wait to grow up . . . that, to him, childhood was a nightmare . . .

LYLE:   Then why all the nostalgia?

MRS. E:   It wasn't that . . . it was . . . like an *exorcism* . . . Frank said he'd been haunted by his childhood all the years we'd lived in California . . . This was an attempt to get *rid* of it . . . by facing it . . . seeing that it was really gone . . . that it no longer had any reality . . .

LYLE: What happened on Forest?

MRS. E: We walked down the street to his old address . . . which was just past the middle of the block . . . 3337 it was . . . a small, sagging wooden house . . . in terrible condition . . . but then, *all* the houses were . . . their screens full of holes . . . windows broken, trash in the yards . . . Frank stood in front of his house staring at it for a long time . . . and then he began repeating something . . . over and over.

LYLE: And what was that?

MRS. E: He said it . . . like a litany . . . over and over . . . "I hate you! . . . I hate you! . . . I hate you!"

LYLE: You mean, he was saying that to *you*?

MRS. E: Oh, no. Not to *me* . . . I asked him what he meant . . . and . . . he said he hated the child he once was, the child who had lived in that house.

LYLE: I see. Go on, Mrs. Evans.

MRS. E: Then he said he was going inside . . . that he *had* to go inside the house . . . but that he was afraid.

LYLE: Of what?

MRS. E: He didn't say of what. He just told me to wait out there on the walk . . . Then he went up onto the small wooden porch . . . knocked on the door. No one answered. Then Frank tried the knob . . . The door was unlocked . . .

LYLE: House was deserted?

MRS. E:   That's right, I guess no one had lived there for a long while . . . All the windows were boarded up . . . and the driveway was filled with weeds . . . I started to move toward the porch, but Frank waved me back. Then he kicked the door all the way open with his foot, took a half step inside, turned . . . and looked back at me . . . There was . . . a terrible fear in his eyes. I got a cold, chilled feeling all through my body—and I started toward him again . . . but he suddenly turned his back and went inside . . . The door closed.

LYLE:   What then?

MRS. E:   Then I waited. For fifteen . . . twenty minutes . . . a half hour . . . Frank didn't come out. So I went up to the porch and opened the door . . . called to him . . .

LYLE:   Any answer?

MRS. E:   No. The house was like . . . a hollow cave . . . there were echoes . . . but no answer . . . I went inside . . . walked all through the place . . . into every room . . . but he wasn't there . . . Frank was gone.

LYLE:   Out the back, maybe.

MRS. E:   No. The back door was nailed shut. Rusted. It hadn't been opened for years.

LYLE:   A window then.

MRS. E:   They were all boarded over. With thick dust on the sills.

LYLE:   Did you check the basement?

MRS. E: Yes, I checked the basement door leading down. It was locked, and the dust hadn't been disturbed around it.

LYLE: Then . . . just where the hell did he *go*?

MRS. E: I don't *know,* Lieutenant! . . . That's why I called you . . . why I came here . . . You've got to find Frank!

## END FIRST TRANSCRIPT

NOTE: Lieutenant Lyle did not find Franklin Evans. The case was turned over to Missing Persons—and, a week later, Mrs. Evans returned to her home in California. The first night back she had a dream, a nightmare. It disturbed her severely. She could not eat, could not sleep properly; her nerves were shattered. Mrs. Evans then sought psychiatric help. What follows is an excerpt from a taped session with Dr. Lawrence Redding, a licensed psychiatrist with offices in Beverly Hills, California.

Transcript is dated August 3, 1975, Beverly Hills.

REDDING: And where were you . . . ? In the *dream,* I mean.

MRS. E: My bedroom. In bed, at home. It was as if I'd just been awakened . . . I looked around me—and everything was normal . . . the room exactly as it always is . . . Except for *him* . . . the boy standing next to me.

REDDING: Did you recognize this boy?

MRS. E: No.

REDDING:   Describe him to me.

MRS. E:   He was . . . nine or ten . . . a *horrible* child . . . with a cold hate in his face, in his eyes . . . He had on a red sweater with holes in each elbow. And knickers . . . the kind that boys used to wear . . . and he had on black tennis shoes . . .

REDDING:   Did he speak to you?

MRS. E:   Not at first. He just . . . smiled at me . . . and that smile was so . . . so *evil!* . . . And then he said . . . that he wanted me to know he'd won at last . . .

REDDING:   Won what?

MRS. E:   That's what I asked him . . . calmly, in the dream . . . I asked him what he'd won. And he said . . . oh, my God . . . he said . . .

REDDING:   Go on, Mrs. Evans.

MRS. E:   . . . that he'd won Frank! . . . that my husband would *never* be coming back . . . that he, the boy, *had* him now . . . forever! . . . I screamed—and woke up. And, instantly, I remembered something.

REDDING:   What did you remember?

MRS. E:   Before she died . . . Frank's mother . . . sent us an album she'd saved . . . of his childhood . . . photos . . . old report cards . . . He never wanted to look at it, stuck the album away in a closet . . . After the dream, I . . . got it out, looked through it until I found . . .

REDDING:   Yes . . . ?

MRS. E:   A photo I'd remembered. Of Frank . . . at the age of
ten . . . standing in the front yard on Forest . . . He was smiling . . . that same, awful smile . . . and . . . he wore a sweater
with holes in each elbow . . . and knickers . . . black tennis
shoes. It was . . . the *same* boy exactly—the younger self Frank
had always hated . . . I *know* what happened in that house now.

REDDING:   Then tell me.

MRS. E:   The boy was . . . waiting there . . . inside that awful,
rotting dead house . . . waiting for Frank to come back . . . all
those years . . . waiting there to claim him—because . . . . . . *he*
hated the man that Frank had become as much as Frank hated
the child he'd once been . . . and the boy was *right*.

REDDING:   Right about what, Mrs. Evans?

MRS. E:   About winning . . . It took all those years . . . but he
won . . . and Frank lost.


END TRANSCRIPT

# The Judge's House

## by Bram Stoker

When the time for his examination drew near Malcolm Malcolmson made up his mind to go somewhere to read by himself. He feared the attractions of the seaside, and also he feared completely rural isolation, for of old he knew its charms, and so he determined to find some unpretentious little town where there would be nothing to distract him. He refrained from asking suggestions from any of his friends, for he argued that each would recommend some place of which he had knowledge, and where he had already acquaintances. As Malcolmson wished to avoid friends he had no wish to encumber himself with the attention of friends' friends, and so he determined to look out for a place for himself. He packed a portmanteau with some clothes and all the books he required, and then took ticket for the first name on the local time-table which he did not know.

When at the end of three hours' journey he alighted at Benchurch, he felt satisfied that he had so far obliterated his tracks as to be sure of having a peaceful opportunity of pursuing his studies. He went straight to the one inn which the sleepy little place contained, and put up for the night. Benchurch was a market town, and once in three weeks was crowded to excess, but for the remainder of the twenty-one days it was as attractive as a desert. Malcolmson looked around the day after his arrival to try to find quarters more isolated then even so quiet an inn as "The Good Traveller" afforded. There was only one place which took his fancy, and it certainly satisfied his wildest ideas regarding quiet; in fact, quiet was not the proper word to apply to it—desolation was the only term conveying any suitable idea of its isolation. It was an old rambling, heavy-built house of the Jacobean style, with heavy gables and windows, unusually small, and set higher than was customary in such houses, and was surrounded with a high brick wall massively built. Indeed, on examination, it looked more like a fortified house than an ordinary dwelling. But all these things pleased Malcolmson. "Here," he thought, "is the very spot I have been looking for, and if I can get opportunity of using it I shall be happy." His joy was increased when he realised beyond doubt that it was not at present inhabited.

From the post-office he got the name of the agent, who was rarely surprised at the application to rent a part of the old house. Mr. Carnford, the local lawyer and agent, was a genial old gentleman, and frankly confessed his delight at anyone being willing to live in the house.

"To tell you the truth," said he, "I should be only too happy, on behalf of the owners, to let anyone have the house rent free for a term of years if only to accustom the people here to see it inhabited. It has been so long empty that some kind of absurd prejudice has grown up about it, and this can be best put down by its occupation—if only," he added with a sly glance at Malcolmson, "by a scholar like yourself, who wants its quiet for a time."

Malcolmson thought it needless to ask the agent about the "absurd prejudice"; he knew he would get more information, if he should require it, on that subject from other quarters. He paid his three months' rent, got a receipt, and the name of an old woman who would probably undertake to "do" for him, and came away with the keys in his pocket. He then went to the landlady of the inn, who was a cheerful and most kindly person, and asked her advice as to such stores and provisions as he would be likely to require. She threw up her hands in amazement when he told her where he was going to settle himself.

"Not in the Judge's House!" she said, and grew pale as she spoke. He explained the locality of the house, saying that he did not know its name. When he had finished she answered:

"Aye, sure enough—sure enough the very place! It is the Judge's House sure enough." He asked her to tell him about the place, why so called, and what there was against it. She told him that it was so called locally because it had been many years before—how long she could not say, as she was herself from another part of the country, but she thought it must have been a hundred years or more—the abode of a judge who was held in great terror on account of his harsh sentences and his hostility to prisoners at Assizes. As to what there was against the house itself she could not tell. She had often asked, but no one could inform her; but there was a general feeling that there was *something,* and for her own part she would not take all the money in Drinkwater's Bank and stay in the house an hour by herself. Then she apologised to Malcolmson for her disturbing talk.

"It is too bad of me, sir, and you—and a young gentleman, too—if you will pardon me saying it, going to live there all alone. If you were my boy—and you'll excuse me for saying it—you wouldn't sleep there a night, not if I had to go there myself and pull the big alarm bell that's on the roof!" The good creature was so manifestly in earnest, and was so kindly in her intentions, that Malcolmson, although amused, was touched. He told her kindly how much he appreciated her interest in him, and added:

"But, my dear Mrs. Witham, indeed you need not be concerned about me! A man who is reading for the Mathematical Tripos has too much to think of to be disturbed by any of these mysterious 'somethings,' and his work is of too exact and prosaic a kind to allow of his having any corner in his mind for mysteries of any kind. Harmonical Progression, Permutations and Combinations, and Elliptic Functions have sufficient mysteries for me!" Mrs. Witham kindly undertook to see after his commissions, and he

went himself to look for the old woman who had been recom-
mended to him. When he returned to the Judge's House with her,
after an interval of a couple of hours, he found Mrs. Witham herself waiting with several men and boys carrying parcels, and an
upholsterer's man with a bed in a car, for she said, though tables
and chairs might be all very well, a bed that hadn't been aired for
mayhap fifty years was not proper for young bones to lie on. She
was evidently curious to see the inside of the house; and though
manifestly so afraid of the "somethings" that at the slightest
sound she clutched on to Malcolmson, whom she never left for a
moment, went over the whole place.

After his examination of the house, Malcolmson decided to
take up his abode in the great dining-room, which was big
enough to serve for all his requirements; and Mrs. Witham,
with the aid of the charwoman, Mrs. Dempster, proceeded to
arrange matters. When the hampers were brought in and un-
packed, Malcolmson saw that with much kind forethought she
had sent from her own kitchen sufficient provisions to last for
a few days. Before going she expressed all sorts of kind
wishes; and at the door turned and said:

"And perhaps, sir, as the room is big and draughty it might
be well to have one of those big screens put round your bed at
night—though, truth to tell, I would die myself if I were to be
so shut in with all kinds of—of 'things,' that put their heads
round the sides, or over the top, and look on me!" The image
which she had called up was too much for her nerves, and she
fled incontinently.

Mrs. Dempster sniffed in a superior manner as the landlady
disappeared, and remarked that for her own part she wasn't
afraid of all the bogies in the kingdom.

"I'll tell you what it is, sir," she said; "bogies is all kinds and
sorts of things—except bogies! Rats and mice, and beetles; and
creaky doors, and loose slates, and broken panes, and stiff
drawer handles, that stay out when you pull them and then fall
down in the middle of the night. Look at the wainscot of the

room! It is old—hundreds of years old! Do you think there's no rats and beetles there! And do you imagine, sir, that you won't see none of them? Rats is bogies, I tell you, and bogies is rats; and don't you get to think anything else!"

"Mrs. Dempster," said Malcolmson gravely, making her a polite bow, "you know more than a Senior Wrangler! And let me say, that, as a mark of esteem for your indubitable soundness of head and heart, I shall, when I go, give you possession of this house, and let you stay here by yourself for the last two months of my tenancy, for four weeks will serve my purpose."

"Thank you kindly, sir!" she answered, "but I couldn't sleep away from home a night. I am in Greenhow's Charity, and if I slept a night away from my rooms I should lose all I have got to live on. The rules is very strict; and there's too many watching for a vacancy for me to run any risks in the matter. Only for that, sir, I'd gladly come here and attend on you altogether during your stay."

"My good woman," said Malcolmson hastily, "I have come here on purpose to obtain solitude; and believe me that I am grateful to the late Greenhow for having so organised his admirable charity—whatever it is—that I am perforce denied the opportunity of suffering from such a form of temptation! Saint Anthony himself could not be more rigid on the point!"

The old woman laughed harshly. "Ah, you young gentlemen," she said, "you don't fear for naught; and belike you'll get all the solitude you want here." She set to work with her cleaning; and by nightfall, when Malcolmson returned from his walk—he always had one of his books to study as he walked—he found the room swept and tidied, a fire burning in the old hearth, the lamp lit, and the table spread for supper with Mrs. Witham's excellent fare. "This is comfort, indeed," he said, as he rubbed his hands.

When he had finished his supper, and lifted the tray to the other end of the great oak dining-table, he got out his books again, put fresh wood on the fire, trimmed his lamp, and set himself down to a spell of real hard work. He went on without pause till about eleven o'clock, when he knocked off for a bit to fix his fire and lamp, and to make himself a cup of tea. He had always been a tea-drinker, and during his college life had sat late at work and had taken tea late. The rest was a great luxury to him, and he enjoyed it with a sense of delicious, voluptuous ease. The renewed fire leaped and sparkled, and threw quaint shadows through the great old room; and as he sipped his hot tea he revelled in the sense of isolation from his kind. Then it was that he began to notice for the first time what a noise the rats were making.

"Surely," he thought, "they cannot have been at it all the time I was reading. Had they been, I must have noticed it!" Presently, when the noise increased, he satisfied himself that it was really new. It was evident that at first the rats had been frightened at the presence of a stranger, and the light of fire and lamp; but that as the time went on they had grown bolder and were now disporting themselves as was their wont.

How busy they were! and hark to the strange noises! Up and down behind the old wainscot, over the ceiling and under the floor they raced, and gnawed, and scratched! Malcolmson smiled to himself as he recalled to mind the saying of Mrs. Dempster, "Bogies is rats, and rats is bogies!" The tea began to have its effect of intellectual and nervous stimulus, he saw with joy another long spell of work to be done before the night was past, and in the sense of security which it gave him, he allowed himself the luxury of a good look round the room. He took his lamp in one hand, and went all around, wondering that so quaint and beautiful an old house had been so long neglected. The carving of the oak on the panels of the wainscot was fine, and on and round the doors and windows it was beautiful and of rare merit. There were some old pictures on the walls, but they were coated so thick with dust and dirt that he could not distinguish any detail of them, though he held his lamp as high as he could over his head. Here and there as he went round he saw some crack or hole blocked for a moment by the face of a rat with its bright eyes glittering in the light, but in an instant it was gone, and a squeak and a scamper followed. The thing that most struck him, however, was the rope of the great alarm bell on the roof, which hung down in a corner of the room on the right-hand side of the fireplace. He pulled up close to the hearth a great high-backed carved oak chair, and sat down to his last cup of tea. When this was done he made up the fire, and went back to his work, sitting at the corner of the table, having the fire to his left. For a little while the rats disturbed him somewhat with their perpetual scampering, but he got accustomed to the noise as one does to the ticking of a clock or to the roar of moving water; and he became so immersed in his work that everything in the world, except the problem which he was trying to solve, passed away from him.

He suddenly looked up, his problem was still unsolved, and there was in the air that sense of the hour before the dawn, which is so dread to doubtful life. The noise of the rats had ceased. Indeed it seemed to him that it must have ceased but lately and that it was the sudden cessation which had disturbed him. The fire had fallen low, but still it threw out a deep red glow. As he looked he started in spite of his *sang froid.*

There on the great high-backed carved oak chair by the right side of the fireplace sat an enormous rat, steadily glaring at him with baleful eyes. He made a motion to it as though to hunt it away, but it did not stir. Then he made the motion of throwing something. Still it did not stir, but showed its great white teeth angrily, and its cruel eyes shone in the lamplight with an added vindictiveness.

Malcolmson felt amazed, and seizing the poker from the hearth ran at it to kill it. Before, however, he could strike it, the rat, with a squeak that sounded like the concentration of hate, jumped upon the floor, and, running up the rope of the alarm bell, disappeared in the darkness beyond the range of the green-shaded lamp. Instantly, strange to say, the noisy scampering of the rats in the wainscot began again.

By this time Malcolmson's mind was quite off the problem;

and as a shrill cock-crow outside told him of the approach of morning, he went to bed and to sleep.

He slept so sound that he was not even waked by Mrs. Dempster coming in to make up his room. It was only when she had tidied up the place and got his breakfast ready and tapped on the screen which closed in his bed that he woke. He was a little tired still after his night's hard work, but a strong cup of tea soon freshened him up and, taking his book, he went out for his morning walk, bringing with him a few sandwiches lest he should not care to return till dinnertime. He found a quiet walk between high elms some way outside the town, and here he spent the greater part of the day studying his Laplace. On his return he looked in to see Mrs. Witham and to thank her for her kindness. When she saw him coming through the diamond-paned bay window of her sanctum she came out to meet him and asked him in. She looked at him searchingly and shook her head as she said:

"You must not overdo it, sir. You are paler this morning than you should be. Too late hours and too hard work on the brain isn't good for any man! But tell me, sir, how did you pass the night? Well, I hope? But my heart! sir, I was glad when Mrs. Dempster told me this morning that you were all right and sleeping sound when she went in."

"Oh, I was all right," he answered smiling, "the 'some-things' didn't worry me, as yet. Only the rats; and they had a circus, I tell you, all over the place. There was one wicked-looking old devil that sat up on my own chair by the fire, and wouldn't go till I took the poker to him, and then he ran up the rope of the alarm bell and got to somewhere up the wall or the ceiling—I couldn't see where, it was so dark."

"Mercy on us," said Mrs. Witham, "an old devil, and sitting on a chair by the fireside! Take care, sir! take care! There's many a true word spoken in jest."

"How do you mean? Pon my word I don't understand."

"An old devil! The old devil, perhaps. There! sir, you needn't laugh," for Malcolmson had broken into a hearty peal. "You young folks thinks it easy to laugh at things that makes older ones shudder. Never mind, sir! never mind! Please God, you'll laugh all the time. It's what I wish you myself!" and the good lady beamed all over in sympathy with his enjoyment, her fears gone for a moment.

"Oh, forgive me!" said Malcolmson presently. "Don't think me rude; but the idea was too much for me—that the old devil himself was on the chair last night!" And at the thought he laughed again. Then he went home to dinner.

This evening the scampering of the rats began earlier; indeed it had been going on before his arrival, and only ceased whilst his presence by its freshness disturbed them. After dinner he sat by the fire for a while and had a smoke; and then, having cleared his table, began to work as before. Tonight the rats disturbed him more than they had done on the previous night. How they scampered up and down and under and over! How they squeaked, and scratched, and gnawed! How they, getting bolder by degrees, came to the mouths of their holes and to the chinks and cracks and crannies in the wainscoting till their eyes shone like tiny lamps as the firelight rose and fell. But to him, now doubtless accustomed to them, their eyes were not wicked; only their playfulness touched him. Sometimes the boldest of them made sallies out on the floor or along the mouldings of the wainscot. Now and again as they disturbed him Malcolmson made a sound to frighten them, smiting the table with his hand or giving a fierce "Hsh, hsh," so that they fled straightway to their holes.

And so the early part of the night wore on; and despite the noise Malcolmson got more and more immersed in his work.

All at once he stopped, as on the previous night, being overcome by a sudden sense of silence. There was not the faintest sound of gnaw, or scratch, or squeak. The silence was as of the grave. He remembered the odd occurrence of the previous night, and instinctively he looked at the chair standing close by the fireside. And then a very odd sensation thrilled through him.

There, on the great old high-backed carved oak chair beside

the fireplace sat the same enormous rat, steadily glaring at him with baleful eyes.

Instinctively he took the nearest thing to his hand, a book of logarithms, and flung it at it. The book was badly aimed and the rat did not stir, so again the poker performance of the previous night was repeated; and again the rat, being closely pursued, fled up the rope of the alarm bell. Strangely too, the departure of this rat was instantly followed by the renewal of the noise made by the general rat community. On this occasion, as on the previous one, Malcolmson could not see at what part of the room the rat disappeared, for the green shade of his lamp left the upper part of the room in darkness, and the fire had burned low.

On looking at his watch he found it was close on midnight; and, not sorry for the *divertissement,* he made up his fire and made himself his nightly pot of tea. He had got through a good spell of work, and thought himself entitled to a cigarette; and so he sat on the great oak chair before the fire and enjoyed it. Whilst smoking he began to think that he would like to know where the rat disappeared to, for he had certain ideas for the morrow not entirely disconnected with a rat-trap. Accordingly he lit another lamp and placed it so that it would shine well into the right-hand corner of the wall by the fireplace. Then he got all the books he had with him, and placed them handy to throw at the vermin. Finally he lifted the rope of the alarm bell and placed the end of it on the table, fixing the extreme end under the lamp. As he handled it he could not help noticing how pliable it was, especially for so strong a rope, and one not in use. "You could hang a man with it," he thought to himself. When his preparations were made he looked around, and said complacently:

"There now, my friend, I think we shall learn something of you this time!" He began his work again, and though as before somewhat disturbed at first by the noise of the rats, soon lost himself in his propositions and problems.

Again he was called to his immediate surroundings suddenly. This time it might not have been the sudden silence only which took his attention; there was a slight movement of the rope, and the lamp moved. Without stirring, he looked to see if his pile of books was within range, and then cast his eye along the rope. As he looked he saw the great rat drop from the rope on the oak armchair and sit there glaring at him. He raised a book in his right hand, and taking careful aim, flung it at the rat. The latter, with a quick movement, sprang aside and dodged the missile. He then took another book, and a third, and flung them one after another at the rat, but each time unsuccessfully. At last, as he stood with a book poised in his hand to throw, the rat squeaked and seemed afraid. This made Malcolmson more than ever eager to strike, and the book flew and struck the rat a resounding blow. It gave a terrified squeak, and turning on his pursuer a look of terrible malevolence, ran up the chair-back and made a great jump to the rope of the alarm bell and ran up it like lightning. The lamp rocked under the sudden strain, but it was a heavy one and did not topple over. Malcolmson kept his eyes on the rat, and saw it by the light of the second lamp leap to a moulding of the wainscot and disappear through a hole in one of the great pictures which hung on the wall, obscured and invisible through its coating of dirt and dust.

"I shall look up my friend's habitation in the morning," said the student, as he went over to collect his books. "The third picture from the fireplace; I shall not forget." He picked up the books one by one, commenting on them as he lifted them. "*Conic Sections* he does not mind, nor *Cycloidal Oscillations,* nor the *Principia,* nor *Quaternions,* nor *Thermodynamics.* Now for the book that fetched him!" Malcolmson took it up and looked at it. As he did so he started, a sudden pallor overspread his face. He looked round uneasily and shivered slightly, as he murmured to himself:

"The Bible my mother gave me! What an odd coincidence." He sat down to work again, and the rats in the wainscot renewed their gambols. They did not disturb him, however; somehow their presence gave him a sense of companionship. But he could not attend to his work, and after striving to master the subject on which he was engaged gave it up in despair, and went to bed as the first streak of dawn stole in through the eastern window.

He slept heavily but uneasily, and dreamed much; and when Mrs. Dempster woke him late in the morning he seemed ill at ease, and for a few minutes did not seem to realise exactly where he was. His first request rather surprised the servant.

"Mrs. Dempster, when I am out today I wish you would get the steps and dust or wash those pictures—specially that one the third from the fireplace—I want to see what they are."

Late in the afternoon Malcolmson worked at his books in the shaded walk, and the cheerfulness of the previous day came back to him as the day wore on, and he found that his reading was progressing well. He had worked out to a satisfactory conclusion all the problems which had as yet baffled him, and it was in a state of jubilation that he paid a visit to Mrs. Witham at "The Good Traveller." He found a stranger in the cosy sitting-room with the landlady, who was introduced to him as Dr. Thornhill. She was not quite at ease, and this, combined with the doctor's plunging at once into a series of questions, made Malcolmson come to the conclusion that his presence was not an accident, so without preliminary he said:

"Dr. Thornhill, I shall with pleasure answer you any question you may choose to ask me if you will answer me one question first."

The doctor seemed surprised, but he smiled and answered at once, "Done! What is it?"

"Did Mrs. Witham ask you to come here and see me and advise me?"

Dr. Thornhill for a moment was taken aback, and Mrs. Witham got fiery red and turned away; but the doctor was a frank and ready man, and he answered at once and openly.

"She did: but she didn't intend you to know it. I suppose it was my clumsy haste that made you suspect. She told me that she did not like the idea of your being in that house all by yourself, and that she thought you took too much strong tea. In fact, she wants me to advise you if possible to give up the tea and the very late hours. I was a keen student in my time, so I suppose I may take the liberty of a college man, and without offence, advise you not quite as a stranger."

Malcolmson with a bright smile held out his hand. "Shake! as they say in America," he said. "I must thank you for your kindness and Mrs. Witham too, and your kindness deserves a return on my part. I promise to take no more strong tea—no tea at all till you let me—and I shall go to bed tonight at one o'clock at latest. Will that do?"

"Capital," said the doctor. "Now tell us all that you noticed in the old house," and so Malcolmson then and there told in minute detail all that had happened in the last two nights. He was interrupted every now and then by some exclamation from Mrs. Witham, till finally when he told of the episode of the Bible the landlady's pent-up emotions found vent in a shriek; and it was not till a stiff glass of brandy and water had been administered that she grew composed again. Dr. Thornhill listened with a face of growing gravity, and when the narrative was complete and Mrs. Witham had been restored he asked:

"The rat always went up the rope of the alarm bell?"

"Always."

"I suppose you know," said the doctor after a pause, "what the rope is?"

"No!"

"It is," said the doctor slowly, "the very rope which the hangman used for all the victims of the Judge's judicial rancour!" Here he was interrupted by another scream from Mrs. Witham, and steps had to be taken for her recovery. Malcolmson having looked at his watch, and found that it was close to his dinner hour, had gone home before her complete recovery.

When Mrs. Witham was herself again she almost assailed the doctor with angry questions as to what he meant by putting such horrible ideas into the poor young man's mind. "He has quite enough there already to upset him," she added. Dr. Thornhill replied:

"My dear madam, I had a distinct purpose in it! I wanted to draw his attention to the bell rope, and to fix it there. It may be that he is in a highly overwrought state, and has been studying too much, although I am bound to say that he seems as sound and healthy a young man, mentally and bodily, as ever I saw—but then the rats—and that suggestion of the devil." The doctor shook his head and went on. "I would have offered to go and stay the first night with him but that I felt sure it would have been a cause of offence. He may get in the night some strange fright or hallucination; and if he does I want him to pull that rope. All alone as he is it will give us warning, and we may reach him in time to be of service. I shall be sitting up pretty late tonight and shall keep my ears open. Do not be alarmed if Benchurch gets a surprise before morning."

"Oh, Doctor, what do you mean? What do you mean?"

"I mean this; that possibly—nay, more probably—we shall hear the great alarm bell from the Judge's House tonight," and the doctor made about as effective an exit as could be thought of.

When Malcolmson arrived home he found that it was a little after his usual time, and Mrs. Dempster had gone away—the rules of Greenhow's Charity were not to be neglected. He was glad to see that the place was bright and tidy with a cheerful fire and a well-trimmed lamp. The evening was colder than might have been expected in April, and a heavy wind was blowing with such rapidly increasing strength that there was every promise of a storm during the night. For a few minutes after his entrance the noise of the rats ceased; but so soon as they became accustomed to his presence they began again. He was glad to hear them, for he felt once more the feeling of companionship in their noise, and his mind ran back to the strange fact that they only ceased to manifest themselves when that other—the great rat with the baleful eyes—came upon the scene. The reading-lamp only was lit and its green shade kept the ceiling and the upper part of the room in darkness, so that the cheerful light from the hearth spreading over the floor and shining on the white cloth laid over the end of the table was warm and cheery. Malcolmson sat down to his dinner with a good appetite and a buoyant spirit. After his dinner and a cigarette he sat steadily down to work, determined not to let anything disturb him, for he remembered his promise to the doctor, and made up his mind to make the best of the time at his disposal.

For an hour or so he worked all right, and then his thoughts began to wander from his books. The actual circumstances around him, the calls on his physical attention, and his nervous susceptibility were not to be denied. By this time the wind had become a gale, and the gale a storm. The old house, solid though it was, seemed to shake to its foundations, and the storm roared and raged through its many chimneys and its queer old gables, producing strange, unearthly sounds in the empty rooms and corridors. Even the great alarm bell on the roof must have felt the force of the wind, for the rope rose and fell slightly, as though the bell were moved a little from time to time, and the limber rope fell on the oak floor with a hard and hollow sound.

As Malcolmson listened to it he bethought himself of the doctor's words, "It is the rope which the hangman used for the victims of the Judge's judicial rancour," and he went over to the corner of the fireplace and took it in his hand to look at it. There seemed a sort of deadly interest in it, and as he stood there he lost himself for a moment in speculation as to who these victims were, and the grim wish of the Judge to have such a ghastly relic ever under his eyes. As he stood there the swaying of the bell on the roof still lifted the rope now and again; but presently there came a new sensation—a sort of tremor in the rope, as though something was moving along it.

Looking up instinctively Malcolmson saw the great rat coming slowly down towards him, glaring at him steadily. He dropped the rope and started back with a muttered curse, and the rat turning ran up the rope again and disappeared, and at the same instant Malcolmson became conscious that the noise of the rats, which had ceased for a while, began again.

All this set him thinking, and it occurred to him that he had not investigated the lair of the rat or looked at the pictures, as he had intended. He lit the other lamp without the shade, and, holding it up went and stood opposite the third picture from the fireplace on the right-hand side where he had seen the rat disappear on the previous night.

At the first glance he started back so suddenly that he almost dropped the lamp, and a deadly pallor overspread his face. His knees shook, and heavy drops of sweat came on his forehead, and he trembled like an aspen. But he was young and plucky, and pulled himself together, and after the pause of a few seconds stepped forward again, raised the lamp, and examined the picture which had been dusted and washed, and now stood out clearly.

It was of a judge dressed in his robes of scarlet and ermine. His face was strong and merciless, evil, crafty, and vindictive, with a sensual mouth, hooked nose of ruddy colour, and shaped like the beak of a bird of prey. The rest of the face was of a cadaverous colour. The eyes were of peculiar brilliance and with a terribly malignant expression. As he looked at them, Malcolmson grew cold, for he saw there the very counterpart of the eyes of the great rat. The lamp almost fell from his hand, he saw the rat with its baleful eyes peering out through the hole in the corner of the picture, and noted the sudden cessation of the noise of the other rats. However, he pulled himself together, and went on with his examination of the picture.

The Judge was seated in a great high-backed carved oak chair, on the right-hand side of a great stone fireplace where, in the corner, a rope hung down from the ceiling, its end lying coiled on the floor. With a feeling of something like horror, Malcolmson recognised the scene of the room as it stood, and gazed around him in an awestruck manner as though he expected to find some strange presence behind him. Then he looked over to the corner of the fireplace—and with a loud cry he let the lamp fall from his hand.

There, in the Judge's arm-chair, with the rope hanging behind, sat the rat with the Judge's baleful eyes, now intensified and with a fiendish leer. Save for the howling of the storm without there was silence.

The fallen lamp recalled Malcolmson to himself. Fortunately it was of metal, and so the oil was not spilt. However, the practical need of attending to it settled at once his nervous apprehensions. When he had turned it out, he wiped his brow and thought for a moment.

"This will not do," he said to himself. "If I go on like this I shall become a crazy fool. This must stop! I promised the doctor I would not take tea. Faith, he was pretty right! My nerves must have been getting into a queer state. Funny I did not notice it. I never felt better in my life. However, it is all right now, and I shall not be such a fool again."

Then he mixed himself a good stiff glass of brandy and water and resolutely sat down to his work.

It was nearly an hour when he looked up from his book, disturbed by the sudden stillness. Without, the wind howled and roared louder than ever, and the rain drove in sheets against the windows, beating like hail on the glass; but within there was no sound whatever save the echo of the wind as it roared in the great chimney, and now and then a hiss as a few raindrops found their way down the chimney in a lull of the storm. The fire had fallen low and had ceased to flame, though it threw out a red glow. Malcolmson listened attentively, and presently heard a thin, squeaking noise, very faint. It came from the corner of the room where the rope hung down, and he thought it was the creaking of the rope on the floor as the swaying of the bell raised and lowered it. Looking up, however, he saw in the dim light the great rat clinging to the rope and gnawing it. The rope was already nearly gnawed through—he could see the lighter colour where the strands were laid bare. As he looked the job was completed, and the severed end of the rope fell clattering on the oaken floor, whilst for an instant the great rat remained like a knob or tassel at the end of the rope, which now began to sway to and fro. Malcolmson felt for a moment another pang of terror as he thought that now the possibility of calling the outer world to his assistance was cut off, but an intense anger took its place, and seizing the book he was reading he hurled it at the rat. The blow was well aimed, but before the missile could reach him the rat dropped off and struck the floor with a soft thud. Malcolmson instantly rushed over towards him, but it darted away and disappeared in the darkness of the shadows of the room. Malcolmson felt that his work was over for the night, and determined then and there to vary the monotony of the proceedings by a hunt for the rat, and took off the green shade of the lamp so as to insure a wider spreading light. As he did so the gloom of the upper part of the room was relieved, and in the new flood of light, great by comparison with the previous darkness, the pictures on the wall stood out boldly. From where he stood, Malcolmson saw right opposite to him the third picture on the wall from the right of the fireplace. He rubbed his eyes in surprise, and then a great fear began to come upon him.

In the centre of the picture was a great irregular patch of brown canvas, as fresh as when it was stretched on the frame. The background was as before, with chair and chimney-corner and rope, but the figure of the Judge had disappeared.

Malcolmson, almost in a chill of horror, turned slowly round, and then he began to shake and tremble like a man in a palsy. His strength seemed to have left him, and he was incapable of action or movement, hardly even of thought. He could only see and hear.

There, on the great high-backed carved oak chair sat the Judge in his robes of scarlet and ermine, with his baleful eyes glaring vindictively, and a smile of triumph on the resolute, cruel mouth, as he lifted with his hands a *black cap*. Malcolmson felt as if the blood was running from his heart, as one does in moments of prolonged suspense. There was a singing in his ears. Without, he could hear the roar and howl of the tempest, and through it, swept on the storm, came the striking of midnight by the great chimes in the market place. He stood for a space of time that seemed to him endless still as a statue, and with wide-open, horror-struck eyes, breathless. As the clock struck, so the smile of triumph on the Judge's face intensified, and at the last stroke of midnight he placed the black cap on his head.

Slowly and deliberately the Judge rose from his chair and picked up the piece of the rope of the alarm bell which lay on the floor, drew it through his hands as if he enjoyed its touch, and then deliberately began to knot one end of it, fashioning it into a noose. This he tightened and tested with his foot, pulling hard at it till he was satisfied and then making a running noose of it, which he held in his hand. Then he began to move along the table on the opposite side to Malcolmson keeping his eyes on him until he had passed him, when with a quick movement he stood in front of the door. Malcolmson then began to feel that he was trapped, and tried to think of what he should do. There was some fascination in the Judge's eyes, which he never took off him, and he had, perforce, to look. He saw the Judge approach—still keeping between him and the door—and raise the noose and throw it towards him as if to entangle him. With a great effort he made a quick movement to one side, and saw the rope fall beside him, and heard it strike the oaken floor. Again the Judge raised the noose and tried to ensnare him, ever keeping his baleful eyes fixed on him, and each time by a mighty effort the student just managed to evade it. So this went on for many times, the Judge seeming never discouraged nor discomposed at failure, but playing as a cat does with a mouse. At last in despair, which had reached its climax, Malcolmson cast a quick glance round him. The lamp seemed to have blazed up, and there was a fairly good light in the room. At the many rat-holes and in the chinks and crannies of the wainscot he saw the rats' eyes; and this aspect, that was purely physical, gave him a gleam of comfort. He looked around and saw that the rope of the great alarm bell was laden with rats. Every inch of it was covered with them, and more and more were pouring through the small circular hole in the ceiling whence it emerged, so that with their weight the bell was beginning to sway.

Hark! it had swayed till the clapper had touched the bell. The sound was but a tiny one, but the bell was only beginning to sway, and it would increase.

At the sound the Judge, who had been keeping his eyes fixed on Malcolmson, looked up, and a scowl of diabolical anger overspread his face. His eyes fairly glowed like hot coals, and he stamped his foot with a sound that seemed to make the house shake. A dreadful peal of thunder broke overhead as he raised the rope again, whilst the rats kept running up and down the rope as though working against time. This time, instead of throwing it, he drew close to his victim, and held open the noose as he approached. As he came closer there seemed something paralysing in his very presence, and Malcolmson stood rigid as a corpse. He felt the Judge's icy fingers touch his throat as he adjusted the rope. The noose tightened—tightened. Then the Judge, taking the rigid form of the student in his arms, carried him over and placed him standing in the oak chair, and stepping up beside him, put his hand up and caught the end of the swaying rope of the alarm bell. As he raised his hand the rats fled squeaking, and disappeared through the hole in the ceiling. Taking the end of the noose which was round Malcolmson's neck he tied it to the hanging-bell rope, and then descending pulled away the chair.

When the alarm bell of the Judge's House began to sound a crowd soon assembled. Lights and torches of various kinds appeared, and soon a silent crowd was hurrying to the spot. They knocked loudly at the door, but there was no reply. Then they burst in the door, and poured into the great dining-room, the doctor at the head.

There at the end of the rope of the great alarm bell hung the body of the student, and on the face of the Judge in the picture was a malignant smile.

# The Tearing of
# Greymare House

## by Michael Reaves

When he had first seen the old house, Lamar Warren had thought, I can make a pile of money off this job. His next thought had been, Ain't it a goddamn shame.

He had not wanted to take the job, despite the money to be made. But these were not good times for the wrecking business. The bank had him good, and their grip kept getting tighter. With the economy the way it was, few new buildings were being built, and so few old ones were being wrecked. The Warren Wrecking Company nearly folded this year. It didn't seem fair, Lamar had told his wife dryly, for the country to be falling apart without his even getting to swing a ball at it.

And so he had taken the Greymare job, despite his feelings about it. The contractor was a firm in Philadelphia, and they had not even taken bids—they had simply called and offered him a price he could not refuse. With that, and the salvage that was his, he stood to make a good profit. He tried to feel enthusiastic about that.

The truck lurched as one of the outside tires ground gravel on the narrow road's edge. George Colby cursed and wrestled with the wheel. "These damn roads ain't graded worth a damn," he said. "And there's another goddamn bridge up ahead," as the fifth in a series of narrow wooden creek crossings came into view. The wide GMC dump trailer barely squeezed through, and the old planks creaked ominously. Lamar watched in the side mirror as the crane truck and the rest of the caravan followed. They had a couple of irritated motorists behind the procession, he noticed. Well, that could not be helped.

The last truck rumbled over the bridge. "Our luck ain't gonna hold out forever," George said.

"That's why I brought a light crane."

"Yeah, it ain't but three times as heavy as these bridges were built to take." George spat out the window. "I got a bad sense about this job, Lamar."

Lamar looked out the window. He had watched the wide rolling fields slowly give way to swampy land, shaded by cypress and filled with tiger lilies and palmetto ferns. He had never liked the lowland country. It was getting toward noon, and hot, the drowsy, humid warmth of early summer. It had been over an hour's drive to Blessed Shoals, the Shadman County seat, and it was nearly another hour from there to the job. Lamar grimaced. Four hours of travel time out of every day. He mopped his bald, sweating head with a blue handkerchief. It would be worth it, he told himself. Even with the overtime, the gas and hauling expenses, it would be worth it.

Still, he wished he hadn't had to take the job.

It was not because of Greymare's reputation. That did not bother him. But when the contractor had offered him the job he had driven out and looked at the place, peered in the windows and walked around the grounds. Greymare was a magnificent house still, despite its dilapidated condition. It did not deserve to be destroyed. Lamar loved well-built structures, no matter what the style or period. He had no difficulty in reconciling that love with his work. Demolishing old buildings was a necessary part of raising new ones. He saw his work at times as

granting a quick death to buildings that had grown old in service and deserved to die honorably beneath the crushing blow
of the ball, rather than degenerate into ruin. The wife said he
was crazy, but he didn't mind being a little crazy. Being a little
crazy was the only way to stay sane in this world.

But this house was not ready to go. Despite its weathered exterior and broken windows, it was still in good shape; restored,
it could easily last another century.

No, it did not deserve to be destroyed. But, he reminded
himself, he did not deserve to go broke either. It was him or the
house, and he did not intend to be the one brought down.

Because of the winding road and the trees, they were upon the
plantation before they saw it. It was on higher land, surrounded
by what had been rice and cotton fields and were now overgrown
with witch grass and thistles. Greymare had once been the largest
plantation in the state, before the Civil War. Lamar could see the
overgrown clumps that had been the barn and outdoor kitchen
and slaves' huts; rebuilt, he had been told, several times in an attempt to restore Greymare to the status of a landmark, but always
abandoned and left to rot again. Nothing worth salvaging there; a
single run with a dozer would bring them down.

The house, however, still stood, old but unyielding. It would
take all that they had to knock it down.

That's an odd way to look at it, he thought.

The truck's wide tires rolled across the overgrown lawn and
stopped. Lamar climbed down from the cab stiffly, putting both
hands over his kidneys and leaning backward to stretch. He
watched the rest of the equipment arrive: the other dump trailer,
the crane and forklifts. Following them were five old Ford
Econolines carrying the crew, and a flatbed truck with the
portable heads. Clouds of diesel smoke drifted low over the grass
as the engines shut down. The crew disembarked, cursing tiredly
about the long ride, a few finishing jokes and stories. All of them
gradually became silent as they turned to stare at the mansion.

Lamar looked at them looking at the house. Some of the

crew were new, for he had hired several men for loading and cleanup in Blessed Shoals. One of these, a young fellow named Jim Driffs, crossed himself as he looked at the house. Lamar looked at his own crew, most of whom had been with him for years. George Colby had helped him start the company nine years previously; the tall black man was one of his closest friends. He stood now beside the dump trailer, fingers hooked in suspenders, staring at the mansion.

Beside him was Alice, the crane operator, tucking her hair under her hard hat. Alice was the only woman in the crew; as far as he knew, she was the only woman in any wrecking crew in the state. She was forty-seven, a stocky, solid woman, not beautiful at all until one got to know her. She had lost a husband in Korea and a son in Viet Nam, and was possibly the best crane operator Lamar had ever seen.

Those two had been with him the longest. The others had joined as the firm grew—Freddie and Larry Tom, the drivers, Dawson, Pettus and the other loaders, and the trimmers and bar men. And there was Randy Warren, the latest addition to the crew. He was twenty years old, the youngest on the crew. He looked uneasy and out-of-place, too soft for the hard hat and coveralls he wore. Lamar frowned, wondering if he should have brought his nephew along. This was only summer work for Randy, before he went back to college. Lamar did not want any valuable scrap damaged due to inexperience. He shrugged. The boy deserved a chance.

The crew's silence he took to be what he felt: appreciation, even awe, for the majestic old house. Lamar walked through the tall grass, waving absently at the clouds of midges, and stopped at the steps leading to the wide, porticoed entrance. Leaning back, he admired the house. The style was mixed: classic pilasters were combined with Gothic gables, lancet windows and Tudor half-timbered walls. But the effect was unifying and impressive. Though it had stood vacant for almost five years and the storms and seasons had weathered it sadly, still it was imposing. It was three stories tall, wide and sprawling. To keep most of the salvage it would have to be hand-torn, and that would take a month or more. Lamar sighed. It was a crime to do it—more than a crime, almost a sin, almost as if he were destroying a life. . . .

"Lamar?" George had approached him and now tapped him on the shoulder. Lamar turned quickly, startled, and George retreated a step. "We'd better get started," he said quietly. "It's noon already."

". . . Sure. Just daydreaming, I reckon. Let's get on it."

He glanced toward Randy and noticed the boy sitting in the shade of one of the vans. That annoyed him slightly—he hoped Randy didn't think he could slough off just because he was family. He did not know the boy all that well; Grace, Lamar's sister, lived in Atlanta, which was a considerable trip. Well, now he would see what Randy was like.

"Randy! Come on, we're gonna open it up. Get your boots and gloves—no telling what varmints have moved in." Randy looked up, then grinned reluctantly. Lamar nodded; the boy at least could make the best of a situation.

He named several others to accompany his nephew. To his surprise, not only Randy looked reluctant—they all did. It must be the heat, he thought. No one wants to work. Well, neither did he, but that was the way it was.

They approached the door, a large, carved oaken panel secured by a rusted padlock and hasp. There was no result from Lamar's key; he tugged at the lock, then took an adze from one of the men, lifted the heavy wrecking tool and brought the blunt end down on the lock. The sound of metal against metal was very loud. It took three blows to shatter it, and then the door swung open. It did not creak, as Lamar had expected; instead, it opened silently and slowly, revealing the shadowed foyer.

Lamar looked inside, then back at the men on the porch. They stood in a tight, silent group. "So what the hell is wrong with everyone?" he asked. "I've seen mules in quicksand move faster!" He looked at his nephew. "You planning on working like this all summer long?"

Randy looked back at him intently. "Don't you feel it?"

"Feel what? And what the hell are you whispering for?"

"This house."

"What about it?"

Randy glanced at the rest of the crew, then shrugged and said, "Well, this may sound silly, Uncle Lamar, but I don't think this house wants us here."

Lamar looked from Randy to the rest of them, all poised in uncomfortable stances, hands shoved into back pockets, heavy boots shuffling. But no one said anything further, and at last he had to ask, "What in hell does *that* mean?"

It was Jim Driffs, one of the hired loaders from Blessed Shoals, who answered nervously. "Well, Mr. Warren, there's been an awful lot of stories about this place." He swigged down the last bottle of warm Pepsi. "Lot of people lived here and died here, and there's those that say none of them people every really left. That there's something in this house that keeps them here. Something evil. And if you tear the place down—it might not like it."

"You didn't seem too worried about all this when I hired you," Lamar said.

Jim Driffs shrugged. "I needed the money. And Greymare was a good forty miles away. Now I'm standing on the front porch, and I wonder how bad I need that money." He looked about at the others, somewhat embarrassed at his speech, and seemed relieved when it was obvious that many of them felt the same way.

Lamar almost made the mistake of laughing—but then he looked closer at each of them, and realized that the house really did scare them, all of them. Even George Colby, who usually had a head as level as a bulldozed lot, seemed nervous.

"Y'all wait here," he said, and walked back to the trucks. Stepping out into the sunlight, he blinked at the sudden heat and light. He hadn't realized just how cool it had been on the porch.

He got several six-battery flashlights, and when he approached the porch again it was with an odd reluctance, considering how hot the sun was. He handed the flashlights to Randy, George and the others. "Let's go," he said cheerfully, and stepped across the threshold.

The cool air inside raised gooseflesh on his arms. He wrinkled his nose at the musty odor, the smells of dead insects and rotting fabric. The foyer opened into a huge main room, of which shuttered windows and heavy curtains made a vast, dim cavern. Lamar flicked on his light, and the powerful beam cut the darkness. There was no furniture left, which made the room seem even more gigantic. A huge, cut-crystal chandelier hung from the ceiling. Lamar turned the light into corners and along the walls, checking to make sure no vagrant lay asleep in a pile of rags. He could hear the squeak and scurry of rats, and he suppressed a shudder. Dealing with vermin was part of the wrecking business, but still, he hated rats. He remembered once demolishing an entire block of tenements; as each building came down, the rats had fled to the next, until at last they were all hiding in the last structure to be blasted. The old brick walls had fairly hummed with the sound of hundreds of thousands of panicked rodents. He had had to go in to plant the charges . . .

He gulped a sour taste and let the light ripple up a wide, balustraded staircase that led to the second floor. "Gonna flake that whole thing loose, if we have the time," he said, and the echoes of his voice made Randy and the others start. They had followed him in, as he knew they would—he was a good man to work for, and he inspired loyalty in his crew. They would not let him go in here alone. Lamar smiled as he looked at the hardwood floor, which had ornamental borders of teak. Against the far wall was a carved mahogany mantel framing a fireplace large enough to stand upright in, with a cast iron fireback. The house was a palace, no doubt of it. There was plenty of money in this room alone, and eighteen other rooms awaited his inspection.

He flashed the light back at Jim Driffs, who ducked as

though struck at. "Some of you open these windows, let a little light and air in here! That should chase the spooks away!" He was immediately sorry he had added that—it sounded too contemptuous. Then he became angry at his regret as he watched them move reluctantly into the darkness, their flashlight beams shimmering off curtains of cobwebs. Was he going to have to mollycoddle the whole crew through this job?

He speared Randy and George with his light. "Come on, you two! Let's give this place the once-over."

To the left, a huge, linteled archway opened into the dining room. The dark walls gave off no reflection. From the ceiling hung an anachronism: a 1920's style ceiling fan with wooden blades, which the movers had somehow overlooked. Lamar trod on something that crackled; his light revealed the shed skin of a rattlesnake. "Watch your step," he said, and heard Randy gulp.

They continued into the kitchen, which had been a later addition to the mansion, replacing the outdoor kitchen of plantation days. A windowed rear door provided faint light. The gritty smell of decomposition came from a bloated dead rat under the double-basin sink. Lamar turned away to a door by the recessed pantry. As he reached for the glass knob, Randy said abruptly, "Don't open it!"

Lamar paused with his hand on the knob. "And why not?"

Randy looked sickly pale in the reflected brilliance of the flashlights. "It's probably . . ."

"Probably the cellar," George said. "Lots of rats, most likely."

Lamar glared at both of them. "I've about near had it with all of you," he said. "This ain't nothing more than an old house! Now we got to check out the cellar, same as everyplace else." He realized he was raising his voice because he was nervous himself; the feeling puzzled and angered him. There was nothing to be frightened of in Greymare House. Outside of the rats . . .

He released the knob. "All right. It don't matter what order we go through the place. Randy, you and I will try that staircase," and he pointed toward another half-open door, with a flight of steps leading upward. "George, get outside and set the trimming crew to marking the place."

"You don't have to tell me twice." George started out of the kitchen, then looked over his shoulder at them. "Be careful up there," he said, and left.

The steep, narrow staircase was most likely the slaves' route to the upper quarters of the house, Lamar thought. It was dusty and close, and once a rat skittered down the steps causing them both to jump. It opened onto a vast hallway on the second floor, one side of which had windows looking down on what had been an orchard. On the other side were four bedroom doors. Lamar stepped forward, then stopped in surprise.

"What is it?" Randy was still on the stairs.

"Chilly here," Lamar said. He waved one hand in the air as he advanced. After five steps, the feeling of cold air surrounding him lessened, and the humid summer warmth returned. He walked down to the other end of the hallway, but there was no further change in temperature. Then he turned and looked at Randy, who still stood on the last step, staring at him with wide eyes.

"Well, come on," Lamar said. "You scared of catching a cold now?"

Randy stepped into the hallway, then stopped. His eyes grew even wider, and he wrapped his arms about himself.

"It's not *that* cold," Lamar said impatiently.

"Yes, it is!"

Lamar could hear his nephew's teeth chattering. He stepped again into the chill area, which did not seem nearly as cold to him as it evidently did to Randy, took his nephew's arm and pulled the young man forward. "See? Nothing to be afraid of. Just a little draft. Hot as a turkey in the oven here, ain't it?"

Randy looked over his shoulder. "I'll be—" he did not finish the sentence. "It's a genuine cold spot."

"I don't need to be told it was cold."

"I mean it's a classic psychic phenomenon." Randy started to extend his hand into it, but did not. "I've read about them— they're a common occurrence in haunted houses."

Lamar sighed. "I can't believe that you, a college-educated boy, believes in ghosts." He was disappointed; he had admired Randy at least for his book learning.

"I didn't say I believe in ghosts, if you mean dead folks' spirits. But there's something wrong with this mansion, Uncle— and a lot of college-educated people would agree with me. I've talked to scientists at the university who say that ghosts are as good an explanation for the way the world works as anything else." Randy looked around him and shivered, though he was no longer in the cold spot.

"What, *scientists* believing in *spooks?*"

"Physicists," Randy said. "You'd be surprised at some of the things they believe in. Listen—let's go downstairs. We don't need to go through the rest of Greymare House, do we?"

"If you're doing a job," Lamar said, "you got to do it all the way, even if no one knows it but you. Come on, now." He started down the hall, and to his satisfaction saw Randy take a deep breath and follow him.

He entered the first bedroom, dimly lit by the hall windows. It was empty of furniture; Lamar looked with satisfaction at the ornate wainscoting and parquet floor pattern. In the second bedroom the walls were covered with peeling, patterned wallpaper. He glanced behind the door perfunctorily and almost missed the mirror. He swung the door almost shut and looked at it. It was full-length, the glass acid-etched with tracery, the frame brass, with finials and candlestick holders. It was a beautiful piece of work, and it was all his. He looked at his reflection in the gloom: a short, solid man with a fringe of gray hair and lines, broken veins in the nose. Despite the belly pushing over the belt, he felt he could say he was still in good shape.

He frowned and looked closer at his reflection. There was something slightly odd . . . perhaps it was just the lack of light. The reflection of the room looked different. Lamar squinted. There was nothing in the room, nothing in the reflection, and yet. . . .

The walls, that was it. The wallpaper was not faded and peeling, and cobwebs did not hang in the corners. Just the darkness? No, for he could see the pattern very clearly where the light from the door struck it.

Something moved in the shadows of the mirror.

He wheeled about, and at the same time he heard the scream. He aimed his flashlight as he would a gun, illuminating nothing but cobwebs; at the same time he pulled the door open and ran into the hallway, in time to see Randy staggering back from the open door of the last bedroom. The boy's face was plaster white, and one hand was out in front of him. He turned and stumbled into Lamar, who took him by the shoulders and held him up. Lamar's heart was pounding. "What? What was it?" he demanded.

"The—the bed . . . blood. . . ."

Lamar released him and started toward the last bedroom.

It took considerable effort on his part to do so. Randy's constant prattling about Greymare being haunted was obviously beginning to affect him. He could have sworn he saw something large and dark come toward him in the mirror. . . .

He took a deep breath and stepped into the room.

It was empty, save for a large, brass-framed double bed. It had evidently been standing there for years; it was still covered with a patchwork quilt, dusty and faded now. But there was nothing unusual about it, except that, like the mirror, it should not be there. He could understand the movers overlooking the mirror, but how could they have passed over such a large piece of furniture?

Whatever the reason, it was his now. He walked around it, admiring the brass frame. There was no trace of blood, on the quilt or on the floor. A floorboard creaking behind him brought him around quickly. Randy stood there, staring at the bed.

"Well?" Lamar asked quietly.

"I—I don't—" he exhaled hard and tried again. "The floor was covered with blood. The bed was soaked in it. I never knew there could be so much blood. It was pouring off the quilt. . . ."

"I don't see any blood."

"Neither do I—now."

Lamar turned away from him in disgust. This had gone too far. He had tried to be patient, but by God, enough was enough! He pointed his finger at his nephew. "If I hear one more word about this place being haunted—"

There was the sound of heavy footsteps running up the front stairs.

In spite of himself, Lamar jumped. Randy turned around with a gasp. Then George Colby came into the room, breathing hard and obviously frightened. "Thought I heard someone holler," he said.

Randy stood quite still. "You didn't," Lamar replied, and saw his nephew relax slightly. "Just a squeaking hinge. How are things downstairs?"

George looked uncomfortable. "Goin' slow, frankly. Things keep happening."

"Such as?"

"Such as a casement window banging shut on Frank Scully's head. Or Pettus burning his hands."

"How did *that* happen?"

George shrugged. "He went into the fireplace to see how that back was mounted. Minute he touched it, he came out yellin' his hands were burned."

"That's impossible," Lamar said.

George shrugged again.

Lamar looked back at Randy. His nephew's face was expressionless. "Randy, go on back downstairs and see if you can help. George and I will go on up here."

He saw the relief in Randy's eyes, balanced by the reluctance in George's. Then Randy was out of the room and down the stairs, the echoes of his retreat fading slowly in the thick warm air.

"I'm tired of wetnursing him," Lamar said. "All the time talking about ghosts, seeing things. I know you won't panic, even if this place does get on your nerves." He saw George's jaw tighten, and knew the man would not back down now.

The inspection of the rest of the floor went by without incident. They hurried through the rooms, saying little, and Lamar had to admit that even he was beginning to be bothered by Greymare House. He did not let any of this be noticed by George, however, who finally said, "I got to admire you, Lamar. I confess this place has me as nervous as a cat in a roomful of rocking chairs. But you don't feel it, do you?"

"I never was one to let my imagination run away with me," Lamar replied. "Never was scared of the dark when I was a kid—never understood why other kids were. My Grandpa used to tell us kids ghost stories, and my brothers and sisters would tie themselves into knots." He paused. "Just seemed silly to me. There's so much on this old world that can hurt you—why make up more things?"

"Knew a fella like that once," George said. "He'd spit in the Devil's eye on Halloween. He was like those folk what can't tell about music, what's the word?"

"Tone deaf?"

"Right, like that—'cept he was tone deaf to the supernatural."

"That's me, too." But Lamar did not feel comfortable saying it. For the first time in his life, he was feeling uneasy without knowing the cause of it. The creaks and groans of the old house as they walked through it made him nervous and jumpy. And, though he would not admit it, he was glad to have George with him.

"Ain't nothing left to check 'cept the attic," George said finally. Lamar nodded, believing it for a moment, and then realized that George was wrong. There was still the cellar to be investigated.

His stomach tightened at the thought. It's the rats, he told himself. Only the rats.

The door to the attic was squat and wide, set at an incline

against the stairs. It took both of their shoulders against it to open it.

Lamar was thinking about something Randy had said. He had an uneasy respect for science that he did not have for the supernatural. If scientists now believed in ghosts—well, that was very disturbing. After all, scientists had put men on the moon, you couldn't deny that, unless you were like old Abe Jeffries who still insisted it was all a hoax. But when you got right right down to it, what was more incredible—men walking on the moon, or ghosts walking the halls of Greymare?

It was not quite dark in the attic; some light and air came through the venting eaves and the shuttered windows. But it was dark enough. The attic was L-shaped, bending about the inclined doorway. Lamar flashed his light toward the large side of the room. He saw nothing except dust and webs, some scraps of cloth and paper. A hornets' nest hung near the ladder to the cupola. Lamar heard the whispering movements of the rats. It sounded, he suddenly thought, almost like someone or something chuckling.

It was then that George said, in a careful calm voice, "Randy ain't the only one who's seeing things, Lamar."

Lamar turned and looked at him. George was staring at one of the rafters near the bend in the room. He was standing quite still, save that his hands were trembling.

Lamar saw nothing. "What is it, George?"

"You mean to say you don't see it?"

"Not a thing." And that was true. But he *felt* something; it was as though the nervousness he was feeling somehow seeped out of him and poisoned the air about him. It was a heavy, close sensation, and he felt his muscles tightening in response, his breathing growing more rapid. The scurrying of the rats increased, and the sound seemed more and more like dry, whispery laughter, the laughter of something old and evil.

"Describe it to me, George."

George said slowly, "I see a body hanging from that there

beam, by a hemp rope. It's the body of a Confederate soldier, looking like it was hung yesterday. And underneath that, there's a Union soldier, lying in his blood. I swear I see those things as plain as I see you."

Lamar went forward and stopped beneath the beam. His heart was beating fast enough to make him dizzy, but he was determined to show none of his fear. "Here?" he asked. He flashed his light up at the rafter, saw nothing but wood.

"You—you're right beside 'em, Lamar. You're standing in that Yankee's blood. Please—don't go no closer. I'm awful scared that they're gonna move. . . ."

Lamar still could not see anything, but now he most definitely felt something. His heart was pounding like a jackhammer, and the hair on his arms was standing up. The air seemed charged with electricity. He forced himself to breathe slowly.

He stepped around the corner to see what lay beyond it.

As he did, he felt as though he broke through a wall of spiderwebs—that insubstantial, yet at the same time very strong. The feeling of electricity in the air vanished. Behind him, he heard George say in amazement and relief, "They're gone! Just like soap bubbles!"

Lamar put a hand against the wall to keep himself upright. The release of tension left him feeling weak. "Well, then," he said, "come on and see what they were hiding."

George approached and looked around the corner. He still looked calm, but there was a jerkiness to his movements and a bright sheen of sweat on his brown temples.

Before them was a small rolltop desk.

"Do you suppose they was hiding it?" George whispered.

"I don't know what to think," Lamar replied, "except that we've been finding more booty in this house than in Cap'n Kidd's cave." He examined the lock on the desk. It was locked, and he had no intention of forcing it open. "We'll figure a way into it later, maybe," he said. "Let's get it out of here."

It was not heavy. They carried it down to the second floor

hallway. Lamar mopped his face with his handkerchief. "We'll leave it here for the crew to take out. Let's get downstairs. We got work to do."

It took all his willpower to walk slowly down the wide, curving staircase.

Most of the crew had assembled outside. There was little talk among them, Lamar noticed. Other items had been found, and assembled on the overgrown lawn: a wingback chair, a dry sink, a gate-leg table. Lamar looked at them in satisfaction. There were antique dealers who would pay a great deal for treasures like these. Outside the house, in the bright warm sun, he realized how foolish he had been to let the others' fears get to him. It was unfortunate about the bruise on Skully's head—unfortunate, but hardly the work of ghosts. The old counterweight ropes in the window had no doubt broken, that was all. As for Pettus' hands, that would be a bit harder to explain, but he was sure there was a reason. Fire ants, possibly.

"Well, time's wasting," he said. "Let's get started. We'll break down the attic first—"

He stopped abruptly, for he had once again remembered the cellar. He had not looked down there, nor had anyone else. Let it go, he told himself. After all, the tearing started at the top; it would be weeks before they had to concern themselves with the cellar. Let it go, or send someone else down. But as he looked at the faces of his crew, watching him, he knew none of them would do it. Could he ask one of them to go where he was reluctant to go?

His words to Randy came back to him: You got to do a job all the way, even if no one knows it but you.

This is foolish, he told himself angrily. It's only a cellar. There's nothing down there except a few old boxes, possibly some old furniture. . . .

And the rats.

The thought made Lamar ill. Nevertheless, his voice was steady as he continued, "Start trimming down the attic, while I check out the cellar." He turned back toward the house, feeling some small amusement at the surprised and worried looks his announced intention had caused.

As he stepped back onto the porch, Randy called, "Uncle Lamar—!" and stopped, as though unable to finish.

Lamar looked back at him and said, "George'll get you started on a job." He looked at George, who was staring at him in disbelief and worry, and said with as much cheeriness as he could, "Be back in a minute." Then he was inside the house again, listening to his footsteps echo as he walked toward the kitchen.

When he opened the cellar door, he could not help recoiling a step from the sheer intensity of the darkness—it was like a black curtain. There was also the damp, earthy smell of mold and rat dung. Lamar started down the steps, holding the flashlight out before him. The beam, more than enough for the darkness upstairs, seemed almost absorbed by the close cellar night.

There was nothing to be afraid of, he told himself. All right, so maybe there was something wrong with Greymare House— maybe it *was* haunted. Just because he had never seen a ghost did not mean there wasn't something to the idea. But he had heard somewhere that there was no record of ghosts having hurt people—the most they could do was appear and frighten. And perhaps they could not even do that to him, for he had not even seen what Randy and George saw—

The risers under the last step were loose—he tripped and almost fell on the slippery stone floor. One hand, flailing to regain his balance, ripped through the sticky gauze of a spiderweb above him. He ducked, feeling the back of his neck prickle with the expectation of something loathsome dropping down his shirt. He almost turned and bolted back up the stairs. Calm *down!* he told himself fiercely. He struck out with the flashlight beam against the darkness. He had never been afraid of the dark before in his life, but this darkness was different— he could almost feel it, wrapping about him, seeking to smother him.

He flashed the light around the cellar.

It was very large—much larger than he had expected. As the light swung about, he heard the scrabbling sound of rats running, could see the green gleam of their eyes. The smell of them, mixed with the other smells of decay and dampness, made him feel ill. It was not cool in the cellar, not even as cool as it had been on the porch. Instead, it was oddly warm, a humid, jungle warmth.

He could see the chewed remnants of cardboard boxes and old newspapers, shredded by rat teeth and claws to make nests. There were a lot of nests. Somehow, he could never manage to catch the rats in the light longer than momentarily. But he could see enough to know that they were big.

Lamar walked out into the cellar, turned and shone the light under the steps. Nothing there but webs; he saw one huge black widow spider frozen by the beam, the hourglass like a drop of blood. He backed away, his back still hunched, though the joists were far over his head. He turned around again, panning the light, causing the rats to jump and burrow into their nests in an attempt to escape it. God, he thought, how the scratch and patter of all those claws did sound like dry, sinister laughter.

He turned back toward the stairs. There was nothing down here worth having. But, as much as he wanted to leave the cellar, he hesitated. There was something about the floor. . . .

Lamar shone the beam over the floor again. The pool of light stopped on a large square that was a different shade of black. It was a trap door, old and moldy, with a ring handle near one end. Greymare House had a subcellar.

Lamar stared at it, not breathing, thinking: I've got to check it out, too.

He shook his head, feeling gooseflesh alive all over him. I can always say I didn't see it, he told himself. But instead of retreating, he approached the trapdoor with stiff, numb legs until he stood over it, looking down at it, the moldy wood shining in the light.

The rats were quiet now, he realized. As though they were waiting. Not one moved, but he could still hear the laughter, papery and evil and coming closer . . .

The trap door moved.

He screamed, and suddenly the cellar was alive with rats, rushing everywhere, startled by his scream; he kicked them and trod upon them as he ran toward the stairs. He tripped on the loose step, falling; the flashlight slipped from his fingers, hit the floor and the darkness was complete about him, suffocating him as he went up the steps on his hands and knees, feeling rats running over him, the sound of them deafening. He crawled for a lifetime, driving splinters into his fingers and knees, until suddenly he was lying on the tiled kitchen floor and kicking shut the cellar door.

He lay there for a moment, sobbing and shuddering. Then he stood, leaning against the wooden counter until his breathing returned to normal. Then he yanked open the back door and walked out into the hot afternoon sunlight.

He stood near the rusting husk of a bell that had once been used to summon slaves from the fields, and looked at the house. It looked no less stately and solid from the back. Lamar looked at it, let his eyes travel up to the dormered attic windows and the cupola. He could hear faint sounds from within as the crew went about stripping the walls of panelling.

For the first time in his life, he had been terrified by his own imagination. It could not be anything else, he told himself. There could not possibly be anything alive in that subcellar.

Nevertheless, he swore he would not see that cellar again until the house above had been ripped away and the sun allowed to burn out the filth and mold.

He stared at the house, feeling none of the admiration and regret he had when he first saw it. All that had changed, now. He was going to enjoy this job.

"I'm gonna bring you down," he said to Greymare House.

* * *

The trimming crew started on the attic and second floor, and soon the sultry afternoon air was full of the sounds of nails shrieking loose from wood and chisels stabbing into plaster. Lamar looked in satisfaction at the amount of salvage that began to come out of the house. Greymare was a treasure trove of woodwork alone: the carved walnut window casings, the redwood ceiling beams and corbels, the mahogany railings . . . all this would resale at a fine price. He had to make a good profit at this job, he thought grimly; otherwise, the Warren Wrecking Company would not last much longer. He could not afford for things to go wrong.

But things did go wrong.

One of the first jobs was flaking loose the cupola from the roof and lowering it with the crane. This was Alice's job. She sat in the worn green leather chair in the open cab, her grinning face protected by a visored helmet, and worked the hoist and swing levers with a delicate touch. The heavy ball and hook at the end of the cable came within reach of the crew men on the roof, and was secured to the ropes woven around the cupola. Lamar listened to the heavy chugging of the diesel engine as the cupola lifted free of the roof, hovered a moment and then swung slowly away from the roof as the crane house turned. He watched Alice fondly. He had often claimed she could lift a baby from a carriage without waking it. Which is why he was so shocked to see the boom suddenly jerk slightly, and the dangling cupola suddenly snap free of its ropes and plummet downward. It was a large cupola, almost big enough for a man to stand upright in, with an iron weathervane tipped with an arrow. The men in the flatbed truck beneath it, who had been waiting to guide the cupola to its resting place on sawhorses, stood frozen in disbelief; then they leaped over the sides of the truck as the cupola crashed into it, shattering a chair and table set that had already been roped into place.

Lamar and the rest of the crew ran to the truck. The cupola and the majority of the furniture on the truck had been smashed to kindling, though thankfully no one had been hurt. Lamar felt a hand on his shoulder and turned to see Alice, her square face pale with shock and disbelief.

"I swear I don't know how it happened, Lamar."

"It's okay," he said. She was blinking back tears; he held her wide shoulders soothingly, attempting to calm her. "It's okay. You've gone for nine years without an accident—you're still 'way ahead of the game." She looked at him gratefully. He turned back to look at the damage done and saw George Colby standing nearby, looking at him. The tall man's face was non-committal, but for some reason Lamar felt quick rage rise up within him. "What the hell you staring at, George? Ain't we lost enough time and money? C'mon, let's get back to work!"

George merely nodded without comment, and turned and walked briskly back toward the house. But Lamar could see him slow for a moment as he crossed the threshold, as though reluctant to enter.

He turned away from the others, who were looking at him in surprise at his outburst. It was unlike him, he knew. Well, Christ, if Alice was allowed an accident, he was certainly allowed to get upset over it.

He looked back at the house, and muttered a curse.

The work continued. Shingles fell from the roof like dirty brown leaves. Tied wood joints were cut, and the bargeboard came down. By the time the long slow summer evening was complete, a large hole in the roof had been opened and the attic stripped bare. One man had been wasp-stung from the nest there, and another had cut his arm on the flange of a metal vent, but such minor injuries accompanied every job. There was nothing, really, to indicate anything out of the ordinary was going on, Lamar told everyone repeatedly. Yet, as the sun sank behind the trees and dark, knifelike shadows slid over the grounds, the crew made haste to vacate Greymare House. They assembled around the trucks, silent and pensive for the most part. A few among them professed to sense nothing wrong with the house, but they did not voice their opinions very loudly.

Lamar did not know what he could say to the crew to cheer them up. For the first time since he had started this company, he felt unable to talk to his employees. It was all foolishness, he told himself irritably; and the worst of it was, he was being affected by it. He flushed at the thought of his behavior in the cellar, though no one knew about it but him. There could not be anything down there. This house was simply a job, like any other.

Still, as the truck pulled away from the grounds and he looked back at the house, limned in the red sunset, he could not help shuddering. If ever a house should be haunted, Lamar thought, Greymare House was it.

They arrived early the next morning, and the work continued. Forklifts carried wood and debris to the loaders, wrenches loosened bolts, screwdrivers removed screws and hinge pins. While work proceeded on the main house, Lamar instructed Bill Antoine to dozer down the mounds of rotting wood and kudzu that had once been the rebuilt slaves' cabins.

The yellow scoop dozer rolled down toward the old buildings, its wide tires crushing elephant's-ear plants and Judas vine, the engine firing slowly, sending puffs of blue smoke from the upright exhaust. Antoine lowered the blade, and the wide curved wall of metal hit the gray wood, pushed it forward with hardly a change in the engine's sound, grinding it into the red dirt like a lawnmower running over an ant hill. Lamar, watching, could smell the strong sweet smell of crushed plants mingling with diesel smoke. He felt a fierce satisfaction as the first building collapsed. See that, house? he thought, amused at his feelings but nevertheless enjoying them. See that? You're next.

The dozer struck the second building. A yellow explosion of sunflower birds scattered from beneath the eaves as their home was destroyed. Lamar turned away toward the house, intending to go inside and get out of the heat. He stopped at the sight of Randy, standing near a skiploader with Jim Driffs and several other men. Randy was talking; the others were listening and nodding.

Lamar started toward them; at that moment, nephew or not, he was ready to fire Randy. Why prolong a bad situation? The boy was obviously not taking his work seriously. Let him go back to college and his crazy professors.

But he had not taken three steps when he heard a scream from behind him, coming just after the crash of the dozer into another building. Lamar spun around, shocked, and saw Antoine leap down from the dozer, tearing his helmet off, to stand staring in horror at the structure he had just brought down.

Lamar ran back to him, puffing in the humid heat. He reached into the open cab of the dozer and shut off the motor. In the loud, throbbing silence that followed, he could hear Antoine's rasping breaths, verging on sobs, as he stood there with his face hidden in his hands. "What is it, Bill?" he asked. "What's happened?"

Antoine's voice was muffled behind his hands; his fingers were digging into his forehead, the nails drawing blood. His body rocked as the words came out. "I didn't know anybody was in there, Lamar, honest to God I didn't—oh, God, I'm sorry, I'm sorry, that poor little girl. . . ."

Lamar looked down at the crushed and oozing tangle of plants and wood. There was no sign of a body in the wreckage. A shadow fell across the scene, and he looked up to see George. Remembering what had happened in the attic, he pointed to the ground beneath the blade and asked, "See anything?" dreading the answer.

George shook his head.

Lamar sighed in relief. "It's okay. Bill." He tried gently to pull the man's hands from his face.

"No—don't make me—I don't want to see her—"

"Ain't nothing to see. Look."

Antoine's hands crept slowly down his face. He looked, and blood followed the lines on his forehead as his eyes went wide. "Oh, thank the Lord!"

"Tell me what you saw."

"It was a young black girl—no more'n a child—the—" he shuddered. "—the blade had took off the top of her head—her eyes still open—" He covered his own eyes again.

Lamar looked down at the crushed cabin again. Then he said to George, "Take care of him," turned and walked away. The members of the crew that had gathered parted to let him through. "Keep working," he said in a low voice, and slowly, reluctantly, they returned to their jobs.

During the rest of the day minor accidents plagued them. A loader, his arms full of panelling, tripped over a bootscraper outside the back door and cut his shin. The engines on the machinery would sputter and die for no reason. A trimmer was bitten by a rat and had to be rushed to the Blessed Shoals Hospital.

Lamar told himself that such misfortunes could happen on any job. But he could not explain the hallucinations more and more members of his crew were having, or the feeling of tension in the air. A worker would rip a section of wainscoting from a wall and suddenly stop in a cold sweat and stare over his shoulder. Lights were strung everywhere, banishing the darkness, and by unspoken agreement no one went into any of the rooms alone.

Riding back along the winding, twisted roads, hemmed in by darkness, Lamar stared at the black and white glare of the headlights on the road. Only the second day, he thought, and already they were behind schedule.

There were more ways than one to demolish a house. He remembered the tenement building, and the living carpet of rats he had crossed to plant the dynamite that had brought the building down. He looked out the side window, into the darkness, and saw the brief glimmer of foxfire in the swamp. He shivered.

*    *    *

The next day, most of the loaders Lamar had hired locally did not return. "There ain't much we can do about it," George told him. "We won't be able to get anybody from that town to help tear this place now."

"We'll have to just get on as best we can," Lamar said. The walkout had come as a shock to him. But they had to keep going; the company's future depended on their completing this job.

This day went no better. One of the small bobcat dozers punctured a dump loader's tire with the corner of its sharp blade as the driver was swinging around. A large section of masonry simply fell from one of the gables, narrowly missing several men. The crew worked with the grim, leaden determination of convicts on a road gang.

At noon, Lamar was sitting under a large catfaced pine, eating a bologna sandwich. He sat alone. He noticed Randy and Jim Driffs—who, oddly, had not quit with the others—bending over the rolltop desk in the back of the flatbed. Lamar stood and walked quickly to the truck. He had spoken little to his nephew since the episode in the bedroom, but he had not been happy with Randy. The boy had refused to enter the house again, working instead outside on the cleanup crew. He had continued to talk to others, asking them what they thought of the house and of the strange things that had happened. Lamar felt he had bent over backwards to give Randy a chance to come around. He could not continue to let the boy stir up more anxiety; this job was causing him too much trouble as it was.

He also did not want him damaging the few pieces of furniture left intact, and so he leaned over the side of the truck. He saw Jim Driffs probing the desk's lock with a wire; before he could say anything there was a *click!* and Jim slid the top up. Lamar swung himself up into the truck with a grunt. Randy and Jim looked up in surprise, but Lamar's curiosity had made him forget his anger. They investigated the contents of the desk together.

The many shelves and drawers were crammed with the usual heterogenous collection that accumulates in desks: a brass candlestick with the melted remnant of a candle in it; a plate with a blue Currier and Ives design; several soiled and faded anti-macassars. There were also a great many yellowed papers and envelopes—and a diary.

All three of them reached for it—Randy seized it and opened it. Lamar covered the pages with his hand. "I'll read it," he said, surprised by the surliness in his voice.

Randy looked at him levelly for a moment, then handed the diary to him without comment. Lamar glared at the pages in confusion for a moment before he realized what was wrong. He felt heat creep up the back of his neck.

"What is it?" he growled.

"French."

Lamar gave the book back to him. Randy looked at the first page.

"It belonged to a woman named Danielle Avinaign . . . the first entry is dated October 15th, 1975. She must have been the last tenant . . . 'How happy Arnaud and I shall be here! This is a house much like the ones of which my mother told me; solid and spacious, with a depth and charm we could find nowhere in New Orleans' highly touted architecture. The movers have finally finished, and we are starting now to make sense of the great chaos they have left us. Arnaud says we will have to make do by ourselves for a time until proper servants can be found; this area is, after all, hardly the height of civilization! Nevertheless, it is what we have chosen for our remaining years; a simple and, God provide, peaceful existence—' " Randy frowned. "The page is torn slightly here, and inkstained—I think something startled her and she slashed the paper with the pen . . . uh-huh, listen: 'I must tell Arnaud to purchase some traps immediately. There are rats here.' " He stopped.

"That all?" Jim Driffs asked.

"All for that day." Randy turned over several pages.

"Sounds like she's trying to make the best of a bad situation," Lamar said, interested enough to forget his anger.

Randy glanced at him, then at the house behind them. "Doesn't it." He began to read again.

" 'The local inhabitants—in particular, one Eudora Hines, a local termagant with seemingly not a good word to say for anyone—have gone to great effort to acquaint me with the sordid history of Greymare. I have learned much that Arnaud did not tell me, though my sources can hardly be called reliable. If they are to be believed, Greymare is a veritable House of Usher. Since its antebellum origins, it has evidently been the site of constant murder and rapine. A few of the less disgusting events, as recounted to me by the salacious Madame Hines:

'The house was built by Claiborne Greymare in the late 1700's as a retreat for his ailing wife. She complained constantly of being cold, even in the summer, and she hated the house. Evidently she went quite mad, for she at last immolated herself in the downstairs fireplace. Greymare sold the house to William Jared, a cotton baron and from all accounts a devil in human form. He beat and tortured his slaves; Eudora has described how a slave was tied to what she terms "That catfaced pine out front," and whipped until he chewed the bark away in his pain. They say it has never grown back. This continued until the Civil War, whereupon the slaves rose up in revolt and literally hacked Jared to pieces while he slept, soaking his bed in blood—' " Randy stopped with a sudden gasp. "The bed!"

Lamar knew what he meant. "Now wait," he began. "That couldn't be the same bed—"

"Why couldn't it? I saw the blood, Uncle Lamar!"

"I don't think you better read any more." Lamar reached for the diary. Randy backed out of reach and continued reading rapidly.

" '—Evidently Greymare drew crimes of passion to it. During the war a young man in the Confederate Army stalked his brother, a Union soldier, through the house, killed him and then hanged himself—' "

"George Colby saw them in the attic!" Jim Driffs shouted.

Lamar was aware of others in the crew gathering around and listening to Randy's rising voice. He felt panic beginning within him—this could cause them all to walk out. "I said give me that!" he snapped, grabbing the diary from Randy's hands. Randy stumbled backward, sprawled over the desk and into a clutter of furniture and lumber.

The silence that followed was quite intense. Lamar and Randy looked at each other in shock. Finally, "I'm sorry, Randy," Lamar said. He leaned forward, offering a hand to his nephew. "This job's been a considerable strain to me—"

Randy ignored Lamar's hand as he got to his feet. "Uncle," he said quietly, "What's a catfaced tree?"

Lamar did not answer him. He did not seem to be able to organize his thoughts.

Jim said slowly, "It's what they call a scar on a tree that's healed around. Like that pine yonder," and he pointed to the tree under which Lamar had been sitting.

"That's a big tree," Randy said. "It's probably over a hundred years old."

He and Jim looked at each other. Then they both leaped from the truck bed and ran toward the tree, followed by several others who had been listening.

Lamar watched them helplessly. If only he knew the right things to say, he thought; the words that would bring them all to their senses, that would stop this increasing madness. . . .

"There!" Randy shouted, pointing at a spot on the tree trunk. "There it is!"

Lamar stared with the rest of them. He could see it quite clearly across the hot green distance: a white wound on the dark body of the tree, glistening with fresh sap.

The next day, half of the crew did not show up for work. George Colby arrived quite late. When Lamar saw him, he began to shout. "Goddamn them! They know this is a make-or-break job for us! How could they—"

"They could real easy," George said. "It ain't that easy for me, Lamar—but I got to do it anyway. I just come to tell you I won't be on this job no more."

Lamar stared at George. It was late afternoon, and they stood by Alice's crane, watching the few crew members left go about the day's work. "George," Lamar said slowly, "You're my right-hand man. You're co-owner of this here company. You—you were never one to lose your common sense, George. You've always had nerve. Remember that burnt job we had over in Beatriceville? We were in there with the scoop when half that burnt-out roof started falling."

"I remember."

"You never turned a hair," Lamar went on, his voice quietly desperate. "You just raised that blade over us like an umbrella. You saved both of us. Now you want to ruin me, George?"

"It won't work, Lamar," George said. "You got to remember—you don't feel what most of us feel in this house. Everytime a man puts a bar to it, seems like it cries out in pain—pain and hatred. You can't feel that. But those men that quit felt it. And I feel it. We stayed as long as we did because of you. But we can't stay no longer. Don't try to make us. Please. You don't know how it feels."

Lamar thought of the cellar; the thick warm darkness, and the cold gleam of the rats' eyes. The hell I don't feel it, he thought angrily. I'm as scared as you all are. But I've got a job to do. Aloud he said, "Go on then, if that's all the spine you have. But we ain't no union company. Don't think you can get your jobs back."

George looked at him with great sadness. "This ain't at all like you, Lamar. I don't know why you're being this way—but it don't change anything. We can't stay here! I'm telling you that house is *alive,* and it's fighting for its life! I'm telling the crew to pull out!"

"You'll put this company underground if you do!" Lamar grabbed George by his shoulders. "You're going to ruin us!"

"If I don't," George said, "Greymare House will!" He pulled free and started toward the house.

Lamar looked after him, seeing through a red filter of fury. They *had* to finish tearing this house! He could not let anything stop him—not the house, not the rats, and not George.

He started to run after him, but at that moment he heard a car pull onto the grounds behind him. He turned to see Randy's Volkswagen come to a stop. His nephew got out and ran toward him, the diary clutched in one hand. His face was quite pale, but full of determination.

"I read it," he said. "The whole thing, last night." He opened the book. "Listen to this: 'I am now convinced that Greymare House is the haven of some hostile, preternatural force, a malignancy that brings out and thrives upon the worst in people. It dwells within the cellar, or in the ground beneath Greymare and drives people to their deaths. But then—ultimate horror!— *it does not let them die.* Their spirits remain, tied to the halls and rooms of Greymare. I know this is true. I have seen in the empty cabins slaves William Jared tortured, such as the truncated specter of a little girl. I have seen his bloodied bed. In the mirror on my bedroom wall I have seen reflected things of which I cannot write.' " Randy turned the pages. "This is the last entry: 'It has taken Arnaud; driven him mad with horror. He has gone to it. The house will not let us leave. The doors close and lock themselves; the shutters cannot be forced. As I write this, the sun is setting. So far I have been able to keep my sanity, but its power is greater at night.

'The sun is almost down. I write this in the attic, as far away from the evil locus as possible. I can hear Arnaud's mad laughter far below. I can see the slain forms of the brothers, one lying in his blood, the other twisting slowly above him. And now the rats are appearing in the dusk . . . they seem quite fearless. . . .' "

Randy shut the diary with a snap. "That's all. Don't you see, Uncle? That spirit, or force, or whatever it is, is still there!"

Lamar looked at Randy, but could not see him clearly; there seemed to be a roaring in his ears, a soundless pounding that made his head ache. "It's impossible," he said slowly. "You're making it up. Can't nobody here but you read it—"

Before Randy could reply, they heard shouting from within Greymare House.

Lamar turned and ran toward the house. Randy hesitated a moment, then followed. Lamar pounded up the steps, colliding with men on their way out, running, clawing, fighting with each other to get through the door. Lamar pushed and shoved against them, at last tumbling into the dark interior.

Randy followed him in. George Colby was the only one still there. He stood staring into the fireplace. Lamar looked; at first he saw nothing. He stared, shaking with intensity, feeling it somehow very important that he see what they had seen.

Gradually, the room seemed to fill with flickering orange light. The huge stone fireplace became ablaze with flame; he could hear the crackling of pine knots and smell the smoke. And in the midst of the flames stood a woman. She had evidently just stepped into the fire, for her nightgown was still burning, her hair just beginning to ignite. As Lamar watched, rooted with horror, he saw her turn and stare at him; her blue eyes, at first filled with the calm of madness, suddenly widened as the agony brought realization. She threw back her head and screamed, as her skin began to blacken and shrivel. . . .

And then the scene seemed to waver, to ripple like disturbed water, and was gone. The fireplace stood empty and cold.

George turned to Lamar. "You saw that," he said quite calmly.

Lamar slowly nodded.

George turned and walked out the door. Outside was the sound of engines turning over. The men had piled into the old

Ford vans and the flatbed. Through the front door he could see them driving away at breakneck speed.

Randy grabbed his arm. "Uncle, we've got to get out of here!"

Lamar blinked. There were quite a few rats in the shadows he noticed—all still, all watching. He shook Randy's hand away and turned to face him. "This is your fault," he said thickly. "All of it. You turned my crew against me. . . ." He swung the back of his fist at Randy, felt his knuckles strike the boy's cheekbone, splitting the skin. Randy fell away from him and sprawled on the floor. He scrambled to his knees and ran, away from Lamar and the front door, toward the arch that led to the dining room.

Lamar looked blankly at his smarting hand, then after his nephew. The blow he had struck Randy seemed to have struck him as well, shocking him out of his rage. "Randy," he shouted. "Are you all right?" He ran after him.

He came through the archway and stopped. Randy stood in the middle of the dark, empty room, eyes wide and face bloodless, staring at the floor in front of him. Lamar heard the dry, sinister rattle even before he saw the snake. It was a huge diamondback, coiled a foot from Randy. Randy stood very still.

"Easy," Lamar whispered. "Take it easy," as he looked about for something to use as a weapon. There was nothing. Then, suddenly, his eyes caught a flicker of motion in the darkness above Randy. Lamar stared upward, unable to believe what he saw.

The ceiling fan was beginning to turn.

There was no electricity to power it, yet the fan was spinning; slowly at first, then faster. Randy looked up as the musty air breathed over him. The fan was spinning quite fast now, faster than it had been designed for. Lamar could feel the floor beginning to vibrate, could hear the high, keen whine of the wooden blades cutting the air. The fan was beginning to shake, but still it spun, faster and faster, producing a propwash that tore at their hair and clothes. Randy stood beneath it, staring alternately at it and the coiled rattlesnake. He closed his eyes and began to sob. A fine powder of ceiling plaster frosted the air. . . .

*No!"* Lamar screamed, as the fan tore loose from the ceiling and hurtled downward. He hid his face behind his arms, but could not avoid hearing Randy's scream, or the hideous sound that cut it off. He felt a wet mist on his arms as he hurled himself backwards, running across the floor under the watchful gaze of the rats.

He burst from the house and ran toward the abandoned heavy equipment. He sagged to his knees against the dump loader and was sick.

Then he stood, slowly, and stared back at Greymare House.

It stood, quiet, substantial and ominous against the afternoon sun. Most of the roof was gone, and part of the upper walls, but it had not been defeated. Lamar stared at it for a long time, feeling his horror and sorrow subside slowly, leaving nothing but icy determination.

He was alone. The crew had left, and Randy . . . Randy was dead. It was him against the house, now.

He would have to bring it down alone.

Lamar turned and climbed into one of the transport trucks. From a locked cabinet he brought forth an extra heavy pair of coveralls, gloves and a face visor. Then he lifted out a stout wooden box, and a wooden chisel and mallet. He stood the box on one end, and carefully tapped the cover loose. Within were the long, brick-red cylinders, packed in sawdust. He had packed the box two days before, telling no one. I could have lost my license for improper transportation of explosives, he thought, and let go a single note of dry laughter.

He worked slowly and carefully, refusing to let himself think about anything but the job. He snapped blasting caps onto each stick of dynamite, attached the black and red wires to each cap. He wired them in parallel, five to a set, and each set to a small radio receiver unit. Then he donned the coveralls, gloves and

visor, gathered up the dynamite and turned toward the house
again.

The sun was near the horizon, but it had not yet set. The
diary had said Greymare's power was weaker by day. And perhaps it would be weaker still after the effort it had just ex-
pended. In any event, he would have to take the chance.

Lamar took a deep breath, and walked toward the house.

The door had swung shut, and would not open until he used
a crowbar on it. He went inside.

It was as he had feared: the rats were there, everywhere, covering the floor in a dirty flood, the sound of their restless
prowling filling the room, sounding so much like laughter. . . .

Lamar swallowed bile and forced himself across the floor toward the fireplace, one of the structural strong points of the
house. The rats tore at his heavy boots, scrabbled up his legs,
slashing at his two pairs of coveralls with teeth and claws. He
clubbed them off with the crowbar. He put one of the sets of
dynamite on the mantel, where the rats could not reach it, then
turned and fought his way toward the kitchen, not looking at
Randy's body in the dining room. He left another of the sets on
the counter. As he did, a creaking sound swung him around,
and what he saw tore a scream from his throat. He turned and
clawed his way up the back stairs against the tide of rats. The
cellar door was opening. . . .

He ran, planting the rest of the dynamite against the supporting walls upstairs. The rooms and corridors were like a
maze; they seemed to twist and turn back on themselves, night-
marishly, as he searched for the front staircase. And everywhere were the rats, tearing at him, biting and clawing. But
even that was not the worst of it, for through the sound of the
rats he could hear laughter, coming closer, and he knew that
something was following him, something that had come from
the cellar to drag him back to it, something dark in the darkness
of the corridors, grinning, and gaining on him.

Lamar's clothes and gloves were ripped to shreds now, and

he had lost his visor. A rat leaped at him, sinking its teeth into his arm—he staggered back, and suddenly there was the staircase. He fell down it, dropping the crowbar, the bodies of rats cushioning his fall. He managed somehow to get to his feet. As he ran across the floor he glimpsed the huge chandelier above him swaying—he dodged to one side as it fell, crashing to the floor and spraying him with crystalline fragments. The front door was closing; Lamar hurled himself forward, twisting through the narrow opening. Then he was outside, stumbling across the grass in the bloody evening light.

Behind him, he heard the door open again.

Lamar did not look back. He ran toward the truck where he had left the detonator. Behind him something was coming, something even more horrible than the formless terror his mind pictured. It was close upon him, he knew, perhaps already reaching for him as he seized the detonator and, knowing he was still too close to the house, jammed both thumbs onto the button.

Then a huge, slamming sound, more felt than heard lifted and hurled him. Lamar felt himself turn completely over once. He did not feel himself hit, or hear the echoes of the explosion rumble away into the pattering rain of debris, and finally into absolute silence.

The last thing Lamar heard as he lost consciousness was the laughter.

When Lamar woke, it was night.

His awakening took a long time. He was semiconscious several times, feeling dimly the night breeze on his face and body, before sinking once more into blackness. At last he became fully conscious. One of the first things he noticed was the acrid smell of cordite. He tried to open his eyes, could only open one—the other seemed crusted over. He looked at a strange, upside-down scene: the blasted ruins of Greymare House.

The moon, just past full, illuminated everything in stark black and white. He had placed the charges well, Lamar thought, feeling absurdly proud of himself. Most of the house had been blown apart. The fireplace and chimney, the spine of the structure, had been broken, and the other blasts had disintegrated the already-weakened upstairs. One wall had collapsed completely, and only fragments of the other three stood. The first floor had caved in. Everywhere were scorched and twisted pieces of wood and metal, fragmented beams, shattered glass and tile. The front window had been blown out on one of the trucks, but he could see no other damage to the equipment.

Lamar was lying upside down in the bank of kudzu where he had been thrown by the explosion. Surprisingly, he did not feel much pain—not until he moved. Then a burst of agony from his left arm told him that it was probably broken. He was bleeding from cuts caused by the blast and the crashing chandelier, but none of them seemed too serious. All in all, he realized, he had been extraordinarily lucky. The plant wall had cushioned his fall and saved him from major injuries.

His movement, slight as it was, overbalanced him, and he slid slowly downward and toppled over, clenching his teeth against the pain as his arm was twisted. He grabbed a broken balustrade from the staircase that lay nearby and used it as a cane to pull himself to his feet. He put his hand to his eye to explore the damage, and took it away again quickly; most of the eye seemed to be gone. He felt faint and sick from his injuries, and he did not know how far he could walk. But he was alive. He was alive, and Greymare House was dead.

The night was very quiet, he thought. Then he realized that he had been deafened by the explosion. He looked up at the stars—his neck crackled painfully, but he kept his head up. I did it, he thought. I brought Greymare down.

He looked at the ruins again, and saw the rats.

There were not nearly as many as there had been. They were crawling about the ruins, and paid no attention to him as he limped painfully toward the truck. They were not interested in him, now that Greymare and its evil had been destroyed.

It would not be a comfortable ride back to Blessed Shoals—he did not know how he would shift gears with a broken arm. But he would manage somehow. He had already been through the worst, he told himself, as he made his slow way past Alice's crane.

The crane moved.

Lamar stopped, turned his head and stared at the crane. No, he said to himself. No. Please, no.

But as he watched, it moved again.

There was no mistaking it; the housing moved slightly, left, then right, like an animal sniffing. The boom lowered slightly, and the steel cables tightened.

Then it began to roll toward him.

Lamar backed up slowly, not thinking at all, simply watching. He could see the crane quite clearly in the moonlight, could see the deep, scarlike paths the treads were leaving in the ground, could see the empty cab, where no one was riding, no one pulling the hoist lever back. And yet the drum was slowly turning, the cable winding, and the clam shell bucket that had been used to pick up salvage was slowly rising, and opening.

The silence was the worst part of it. His deafness prevented him from hearing the creakings of the boom and cables, the clacking roll of the treads. But he knew that the engine was not running—he might not have heard the starter engine crank, but the heavy pounding of the diesel was a subsonic, gutwrenching sound that shook the ground. No, the motor was off—but the crane was moving.

It's not fair, he thought.

He stepped backwards again and stumbled, then slid down an embankment of loose earth, tumbling, crying out in agony.

He opened his one eye and realized he was in the cellar.

It had survived the dynamite quite well. Over half of the floor sagged, making a brooding cave. The rest was bathed in moonlight, the jointed stone a cold silver over which rats flickered like shadows. Lamar stood, staring at the center of the floor.

The trap door was open.

Of course, he thought quite calmly. It's stronger at night.

A movement overhead made him look up. The crane boom was swinging over him—and the bucket was dropping!

Lamar scrabbled to one side, feeling the vibration as the heavy steel bucket slammed into the stone beside him. He stared at it as it rose again, the welded bolts covered with dirt, the cables drawing open the serrated halves like giant jaws.

He half-ran, half-limped into the darkness beneath the first floor. A moment later the broken floor beams shook as the bucket dropped on top of them. Lamar hid under his good arm as small pieces of wood and plaster rained down on him.

The bucket struck again. The floor sagged. It was coming apart. He knew he could not remain under it.

He ran out, holding his broken arm in his good hand, trying to use his feeble momentum to carry him up the embankment. It was useless; he slid back down.

The bucket hit the stone beside him again. Lamar backed away, felt nothing under one foot—and then he was falling. . . .

He did not fall far. The impact knocked him breathless nonetheless. He tried to stand and could not.

He was in darkness, lying on a damp dirt floor. He looked up—the trap door was well out of reach.

He thought longingly of how the eventual sunrise would burn out the evil that had dwelt so long beneath Greymare. But it would not come in time for him.

Though he was deaf, he could still somehow hear the dry, crackling laughter—or was it the scrabbling of the rats? Something touched his ankle, began to creep up his leg.

Oh please, he thought; please—let it be a rat.

**Robert Aickman** (1914–1981) wrote fantasy and horror for much of the latter half of his life. Other stories of his appear in *The Dark Descent, Vampires,* and *Shudder Again.* He also edited the first eight volumes of the *Fontana Books of Great Ghost Stories.*

**Robert Bloch** (1917–1994) was known worldwide as the writer of the book *Psycho,* the basis for Alfred Hitchcock's famous film of the same name. He got his start writing stories for pulp magazines such as *Weird Tales, Fantastic Adventures,* and *Unknown.* Later in his career he wrote the novels *American Gothic, Firebug,* and *Fear and Trembling,* among many others. He also edited several anthologies, including *Psycho-paths* and *Monsters in Our Midst.*

**Elizabeth Bowen** (1899–1973) wrote primarily Victorian ghost stories, exposing the evil behind the nuanced manners of the period. Her short stories have been reprinted often in anthologies, and with good reason, as the included story illustrates.

**Edward Bryant** began writing professionally in 1968, and has since published more than a dozen books. His latest short story collection, *Flirting With Death,* was published in 1995. His work has appeared in such anthologies as *Orbit, Night Visions,* and *Blood Is Not Enough,* as well as such magazines as *Omni, Writer's Digest,* and *Locus.* He's won the Nebula Award (twice) and is currently living in North Denver finishing his next novel.

**Hugh B. Cave** was a mainstay author of many pulp magazines in the 1940s and 1950s. Later in his career he wrote several remarkable novels, including *The Cross on the Drum,* one of the few excellent novels examining the theme of voodoo. Other novels include *The Nebulon Horror, Disciples of Dread,* and *The Lower Deep.* His dozens of short stories have been collected in several anthologies, including *Murgunstrumm and Others, The Witching Lands,* and *Death Stalks the Night.*

**Jack L. Chalker** has written over thirty novels, including several series such as Well World, Changewinds, G.O.D., Inc. Ring of the Master and others, each containing several books. Before turning to writing he served in the Air Force and the Air National Guard and taught English, history and geography in Baltimore high schools. He lives with his wife, Eva, and his son in Westminster, Maryland.

**Charlotte Perkins Gilman** (1860–1935) is most famous for the following story, a tale of one woman's descent into madness and the house that begins the journey.

**Charles L. Grant** first rose to prominence in the horror field with his novels and short stories about Oxrun Station, a small Connecticut town which is occasionally visited by the supernatural. He later edited the acclaimed *Shadows* anthology series, which marked his standing in the field and set a new level of excellence for horror writers and fans everywhere. Other notable novels of his include *The Nestling, The Pet, In a Dark Dream,* and *Something Stirs.*

**H.P. Lovecraft** (1890–1937) was best known for his creation of Arkham County and the Cthulhu Mythos, where ancient unnamed gods, the "Old Ones," attempt to open a portal from another dimension to conquer Earth. A prolific contributor to *Weird Tales* magazine, his redefinition of the pulp horror tale, sparked new life into the genre. The lush, poetic descriptions and all-consuming sense of inescapable doom found in his work inspired such writers as Clark Ashton Smith and Manly Wade Wellman, and continues to draw interest today.

**William F. Nolan** is best known for his Logan Trilogy, *Logan's Run, Logan's World,* and *Logan's Search,* which detail a future world ruled by the young, where the most heinous crime is growing old. However, during his more than forty years as a professional writer, he has turned out over a thousand short stories and nonfiction works, as well as dozens of novels, scripts and teleplays in all genres and styles.

**Joyce Carol Oates** is renowned for her novels of psychological suspense, including *Zombie,* a recent Stoker nominee for best novel. Her short fiction has appeared in magazines such as *Omni, Glamour, Playboy,* and anthologies such as *Dark Forces.* Her non-fiction articles have been published in *The New York Times Review of Books,* among others.

**Michael Reaves** has worked in several facets of the fantasy genre, collaborating with fellow author Steve Perry on novels such as *The Omega Cage* and *Sword of the Samurai,* publishing his own work, the Shattered World series, and writing various episodes of the revived *Twilight Zone* and animated series such as *Centurions* and *The Spiral Zone.*

**Ruth Rendell** is the multiple award-winning author of dozens of novels, including *A Judgement in Stone, A Demon in My View,* and *King Solomon's Carpet.* Although she writes a detective series featuring Inspector Reg Wexford, many critics feel that her non-series novels are her most powerful, often dealing with adult themes and relationships in a frank and realistic manner. She lives in Colchester, England.

**Henry Slesar** is one of the great pulp writers of all time, with many of his stories appearing in *Alfred Hitchcock's Mystery Magazine, Ellery Queen's Mystery Magazine, Playboy* and many others. Alfred Hitchcock produced several of his short stories on his television show *Alfred Hitchcock Presents.* These stories were collected in the anthology *Death on Television: The Best of Henry Slesar's Alfred Hitchcock Stories.*

Born in Kansas in 1911, **Margaret St. Clair** is known for her novels of distant futures both adventurous and beautiful. Particularly noteworthy are *Vulcan's Dolls* and *The Shadow People*. Before she became a writer, she attended college at the University of California and worked in horticulture for several years.

**Bram Stoker** (1847–1912) is widely considered the father of the vampire story, with his novel *Dracula* setting the standard by which all later Gothic fiction was judged. He wrote several other horror novels, including *The Jewel of the Seven Stars, The Lady of the Shroud,* and *The Lair of the White Worm.* Most of his life was actually spent as actor Henry Irving's business manager, but in his spare time he managed to write not only novels but several short stories, which were collected in the book *Dracula's Guest.*